I0636484

# Conquer my Heart

Payton Lee Publisher
For information address:
14122 Hunters Grove Drive
Orlando, FL 32828
www.paytonlee.com


Contact Payton Lee at
Email: pyoung8@cfl.rr.com

This is a work of fiction. Names, characters, places, and incidents either are the product of the author's imagination or are used fictiously. Any resemblance to actual events, locales, organizations or persons, living or dead is entirely coincidental and beyond the intent of the author.

ISBN 978-0-6151-8161-5
Printed in the United States of America

# Dedication

I wish to dedicate this book to you the reader. It is for you I write. Please enjoy the movies of my mind. I would love to hear from you, take a moment and drop us a line to let me know if you enjoyed the story.

Payton Lee

# Chapter 1

"Our Lord High King," John de Redvers said bowing slightly. The pain in his shoulder prevented him from exerting his body too strenuously.

"Prithee, come and sit with us, Earl of Devon," King Edward III invited, opening his palm to the ornately carved chair by the desk he was using. "Thy wound still pains thee?"

"Yea," John acknowledged rubbing his shoulder.

"King Edward sat back against his chair, "Thee art getting to old for battle we fear."

"Yea," John agreed and cast the king a wry smile. "At least some battles."

"We refer to war with France," King Edward chortled. "Thee be a fine and noble knight, Sir John."

"Thank you my Lord King," John replied graciously.

"Whither be thy petition?" King Edward questioned. "We trow thee need to be off to thy bailey to recover instead of tarrying so and seeking an audience with us. Whither be so grave our Goodman?"

John de Redvers hesitated a moment. He cast his eyes upon the large tapestry draped over the king's chair. The king was dressed informally for this audience wearing his chausses, velvet red slippers, and red brocade ermine lined mantle covering a simple red woolen tunic. A simple gold crown with only a few precious stones circled his head. John knew King Edward was trying to make him feel comfortable since he had never requested an audience until now.

"Come our Goodman and noble knight," King Edward pursued. "We wouldst grant thee favor if it is within our power and capability."

Quietly John began, "Thus be regarding our daughter. Our only surviving child."

"Yea, our Goodman. We at court mourned with thee when we heard of the deaths of thy two sons. They died bravely in battle," King Edward replied bending over and touching John's hand.

John's heart saddened again. His sons had died in the battle of Neville's Cross. His sons had joined their father serving England's throne, under Queen Phillippa's con ' ' ' the Scots king. He had survived but lost his heirs. John watche s were buried on the battlefield. He would find it difficult to face ther of his boys. John wished he would battle once more instead of returning home without Robert and John. It was fortunate for him that King Edward returned first to Westminster Palace instead of Surrey Castle. John de Redvers was in London to collect his seventeen-year-old daughter from her fostering care. He had rested a few days to watch the tournaments with King Edward in celebration of the King's son obtaining his spurs. Prince Edward's consecration of knighthood would soon follow. These festivities had also given him more reason to rest and recover from his wound before riding to the Convent of St. Giles to collect his daughter, Leticia. John broached the subject on his mind, "Thus be regarding our daughter. She is ten and seven and hitherto unbetrothed."

"We understand," King Edward responded thoughtfully. "Thee have lost thy heirs and Okehampton Castle would be subject for conjecture upon thy demise. Thee be looking for a political alliance mayhap?"

"My Lord King, We look for strength and political alliance to protect our lands. Thus man to wed our daughter must be powerful knight to protect Okehampton from attack by the French and others most jealous of our lands," John said firmly sharing his most inner thoughts with his king. "Thus man must also be young enough to provide heirs."

King Edward leaned back against his chair once more and laughed, "We believe thee have some knight in mind?"

John de Redvers nodded sheepishly.

"Well considering the winner of the jousting tournaments and thus eligible knights be currently in London," King Edward leaned forward and whispered jokingly. "Our guess would be Sir Vincent de Courtenay since our son be only other choice and hath just won his spurs. He will be knighted thus next holy day."

"Prince Edward be young for our daughter," John agreed feeling more comfortable with his request of the king. Well, a little more comfortable.

"Verily! We trow so well! We married Queen Phillippa whence we were only ten and six," King Edward laughed loudly remembering his own youthful marriage. "Sweet Jesu! We trow naught whither happen with a maiden in bed. Thus took us many Easters of practice to finally create a child."

"Do thee warrant thus would be a good union, our Lord King?" John queried hoping for approval. He was still a bit nervous and the palms of his hands were beginning to sweat profusely.

"We warrant tis an excellent union," King Edward concurred. "We wouldst write proclamation fore with, but we wouldst first speak with Sir Vincent."

"Bless thee our Lord King," John breathed with relief. He was certain of his choice. The King's choice might be completely different. It was the King that must decree the betrothal. "We wouldst leave and await thy word."

"Nay, nay!" King Edward declared. "Rest and be comfortable. We wouldst have thee present when we speak with Sir Vincent." The King called for Hanley, his clerk who stood nearby. "Hanley, fetch Sir Vincent for us. We saw him last in Great Hall enjoying attentions of our many ladies of court. Make haste."

4

"We noticed he be favorite of the ladies," John chuckled.

"We believe we can be assured that unlike us, he wouldst naught need guidance in the fine art of procreation," King Edward snickered. "Thee wouldst have thy heir quickly."

"Thee do trow de Courtenay wouldst be faithful?" John asked suddenly wondering just how his daughter would adjust to a wandering husband.

"Our de Courtenay be most noble knight," King Edward assured. "Cause be Sir Vincent remains unfettered. Our knight be allowed to sample sweetmeats. Once united before our Lord, Sir Vincent wouldst remain faithful."

Vincent instinctively knew Hanley was coming for him and it was a great relief. For several hours the many ladies of court had besieged him. Vincent sighed with relief when Hanley approached him and whispered in his ear. He had only come into the Great Hall to eat his meal. Bowing politely he said to the ladies surrounding him, "Please forgive our departure fair ladies, the Lord King hath summoned us."

"Oh how impossible," Lady Celeste pouted. "We hoped thee wouldst choose to walk in the gardens with us."

"Our dear Lady Celeste, we fear thee must ask thy husband to accompany thee," Vincent grinned deviously. "We hear thy husband be but a league away."

"Lord Miles is certain to occupy thee for sometime upon his return," Lady Elizabeth cooed. "Even thy son hath been fostered for some time. We be certain thy husband will be looking for thee to warm thus bed and create new child."

The women placed their hands upon their lips to stifle the giggles at Lady Celeste's expense. The women in the hall were all wed or betrothed, but with their husbands gone they played wherever they could and the powerful handsome knight Sir Vincent de Courtenay was fair game.

Lady Juliet placed her body in front of the retreating knight. Her hands pressed firmly upon the blue woolen tunic and played delicately with the brass buttons. "Evade us naught and be gone too long, Sir Vincent. We hath a book of poems to show thee."

Vincent cocked a brow, "A book of poems?"

Lady Juliet breathed sensually, "We be aware of thy love for literature. It is in our rooms. Come hither to us this eventide and we wouldst share with thee." There was definitely more than a subtle innuendo here.

Vincent simply was not interested in the manly arts this evening. He had spent four days in jousting and was bone tired. All he wished to do this evening was sit in front of a warming fire and have a drink of fine Bordeaux wine. He was looking forward to a warm bath as well. "First we must see to our Lord King's summons," Vincent replied chivalrously brushing his lips across her soft knuckles as he removed her hands from his chest. Vincent began walking briskly toward the passage to the staircase.

Hanley had a difficult time keeping up with Vincent de Courtenay. The powerful knight was more than six feet tall compared to his diminutive height of only five and a half feet.

Vincent was hardly paying attention to the clerk. His mind was filled with relief to finally have a plausible excuse to leave the hall. He felt like kissing King Edward for his most advantageous summons.

In moments they had crossed the Great Hall and up the narrow circular stairs to the second floor offices of the King. While in residence the King would live on the third floor chambers of Westminster Castle. During this time of day the King would be found on the second floor. Torches lit the stairs and the narrow passage to the large office chambers.

Vincent stood outside the closed golden gilded oak door that led to the offices. He realized then he had out distanced poor Hanley.

The clerk caught up with swarthy knight and caught his breath before approaching the king's guards. Hanley nodded to the guardsmen who opened the large doors outward to the passageway.

"Ah, Vincent!" King Edward greeted. "Enter and be seated by Sir John."

Vincent bowed to the King and acknowledged the Earl of Devon, "Thy servant." He took a chair next to the elder knight.

"Dost thee enjoy company of our ladies?" King Edward quipped.

"Dost one enjoy being fox in center of packs of hunting dogs?" Vincent snorted in return.

King Edward suddenly became serious, "Thus be right time to remind thee of thy Christian obligation."

Vincent's smile disappeared instantly. "My Lord King?"

"Tis time for thee to take Goodwife," King Edward snorted once more. "The court will be relieved of all thus feminine squabbles thus arise whence thee be present in our court."

"A Goodwife?" Vincent choked out. "As in marriage?"

"As in proclamation," King Edward chortled handing the hand written document to the educated knight.

Vincent took the parchment and read the royal declaration carefully. "Thy daughter?" he asked looking at the Earl of Devon.

"Leticia be of age. Our daughter hath been fostered by holy Sisters of St. Giles," John de Redvers revealed.

Vincent sank into the chair and groaned, "A nunnery?"

"Thus strict and catholic upbringing provide virtuous and obedient wife," John countered with surprise.

"Thus bed frigid with ice," Vincent complained under his breath. Oh, he had heard about those convent-raised girls. His friends had married some of them and were soon happily involved with mistresses. They had told him the act of procreation was as wonderful as having intercourse with an oaken board and just as comfortable.

King Edward watched the knight and his reactions with scrutiny. Edward had not expected this to be easy. He rose from his chair to his full stature indicating for the two men to remain seated. He crossed his arms while he paced back and forth until he spoke. "Sir Vincent, thee be aware our Earl, John de Redvers, hath lost two sons. Verily, Sir John hath naught any heirs to protect Okehampton Castle and our coast from French. We be in need of good and powerful knight such as thyself to provide for both."

"Our daughter hath reached marriageable age and we wouldst require heir for our bailey," John added in support for the union.

Vincent raised a brow and countered, " Wouldst thy daughter be amendable to thus union?"

King Edward eyed the knight warily. Just what exactly was that question supposed to mean? If he as the king decreed a union, it would be.

"Leticia be reared in virtue and obedience. Whither our daughter feel matters naught," John replied arrogantly. "Leticia wouldst do as our Lord King and father order."

"And if thy daughter dost naught?" Vincent queried innocently. "We wouldst naught tolerate belligerence."

King Edward did not refrain from an immediate response to this statement. "Sir Vincent de Courtenay. Thee hath fought by our side and defeated French at Crecy. Thee have led armies with us and once more defeated Scots. Thee joust in tournaments and remain undefeated. Dost thee fear de Redver's mere wisp of maiden daughter?"

Vincent jerked at the King's remark. *Coward? We coward? Afraid of marriage? We fear naught!* It was also true that the time had come to wed and produce heirs. He changed the subject quickly directing the next questions to the Earl of Devon. "Wouldst we be Lord of Okehampton? Wouldst thee concede land to us upon marriage?"

"Our Goodwife and our person wouldst retire to Tiverton leaving thee in complete control of all Devon," John de Redvers conceded quickly. "We be tired. We be weary. We wish to live out the rest of our life in peace and see our grandchildren grow."

"We wouldst write all of thus as part of proclamation. Thus documents wouldst be presented to church records as Leticia's dowry," King Edward added to assure the young knight of the King's promise.

Vincent nodded in agreement and rose to grasp the hand of John de Redvers. He thought to himself that it was surely time to marry and this was an opportunity to marry well. He would receive land and title. A wife would be worth it all. If she were difficult he would just send her back to the nunnery after she provided him with an heir.

"Good!" King Edward exclaimed acknowledging the hand grasp. "Let us celebrate the betrothal of Vincent and Leticia. Hanley, bring us wine!"

It was then they noticed a disturbance in the curtains by the windows close to the staircase.

"Who be hither?" King Edward demanded angrily. Perhaps someone had been eavesdropping on the conversation?

"My Lord King," a young male voice replied. "Tis thy son."

"Edward!" the king recognized. "Enter and be with us. We celebrate marriage proclamation of thy noble liege and mentor, Sir Vincent!"

Edward did not confess that he had been listening to the entire conversation. He had heard Sir de Redvers had sought an audience with the

King and that he was in London to retrieve his daughter, Leticia. He had hoped Leticia was with them and then he heard of the alliance and proclamation. Even his father the king did not know of his childhood friendship with Leticia. She was fostered at St. Giles Convent and that was next to Lord Gilroy's manor where he was fostered. No one knew of a secret underground passage between the two buildings. No one knew except Leticia and himself. They had both found the secret place by accident and both had used it as refuge when they wanted time to be alone. He and Leticia had become great friends and soon met secretly to share their sorrows, triumphs, and secrets. Both were fostered and both were kept separated from family and siblings. Together they had created a warm and caring brother and sister bond.

"Felicitations," Edward offered to his former mentor. He couldn't wait to leave and ride to St. Giles. It would be fun to let Leticia learn of her betrothal. They had developed a secret sign to let each other know when they would meet in the secret chamber between the two houses. He would place a black silken cloth on the hedgerows between the properties and she would place a white silken cloth. "My Lord King, I came to ask thee to join us in ride. Since thee be involved, we wouldst take leave and take our ride." It was a poor and quick excuse but it was an excuse to leave Westminster and find Leticia. He couldn't wait to tell her. She would wed the very knight he had served as squire.

"Go our son," King Edward allowed. "Thee be verily a knight of the realm. Thee may come and go as thee desire." He was proud of his handsome and powerful son. It was rare for a lad to obtain knighthood at such a young age. His son, Edward, had achieved this!

When the Prince had left the office King Edward again returned to the matter at hand. He addressed John, "We desire to observe thy Leticia. Thee wouldst bring thy daughter's countenance to royal court."

"We obey my Lord King," Sir John acquiesced quickly. "Leticia wouldst be introduced to court and become accustomed to it as dutiful Goodwife of a noble knight."

King Edward turned to address Sir Vincent, "Our Lady Leticia wouldst be placed under thy protection from thus moment. Thee be Lady Leticia's future husband tis thy obligation to escort thy lady to Westminster Court."

"Whence wouldst thee send us to fetch our lady?" Vincent asked somberly.

"We wish Lady Leticia to be hence for knighting of our son. Bring thy lady on the morrow," The king commanded. "We wouldst send three ladies of court with thee as thy lady's companions and chaperones."

"Thy obedient servant," Vincent bowed. "Mayhap whence women of court wouldst be selected?" There were some women of the court that would not be a good selection while bringing his future wife to the court.

"We wouldst leave thus for our Goodwife, Queen Phillippa," King Edward volunteered. King Edward relied on his wife's sensibilities completely and without question.

"Prithee, and whence be left for us?" Queen Phillippa asked sweeping into the room with grace and beauty. Her head adorned with silken wimple circled by a golden crown. The queen looked lovely and elegant. "We hath only come to see why our husband Lord King wouldst be detained so long from our guests."

"My love," King Edward replied smiling broadly. "We hath concluded betrothal of Lady Leticia de Redvers and Sir Vincent de Courtenay. We hath volunteered thy wisdom to select three ladies of court to accompany Sir Vincent to fetch thus betrothed and serve our Lady Leticia."

Queen Phillippa recognized Sir John and walked to his side offering her hand. "Our condolences on loss of thy sons."

Sir John took the queen's offered hand and whispered sadly, "God grant thee mercy!"

Queen Phillippa stroked the elder knight's head gently with her hand. "Husband, We fear we wouldst need many knights to keep peace in our Great Hall and throughout our land when ladies learn Sir Vincent de Courtenay be betrothed."

"We wouldst call all my knights from abroad to keep peace in our lands," King Edward teased lightheartedly.

"'Tis most difficult to select from our court ladies. Thus courtly ladies be dangerously jealous of Lady Leticia, verily let us contemplate," Queen Phillippa said placing her forefinger to her lips. "Lady Rosamund be likely candidate. She be mature with years and hath served court faithfully for many years. We warrant Lady Agnes and our young and good Lady Organa."

"Lady Organa?" The king questioned. "She be naught but child herself?"

"A young woman in need of training," Queen Phillippa replied. "Organa wouldst do well fostered under the training of Lady Leticia as she herself learns how to be a Goodwife."

"Thy wisdom be great, my queen," King Edward pronounced proudly. "Wouldst thee see for it thy ladies be ready to accompany Sir Vincent on the morrow? As for our guests, we wouldst celebrate thus auspicious occasion with our knights and then join thee and our guests. Thee hast our word."

Queen Phillippa smiled at her husband and then just as silent and swift as her entrance, she left the offices.

Hanley brought in a tray of golden goblets filled with Bordeaux Wine. Each man took a goblet and drank to the betrothal. Hanley saw to it that the goblets were refilled several times before the king waved his hand.

"Excuse us, we must see to our guests," King Edward stated.

"And we be weary," Sir John agreed. "We wouldst rest and accompany thee about collecting our daughter on the morrow."

"Then we must seek solitude and rest so we be presentable for our lady," Sir Vincent replied following suit. He wanted his bath and his room. This betrothal was something he needed time, rest, and his friends to help him adjust.

Prince Edward had mounted his black Destrier, a gift from his father for achieving knighthood, and was quickly on his way to St. Giles Convent.

Leticia worked laboriously on the tapestry before her. Sister Agatha sat next to her scrutinizing every stitch.

"Sister Agatha, we request of thee permission to stand up and walk?" Leticia asked respectfully. Her legs were beginning to fall asleep after the long hours of stitching. She wanted to run across the lawns in her bare feet and run from this place forever, but where could she go?

"Thee be excused for thus den," Sister Agatha allowed.

Then Leticia saw the black silken cloth on the hedgerow. Her heart leaped with joy. Prince Edward was here and waiting in their secret place!

# Chapter 2

Leticia checked behind her and then scanned the open garden for signs of anyone. She especially looked for Sister Mary Martha. Whenever she was up to something Sister Mary would appear out of nowhere. Seeing no one about, Leticia removed her slippers and ran across the garden lawn staying close to the boundary hedgerows. It gave her some cover from penetrating eyes. The grass was cool under her feet as she sprinted toward the large statue in the corner of the garden. Her sun streaked golden brown hair trailed behind flying like a soft pennant. Her gown hem securely held up by both hands as she ran in and out of the trees and hedges. Her goal in sight, Leticia was breathing hard for the run and the excitement of seeing Prince Edward after a two-year absence. Finally reaching the base of the statue, Leticia steadied her breathing and beating heart before pulling the lever that moved the stone allowing her to enter the secret passage to the secret garden of rocks. The marble stone of the passage was cold to her feet and slippery for the moss upon it. She wasn't afraid for darkness. Prince Edward had signaled her and he would have the torches lit. Leticia took a moment to put her slippers back on before pulling the ring to close the opening. She proceeded down the passage following the dim light of the distant torches.

Crossing the intersection Leticia continued straight until she came to the bright light of the open rock garden. There she saw a shadowed figure in the distance dressed in black. "Edward!"

The dark mantled figure turned to her voice. "Leticia!"

They ran to meet and embraced each other with strong hugs.

Leticia pulled back and put the handsome prince's head in her hands. "Thy countenance be wonderful. Thee hath grown so tall and strong in thy absence," Leticia bubbled. "We heard thee received thy spurs and thee wouldst be knighted thus next eventide!"

"And thee hath grown up as well," Edward marveled removing her hands from his face. He took her hands and straightened his arms to look at her. "Our fostered sister and child maid has turned into a woman. We admire thus change."

Leticia blushed in embarrassment. "We haven't seen each other in such length of time, tell us instead all about thee! When thee left, thee be squire to noble knight."

"Our life hence hath filled of adventure and growth," Prince Edward bragged. "We hath learned all thus good knights wouldst trow of warfare and chivalry."

"Whence cometh thee? Wherefore lands hast thee journeyed?" Leticia asked eagerly devouring Edward's every word.

"We hath been to Bordeaux, Crecy with our father and Lord Knight, and then our triumph at Neville's Cross," Prince Edward said enthusiastically. "Telling thee our stories be naught purpose we have come hither to thee thus den."

"We always shared our stories hither!" Leticia stated in surprise. "We be anxious for hearing about thy travels."

Prince Edward took Leticia's tiny hand in his large one. "Our dearest fostered sister, thus may be our last time we meet e'er again."

Those words put a strangle hold on Leticia's throat. "We comprehend naught. Whither be wrong? Whence hath occurred?"

"Leticia, thus be naught delicate way for telling thee," Edward hesitated. He looked lovingly into her deep brown eyes. "Thy brothers, John and Robert, hath been killed in battle."

"We be so sorry for our father," Leticia offered weakly at the sad news. "We trow sadness, but we trow naught our brothers as well as we trow naught our father. Prithee, whither dost thus do with us?"

"Thee be thy father's only surviving child. Thee art Sir John's only means for Devon's heir," Prince Edward shared knowing she would understand what he just said to her.

Leticia's eyes grew wide when his words brought comprehension.

"We hath just arrived from our father, Lord King's offices. Thy father and Lord King hath arranged betrothal for thee. Thee wouldst be married in a fortnight," Prince Edward told her quietly still holding her hand.

"So our person be naught more than vessel for heir?" Leticia retorted angrily. "We trow our father hath naught care for us, but surely our mother wouldst protect us from this fate!"

"Thy mother dost naught trow thus proclamation. Thus be only person thus trow thy fate," Prince Edward smiled half-heartedly. "Thee be dearest sister of our heart. We wished to give thee knowledge before thy father and thy betrothed collect thee."

"We wouldst hope we might obtain opportunity of love and naught pawn for politics," Leticia whispered choking back her tears.

"Demise of thy brothers hath changed all thus," Prince Edward advised lovingly. "Thus be thy duty. Thee hath been raised in nobility and understand duty same as we understand it."

The tears streamed down Leticia's cheeks as she nodded in agreement. "Whence be thus betrothed? We pray tis naught some old foul smelling man."

Edward's face brightened. "Tis Sir Vincent de Courtenay!"

"Wouldst naught thee be de Courtenay's squire?" Leticia queried from past conversation. She wiped her eyes with her sleeve.

"Yea. Sir Vincent be fine and noble knight," Edward announced happily. "Our former liege be naught old. Sir de Courtenay be handsome, and all women for our king's court fawn upon him. Thee wouldst be envied by many women for court."

"Whence kind of man be thus Vincent de Courtney?"

"We just told thee," Edward laughed. "Sir Vincent naught to old…"

"We asked, verily whence type of man?" Leticia pouted. "Be Sir Vincent cruel? Be Sir Vincent self-indulgent or vulgar? Dost Sir Vincent smell foul? Dost Sir Vincent own a bad temper? Dost Sir Vincent drink heavily?"

"Sir Vincent is patient and thoughtful, but rigid and strict. Tis his way, or naught way. Sir Vincent be quite clean and dost naught smell foul," Edward laughed. "He hath been known to drink heavily, but naught problem drinker. He dost possess bad temper. One learns quickly to avoid thus temper."

"Wouldst thy knight beat us?" Leticia asked fearfully.

"Sir Vincent be noble and chivalrous knight. We doubt wouldst e'er raise hand for maiden fair, yet we have seen Sir Vincent get so angry our liege wouldst be vengeful angel," Edward admitted. "Our liege hath won all disagreement, battle, and joust."

"Wouldst thy liege be faithful as husband?" Leticia asked tentatively unsure if she should broach such a personal subject with her fostered brother of heart. "Thee told us Sir Vincent be sought out by ladies at court."

"We wouldst naught answer thus," Edward blushed profusely considering his own first experience that occurred while a squire to Sir Vincent. A young woman dismayed at not being selected for the night by the noble and handsome knight took the young prince and squire for pleasures that evening after Neville's Cross.

Leticia noticed Edward's red face. "Thee be naught a virgin any longer, art thee?" she teased. "Tell us troth!"

"A noble chivalrous knight ne'er tells tales! Especially for fostered sister of heart," Edward chuckled. "Enough of thus!"

"We know tis troth," Leticia continued in teasing. "Instead tell us about ladies thy noble knight, Sir Vincent, likes to take for warmth in pallet."

"Leticia!" Edward shrieked in surprise. "Thee be raised in St. Giles nunnery. How can thee trow of such things?"

"Thus be more secret passages in thus convent other than thus one," Leticia informed. "As child in Okehampton we always managed to find secret passages and in night darkness with a small candle watched many strange things."

"Whence?" Edward gasped.

"Hither we find many same strange things in night wandering through secret passages," Leticia grinned wickedly. "Such difference be we understand thus moaning and groaning. Or methinks we do."

"Leticia, thee continue to shock us," Edward chortled. Leticia always surprised him with her wit, charm, intelligence, and unusual demeanor.

"Verily, tell us all!" Leticia declared. "Whence type of lady dost thy noble knight find attractive?"

"Thus alas, naught any special kind," Edward admitted. "Some be tall and some be short. Some be golden haired and some be raven-haired. Some be beauteous and some not so handsome. Some be married and some be not. We believe thus be convenience."

"So thy noble chivalrous knight hath naught specific tastes?" Leticia growled. "Thy knight sleeps around like mongrel dog?"

"Thus be unfair Leticia," Edward defended. "We men hath our needs met, especially since we hath naught a Goodwife."

"Unfair? Whence wouldst woman go for such needs? Such lady wouldst be condemned for seeing about such needs with another?" Leticia complained angrily. She stood and began pacing. "We be holy and virtuous allowing our bodies to be used by politics and men for vessels holding heirs. Thusly men may see to such needs like mongrel dogs spreading seed upon any bitch."

"Leticia!" Edward choked on her use of words. "A chivalrous noble knight be faithful to such wife."

"Be thus so? Whence do all these noble knights take mistresses?" Leticia argued. "We hath seen many fettered man cavorting with other than such wives in thus place!"

"And we have seen ladies of court throw themselves upon the noble knights while such husbands be absent," Edward countered.

Leticia pointed her finger at him declaring, "thee understand? Whence be purpose of thy holy and sacred pledge of nuptials? Thus such vows be only means for creating an heir!" After her angry words she once again sat next to Edward and began to cry.

"Whence vexes thee? Verily, whence causes thy vexation?" Edward offered extending his arm and placing it around her shoulder.

"Our father trow us naught. Suddenly our father takes interest in us just to wed us off and obtain heir," Leticia sobbed into Prince Edward's arms. "Sir John hath ne'er acknowledged us once or e'er said love words for us. Only our mother hath cared for us."

"Thee hath wonderful visits with thy mother. We remember thee telling us," Edward replied softly whispering against her silken hair.

"Our mother wouldst come hence often to spend time with us, and in cold times she wouldst take us home," Leticia said weeping. "E'en if our father be at home, thus man wouldst naught seek us. Our father wouldst naught speak with us. Instead thus time be devoted for John and Robert. We trow naught our brothers either. We only trow our two little sisters who hath perished whence we be at St. Giles."

"Thus be our life for nobility," Edward assuaged patting Leticia gently on her back. "We hath discussed the matter many times."

"We trow," Leticia agreed. "Thus hurts so, and now we be married to knight we wouldst trow naught."

"We hath served as Sir Vincent's squire," Edward stated. "Sir de Courtenay be a good and noble knight, and quite handsome of face."

"Tell us, be thus noble and grand knight afraid of naught?" Leticia questioned humorously trying to get herself out of her unhappy mood.

Edward laughed loudly, "Oh there be naught man or beast he fears, yet...."

"Yet?"

"Sir Vincent be terrified of arachnids and frogs," Edward shared. "I warrant he hath been frightened by them as a lad. Thee hath naught seen such fear on face. Tell naught anyone we told thee, take oath?"

"We wouldst naught say to soul," Leticia promised. "And wouldst naught speak of thy fear for cats!"

"We wouldst share naught thee be afraid of snakes," Edward teased in retribution. "We must go leave anon ere we be missed."

"Oh Edward," Leticia whimpered placing her arms around his muscled chest. "Trow thee we treasured thy visit. We only wish we wouldst be at thy knighting."

"We wish thee wouldst be there as well," Edward hoped. "We trow naught of plans thy betrothed hath made for thee."

"We be glad thee told us whither our father hath done," Leticia said wiping away another tear with her hand. "Tis naught too much surprise and wouldst be able to conduct our person in proper manner."

"Whence be thy meaning?" Edward queried warily raising his eyebrow. "We trow naught thee for conducting thyself in proper manner since we be children."

"Except in front of our convent's sisters," Leticia reminded. "Our peers trow of us as nearly perfect child."

"Yea, thee be fine deceiver," Edward agreed with a smile crossing his lips.

"Whence one must," Leticia winked. "As we all must be whence required. E'en thee!"

"Prithee only thee and few hath viewed our real person," Edward chuckled. He stood to his great height and bent over to brush a brotherly kiss across Leticia's brow. "Thee best return before thee be missed. We wouldst wait for few moments and thus remove torches."

"Adieu our Goodman and brother," Leticia whispered sadly. She turned and left their secret garden. In a few moments she had returned to her rooms in the convent. There she lay upon her pallet and wept until sleep overtook her.

"Maynard!" Vincent bellowed to his squire upon entering his rooms.

"My Lord?" Maynard replied immediately from a darkened corner. He had been sitting for a rest after he had polished Vincent's armor.

"Fetch us bath. Make haste!" Vincent growled taking out his frustration on the poor young squire.

Lionel rose from his chair facing the hearth. "Prithee, from whence hath such foul mood grown, Goodman?"

Vincent walked briskly across the room and grabbed the goblet of wine from his friend's hand. "Thee be looking at man about to be fettered."

"Ho!" Lionel laughed. "Verily, thee art jesting with us?"

"Nay," Vincent answered seriously while draining the goblet dry in one swallow. "King Edward hath betrothed us to daughter of Sir John de Redvers. We wouldst be Lord Earl of Devon."

"Felicitations!" Lionel replied taking the goblet and refilling it once more. He handed the full goblet back to Vincent. "Thee be hence land owner. Many knights wouldst wish to be in thy place. Whence be good fortune."

"Thus lady be raised in nunnery!" Vincent growled. "We desired to wed for love after we hath obtained land, naught before. We certainly wouldst naught chosen a maiden from nunnery."

"Whence difference wouldst thee like her naught or do? Thee gain much for union," Lionel cajoled. "'Tis time thee wed and thee trow thus for troth."

"Thee speak naught for thy Goodwife," Vincent noted. "Be thy union fain?"

"Our Goodwife be our treasure guarded," Lionel admitted. "Our Goodwife dost bring us great joy and love. We dost boast four children. Three sons and daughter."

"We trow she be naught raised in a convent?" Vincent pursued to justify his upset.

"Nay, naught convent, yet still maiden virtuous," Lionel shared. "Thee seem in haste for judging thus maiden without meeting."

Maynard returned with servants carrying the great wooden tub and hot water for his lord's bath.

Vincent allowed Maynard to remove his slippers, hose, and tunic. Still wearing his braies he walked to the tub and then removed them. He eased into the sweet smelling hot water and let out an oath, "By arms blood and bones tis good to be unbraced!"

"Thee wouldst enjoy more when thus soft hands of thy Goodwife massage those tired bones," Lionel teased.

"If such lady wouldst naught run in fear of our nakedness," Vincent countered belligerently.

"Yea, thus wouldst be thy error, not hers!" Lionel snarled in debate.

"Prithee?"

"Train her early and train her well with loving hand of thine own!" Lionel reprimanded. "As we be taught, so we learn. Thee be great knight and consul thy squires well. Doeth same in thus art of loving."

Vincent cocked his brow and stared at his friend, "Dost thee believe thus troth or thy experience?"

"Both, Goodman!" Lionel laughed loudly. "We trow more life experience than thee and hath served us well."

"Goodman, We wouldst need thy consul," Vincent stated washing his body with his favorite sandalwood scented soap. "Whence cost dost thee ask for our instructions for thus delicate of matters?"

"We ask naught," Lionel replied taking the goblet of wine and sipping it. "We wouldst bestow upon thee our knowledge, yet each maiden be unique. Thus teaching wouldst require great amounts of patience from thee. Yea, thus be half our fun of wedded life. Learning anew."

Lionel stayed the night discussing all he knew of bedding, loving, and the art of husbandry.

After only a few hours of sleep, Vincent rose and had his squire dress him in one of his finest tunics of green brocade with gold buttons. He wore his tightest hose to accent his muscular legs. He chose pointed slippers of green velvet and leather. He wore a girdle of golden embroidered and jewel studded leather. Attached to the girdle was his jeweled case holding his golden and jeweled dagger. The green velvet tunic was short sleeved with ermine trim. Beneath the tunic he wore a brocaded long sleeve shirt. A chamberlain was sent for to comb his dark, almost black, hair. The crown of his head was accented with a golden embroidered and braided circlet.

Lionel stepped back to look at his friend and noble knight. "Thee wouldst melt the heart of all virtuous maidens casting such feminine eyes upon thee."

"Goodman, We hath taken all thy words to heart. We pray thus lady wouldst naught make our life hell," Vincent replied. "Wouldst such lady doeth thus, tis naught fault of ours."

There was a knock at the door.

Maynard scurried quickly to answer the knock. He returned to his lord. "Our King hath sent messenger informing thee our Sir de Redvers be awaiting thee forthwith in thus courtyard."

Vincent turned to his good friend. "Dost thee honor us to accompany us thus den and fetch our betrothed?"

"Verily, we dost believe thou be afraid, Goodman," Lionel snickered. "Verily we dost consider thus our honor for protecting thee from such venomous lady thou dost fear."

"We fear naught!" Vincent snapped in return. He would not admit even to himself he was terrified of this maiden, of marriage, of becoming Earl of Devon. He was just as afraid of spiders and frogs, but fortunately only his squire, Prince Edward had seen his fear of spiders and frogs.

"Come, let us be done with thus," Lionel ordered walking to the door and opening the heavy oaken door leading to the castle halls.

Vincent and Lionel proceeded to the courtyard. Before the men were two empty carts for Leticia's belongings. Lady Rosamund, Lady Agnes, and Lady Organa strained their heads to look at the noble and well-dressed knight as he approached the small mares they were seating. Sir John led the group holding the reins of a small Palfrey horse that would be a wedding gift to his daughter. Two unseated Destriers awaited their masters.

Lionel and Vincent mounted and began the short ride to St. Giles Convent. The King had also sent along a small royal escort. It was a symbol to all of the royal decree.

Leticia had been woken early before prime.

Sister Clarice shook Leticia gently, "My Lady, thee be called to our Prioress. Make haste."

Wiping her swollen eyes Leticia rose from her pallet. She walked to the basin Sister Clarice had brought for her and splashed her face. Taking the towel she dried her tear-stained cheeks and brushed her hair. Still wearing the simple bliaut she wore the day before, Leticia smoothed the wrinkles and walked with Clarice to the chambers of the Prioress.

"Come hither my daughter," the Prioress greeted upon Leticia's entry. "We bring thee news of great joy."

Inwardly Leticia groaned. It was not joy for her.

# Chapter 3

"Trow thee our king's proclamation thee be betrothed to Sir Vincent de Courtenay, most noble and favored knight of our Lord High King," the Prioress announced excitedly. "We wouldst receive word late last eventide to ready thee for thy betrothed. Sir Vincent wouldst arrive before sexte for collecting thee."

"Sir Vincent arrives forthwith?" Leticia choked. She had hoped for some time with her mother at Okehampton before the nuptials and she would be forced to be his possession. Instead he was taking immediate possession.

"Thee be under thy lord's protection henceforth," the Prioress replied quizzically. "Verily, tis a great honor for protection of thy betrothed forthwith."

"Thus be naught time for prattle," Sister Agatha blurted out taking Leticia's hand. "We wouldst find thy most beauteous gown, bathe thee, and make thee presentable for thy betrothed. We wouldst school and prepare thee for thy most auspicious occasion."

Leticia allowed Sister Agatha to drag her to her rooms. She would once more play the role of the dutiful maiden. It occurred to Leticia that the sisters were far more excited than she was. Sister Agatha and Sister Beatrice pulled out one gown after another from her wardrobe. The two finally decided upon the white silver damask with silver buttons in the front. Sister Beatrice selected a royal blue mantel edged with white ermine, and a white silken wimple. Sister Madeline had prepared a scented bath for Leticia and washed her lovingly humming through the entire bath. After washing Leticia's hair, Sister Madeline helped her from the tub and dried her. The sister carefully brushed and braided Leticia's waist length sun kissed golden brown hair. Sister Agatha dressed her charge and after placing the silken wimple on her head covering Leticia's hair she started to secure the wimple with a silver circlet.

"We wouldst wear face veil," Leticia interrupted.

"Such a beauteous face shouldst naught be covered for thy betrothed," Sister Agatha protested.

"Prithee, We shouldst meet our betrothed for the first time. We be unsure of our heart and wouldst naught cause revealing of our soul through our eyes," Leticia countered logically. She was going to protect herself from revealing her emotions. If she were to play act it would be better to play act behind a mask, or in this case, veil.

"Our lady be correct Sister Agatha," Sister Madeline agreed not truly understanding Leticia's feelings, but bubbling in her own ideas of what Leticia should be feeling. "A lady wouldst naught appear to bold or eager."

Leticia smiled demurely. *Bold? Eager? Those be hardly our feelings. We be naught more than a possession of one unknown man passed to another unknown man. Fie on all the males of the realm. Well, mayhap excluding Prince Edward.*

Sister Agatha chose a matching silken veil and placed it upon the wimple. Leticia's face was covered to her lips. Satisfied with the veil, Sister Agatha secured the silver circlet.

Sister Madeline placed the blue satin mantel over Leticia's shoulder and secured with chain pins bearing the carved and painted coat of arms of the de Redvers.

"Thee appear in troth beauteous," Sister Beatrice sighed and her attention was immediately drawn to the courtyard. The royal entourage had entered.

Sister Agatha and Sister Madeline ran to the window.

"Whence be Sir Vincent?" Sister Agatha queried. "The older handsome man wouldst be Leticia's father. Whence of two handsome knights wouldst be Sir Vincent?"

"We wouldst believe him thus tall raven haired knight dressed in green," Sister Beatrice sighed dreamily.

"Nay, thus handsome sandy haired knight," Sister Madeline disagreed. "He be the knight older and more noble in appearance of thus two."

"Leticia, do thee peek with us?" Sister Madeline asked surprised that her lovely charge had not joined them.

"We wouldst meet them all anon," Leticia replied and walked to her chair sitting down with a plop.

"Thy betrothed hath brought three ladies with his entourage," Sister Agatha observed. "Mayhap thy most noble betrothed be wealthy and providing for thy care."

"Yea, mayhap," Leticia replied quietly. She laid her head upon her hand. *Out of the care of women to the care of more women. Wouldst we e'er live our own life? Oh how we ache to be chafe.*

"Our Prioress wouldst send for us anon," Sister Madeline giggled. "She wouldst be pleased with our work."

Leticia reached for her hose and garters.

"We wouldst accomplish this," Sister Beatrice said quickly running to Leticia's side. "We fain for thee." Sister Beatrice raised Leticia's gown hem and put the hose and garters on.

"Thee wouldst wear thy leather boots," Sister Agatha noted. "We trow thy lord brought beauteous Palfrey mare for thee to seat."

"Our own mount?" Leticia shrieked jumping up from the chair and running to the window.

Sister Agatha was shocked. "Thee cares naught to see thy betrothed, yet leap to see mount?"

"We hath naught e'er received our own mount," Leticia bubbled with happiness.

"Thee hath naught acquired such betrothed," Sister Agatha countered.

"We be our betrothed's possession," Leticia argued while admiring the Palfrey mare from the window. "Our beauteous mount be our possession."

Sister Beatrice laughed heartily. "My lady hath point hitherto."

"Oh our Palfrey be most fine," Leticia admired joyfully. There were some good points being betrothed to a noble knight. Gifts!

It was at that moment Vincent looked up and saw Leticia in the window. Her damask sparkled like thousands of diamonds in the sun. He noticed her shapely figure and hoped that little waif would be his betrothed. He squinted to see her face but she turned quickly and returned to her room. He dismounted the Destrier and walked with Sir John and Lionel to the great door of the Priory.

A diminutive sister opened the great door and showed the entourage to chairs in a large room. Another sister walked briskly to the offices of the Prioress.

The Prioress rose and sent yet another sister to call Leticia. Hopefully she was ready since the knight had come to claim his betrothed early. It was just a little past terce.

Upon entering the great room the Prioress greeted the knights. "May thus please thee, Lady Leticia be in her rooms preparing."

"Our daughter be told?" John queried the Prioress.

"We woke thy daughter in morn and related thus joyous decree," the Prioress stated. "Whither of thee be Lady Leticia's betrothed?"

Sir Vincent stood from his chair and bowed politely, but said nothing. He found his knees were shaking. It was coming to reality. He was going to be fettered.

The great staircase was in sight of the room and all eyes turned as to a silver and blue figure descending gracefully down the stairs. Three sisters of the Priory descended behind her and carried her mantel hem.

Though completely covered, Vincent held his breath. The sight of this maiden was akin to the descent of an angel from the heavens. She showed a perfect form in her gown. Her grace and bearing was obvious. This maiden would be a good and prized possession.

John rose from his chair and walked to the staircase. He offered his arm as she stepped on the last stair. "Thee hath grown into fair maiden."

For the first time in her life her father had noticed her. "Good den, my lord father." A small glimmer of happiness came from that simple paternal statement.

Vincent was already standing but found that he could not move.

Lionel pushed him gently from behind. "Chivalry requires thee claim possession of thy betrothed from the lady's father," he guided.

Slowly Vincent approached the young maiden and offered his arm.

John addressed the knight, "We give thee our daughter's hand henceforth. Lady Leticia be thine for protection and defense."

Leticia was grateful for the veil. Her eyes rolled in anger. *Thine! Methinks naught! We wouldst naught be owned by any man of King Edward's realm.* She obediently placed her hand upon Sir Vincent's extended arm. She would play act this role to obtain a little freedom. Leticia believed that a married woman could have more freedom than an unmarried maiden. She had to believe this. These thoughts were her only comfort. She failed to even look at her future husband.

The accompanying sisters sighed with envy when the handsome and well-structured knight took Leticia's arm.

When she touched him a breeze swept through the room and he inhaled a sweet flowery scent that was the Lady Leticia. This scent and her touch sent a fire through him that he had never felt before. She was to be his wife. Instantly his manhood became hard. No woman had ever had such an effect on him. "My Lady, thy father hath bestowed thee with nuptial gift, thus Palfrey horse. Methinks for thus ride to Westminster we wouldst prefer thee saddle with us." He felt immediately protective and wanted her near to him. *What be these strange thoughts in our head?*

"Sirrah, we hath much experience and wouldst prefer to seat our gift," Leticia responded in above just a whisper. She dare not raise her voice or the anger would spill out. *How dare he? How dare he stop her from riding her mount? Fie on him.*

"Nay." Vincent countered. He gave her no quarter. Was this a test of her obedience? *Yea tis a test!* He would find out if she were given to being a shrew.

Leticia ground her teeth angrily, but said nothing. She walked gracefully with her betrothed to his Destrier and cast a longing glance at the Palfrey mare.

Vincent mounted and Lionel lifted the Lady Leticia to the knight's arms. Vincent settled her on his lap and waited as the others mounted. Quietly he inhaled her essence and squirmed as his manhood hardened more.

Leticia felt the pulsing bump and not knowing anything of men tried to remove her seating from it. She edged forward on the Destrier's withers.

Vincent pulled her back and his hand gently felt for the feminine globe he saw in her form. His thumb gently rubbed her breast's nipple.

Leticia jerked at his touch. Suddenly a fire raced through her body and she felt her nipples harden. No man had ever touched her, much less touched her so intimately. These body reactions were new and strange to her. She suddenly felt fearful.

Vincent's Destrier smelled her fear and began twitching nervously.

Vincent pulled Leticia closer and tightened the reins for control. "Our mount desires to begin thus journey. We wouldst depart."

"Ho!" Lionel called mounting his Destrier. "Thus wagons wouldst naught be loaded hence."

"Thus footmen wouldst bring them later," Vincent called out while reining his Destrier to turn and begin the path back to Westminster Castle. He wanted Leticia right now and in this close proximity he would take her. It would be better to get her to the castle and present her to King Edward. That would give him some time to regain control of his body. How embarrassing. *Thus naught happened to our person since we wouldst be young lad.*

Leticia relaxed a bit on the ride to Westminster Castle. She took the opportunity to look through the veil at her betrothed for the first time. *Sir de Courtenay be a handsome knight. Situations mayhap be worse. Our father wouldst betroth us to old man. Nay, beauteous face means naught. Whence kind of man art thee? Oh great and powerful noble knight, wouldst thee conquer my heart?*

22

In a short time they arrived at Westminster Castle. Vincent dismounted giving the reins to a page by the livery. He picked up Leticia with the effort of picking up a feather and gently placed her upon the courtyard stones.

Leticia was nervous again. What was she supposed to do? She decided to simply stand there and wait for instructions.

A page had run to Vincent and spoke to him. He nodded to the boy and sent him off. Vincent then extended his arm for Leticia. "Our Lord High King hath heard of our arrival. Our king wouldst meet thee thy lady."

Leticia bowed her head and after placing her hand upon Vincent's arm, kept her gaze at her feet while they walked.

Vincent led her past the great hall where they were preparing for a meal into the chambers of the king and his audience room.

Edward was sitting on his throne talking to his wife Phillippa when they entered. Vincent brought Leticia before the king and queen. Together they bowed.

"Come hither," Edward motioned to Leticia.

Removing her hand from Vincent's arm and using it to raise her skirt hem so she would not trip, Leticia approached the king.

"Remove thus hideous nunnery veil," Edward commanded. "We wish to see such face of Sir John's daughter and only surviving child. Thus be betrothed of our favored noble knight, Sir Vincent."

Leticia slowly lifted the veil with her trembling hands. This was incredible. Only yesterday she was an insignificant fostered child. Today she was betrothed to the king's favored knight and presented before the king and queen. *Who wouldst naught be frightened?*

Sir John walked to the side of King Edward's throne. Sir Vincent remained behind his betrothed.

"Thus be prime piece Sir Vincent," King Edward admired. "Methinks we hath chosen well for thee."

"Upon thy betrothal announcement we feared an uprising from our court ladies," Queen Phillippa said thoughtfully. "We wouldst believe herewith thee wouldst be fighting off our noble men for protection of thy betrothed."

Leticia muffled a small laugh, but a smile crossed her face. She had immediately developed a fondness for the queen.

"Come hither daughter," Queen Phillippa commanded. She rose from her throne and took Leticia's hand. "We wouldst prepare chambers near ours. We fear thee wouldst need much protection. We wouldst aide Sir Vincent for thus plight."

"Remove thus accursed nunnery veil!" King Edward shouted in decree after his wife. "Thy daughter be beauteous," Edward said turning to Sir John at his side. "Lady Leticia reminds us for thy Maude."

"Yea, Leticia be her mother's daughter," John agreed. It was strange he hadn't really ever noticed Leticia before. He had never realized how lovely she was and the image of her mother. "Mayhap our king wouldst understand the reasoning for our return to Devon."

"What doth surprise us wouldst be thee hast naught more children," King Edward laughed thunderously. "Methinks we hath kept thee for war too long."

Sir John laughed with the king in agreement.

"For thee, our Goodman," King Edward addressed Sir Vincent. "We wouldst surely allow thee time with thy fair Goodwife."

"Be thee ready for setting thus nuptial date?" Sir John asked Sir Vincent.

King Edward interrupted, "Thus date be set on St. Giles holy day. Thus hath thee time for return to Okehampton. Thus thee wouldst naught wait long to create an heir."

"Ho, the day of our saint and verily the name of the nunnery our daughter be fostered," Sir John chuckled. "Verily thee be our wise and gracious king, majesty."

Sir Vincent was thinking he had not even seen his betrothed's face. He had concentrated on her body. Now he was curious.

"Whence be thou?" King Edward addressed the obviously preoccupied knight. "Thy lady wouldst be in thy bedchamber anon."

Queen Phillippa took Leticia to a chamber of many rooms. It was lavishly furnished with ornately carved wooden and cushioned chairs. A Venetian looking glass in a large oval frame was off to the side. A large hearth was found in the sitting room and the sleeping chamber in the next room. There was an ornate tub for bathing in another room and even a privacy closet. Built into the castle walls were wardrobes with locks. Queen Phillippa told Leticia the handmaiden present would be keeper of the keys.

Leticia was agog at the rooms she had been given. "My Grace, we fear one might be soon lost for such rooms."

Queen Phillippa laughed joyously. "My daughter, methinks we love thee already. Mayhap we wouldst make thy betrothed aware of such good fortune?"

"Our Grace?" Leticia questioned. She wasn't certain of what the queen meant at all.

"Dear child maiden, thy betrothed hath thus court ladies chasing thy knight in constant. Methinks thy Goodman might believe he be quite thus catch," Queen Phillippa chuckled. "Methinks tis our duty for thy knight's proper training. Thee wouldst be glint for all males eye this eventide. Sir de Courtenay wouldst learn his person be thus fortunate for thee."

Leticia cocked her head and simply stared at the queen. "Mayhap thus miracle be done?"

"Naught miracle," Queen Phillippa teased. "Feminine wiles. Thee wouldst come to court much sooner, but tis naught too late for instructions in such ways of femininity." Queen Phillippa instructed her ladies in waiting to bring her own finest gown and plenty of silken thread and needles. They would be redoing a gown of the queen. She then took Leticia to sit in front of the hearth. Each was poured a goblet of wine and the queen shared her plan.

Leticia was delighted and even more elated when the queen instructed her in the power of the wife. Even the king was not spared from the wiles of a woman. It obviously worked. Leticia found herself becoming excited about her new life and soon new freedoms she would have if she did everything right. God bless the queen! Leticia stood perfectly still as the queen's ladies in waiting redesigned the queen's gown according to the queen's instructions.

When the gown had been completed Leticia walked to the Venetian looking glass. She was astonished. She was beautiful. The gown was deep emerald green velvet. The shoulders were dropped and her neckline cut deep and revealing. The neckline and dropped trumpet sleeves were edged with emerald green satin ribbons and decorated with embroidery and precious stones. The gown had been tailored to be tight fitting and accented Leticia's perfectly formed body. Directly under her bosom was a large ornate brooch of gold in a floral design filled with pearls, diamonds, rubies, and emeralds. The brooch was a gift from the queen. The ladies in waiting had also combed and braided Leticia's hair with topaz hairpins, green and gold satin ribbons, and crowned her hair with a small golden circlet.

"Thee wouldst take away breath," Queen Phillippa said admiring her handiwork. "We wouldst stay by our king and keep our husband breathing."

Leticia blushed deeply at the compliment. Truth indeed, she felt beautiful for the first time in her life. She felt very special and wonderful.

"Come daughter, tis past Vespers and the Great Hall wouldst be filling," Queen Phillippa ordered rising to take Leticia's hand. "Let us be about our ways."

Queen Phillippa entered the Great Hall first. She looked for Sir Vincent and found him surrounding by numerous court ladies. She grinned mischievously and walked slowly toward the king. Without turning around Queen Phillippa knew Leticia had entered. A silence covered the hall as all male conversation ceased. Their eyes focused on the radiantly beautiful young maiden stepping into the hall. Trenchers and goblets were put quickly aside and half the room rushed toward the maiden who seemed hesitant and unsure of what to do next.

Sir Vincent looked up to see the beautiful maiden just as Queen Phillippa approached him. The court ladies had moved aside for the queen.

"Sir Vincent, we note thy betrothed enters for thus meal," Queen Phillippa told the bedazzled knight and pointed to Leticia. "Methinks thy betrothed wouldst require thy protection. Think thee naught?"

"Leticia?" Vincent mumbled.

"Yea, thy betrothed, Leticia," Queen Phillippa replied allowing a large smile to appear on her lips. Half of the great hall was up and about surrounding Leticia. This would teach the knight who was the fortunate one. Her plan had worked perfectly.

Vincent bolted toward Leticia. He began pushing the noblemen and knights alike as he made his way toward her. The few moments and numerous

25

bodies he had pushed aside seemed endless. His anger began consuming him and he was furious when he received his first good look at her revealing gown.

"Goodwife!" Vincent shouted when he was at last by Leticia's side.

# Chapter 4

Vincent's face turned crimson with anger when he recognized the tall sandy haired man standing next to Leticia and brushing his lips over her knuckles. "Lionel, by God's teeth, from whence do thus?"

Lionel looked to see his good friend and the fury in his eyes. "Goodman, whence vexes thee?"

With fury Vincent removed Lionel's hand and took Leticia's. He shouted angrily, "Goodwife, from whence comest thee wearing such gown?" He opened his catch brooch and removed his mantel covering Leticia completely with it. He wrapped his mantel around her so tightly she could not move her arms at all and could not breathe.

Lionel's mouth dropped open. "Leticia? Thy betrothed?"

Slowly the gathered men removed their person from the presence of the furious knight and returned to their conversations, wine goblets, and trenchers.

"Yea," Vincent responded yanking the mantel even tighter around Leticia's small frame.

"Sirrah," Leticia wheezed. "We be finding thus difficult for breath!" Leticia started to feel light headed and began to sway.

"In God's Holy Name, Vincent," Lionel growled. "Take thus mantel off our lady's person, or loose it!"

Vincent released his grip on the mantel a moment before Leticia would have fainted. He enveloped her tiny frame with his massive arm giving her support.

It took several minutes for Leticia to regain normal breathing. She looked up and spanning the Great Hall noted that all eyes were upon her. "My Lord, methinks we hath created great scene. Let us be seated for our meal."

"Nay," Vincent snarled. "thee wouldst take thy meal in thy chambers."

"My Lord, from whence cometh thy anger for us?" Leticia whimpered. Everything had been wonderful to this point. Her betrothed was furious and was ordering her to have her meal in her chamber. Leticia wanted to cry. This is what she had been afraid of. She was being ordered around like a nothing and denied the gaiety of the court.

"Sir Vincent, bring thy betrothed to our table," a familiar voice said behind Vincent's back. It was the king.

Vincent turned around and King Edward moved forward to take Leticia's hand. "Queen Phillippa has requested our beauteous guest to sit with us at our table."

Leticia smiled again dropping the mantel off her shoulders leaving Vincent to retrieve it. "My Lord, we wouldst naught disobey our king. We fear we wouldst naught return to our chamber."

Vincent retrieved his mantel and continued growling. He flashed angry and warning eyes to the men staring at his betrothed.

When Leticia had taken her chair next to Queen Phillippa Vincent immediately sat next to her and once more tried to cover her with his mantel.

"Sir Vincent," Queen Phillippa admonished. "We find tis much too warm in thus Great Hall to wear mantel."

"Our Goodwife be chilled," Vincent countered.

27

"We be naught!" Leticia disagreed.

"Thee be chilled!" Vincent replied firmly.

"Nay," Leticia emphasized strongly.

"Sir Vincent," King Edward interceded. "Tis new to thee, but learn quickly thus be naught victory to win in an argument with thy Goodwife."

Leticia smiled over her small victory.

"Thy Goodwife in troth art beauteous, allow our eyes to enjoy thus beauty," King Edward chuckled raising his goblet.

The men within hearing range of the king offered a loud and unison, "Hoo! Hoo!"

Vincent scowled menacingly at the other men throughout the meal. The courtly ladies who had previously surrounded him continued to scowl at the lovely Lady Leticia. Sir John boasted throughout the meal that Leticia was his daughter and the image of her mother.

Leticia enjoyed the attention, conversation, and the company of the wise and wonderful Queen Phillippa. Leticia had followed the queen's instructions throughout the meal. She smiled broadly throughout the evening. It was another feminine victory. Queen Phillippa had told her to keep her goblet far enough away to require a long stretch of her arm placing her shoulder and low neckline in the path of her betrothed's eyes. Doing so, she reveled in his longing looks and then passionate anger upon noticing the other men as they stared at her. Ah, it was wonderful to make a man suffer like that. Leticia wondered why Vincent kept moving about in his seat when offering her meat, vegetable, and bread from his trencher. He looked in pain. If he were, that was good also. Queen Phillippa was a wonderful friend!

Vincent was in severe pain through out the entire meal. His betrothed's soft shoulders and feminine enticements once again made him lose control of this manhood. Every time he would slice and offer her a piece of meat he would become painfully aware of her enchantment. Silently he would groan in agony when she reached for her goblet allowing him full view of her shoulders and inviting breasts. Only the anger of looking up and seeing the other noble men and knights peeking at his property stopped him from collecting Leticia in his arms and ravishing her. This had to be the longest meal in his memory. Was Queen Phillippa purposely extending the length of this meal to torture him? He could not think of any reason for the queen to be angry with him.

King Edward leaned to his wife, "One wouldst naught believe scenes created by thee merely obeying our command to remove thus maiden's wimple."

"We obeyed only thy royal command," Queen Phillippa replied innocently. "We be thy majesty's most humble servant."

King Edward laughed boisterously, "Whither be servant and whither be lord? Trow thee troth, we be subject to thy tender mercies."

"Dost thou be wroth with us?" Queen Phillippa queried again with feminine innocence.

King Edward took his wife's hand and kissed her palm. "Nay! We enjoy our play too much. Before me sits a noble knight undefeated and fearful of nothing until hither comes a fair maiden. Turned from noble knight to young fearful lad by thus said lady. Thus play be too humorous by far! We owe thee debt, our Goodwife!"

"We wouldst collect thus eventide," Queen Phillippa invited sensually.

King Edward raised his brows several times in understanding. "Come hither Goodwife. Let us end thus meal and retire to our lover's chamber."

The departure of the king and queen announced to the hall the end of the meal. With the queen gone, Vincent immediately placed his mantel upon Leticia's shoulders. "Thee be chilled from thus night air!"

"Nay, we feel to warm by far," Leticia responded and attempted to remove the mantel.

Vincent grabbed her hand and removed it from the mantel. "Nay, thee be chilled and wouldst retire to thy chamber."

Leticia remembered Queen Phillippa's advice. *One only goes so far. A woman must know when to allow the man to believe he is in control. Thus she wins even more of a victory.* Leticia smiled and acquiesced to Sir Vincent's unspoken command. She took his extended arm to leave the Great Hall. Meekly she gave the knight instructions to the location of her chambers.

Leticia's three handmaidens had waited for her in the main chamber. Vincent was grateful, for he wanted to continue on to her bedchamber. Instead, he crushed her small frame into his massive muscular body. Holding her tightly he kissed the crown of her hair. His hands gently lifted her face as he bent to kiss her lips. Finally, his anger had receded and he realized this beautiful woman was his and his alone. The kiss gentle at first progressed into passion. Surprisingly his maiden opened like a flower to the realm of his passion. Vincent's tongue delved into the honeyed mouth and probed deeper and deeper.

For Leticia this kissing was a completely new experience. It was an experience she found pleasurable. She felt her body go limp in his strong hold and found his lips tasted sweet with wine. His tongue delicious and tasting of fine Bordeaux wine as he probed deeper and deeper. Soon Leticia felt her head spin and knew her legs would no longer support her. Whatever this strange kissing was, she enjoyed it.

The two handmaidens turned their face as not to interfere in the intimacy, but Lady Organa stared with her mouth agape. Unconsciously she sighed enviously.

The sigh made Vincent remember they were not alone and God help him he had to stop here. His body was burning with passion. He doubted he would be able to wait until the holy day of St. Giles. *God aide thy servant!* Carefully he placed Leticia back on her feet. "Goodwife, methinks thee wouldst naught wear thus gown evermore."

Leticia was still trying to get her breath and bring logic and reason back into her head. "Sirrah, thus gown be our gracious gift from Queen Phillippa."

"We wouldst naught allow thus gown upon thy person evermore," Vincent stated firmly. He would not have her argue with him and his jealousy might not be able to be controlled again. She was his and his alone to gaze upon.

"Our vows hath naught yet spoken," Leticia replied defiantly. "We be our own person!"

"Nay, our betrothal hath declared thee ours!" Vincent answered belligerently. "Thee wouldst obey as Goodwife wouldst!"

Leticia did not respond but stomped her foot and turned her back to begin walking to her bedchambers.

Vincent reached out and grabbed her shoulder pulling her back, "Dost thee comprehend our order?"

Leticia raised her eyebrow defiantly and answered angrily, "Yea, we comprehend thy command!"

Feeling confident he had won this battle of wills, Vincent turned and left the room.

Upon his departure Leticia removed his mantel and threw it at the door. "Fie on thee and thy commands!"

Her handmaidens watched in confusion as Leticia had a temper tantrum picking up items from the room and throwing them at the door. "Mongrel, Knave, kinder of serfs!" Were only some of the expletives that exploded from Leticia's harangue.

Sometime later Leticia allowed her handmaidens to undress her and prepare her for bed. Angrily Leticia tossed and turned until sleep finally overtook her.

The strain of the evening and the stubbornness of his future wife had taken a toll on Sir Vincent's emotions, but not his body. Unfortunately he took his frustration out on his squire.

"Maynard!" Vincent shouted angrily. "Thou slothful squire. Whither thee sleeps

whence thy lord needs thee?"

Maynard had dutifully prepared his lord's bedchambers and had been waiting for him in the bedchamber. He ran quickly into the anteroom at his lord's angry tone.

"Prepare thy lord a bath and make thus water cold!" Vincent growled ripping off his tunic scattering the buttons across the floor.

Maynard ran from the room in terror believing his violently angry lord would whip him in the next moment. He had never seen his lord in this mood. In short time Maynard had servants bring the tub and several were laden with buckets of water. Maynard ran into the room unlocking cabinets and bringing soap and cloth to the tub.

Wearing only his braes to cover his hardened man rod, Vincent watched the servants scurry to prepare his bath as he drank wine to help calm his wrath and need. When the servants had completed emptying the buckets in the tub, Vincent shouted, "Be gone!"

The servants tripped on themselves running out of the room. Maynard stood shaking at the tub holding his lord's soap and cloth.

Vincent shrieked a curse as he lowered his body into the tub, " By arms blood and bones, whence hath thus maiden wrought?"

30

Maynard chewed his lip to prevent a laugh from emitting after noticing the painfully stiff rod of his lord. Dutifully he washed his lord's back, arms, and legs. He dried his Lord when Vincent rose from the tub. Vincent removed his soaking cold braes and climbed into his bed pallet. Maynard closed the bed curtains and breathed a sigh of relief that at last his lord would sleep and he had been spared a beating.

Leticia woke early from her fitful sleep. Wrapping a warm cotton robe about her naked body she stretched at the window and noticed her Palfrey mare was getting exercise by a stable boy. "Fie on thee Sirrah!" Leticia snarled thinking about the beautiful horse Vincent had denied her to ride. Then a wicked smile spanned her lips and a glint of deviltry sparkled in her eyes. Quietly she opened an unlocked chest and pulled out a simple cotton bliaut. She dressed silently putting on her chemise, bliaut, hose, garter, and leather boots. Leticia brushed her hair leaving it flow naturally down her back and put upon her head a small braided circlet. Another unlocked chest held her soft velvet mantel and riding gauntlets.

Leticia attempted to open the door to her bedchamber without sound but failed. The door creaked loudly waking Lady Rosamund.

"My Lady?" Lady Rosamund questioned trying to focus her waking eyes.

"Be naught disturbed," Leticia whispered trying not to wake the others. She hurried her pace to the antechamber door.

"Thee be garmented!" Lady Rosamund gasped recognized Leticia's dress. "My Lady, thee wouldst naught ride alone!"

"Forsooth," Leticia replied quietly. "Peace, Lady Rosamond. Wake naught thus sleeping ladies." She opened the large door and ran through the hall down the steps.

"Abide! My Lady!" Rosamond shouted after Leticia tearfully. There was only one thing to do. She must seek out Leticia's betrothed and tell him. Frantically Lady Rosamund dressed while waking Organa, and Agnes. The two women also became hysterical with worry.

Rosamund left the chambers and asked the guards where the knight Sir Vincent was bedded. They directed her to the other wing of the castle and filled with fear rapped on the heavy oak door.

Maynard responded. He was already awake preparing for his Lord. "Whither be thy vexation lady? Whence dost thee come and wake our lord?"

"Thee must inform Sir Vincent," Rosamund said breathlessly. "Tis our lord's betrothed, Lady Leticia leaves thus castle unescorted."

The noise had wakened Vincent and wrapping himself in a brocade robe he walked into the antechamber. He heard everything Lady Rosamund had told his squire. Vincent grabbed the door slamming it against the wall. "By God's Teeth, whence hath thus trouble taken Lady Leticia's person?"

"Methinks our lady hath gone to thus stables," Rosamund wept fearfully. "My Lady dressed for riding."

Vincent cursed as he walked out to the passage. He shouted over his back to Lady Rosamund, "Return thee to thy rooms. We wouldst manage thus vexing child maiden."

Maynard called his lord, "My Lord, thee be naught garmented!"

Vincent looked at his open robe and cursed once more returning to the room.

Rosamund addressed the furious knight, "Pray thee Lord, for patience. The Lady Leticia trow naught of London city and dangers for such person."

"Return to thy rooms lady!" Vincent growled. "Thy lady behaves as child maiden and wouldst be treated thusly."

That was not comforting to Rosamund. She began to wonder if she had done the right thing to seek out Lady Leticia's betrothed. Slowly she returned to their rooms.

Maynard retrieved the clothes he had already prepared and helped his lord dress quickly.

Vincent bolted from his room. He ran toward the stables to see Leticia riding the Palfrey mare with a stable boy on a mount behind her. He could not imagine what she was thinking going out with him or a guard. A simple stable boy was not capable of protection. He ground his teeth as he quickened his pace. At the livery he did not wait for the stable master but saddled his Destrier. Vincent was mounted and after Leticia just moments later.

Leticia reined her horse toward the open area behind Westminster Castle and was enjoying a gallop with the Palfrey. Her hair flew behind her back and her heavy mantel flapped in the breeze. It was a ride of freedom.

The stable boy's mount was an old mare and could not keep up with the young and agile mare. He heard thundering hooves behind him and his mouth dropped open when he saw the noble men riding a huge Destrier obviously chasing them. As the knight passed him, the boy noticed fury boiling over in the knight's eyes. The boy turned his mount and returned to the stables. He recognized Vincent and knew the knight was after the Lady. She would be safe and he would make a quick exit.

Leticia was enjoying her ride to the extent she did not hear the thundering Destrier come from behind. Suddenly she was yanked off her Palfrey and settled upon the Destrier with a powerful and familiar arm surrounding her. Immediately she began to struggle. "Thou Knave, thee wouldst see us dead? Whence dost thee take our person from our mount? Fie upon you!"

Vincent reined his Destrier to a stop. "Behave anon or we wouldst warm thy bottom!"

Leticia stopped struggling. "Thee wouldst naught?"

"Yea, we wouldst!" Vincent said menacingly. "Thee behaves like child maiden, thee wouldst be treated like one."

"Sirrah, we dost naught ride like child maiden," Leticia snarled completely misunderstanding Vincent's words. "Whence dost thee consistently ruin our joy? Art thou e'er so cruel?"

"Cruel? Dost thee naught comprehend thy danger?" Vincent growled with impatience.

"Thy danger!" Leticia snapped. "Thee wouldst kill my person taking us from our mount thusly!"

"And many that wouldst take thee and hold thee for ransom," Vincent shouted heatedly. "Thee wouldst be beaten, starved, and violated for our golden coins! Dost thee comprehend?"

"Yea," Leticia cracked venomously. "Thee wouldst be angry for parting of thy coins."

It took all of Vincent's resolve not to turn her over his knee and spank her soundly. Instead he spurred his mount to trot to the Palfrey and take her reins. Vincent increased the strength of his hold on Leticia and returned to the castle.

King Edward had risen early and was about to mount for his morning ride when the two returned to the livery.

"Out for morning rides?" King Edward teased. The angry looks on their faces gave away their moods. "Tis happy we be thee art so good together. We wouldst enjoy our den together celebrating thus knighting of our son!"

Vincent first remembered his obligation. He would have to hurry to dress for Prince Edward's vigil. "Yea, my king! Happy be we in celebration," Vincent replied sarcastically. "We wouldst use thy solar to keep our Lady in protection until thus eventide." Vincent jumped from the Destrier handing the reins to the stable boy that had made a hasty return to the livery. Vincent then unceremoniously pulled Leticia from the Destrier and slung her small frame over his shoulder.

Leticia began screaming, "Knave unhand me! Cur! Mongrel!"

Vincent responded by slapping her soundly and with force on her buttocks.

The sting and the embarrassment in front of the king silenced and stilled Leticia.

"Yea, thusly thee become our behaved Goodwife," Vincent chuckled when she stilled and was silent. Vincent proceeded to her rooms with a smug and self-satisfied feeling that he could dominate this free spirit that was about to become his wife. That smugness was soon erased.

Opening the door to Leticia's rooms with Vincent's foot caused the heavy oak door to slam against the wall with a thud. The noise was so loud Leticia's handmaidens jumped in fright. The noise also brought the attention of Queen Phillippa who was about to leave her chambers.

Striding with arrogance and his burden on his shoulder in control, Vincent once more kicked open Leticia's bedchamber door with a thud. He dropped her on the bed as if unburdening himself with a sack of potatoes.

The embarrassment in front of the king and now her handmaidens set off a flood of tears. Leticia was soon sobbing hysterically.

Vincent was at his wits end. This woman had infuriated him, not understood the danger she had put herself in, and now was sobbing. Never before had the noble knight been at a loss as to what to say or do. He was helpless.   He wanted to soothe her, but he was angry with her for her foolishness.  His quandary was ended by a sharp and aristocratic voice behind him.

# Chapter 5

"Whence hast thee wrought such tears to our daughter? Thee be naught noble knight, thou be cur!"

"Majesty," Leticia sobbed leaping from the bed and running to the queen's open arms. "Save us from thus man formed beast. Thus knight hath beat us and caused us shame in witness of our king and handmaidens."

Encircling her mothering arms around Leticia, Queen Phillippa snarled at Vincent, "Get thee from these rooms. Our king shall hear of thus bestial act from one of our lord's own favored noble knights. Sirrah, thee be cur. Be gone from hither!"

"Majesty, tis naught troth," Vincent tried desperately to explain.

"Tis naught thee weeping in our arms so vexed," Queen Phillippa snapped. "One so large against tiny and delicate creature. For shame! Take thy leave anon."

Vincent could do no other than leave the room meekly by the queen's order. He felt his face redden in the embarrassment Leticia had suggested she endured. He cared for Leticia and was worried for her safety. His actions were noble to protect her. Couldn't Leticia and the queen understand that? Vincent bowed his head and allowed his shoulders to sag while walking past the glaring handmaidens and ladies in waiting to the queen. This waif of a woman had clearly beset and defeated him, an undefeated knight. In his very soul he wanted her now more than ever. Leticia had conquered his heart. Vincent silently vowed he would conquer her heart.

The noble knight that walked into the chambers was not the fearful and angry Sir Vincent de Courtenay. Maynard drew a breath of relief. This noble knight entered humbly with head bowed and shoulders sagging as if greatly defeated in combat.

"Squire, Prithee a goblet of wine," Vincent requested quietly. "We be worn to our soul."

Maynard rushed to fill his lord's goblet with wine from the tankard on the chest. "My lord, thee appears vexed and saddened," Maynard asked boldly but in concern. "Sire forgive our words, thee appears beset."

"Yea, most beset! Thus noble knight hath lowered down to his knees by thus most beauteous and virtuous maiden," Vincent replied taking the goblet from his squire. "Devon's wench hath conquered my heart and walks upon it like rushes in the Great Hall. Devon's wench hath naught care for our heart than drops of rain in lake waters."

"Thee speaks of thy betrothed?" Maynard queried.

"Yea, and tis good advice we wouldst seek," Vincent admitted suddenly sitting straight in the chair. "Whence be our Goodman, Lionel?"

"Sir Lionel beg leave at first light," Maynard informed. "Sir Lionel's message for thee was such sudden desire and need for the comforts of Goodwife. Sir Lionel wouldst meet thee at Okehampton Castle prior to thy nuptials."

"Fie!" Vincent shouted slamming his fist upon the chair arm. "We require thus experience of thus happily fettered man."

A little hesitant once more at his knight's anger, Maynard suggested, "Mayhap our Lord High King wouldst help thee. Our King Edward be verily and happily fettered."

"Squire!" Vincent shouted once more rising and grabbing the frightened lad by his arms and rising him off the floor quite easily. "Verily thee be blessing and wise for thy age. Our King! Of course our King!" It was then Vincent remembered his obligation to be with Prince Edward during his vigil. Gently he placed the boy back on the floor. The Holy Mass wouldst begin anon. "Come good squire, aide us to dress for our duty. Whence thus day be o'er we wouldst obtain our king's great wisdom in thus unknown matters set before us."

Queen Phillippa held Leticia patting her gently and speaking to her soothingly. "Weep naught our daughter. We wouldst protect thee and care for thee. Thus beast wouldst not frighten thee anon. We wouldst see to thus."

The warm and loving embrace of the queen did calm Leticia. "Majesty, thee be so kind," Leticia sniffed catching her breath.

The queen offered a silken kerchief to Leticia. "Dry thy tears. Tis naught our way to celebrate thus knighting of our son? Swollen eyes and tear stained cheeks?"

Leticia wiped her eyes. "Celebrate Prince Edward's knighting?"

"Yea, thee wouldst naught attend for tears upon thy cheeks," Queen Phillippa responded taking Leticia's hand in hers and helping wipe her eyes.

"We may attend thus knighting?" Leticia asked in surprise.

"Yea, as betrothed of noble knight, thee be required by protocol to attend," Queen Phillippa reassured. "Thus be some advantages for thy betrothal. Fear not, we wouldst naught allow thy noble knight to raise hand to thee."

"Whence wouldst we do for prevention?" Leticia breathed deeply still trying to control her sobbing.

"We wouldst speak to our Lord King. Sir Vincent wouldst be warned naught to raise hand to thee," Queen Phillippa replied soothingly. "Whence caused thus turmoil?"

"We, we went for ride upon our Palfrey mount thus morn," Leticia sniffled.

"Dost thy betrothed accompany thee?" Queen Phillippa queried.

"Nay, we wished quiet and solitude thus morn," Leticia explained meekly.

"Verily, thee be naught alone?" Queen Phillippa gasped.

"Nay, thus stable page accompanied us," Leticia replied.

"Stable page be naught proper escorting for our daughter. Thee placed thyself in great danger. Sir Vincent sought thee?"

"Yea, Sir Vincent grabbed us from our mount and scolded us fiercely," Leticia clarified. "Hence before our Lord King he threatened us with confinement in thus solar. Thus beast slung us over shoulder like sack of flour, and warmed our bottom most soundly. If thus wast naught evil and cruel, Sir Vincent carried our person thusly before our handmaidens."

Queen Phillippa held back a chuckle. "Thee hath much to learn in thus arts of Goodwife. Yet, we wouldst naught allow Sir Vincent to escape unscathed from thus scene our knight hath created. Our daughter in troth be in great danger and verily thy betrothed justifiably fearful."

"We be naught aware of danger," Leticia choked holding back new tears.

"Verily, a virtuous and beauteous maiden such as thee wouldst be taken captive for ransom. Thee wouldst be beaten and ravaged waiting for thy ransom. Thee wouldst naught leave thus protection of thy betrothed without proper guard. Dost thee give us oath?"

Leticia nodded her head subserviently. "We trow naught of thus happenings."

"Thee wouldst learn court from us. We wouldst instruct thee in thus protocol, joys, and dangers," Queen Phillippa promised. "Thee wouldst stay in our protection."

"God have mercy on thee," Leticia said appreciatively. "Wouldst we apologize to Sir Vincent?"

"Verily Nay!" Queen Phillippa replied emphatically. "Thy betrothed wouldst be more gentle with thee. Sir Vincent be of thus world and trow these happenings. Sir Vincent's patience wouldst be forged. Thy betrothed wouldst be punished for thus error. Learn thus our daughter, thus Goodwife wouldst naught allow our man to lord over us any right."

"We wouldst be thy most willing servant," Leticia smiled joyfully. She did love the queen.

"We wouldst dress thee and in so happening, we wouldst instruct thee," Queen Phillippa laughed. "First we wouldst break the fast with our Lord High King and suggest to our husband thus wrongs of our throne's most noble knight."

The queen left Leticia to join her husband for breakfast. Leticia bathed and dressed to join the king and queen in their private chambers. Queen Phillippa had already spoken to King Edward of Sir Vincent de Courtenay and his wrong doings. King Edward agreed to all of his wife's demands on retribution. King Edward, knowing the truth of what happened, knew his adored wife would not listen to the facts. He laughed inwardly at the punishments his wife had requested. It would indeed teach the knight to be gentler with his betrothed and Sir Vincent should begin to understand the power of femininity. That was a lesson King Edward was readily aware of and had been for some time.

The gossips of the castle had quickly made the courtly rounds about Sir Vincent de Courtenay in record time. Each version was embellished and soon the beastly knight had beaten his lady mercilessly in a fit of jealousy.

Vincent was unaware of the wagging tongues. He was dutifully holding holy vigil with his former squire, Prince Edward.

At vespers the Holy Mass concluded with the Prince's entire family attending. Sir Vincent noticed his fair Lady Leticia standing at the queen's side.

The long mass seemed endless as Vincent wished to be near his betrothed. When the blessings were finally said, Vincent rose to approach Leticia. Another knight's arm stayed him.

"Our Lord King hath ordered thee to attend our king's son, Prince Edward," Martin Bolin instructed. "Thee wouldst accompany thus prince to our Great Hall, whence thee wouldst take thy seat next to our Prince."

Vincent looked up to see Queen Phillippa scowl at him and embrace Leticia protectively. Queen Phillippa guided Leticia toward the doors of Westminster Abbey.

It was amazing how Queen Phillippa managed Leticia and her children at the same time so well. Vincent admired the queen for her talents. Returning to the prince's side, they walked together in the passage to the Great Hall for the festivities.

Vincent was discouraged when he was seated next to the prince who had been seated next to the king. Next to the king was Queen Phillippa, and next to the queen was Leticia. She was served her own trencher. That meant there was no need for Sir Vincent to sit near her. It was an obvious snub to his person. Leticia enjoyed the celebration with light conversation and goodwill of Queen Phillippa.

Vincent noticed many noblemen staring at his betrothed with lustful eyes and he was infuriated at being kept from her. He also noticed the women of the court that usually hung on his every word were avoiding him like he was afflicted with the pox.

Long after he had finished his meal, he found his opportunity to speak to King Edward.

"Majesty," Sir Vincent addressed bowing deeply. "Wouldst thee spare us moment? We need thy great wisdom and experience."

King Edward raised a brow. "Whither wouldst thus greatest undefeated knight of our realm need of our wisdom?"

"Advice from man who be merrily wed, Majesty," Vincent stated almost pleading for help.

"We must hide. Our Goodwife be wroth with thee," King Edward whispered. "Protecting our person, we must naught be viewed in prattle."

"Whence grievance hast we committed against our queen?" Vincent queried. He had only tried to protect Lady Leticia. Surely she must have understood that.

"Thy error matters naught. Our Goodwife be wroth," King Edward warned. "We wouldst naught suffer thy same wroth. Speak with us on the morrow. We wouldst leave for Surrey after first light. Thee wouldst be our riding companion."

"Surrey?" Vincent asked with surprise. "We wouldst be on our way to Okehampton."

"Nay, thy betrothed rides with us to Surrey. Lady Leticia be our ward until thy nuptials. The queen hath decreed it," King Edward informed the knight. Before Vincent could reply he raised his hand for silence. "Depart anon our Goodman, if our queen views thee and our person in conversation, wouldst be most uncomfortable in our bedchamber thus eventide. If thus wouldst happen? We wouldst be angry with thee."

"Majesty," Vincent acquiesced and turned to walk back to the hall.

"Whence goest thee?" King Edward asked grabbing Vincent's arm.

"We wouldst escort our lady to thus solar," Vincent replied in surprise at King Edward's staying hand.

"Nay, Lady Leticia be our ward. Our son, Prince Edward, wouldst be thy lady's escort," King Edward replied firmly. "Depart anon, thy punishment from our queen be separation from thy lady until thee dost learn to be gentle."

Vincent obeyed and like a child petulantly left the Great Hall and returned to his rooms. *How wouldst it be thus great and undefeated noble knight be reduced to discipline of young lad?*

The king attempted to make his way back to his wife's side but was detained by Sir Bolin.

The queen noticed this conversation and noted the conversation seemed intense. Sir Martin's face grew red with anger, but bowed stiffly and left the king.

"Whence happened in thy conversation with Sir Martin Bolin?" Queen Phillippa asked her husband when he took his seat beside her. "Thee appear vexed, our love."

"Sir Bolin hath heard all thus gossip of thus den betwixt Sir Vincent and Lady Leticia," King Edward replied crossly. "Thus dolt requested we cast aside our nuptial decree and make Bolin, Lady Leticia's betrothed."

"Whence be excuse for thus? We trow in troth Sir Martin's purpose be greed," Queen Phillippa queried. This request angered her also. It was well known in court Sir Martin was untrustworthy and greedy, stopping at nothing to attempt title and wealth.

"Yea, troth be greed. Sir Martin carries thus tale he wouldst be gentle and kind to so fair maiden, unlike thus bestial Sir Vincent."

"Okehampton Castle and lands wouldst be fine prize for thus greedy knight," Queen Phillippa recognized. "Thou replied with firm naught?"

"Yea, we trow Sir Vincent to be our most worthy suitor. Thus knight be merely ignorant in thus ways of femininity," King Edward laughed. "Sir Vincent wouldst soon learn thus ways to delight as we trow."

"As thee speaks of nuptial delight, our lord," Queen Phillippa said seductively. "Wouldst thee be tired and need rest in our bedchamber?"

King Edward smiled happily. "Our person be most tired." King Edward leaned over and spoke to Prince Edward. He and the queen then took leave of the Great Hall.

Sir Bolin watched when the king and queen rose to leave. He walked over to Lady Leticia immediately. "Thus be late in den. Wouldst thee retire to thy chambers? We wouldst be honored to take thee hence."

Leticia always believed in her first impressions and feelings. This man made her blood run cold. In the inflection of his words she felt coldness. Sir Bolin smelled of drink and being unbathed for several days. Sir Vincent, although brutish, she did enjoy his presence. Sir Vincent always smelled clean and fresh. But where was he? She craned her neck looking for him. She could not find him. Surely he would escort her to her rooms. Leticia did not know how to turn Sir Bolin down gracefully.

"Lady Leticia, our father, Lord High King, hath requested we escort thee to thy rooms," Prince Edward announced stepping between her and the knight.

Leticia let loose a breath she was unaware she was holding. Before she could answer Sir Bolin objected.

"We wouldst take thus lady to her chambers. We hath previously requested thus."

"Nay, thus be command of our Lord High King," Prince Edward countered. He was no longer the squire, even if a prince. Today he was fully knighted and Prince Edward. He was Sir Bolin's equal and superior by royal blood. Prince Edward inwardly hoped Sir Bolin would challenge him. He knew he could easily defeat the knight grown slothful.

"My lady," Sir Bolin bowed and backed away.

"Edward, brother of our heart. We be in thy debt," Lady Leticia whispered. "We wouldst naught care for Sir Bolin's countenance."

"Sir Bolin hath turned slothful and greedy for title and wealth," Prince Edward whispered into her ear. "We wouldst thee avoid him."

"Quite merrily, dearest brother," Leticia replied. "We be in debt to thee. Whence be our betrothed to spare us such fates?"

"Mother be wroth for Sir Vincent's misconduct," Edward chuckled. "Sir Vincent be punished for thus. Mother hath Father decree thee be our king's ward until nuptials. Sir Vincent may naught be near thee till our mother's wrath wanes."

Leticia giggled at the thought of the big strong night reduced to punishment of a lad. "Doth thy mother, our queen, trow of our secret friendship?"

"Nay, we wouldst tell her anon," Prince Edward answered smiling. "Thus wouldst please her in troth."

Leticia felt as light as a feather and a new found happiness overwhelmed her. She could spend time with her best friend and it was not only acceptable, the king himself had decreed it. Leticia also gained a confidence in her abilities as she discovered her power to bring a noble knight to her control. Leticia chatted happily with Prince Edward. They slipped into their childhood practice of sharing all happenings and feelings. It had been a wonderful day after all.

Sir Vincent returned to his rooms disheartened. He was not only angry to be punished as a child. He found his attraction to Lady Leticia was genuine and he was disturbed at being kept from her. Was this love? Silently he allowed Maynard to remove his clothing and crept into his lonely bed. When the chamberlain closed his lord's curtains, Vincent was thinking of his fair betrothed. He vowed once more he would conquer her heart. He would attempt to be more sensitive to her wants and needs. He would definitely ride next to the king for his advice tomorrow.

Maynard stayed awake for several hours polishing his lord's armor. This knight he squired was very strange. His moods and emotions seemed to change like the tides. In the short time he had been Sir Vincent's squire he noted this change first occurred when his lord was betrothed. Maynard swore a silent oath never to be fettered if a woman had such effects upon a man.

The next morning Vincent woke early ordering his squire to dress him in full armor. Maynard had already been told the evening before to pack for his knight. They would accompany the king to Surrey Castle. Vincent was overly anxious to speak with the king and if not be near his betrothed, at least see her. Vincent broke fast in his room and hurried to the livery to prepare his Destrier. He could not bear to endure the Great Hall to see his betrothed, but not allowed to be near her. At least on the ride to Surrey Castle he would not bear the stares of others. He wasn't even sure why all, even the ladies, shunned him.

"Sir Vincent! A word with thee," Sir John growled.

"My lord," Vincent bowed turning to the titled and land holding knight.

"We warn thee anon, wouldst thee raise thy hand for our daughter e'er, " John snarled angrily. "Thee wouldst feel blade of our sword!"

"Of whence sayeth thou?" Vincent asked with surprise. "We wouldst naught harm thy daughter."

"The court doth say thee beat our daughter for thy jealousy with naught mercy," Sir John accused. "We wouldst naught have our daughter and only child so treated."

"Tis naught troth!" Vincent defended. "Thy daughter deemed to ride unescorted into countryside. We retrieved our lady from folly. Lady Leticia behaved childishly. We merely swatted thus behind, yea only once, to still thy daughter's ranting."

"Troth?" Sir John asked.

"Tis troth," Sir Vincent replied. "Shouldst thee naught believe. Ask of our Lord High King. He wouldst be present for thus moment."

"How be thus a tale running through court?" Sir John queried.

"Thy daughter with hysterics cried out to our queen," Sir Vincent exclaimed. "Our queen heard only thus words of distress from thy daughter. In wroth told our queen thus. Wouldst thee speak to thy daughter? Whence trouble dost we commit?"

"Dost our daughter's wroth vex thee?" Sir John questioned.

"Yea, our lady's wrath dost vex our person greatly," Sir Vincent admitted stroking his Destrier's nose gently.

"We wouldst speak with our daughter," Sir John reassured patting Sir Vincent on his shoulder. Sir John de Redvers was once again confident of his choice in the selection of betrothed, for his only daughter, had been the right one.

Shortly thereafter, the king and his entourage appeared and began mounting their horses for Surrey Castle. Queen Phillippa rode with her younger children and ladies in waiting. She had been told by her son of Lady Leticia's and his secret childhood friendship and secret place. He shared with his parents the brotherly and sisterly love that had grown for each other during their fostering. The king and queen were delighted to know of the friendship. Prince Edward assisted Lady Leticia on her Palfrey and mounted his black Destrier. They rode side-by-side and chatted merrily.

Vincent thought they looked too happy with each other. Once more jealousy started grabbing at his heart.

# Chapter 6

King Edward and Sir Vincent de Courtenay rode side by side at the beginning of the long entourage.

"Mayhap we wouldst be able to speak to our lady anon?" Vincent asked the king being fully aware of his punishment of separation ordered by the queen.

"Mayhap if thou wouldst be gentle and soft of voice," King Edward teased. "Methinks young knight thee be learning thus lesson of thus power of femininity at last."

"My Good King, we fear we trow nothing of thus courting and ladies," Sir Vincent sighed heavily. "We dost our duty in protection only to be treated as if we hath pox."

"Tis time for thee to be instructed. Learn anon thy Goodwife be naught thy possession. Yea thy Goodwife be thy obsession to be treated tenderly and with regard lest thee break thy own heart," King Edward laughed. "Trow thee thus maiden fair hath power to make thy bedchamber heaven or hell?"

"Nay," Vincent declared in disbelief. The king's words already made him feel like an idiot.

"Yea, thus be whence thee fail," King Edward warned. "Thy Goodwife wouldst comfort thee and care for thee most tenderly if thee be kind, gentle, and caring of thy lady's needs."

"Whither be a lady's needs? Doth naught thus lord provide all for thus lady?" Vincent queried with confusion. A knight fought for thus lady, protected thus lady, took count of lands and protected thus lands for wealth, food, clothing, and shelter. Whence be more for thus lady's need?

"Dost thee ask our person? Thee wouldst ask thy lady," King Edward chided. "Thee wouldst comprehend thy Good wife's monthly flow and thus pain thus brings. Thee wouldst comprehend whence her belly be full with thy child and thus discomfort hence. Thee wouldst comprehend whence some den hath been difficult and fraught with problems in thy kitchens, chambers, kinder, or any other vexation."

"Thee be jesting with our person," Vincent snorted.

"Nay, we be most serious," King Edward stated firmly. "Whence thee be considerate and loving about thy lady's needs. Thy lady cares tenderly for thy needs. Thy lady wouldst provide soothing massage whence thy muscles ache from war and jousting. Thy lady tends to thee for thee wouldst drink warm wine waiting for thee in winter cold, and cool wine in summer heat. Thy lady wouldst provide warm stones under thy bed for thy comfort and thy lady's warm body to keep thee warm at night."

"Thee hath endowed to our person thy great wisdom," Vincent acknowledged gratefully. "Methinks thus lady wouldst recite her poetry for our person, and if we listen, our lady wouldst care for our noble and great deeds in battle."

"Yea, as thee gives to thy lady, so wouldst thee receive," King Edward said. "Trow anon and comprehend thy bedchamber wouldst be heaven or hell. Thus place wouldst be thy choice."

"Dost thus simple plan work equally as well in the bedding?" Vincent snorted with mirth.

"Yea, tis better in thus bedding when both share," King Edward laughed boisterously. "If thou be loving and treasure thy precious Goodwife. If thee wouldst take time to explore and kiss every curve upon thy silken treasure, thy rewards be most pleasing!"

"Explore and kiss all soft silken places?" Vincent smirked allowing his imagination to run rampant.

"Yea, all!" King Edward snickered enjoying the manly discussion with his knight. King Edward looked at Sir Vincent and laughed loudly. "Thee dost comprehend!"

"Yea!"

"We wouldst speak with our queen thus eventide and occupy her," King Edward teased joyously and with innuendo. "Speak to thy lady thus eventide. We see to thus be allowed. Whence camp be made, approach thy lady hence."

"May God keep thee, our Lord High King," Vincent appreciated. Throughout the day he watched Lady Leticia. It did not please him to see Prince Edward and his lady laughing and enjoying each other with animated conversation. This did not bode well with him at all. Finally the day ended and the entourage broke for camp. Pavilions were hastily raised and Sir Vincent watched as King Edward took Queen Phillippa into their pavilion and closed the flap so they would not be disturbed.

Vincent had Maynard remove his armor leaving his tunic, hose, and leather boots as dress. He walked to the pavilion where Lady Leticia would stay with the other ladies of the court. He spotted Leticia once more in happy and animated conversation with Prince Edward. Other young ladies stare doe eyed at the Prince. Vincent approached and announced, "Prithee, mayhap we wouldst enjoin in thus conversation?"

Leticia looked up to see her betrothed. He looked forlorn and her heart beat a little faster for that. "Yea, we wouldst be speaking of thee. Prince Edward wouldst be telling us of thy great victories."

"Yea, thou art known far and wide with trembling and fear," Prince Edward agreed.

"Such words be valuable for enemies, but naught for our Goodman and Goodwife," Vincent answered with soft voice. His blues eyes softened with his words to show a tenderness Leticia had never noticed before. "We bring thee poetry from our northern lands. Wouldst thee care to listen to our recitations?"

Prince Edward reached for Leticia's hand, "Therefore thee seest our words be troth. Dost naught we speak of Sir Vincent's love for prose?"

Leticia nodded her head shyly. What would her betrothed think if he realized their primary conversation had been about him? Would he understand Prince Edward admired and respected his former lord and was trying to ease Leticia's way with the betrothal?

Sir Vincent spread his mantel upon the ground and began reading the prose.

Leticia was surprised with the feeling he emitted as he read. *Verily, such a man wouldst be kind and understanding.*

A few hours later, Prince Edward excused himself and many of the ladies retired to the pavilion where the ladies of the court stayed. They had enjoyed listening to the prose also, but it was now time to retire.

"My Lady Leticia, wouldst thee walk with our person?" Sir Vincent asked timidly. "Thee wouldst pain us grievously if thee still be wroth with thy servant."

"Nay, we be naught wroth for thee. Our good and kindly queen explained to us thus peril we hath placed our person. Our good and kindly queen explained to us thee be trying to protect us."

"We attempted to tell thee thusly," Vincent sighed heavily. "Thee wouldst naught hear me thence."

"Our good and kindly queen explained all to us," Leticia quickly snapped. "Thee dost shout at us!"

Curbing his temper Vincent replied apologetically and meekly, "Prithee grant us forgiveness. We wouldst naught raise our voice to thee e'er again."

"Verily, thou dost regret thy injurious misconduct?" Leticia queried skeptically.

"We regret our misconduct deeply and for apologetic heart, my lady," Vincent replied.

Leticia once more enjoyed the savor of victory. This new and different way of life being the betrothed was turning out to be quite fun and an adventure. She took his arm and they walked silently into the clearing of the forest by the lake. "Tis very beauteous."

"Yea, tis lovely, but thy countenance brings shame to all other beauty," Sir Vincent said chivalrously.

"Speakest thee thy heart, Sirrah?" Leticia asked hopefully. "Verily thee be pleased to procure us for thy betrothed? Thee wouldst naught treat us as possession and decree of thy king?"

"Nay my lady. Thee be our obsession, naught possession. A humble knight such as we doth sing in celebration our fortune for our betrothal, " Vincent repeated from the king's previous words. He thought himself quite smart for that one. "Tell us fair lady, whence wouldst us do to win thy heart for troth? Ask us or tell us whence thee requires of thus humble and enchanted knight?" He remembered King Edward's previous advice. Yes this would be easy with help and knowledge of experience. Vincent drew Leticia into his muscular arms. He held her tightly and inhaled her sweet fragrance. His lips brushed her hair searching, seeking, and wanting more.

Leticia melted into his arms and enjoyed the strength and security there. Never before in her life had she been held like that. She felt her resolve weaken. Strange and pleasant feelings enveloped her body.

Vincent used his hands to lift her face and he bent down to kiss those sweet and delicate lips. "Ask us for anything. Whence wouldst bring thee happiness from us?"

Leticia's voice cracked, "We trow....we trow... we trow naught... Ohhh!" She sighed as Vincent covered her mouth with his and his tongue played with her lips finally opening her mouth. Leticia thought she was floating. She no longer felt her arms or legs. Leticia slipped in and out of reality as Vincent's tongue slid deeper and deeper into her mouth, challenging her to a duel of love. There was no doubt she lost this battle.

Steadying his own pounding heart, Vincent breathed heavily, "Wouldst thee walk further with us?" He had to cool down his demanding body.

"Yea," Leticia whispered hoping her betrothed did not hear her pounding heart.

Vincent boldly placed his arm around Leticia's shoulder as they walked to a ledge rising above the lake.

Leticia was grateful for Vincent's embracing arm. She wasn't certain she could walk unsupported.

They stopped upon the ledge and looked down on the quiet lake reflecting the full moon.

"Wouldst thee capture thus place as thee doth capture thus heart," Vincent suggested lovingly. "Mayhap thee wouldst use thy needle for tapestry upon our return to Okehampton?"

Leticia did not hear the love part of Vincent's sentence. She only heard the needle and tapestry part. "Sirrah, whence dost thee believe we handle needle?"

Vincent looked down upon her with confusion. "All ladies be skilled for thus art."

"Fie on thee! Thus lady doth despise needles!" Leticia replied angrily. She hated the needle and tapestry in truth. She hated Sister Agatha watching over her shoulder criticizing every stitch. She hated the hours upon hours forced upon her to learn the art in the nunnery. Many times Leticia would feign illness to seek sanctuary in her secret place. The very place she met Prince Edward. She loved to tell and share tales with Edward. Leticia loved to read and also practiced falconry. She even loved numbers and sums. She loved going into the meadows with Sister Beatrice and learning the plants for food and medicine. She hated tapestries!

"My Lady, thy tongue!" Vincent chided genuinely surprised at the curse she used. He was totally confused at her anger. What on earth did he do wrong now? Women were certainly confusing.

"A pox upon thee!" Leticia snarled and pushed against Vincent with anger.

The movement caused her to slip on the mossy ledge and she quickly lost her balance. As she started falling into the lake, Vincent made an attempt to rescue her but lost his footing and ended up following Leticia into the lake.

Fortunately Vincent was tall and he stood upon the lakebed. The water was up to his neck. He found Leticia paddling with her arms and laughing.

"Whence be thy sudden humor? Wouldst thy wroth be cooled with us?" Vincent asked raising an eyebrow.

"Thee wouldst find humor in thy landing, if thee hath watched thee fall," Leticia laughed. "A brave and noble knight most ungraceful whilst attempting to dive into thus pool."

"Thou didst naught gracefully dive methinks," Vincent chuckled reaching for Leticia.

"Nay, tis troth. Still, thee dost appear quite drenched," Leticia teased.

"Yea, thee dost also appear quite drenched," Vincent snorted. "Thee be naught wroth with thy servant?"

"Nay, thy countenance be too comical for wroth," Leticia replied allowing Vincent to take her in his arms.

"Thus knight hath learned thee dost naught be fond of the needle?" Vincent questioned realizing her anger had to mean that she hated doing tapestries. "Prithee, whence dost delight our lady?"

"Verily, dost thee truly wish to learn?" Leticia queried softly.

"Yea," Vincent replied holding her tightly against his chest.

"Our greatest pleasure be reading and scribing tales," Leticia shared with Vincent. "We enjoy, falconry, sums, and herbs. We dost despise thus needle and tapestry."

"Mayhap thus humble knight wouldst become thy greatest pleasure," Vincent said more for himself than Leticia. "Therefore we dost decree thee wouldst naught raise needle e'er again unless thy desire. Upon our return to Okehampton we wouldst create hunting party and thus knight wouldst see thy falconry skills."

"Verily, for troth thee dost speak?" Leticia asked happily.

"Thee hath our oath for noble and knight, my lady!" Vincent declared. *So thus be whence our king meant by listening to thus lady.* Vincent was slowly beginning to understand. He was extremely happy with the results just as King Edward had advised. Leticia took Vincent's head in her hands and gently placed a kiss upon his lips.

"Thee doth make us joyous," Leticia bubbled with happiness.

Vincent kissed Leticia back and he thought the water was beginning to steam around them. He no longer felt the chill of the lake.

Neither did Leticia feel the lake's chill as Vincent once more encased her body with his arms and kissed her with what she now recognized as passion. The queen had been right. A woman has great power over men, but sometimes a soft voice and explanation of her thoughts was required. Queen Phillippa had told her that men were wise in battle but quite ignorant of life. Yes, Queen Phillippa was very wise.

"By God's teeth!" A rude voice interrupted. "Whence happened hither?"

Vincent broke away from his kiss and looked to see Sir Martin Bolin standing by the lakeshore. He replied angrily, "our lady hath wished for swim thus eventide."

"Yea, and our lord thought to join us," Leticia giggled playfully.

"Thee wouldst catch thus death!" Martin replied drooling with false concern. "Thsu breezes be strong thus eventide and carry chills."

"Mayhap thus be reason thee dost naught bathe?" Vincent quipped sarcastically. He began walking back to shore with Leticia firmly in his arms.

Leticia buried her head into Vincent's shoulder to stifle her amusement at his remark to Sir Bolin.

Vincent felt Leticia quiver in his arms. "Wouldst our lady be chilled?"

Keeping her face buried in his chest, Leticia whispered, "Nay, tis thus troth of thy words, Sirrah. Sir Bolin be for dire need of bathing."

Vincent and Leticia did feel the chill of the breezes on their soaked bodies when they emerged from the lake.

Leticia did shiver as the breezes wafted over her soaked clothing.

Sir Bolin removed his mantel and placed it over Leticia's body. Vincent was still carrying her and found the heavily pungent body odor on the mantel disagreeable to his sense.

Leticia buried her face deeper into Vincent's muscled but wet chest to avoid the odors. However, even bearing the odorous mantel did not stop the chills from overtaking her. As she was carried back to camp her teeth began chattering.

Vincent picked up his pace and upon approaching the camp called to her handmaidens. Lady Organa ran into the pavilion and returned with several warm dry woolen blankets. Lady Rosamund and Lady Agnes wrapped the blankets around Leticia and took her into the pavilion to change her wet clothes. Vincent heard several consecutive "HaaChoos!" from his lady. To him the cool chill was a blessing on his hot body. He was also used to cold baths on the battlefronts. He could withstand the physical environments. A lady could not. He went to his pavilion to change his clothes for a dry shirt to sleep in and hoped Leticia would be taken care of. Inwardly he wished they were already married. He would have dried her and kept her very warm at night.

The next morning, he wore one of his best tunics and tight fitting hose. It was crazy, but he wanted to impress the Lady Leticia. He felt like a peacock strutting his feathers before his mate. But in his mind, it was worth the effort to impress his lady.

Leticia finally emerged from the pavilion and Vincent rushed to her side. Holding a silken kerchief to her face he noticed her eyes were not sparkling as they usually did. "Hath thee malady?" Vincent asked with earnest concern.

"Yea, methinks we be taken for sniffles," Lady Leticia replied weakly.

"Wouldst thee ride with us upon our Destrier?" Vincent questioned hoping she was not too ill.

"Nay, we fear thy mount in troth," Leticia replied honestly. "Wouldst thee assist us upon our mount?"

"Happily," Vincent answered. "We be deeply saddened thou dost fear our mount."

"Tis better to fear thy mount or thee?" Leticia teased lightly. She wasn't really feeling well at all, but hoped as the day progressed she would feel better.

"Our mount," Vincent quickly replied happily. Never before had a woman made him more crazy or more delighted with her company. This would be a wonderful marriage. Vincent was looking forward to making this beautiful woman his wife.

Leticia's body ached and found it difficult even with Vincent's help to mount her Palfrey. Stubbornly she took the reins with determination not to allow this cold to affect her. She smiled at Vincent and after many consecutive HaaChoos, thanked him graciously.

Vincent rode next to Leticia for the remainder of the ride to Surrey Castle. Prince Edward rode on the other side of Lady Leticia. Vincent learned of their special friendship and his jealousy of the handsome young Prince left quickly. Soon he settled into their conversations. Vincent found he enjoyed their conversations filled with barbs, puns, and laughter. The only down side to the ride was Leticia's continual sneezing.

It was near vespers when they arrived at Surrey Castle.

Leticia had been stalwart in her battle with her cold, but once they stopped in the castle courtyard she lost. Blackness enveloped her and she drifted into it.

Vincent noticed her swaying upon her mount and her brown eyes disappeared suddenly by closed eyelids. He jumped from his Destrier and caught her just as she fell. He cradled her limp body and swore loudly, "By God's teeth, our lady's body doth burn with fever!"

Prince Edward turned to see Lady Leticia fall into Vincent's arms. He called to his guard to find his mother, Queen Phillippa. Like any young lad, Prince Edward believed his mother could take care of anything.

The stir had drawn Queen Phillippa's attentions. She heard Sir Vincent's curses and hurried to his side.

"Bring our daughter hither," Queen Phillippa commanded leading the way into the bailey and into the castle. Moving quickly, she led the frightened knight carrying his lady up to the royal private chambers. The queen herself opened the curtains of her eldest daughter's bed and pulled down the covers. She watched as Vincent laid Leticia gently on the soft pallet. When he was done she opened the gown and removed it leaving only Leticia's chemise. Queen Phillippa covered Leticia to her chin with the heavy cotton blanket and ordered her ladies in waiting to bring out the winter's fur blankets and covered Leticia. The queen kept adding covers until Leticia began to sweat.

Vincent watched in concern and dared to ask, "Whence dost thusly? Our lady be burning for fever and thee wouldst cover more?"

"Leave us," Queen Phillippa ordered. "Thee trow naught medicine. We wouldst break thus fever anon." Queen Phillippa's lady in waiting handed her several vials. The queen busied herself mixing several of the herbs in a goblet of wine. She then lifted Leticia's head and held it so Leticia could drink the mixture.

It seemed to take hours before the drink was completed by the delirious patient. Vincent paced back and forth nervously.

When the queen laid Leticia's head back down on the pillow she looked up at the fidgeting knight.

"Dost thee hear us? Leave anon!" the queen ordered angrily. "We wouldst take Lady Leticia's care. Find some battle prattle to keep thee occupied."

"Wouldst my lady live?" the frightened knight asked.

# Chapter 7

"Verily, dost thee for troth care so for thy lady?" Queen Phillippa questioned while she took a cool cloth to Lady Leticia's brow.

"We care sorely," Vincent confessed. "We find our person deeply and vexed with love for our lady."

"Dost thee love thy lady so thee wouldst stay to minister to thy lady's needs?"

"Yea."

"E'en if thee must do so lowly chore as wiping thy lady's brow?" Queen Phillippa queried. "Mayhap forcing medicine into thy lady's mouth?"

"Yea."

"Yea, wouldst thus be for troth, come sit with us and help us," Queen Phillippa proposed.

Vincent quickly grabbed a stool and put it by Leticia's bedside. He took the offered cool cloth from Queen Phillippa and gently began wiping Leticia's brow. "Methinks my lady's malady be fault of ours," Vincent confessed.

"Yea, to take swim in cool of night wouldst cause such malady," Queen Phillippa scolded lightly.

"Thee trow?"

"Yea, wagging tongues of court and thy jealous competitor came with such tales for my person the day long," Queen Phillippa shared. "We be naught wroth with thee. We wouldst suggest thee consider thrice before we take nightly swims once more."

"Thee hath our word," Vincent vowed to the queen.

For hours Leticia stay in delirium. Queen Phillippa covered her mouth several times from outright laughing at Leticia's delirious ranting. The queen also held back tears listening to Leticia's heartbreaking stories.

Leticia used curses several times for Sister Mary Martha and Sister Agatha. She spoke of undoing Sister Agatha's perfect stitches one evening when everyone was asleep. To this day Sister Agatha never knew who had ruined her stitching. Leticia spoke of finding a kitten and bringing it to the secret place to show her foster brother, Prince Edward. She related in detail his terror when he ran away from her and the kitten. She related a tale of her running to her father when he returned from a battle. Her father's Destrier would have stomped her to death if not for the quick action of her mother. She cried in her delirium of how her father had scolded her severely and called her an idiot child maiden of useless worth. She cried at her father's apathy toward her and being fostered so far from the mother she loved so dearly. St. Giles had been her father's choice and she had heard him arguing with her mother about it. Sir John believed the child maiden was stupid and useless and his wife Maude had spoiled her.

To all of the ranting Sir Vincent listened carefully. He understood her fear of Destriers. He chided himself for not considering any fear she might have when he forced her to ride upon his mount from St. Giles. Or the time he

51

removed her from her mount when she left to ride unescorted. Vincent could empathize with her tale of apathy from a parent. In his case, it had been his mother. She quickly fostered him to Coventry. His mother had berated him for being the all so perfect and special son of his father. He had realized later she was jealous of the time his father spent with him. He remembered well the sense of loneliness in fostering. He remembered missing his father's company and trying to understand why his mother didn't love him as he loved her. He tried everything he could think of to make his mother love him.

"Sir Vincent!" Queen Phillippa repeated for the third time. "Whence be thou?"

"Pardons Majesty," Vincent replied woken from his deep thoughts.

"Wouldst thee administer thy lady her broth?" Queen Phillippa asked handing the bowl and spoon to the knight. "We wouldst hold thy lady for thee."

Queen Phillippa sat on the bed and held Leticia upright. Leticia's ranting had become less frequent and she attempted to open her eyes. Queen Phillippa determined this was the right time to get some solid broth into Leticia.

Vincent moved to the other side of the bed and with the queen's help and instructions began to feed Leticia.

Leticia's handmaidens and the queen's ladies murmured between themselves on the gentleness and loving of one of the realm's most feared and noble knights. Most of the ladies sighed dreamy eyed at the knight and wished they could have a knight like him as their husband or suitor.

One lady was furious at the attention Leticia was receiving from Sir Vincent. Lady Juliet had planned to make the noble knight hers. She wanted Vincent and she would have him. Juliet hoped Leticia's condition would turn for the worse. She hoped Leticia would die, then the king's decree would no longer matter and she would be free once more to pursue Vincent.

The next day the queen announced the medicines had worked and Lady Leticia's fever had broken. For the next week Lady Leticia remained in bed.

Vincent left her side more frequently and practiced jousting with his squire. He spent the week with knightly and courtly duties. The ladies of court were once more clamoring for his attention. He found he was not the least interested and left the Great Hall immediately after the meal to spend time with Lady Leticia or the king.

It was at one of these meals the king and Vincent shared an interesting conversation.

"Methinks thee hath acquired comprehension of pleasing thy lady," King Edward said leaning to the side to speak with Sir Vincent de Courtenay. My queen speaks of thee kindly and be naught wroth with thee."

"My person dost grow for wisdom each den, Majesty," Vincent responded. "My lady and our person talk of our youth. We discover secrets we carry within."

"Secrets?" The king asked in astonishment.

"Yea, we all hath deep hurting secrets within. Thus hath we discovered," Vincent shared.

"Thee dost grow for wisdom beyond we hath hoped with haste," King Edward smiled. "Tis our secrets we share so provide us great love."

"Yea," Vincent agreed.

"Tis naught secret our favor for falconry," King Edward stated changing subjects. "We wouldst do falconry hunting for coming days."

"Thus wouldst greatly please us, Majesty," Vincent replied but he wanted to take Leticia to Okehampton and make her his bride. It would be Saint Giles day in ten days and it would take a week just to travel to Okehampton. Lady Leticia was nearly recovered and he wanted to leave tomorrow. "Wouldst thee be wroth with thy servant wouldst we request leave to take my lady to Okehampton? We wouldst make my lady our bride."

"We wouldst alter thy plan. Thy lady and thee wouldst wed here at Surrey. We hath sent messengers to Okehampton bringing de Redvers to court. Thy lady dost recover. Yet, another malady has struck thy lady. Our Goodwife and queen determines thy lady wouldst naught travel."

"Yet another malady?" Vincent's face paled with the thought.

"Be naught vexed, Goodman," King Edward snorted. "Tis only thy lady's monthly flow. Lady Leticia be for complaint of aches. Our queen provides remedy of potatoes and spinach leaf."

"My lady dost naught travel for monthly flow?" Vincent queried in ignorance.

"Goodman, our queen commands thy lady eat and rest. Thus be naught command higher!" King Edward laughed.

"Whence be our queen thus eventide," Vincent questioned. He had wondered why she did not join them for the meal as she usually did.

"Our babe, Margaret hath colic. Our Goodwife tends to our young daughter," King Edward shared. "Our realm be blessed with such queen. Our queen tends to all our children with great knowledge of medicine, and for kind loving heart. Our queen tends to all of our kingdom with love."

"Thus be all manner and reason for obedience and honor to our queen," Vincent added with genuine respect. "Dost thee foster thy seed?"

"Nay. Our queen wouldst tend ours. Prince Edward we hath fostered. From thence our queen forbade it. Our Phillippa wouldst see to all ours," King Edward told Vincent proudly. "My Goodwife dost raise our seed most righteously."

"Methinks my lady wouldst also raise our seed," Vincent said thoughtfully more for himself than the king.

"Yea, thy Goodwife be with our queen tending our Margaret." King Edward remarked taking another sip of wine from his golden goblet. "Our queen dost regard thy lady highly."

King Edward took meat from his trencher and then asked Vincent, "Doth our plans be acceptable?"

"Yea," Vincent accepted thinking of Leticia. "Verily, thus matters naught whence our nuptials be. Hence or Okehampton."

"Methinks thee be smitten, Goodman," King Edward laughed nearly choking on the meat he was chewing. "We be for reference our falconry hunting."

Vincent blushed profusely in embarrassment. "My Lord High King, we wouldst be eager for thy falconry hunt."

"Good! Good!" King Edward chuckled. "First thus falcons hunt, hence thy nuptials."

Sir Martin Bolin approached the king. "We doth hear of thy plans for hunting?"

"Yea," King Edward told the knight. "On the morrow we shall begin our hunt. Hath thee falcon?"

"Yea, my lord. Our falcon, Richard's Crest, be as great as thy falcon, Tribulation," Sir Bolin bragged wiping his mouth with his sleeve.

"Thus be so?" King Edward took the challenge. "On the morrow we wouldst witness thy boast."

"Our falcon wouldst bring near same count as our Lord High King," Sir Martin promised. He faced off to Vincent. "Dost our king be knowledgeable of thy falcon, Sir de Courtenay?"

"Sir Vincent's falcon be, Elizabeth," King Edward answered for Vincent.

Martin roared with laughter, "Thee dost own female bird?"

"Sir Bolin, mayhap thee wouldst trow most females be superior hunters," Vincent answered sarcastically.

"Dost thee challenge us?" Martin growled with superiority taking another long drink of wine.

"Thee wouldst require competition to consider challenge," Vincent replied casually.

The barb struck Martin instantly. "Verily thus be so. Our falcon hath naught equal."

Vincent ignored Martin not wanting to get into a ridiculous conversation.

King Edward on the other hand couldn't help but comment, "Thus score gold crowns for master of falconry on thus hunt for seven den. Whence falcon doth bring us most booty, thus master receive crowns."

"Dost thee pay thy own person?" Vincent teased the king.

"Nay, our falcon be naught in our game," King Edward replied. "Thence be so our decree."

Vincent raised his goblet in acceptance. Martin followed suit.

It was late and Vincent wanted to tell his squire of the planned hunt. He was also tired. He begged to be excused from the Great Hall. King Edward gave him leave. Vincent walked the circular stairs to his guest rooms. They happened to be near the children's nursery and he hoped he might catch a glimpse of Leticia.

Leticia stayed to have her meal with Queen Phillippa. For one to say Leticia was impressed with the queen would be an understatement. The queen seemed to be capable of miracles with everything. Her knowledge of herbs, castle operations, royal protocol, and parenting was phenomenal. It seemed the queen could do it all, and was just short of sainthood in Leticia's observations. Throughout the meal, Queen Phillippa held her infant daughter, Margaret. The queen had kept the baby face down over her knees and gently patted her back. Gas bubble after gas bubble emerged from the infant that slept contentedly on her mother's lap.

"Thy babe sleeps comfortably. Thus colic vanished," Leticia said with admiration.

"Remember thus my daughter. Thy babe eats whence thee eat. Wouldst thee devour gaseous foods, like Margaret's nurse, thy babe wouldst suffer thus," Queen Phillippa advised. "Hence we hath eaten only light food and drink thus den. We wouldst feed our babe thus eventide."

It was a short time later Margaret woke and demanded to be fed. Queen Phillippa opened the front buttons on her gown and provided her breast for the hungry Margaret to feed from.

"Thee dost feed thy own babe!" Leticia exclaimed.

"Yea, tis wonderful and great. Listen naught for tongues thus telling thee other," Queen Phillippa shared. She looked down on her hungrily feeding baby daughter and spoke to her with a chuckle, "Margaret, thee dost feed so greedily as thy father."

Leticia's eyes rounded with surprise at the queen's statement. Her gasp of surprise did not miss the queen's notice.

Queen Phillippa looked up at Leticia and snorted, "We forget thee be virgin still. Consider daughter thus another lesson. Man dost enjoy suckling mother's milk in fervor as thy feeding babe doth enjoy suckle."

Leticia's face turned crimson with the thought of it.

Queen Phillippa laughed harder at Leticia's embarrassment, "Thy time dost arrive anon. Remember thy queen's word."

"All thee dost teach us do we keep securely for our heart and mind," Leticia replied lovingly.

"Hold more favor for us," Queen Phillippa smiled after she fed Margaret. "Put our daughter upon thy lap as we hath previously. Rub our babe's back for us. Thee wouldst obtain thus for practice."

Obediently Leticia took Margaret and followed the example previously given to her. Queen Phillippa buttoned her gown while watching Leticia follow her instructions. A moment later Margaret released a large gas bubble and finding her thumb to suck, fell sound asleep on Leticia's lap.

Leticia was taken with the baby. She found she wanted her own child soon. This was the right time to marry. The curiosity in Leticia caused her to ask the queen, "Whence be child created?"

The queen motioned for the nurse to take Margaret to place in her cradle. Queen Phillippa spent the next hour giving Leticia a short, concise, and accurate sex education lesson.

When Leticia left the royal nursery she spoke to Queen Phillippa, "Thy daughters be most fortunate for thee as mother. Thou art wise, educated, loving, and be sainted."

Queen Phillippa laughed, "We may find humility difficult with thee as our daughter."

Leticia left the nursery rooms and began to walk the passageway stairs to reach her rooms. Leticia was full of hope and anticipation of her marriage to Sir Vincent. The queen had told her wonderful things about the bedding and maternity. There was hope and joy bubbling in Leticia's mind this evening. Leticia was happy until she noticed Lady Juliet talking to her betrothed. A green eyed jealous monster suddenly appeared out of nowhere. After what the queen had told her, the thought of any other woman enjoying her betrothed was too much to bear.

Juliet had stalked Sir Vincent many times over the past week to have just the right opportunity to talk to him. She had hoped he would have drunk too much as he did that one night he returned from battle at Neville's Cross when she crept into his bed and he took her. Juliet smiled remembering Sir Vincent's surprised face when he awoke and found her in his pallet. She had hoped he would take her so she could ask the king for dispensation. Unfortunately that did not happen. Vincent was far to drunk at the time. He was completely passed out and completely incognizant of her presence until he woke up. Another opportunity never arrived. A few days later the king decreed Sir Vincent's betrothal to Lady Leticia. Juliet had been delighted about the problems that seemed to plague the couple, but the king, Vincent, and Leticia kept the decree of betrothal faithfully. She would try once more to seek the affections of Sir Vincent. Before Neville's Cross he had shown some interest in her. Since meeting his Leticia he hand shown no interest.

As Vincent approached the door to his room, Juliet appeared around the corner swiftly to run into Vincent.

"Lady Juliet, wouldst thee be injured," Vincent asked innocently after slamming into her diminutive body broadside. Vincent was completely unaware the collision had been contrived.

"Our breath," Juliet wheezed feigning injury. She felt his arms take hold of her to steady her. It was that moment, Juliet saw Leticia move into the shadows of the passageway. This was a perfect opportunity to create more problems between the betrothed couple. Raising her voice to make sure Leticia heard, Juliet spoke to Vincent sensually, "My lord, Sir Vincent. We enjoyed our moments only to part hence. We obey sadly our Lord High King's decree. Words so cruelly spoken to keep our hearts and bodies apart. Farewell, good dreams sweet knight of my heart."

Those words cut Leticia to the quick. She had interrupted a tryst. While betrothed to her, Vincent had already taken a mistress. *Fie on thee. Pox upon thee!* Leticia cursed under her breath. As she turned to walk down the stairs and obtain a glass of cool well water to squelch her anger she noticed a spider web. A wicked smile slowly pasted on her lips. She ran down the stairs several flights to the basement kitchens. The servants watched in confusion as she took a pot and spoon. To add to their confusion the servants watched with mouths agape as Leticia spooned many spider webs from the store rooms and placed the spiders in her pot.

Vincent creased his brows at Juliet's words. With his back to Leticia, he had no idea the scene had been created for affect by Juliet. "My lady?"

"Sir Vincent, our heart beats for thee, yet we be parted. We shared our bodies and our love, yet our king's decree enters betwixt us," Juliet sighed heavily placing her hands upon Vincent's arms that steadied her.

"Methinks thee be injured. Thee dost speak so strangely," Vincent commented quietly.

Juliet watched Leticia's shadow go toward the stairs. "Tis only our heart needing to share with thee our body and soul."

"Lady Juliet, we be betrothed," Vincent reminded her gently. "Thus one night we shared be error. Thus be error we wouldst naught correct. We wish thee happiness with thy future. We hope thee wouldst wish us happiness equally."

Demurely Lady Juliet fluttered her long lashes. "We wish thee happiness. Verily our happiness still lies with thee in thy pallet."

"Thus wouldst change, Lady Juliet," Vincent said tenderly but with warning. "We wouldst speak with the king about thy betrothal."

Once more Juliet fluttered her eyelashes, "wouldst thee? Whither thee dost still care and worry for our happiness?"

"Yea," Vincent offered with kindness. "Go from us. We wouldst discuss our hunt with our squire."

Juliet released her grip on Vincent's arms and walked away slowly. She had created damage with the Lady Leticia and Sir Vincent she was certain. Juliet could only hope her little scene would be gossiped about and brought to the king's attention by the queen. Queen Phillippa was certainly found of the little waif for some reason. Happily Juliet picked up her pace to go to the rooms of Sir Martin Bolin. He was not the lover Sir Vincent de Courtenay would be. Bolin did take her to his pallet every night. He proved a gentle and caring lover. Leticia needed Bolin's attentions to continue with the rest of her plan.

✦

**Chapter 8**

"My lord," Maynard greeted Sir Vincent upon entering his rooms.

"Good Eve," Sir Vincent answered. "On the morrow we wouldst be part of our Lord High King's hunting party." Vincent removed his tunic handing it to Maynard. "We wouldst wear our woolen tunics, mail, and chausses for our hunt."

"Yea my lord. We wouldst make them ready for our hunt, " Maynard answered laying the tunic neatly over the chest for the servants to wash.

"We wouldst make Henry prepare our Elizabeth," Vincent added removing his hose.

"Yea," Maynard replied with pride. He was as proud of the falcon, Elizabeth, as Vincent was. He was also excited about accompanying Vincent on the hunt. Such an event was always exciting recreation for knights and squires. It was even more exciting when a knight was invited to hunt with the king. Maynard noticed Vincent sat on the chair with his finger over his lips and his elbows resting on the chair arms. He noticed Vincent sat not making a move for several minutes. "My lord? Wouldst thee be vexed by some matter?"

"Yea," Vincent replied but still not moving.

"Thy betrothed?"

"Nay," Vincent answered shifting his body and raising his leg to the seat of the chair. "Tis Lady Juliet. Her conversation be most strange. We still trow or comprehend naught whence thus lady spake or thought."

"Femininity be most strange," Maynard soothed while preparing Vincent's tunic, mail, and chausses. He was thinking how quickly Lady Organa had taken his interest. He hoped he wasn't the same mess of emotions his lord seemed to be.

"Yea, thus be troth!" Vincent answered removing his braies. Maynard turned down the covers for Vincent to climb onto his bed.

Leticia woke up before the sunrise and in the torchlight dressed in a lovely tunic dress of red velvet. She wore a pink damask wimple. The gown was tight fitting and girdled with a golden embroidered belt. She picked up the small brass pot that held her collected spiders. She counted twenty spiders. There were about three different species in her pot. Her favorite were the spiders with small bodies and long legs. She hurried to Vincent's rooms. Leticia listened at the door until she heard voices from within his rooms. She leaned against a stonewall in the passage way for a few moments allowing Vincent a moment to don his robe. Then Leticia knocked at the door.

The door creaked and Maynard peered through the crack. "My Lady?"

"Mayhap we speak to our lord?" Leticia asked innocently.

"Leticia?" Vincent queried upon hearing her voice. He tied his robe tighter and grabbed the door from Maynard's hand. "Enter my lady."

"We hope for troth we disturb thee naught," Leticia oozed with false concern.

"Thee wouldst naught disturb us," Vincent replied. He was thrilled to see her and that she came to him proved in his mind she had missed his company as he had missed hers.

Leticia looked about the room and noticed the rough homespun tunic. "Dost thee ready thy person for departing our court?"

"Nay, we wouldst falcon with our Lord High King," Vincent smiled walking toward her.

"Hunt? Wouldst we join thee?" Leticia said excitedly evading his grasp. She enjoyed acting the tease. "We wouldst enjoy thus."

"We be told thee wouldst be in discomfort time," Vincent didn't want to outright tell her he knew she had her monthly flow.

"Yea, tis troth," Leticia replied allowing a slight blush of embarrassment. She turned her back and opened the pot dumping its occupants onto the woolen tunic. "Mayhap a few den hence?"

"Whence thee wouldst," Vincent offered admiring her backside.

Leticia spun around to face Vincent. "Verily, dost thee be sincere?"

"For troth," Vincent smiled.

Leticia moved to Vincent and using an arm placed on his chest to steady herself, she stretched to plant a kiss upon his cheek. Leticia then spun around several times propelling herself to the doorway and leaving the rooms. She slinked into a dark part of the passage hall and waited to hear the results of her plan of simple retribution for toying with another woman while betrothed to her.


Vincent soaped his face and used the knife blade to shave his face. When he was finished he used the water in the basin to wash and then used the towel Maynard had handed to him. Happily he hummed a ditty and absentmindedly started to dress. After his braies, mail, and chausses he put the tunic on over his head. After a moment or two he felt a strange tickling. There was tickling on his neck, his face, and his hands. He looked down on his chest and saw a small bodied long legged spider crawling down the front of his tunic. On his hands he saw several smaller spiders. He wiped his face and found another large spider. Immediately his face paled with fear and his body swayed.

Maynard looked toward Vincent when he heard his knight screaming curses. He watched in horror as Vincent suddenly ripped off his tunic and rolled his body on the floor screaming as if being tortured on the rack.

Vincent rose from the floor and started tearing his mail off with such power his hands started to bleed. Then suddenly seeing his own blood and small spiders on his hands he fell into a black pit of unconsciousness.

"My lord!" Maynard shouted running toward the seemingly insane knight. Helplessly he watched Vincent collapse to the floor. Now hysterical, Maynard ran out the door shouting for help. Running down the passageway toward the main stairs, he did not see Leticia in the shadows.

Leticia heard the screaming, curses, and thuds of the body rolling on the floor. She bit her lower lip until it bled to prevent her laughter from being heard. Leticia's body was shaking with mirth. When she saw Maynard running out she could no longer contain her laughter. Entering the room Leticia saw Vincent lying on the floor. A flash of fear crossed her mind. Was he frightened to death? Quickly she knelt be his side and placing her cheek next to his mouth. She felt his warm breath and whacked his unconscious body. "Thou wouldst be well, coward," she chuckled. Still holding her pot she collected the spiders walking about the floor and removed the spider that had been splattered by Vincent. Leticia placed the insects back into the little brass pot. Checking her handiwork once more and making certain there was no evidence to be found, she left the room laughing so hard, her ribs were beginning to hurt.

Maynard raced toward the Great Hall. He spotted Prince Edward approaching the room to break the fast and hailed him, "My Lord High Prince. Prithee thy aide. My liege, Sir Vincent be filled with madness. Sir Vincent wouldst rant and scream in agony. My liege doth faint upon our floor."

Prince Edward attempted to listen and understand Maynard's words, but nothing made any sense. "Be thee mad?" Prince Edward queried the hyperventilating squire.

"Prithee, give us aide! My liege be ailing. My liege be filled with madness and agony," Maynard implored screeching in terror.

Prince Edward was annoyed by the squire's raving and asked, "Whence be Sir Vincent de Courtenay?"

"My Lord High Prince, we tell thee," Maynard breathed heavily. "Our liege be on our floor for need of aide!"

Shaking his head in disgust, Prince Edward motioned for two pages to follow him. "Lead on squire!" Prince Edward grouched.

Maynard led him to the rooms and opened the door.

Prince Edward saw Vincent lying on the floor looking quite pale and quite unconscious. He ran to his former liege and friend. Prince Edward kneeled next to Vincent. He felt the knight's soft warm breath and was relieved. Prince Edward rose from the floor to his full six-foot stature and ordered one of the pages, "Bring our mother hither to aide Sir Vincent." To the taller and older page he ordered, "Aide us for lifting Sir Vincent. We wouldst place Sir Vincent upon thus pallet."

In the time the younger page found Queen Phillippa and brought her to Sir Vincent's chamber, Maynard and Prince Edward had undressed Vincent. They placed him in bed and covered him with only a linen sheet.

When Prince Edward picked up the mail and shirt from the floor, a large dead spider fell to the floor. Prince Edward knew immediately why Sir Vincent had appeared insane to Maynard. He was well aware of Vincent's terror of spiders. It was then he noticed two or three smaller spiders smashed into the chain mail. He couldn't be certain how many spiders there were since their body parts appeared to be in various places on the chain mail. "Maynard, whence be thy lord's mail? Hast thee stored thus?"

"Nay, our liege's mail be polished only last eventide," Maynard replied trying to understand Prince Edward asking such a question.

"Since thee polished only last eventide, whence wouldst thee naught see thus arachnids upon it?" Prince Edward questioned showing the smashed insects in the mail to Maynard.

Suddenly Maynard was frightened even more. Would he be blamed for spiders in the tunic and mail? He did polish the mail and he did not see any spiders. "My Lord High Prince, tis troth. We polished our liege's mail, Seest thou? Thus metal doth sparkle in thus sun!"

"Thus metal doth sparkle tis troth. Whence wouldst thee naught see arachnids upon it?" Prince Edward pursued.

"My Lord High Prince, thee wouldst believe our humble squire. Last eventide be naught arachnids," Maynard pleaded. "We wouldst offer oath for it!"

Queen Phillippa entered the room with her ladies in waiting. The women couldn't help but stare at the strong muscular chest of the unconscious knight.

"Whence complaint hath Sir Vincent?" Queen Phillippa asked her son. She walked past Prince Edward. "Thy Goodman doth appear pale!"

Maynard said nothing. He was still afraid he might be punished in some way.

Queen Phillippa sat on his bed and leaned over Vincent's face. "Sir Vincent doth breathe," she announced. Queen Phillippa then examined his head, ears, neck, arms, and chest. Since there was no blood on the sheets, she went no further. She determined her lusty ladies in waiting would see no more of the knight. "We see naught injury or blood save scratches upon Sir Vincent's hands."

"Majesty," Maynard whimpered. "Our liege did beat upon our lord's chest and arms. Sir Vincent screamed in terror and agony as if besieged with devils."

"Madness!" Prince Edward interrupted. "Thee declared Sir Vincent full of madness."

"Thus wouldst be troth," Maynard said softly bowing his head. "Thus be since our liege be betrothed, Sir Vincent behaves most strangely. Thus madness began once our Lady Leticia left our liege."

"Lady Leticia be hence?" Prince Edward questioned. Immediately the spiders, her presence, and Vincent's presumed madness made sense.

"Yea, my Lord High Prince," Maynard answered quickly. "Lady Leticia be hence this morn."

Prince Edward started laughing.

His mother reprimanded, "Mayhap thee wouldst explain thy humor with thy Goodman laying abed?"

"We wouldst believe our Goodman suffers only for fright and wouldst be healed anon," Prince Edward choked holding back his guffaws. "My mother and queen, Sir Vincent fears arachnids. Upon our undressing Sir Vincent, we found several deceased arachnids upon Sir Vincent's person. Thus finding arachnids upon thus person hath frightened our Goodman for strange behavior."

Queen Phillippa noticed a small fuzzy black ball on Sir Vincent's wrist. She picked it up to find another smashed arachnid. "Thus appears need for housecleaning. We wouldst clean our house. Naught more wouldst our guests be subject to such travail. We wouldst clean thus wounds on Sir Vincent's hands and thence clean our house."

The ladies in waiting understood the queen's words and offered her a basin of fresh water and linens from the chest in Sir Vincent's room. Another lady in waiting went to the chamberlain and acquired servants to begin cleaning the castle. Mops, brooms, bucket, and soaps were quickly passed out.

Vincent woke just before Queen Phillippa put the last bandage over his hand. "Majesty, thou be for peril! Tis arachnids loosed!" Vincent warned grabbing Queen Phillippa's wrist. "Run!"

"Our ladies hath cleaned thy room," Queen Phillippa assuaged the terrified knight. "Thy arachnids be deceased and swept clean."

"Tis troth, Goodman," Prince Edward supported. "Thy room be cleaned and swept clean. Thy arachnids be deceased."

"Verily? Thus be five score or more descending and attacking our person," Vincent exaggerated in terror.

Prince Edward raised his brow. "Five Score?" He only found three and his mother found one. That was only four by his sums. It was not even one score.

"Yea, armies of beasts," Vincent embellished.

"Thy army of arachnids be destroyed," Queen Phillippa soothed. She lovingly patted Vincent's arm. "Thee wouldst suffer naught travail hence. We wouldst give thee medicine to rest for thy battle," Queen Phillippa said reaching for the goblet containing medicinal herbs to help him sleep. "Take thee rest."

"Our hunt?" Vincent questioned worriedly. What would the king say if he didn't show up for the royal hunt?

"We wouldst tell our Lord High King thee hath accident and require rest," Queen Phillippa told Vincent helping him drink the concoction.

"May God keep thee," Vincent offered in thanks. He would have been embarrassed if King Edward found out he couldn't go on the hunt because spiders frightened him. He was grateful for Queen Phillippa's wisdom and understanding in the matter.

"Rest," Queen Phillippa ordered and covered Sir Vincent with a warm blanket as a mother would cover her own child. "We wouldst send for thy betrothed for care of thee."

"We wouldst obtain Lady Leticia," Prince Edward volunteered. He had a strong idea of what really happened and wanted to talk to Leticia alone. "Wouldst thee tell our father we wouldst meet him in field for thus hunt?"

Queen Phillippa nodded and patted her son gently on the face. With a regal air, she left the room.

Prince Edward followed his mother and left quickly for his sister's room. He knew his mother had used Blanche's room for Leticia. Knocking on the door he heard a muffled giggle and a pleasant, "Enter."

63

Leticia's face showed tears streaking down her cheeks. Prince Edward guessed they were not from crying but laughing.

"My Lord Prince," Leticia bowed humbly. "Whence good fortune brings thee to our rooms?"

"Good fortune or jest?" Prince Edward growled in attempt to cover his own mirth over the spider episode.

Wide eyed and with innocence Leticia asked demurely, "Jest?"

"Yea, methinks wouldst be jest for arachnids," Prince Edward scowled. "For thee, we be dispatched, by our mother our queen, to bring thee to thy betrothed. Sir Vincent be wounded for battle with arachnids."

Leticia tsked with false sympathy. "We wouldst attend our betrothed anon."

"Wouldst thee admit for thy jest?" Prince Edward chuckled grabbing her arm as she attempted to pass by him.

"My Lord Prince?" Leticia replied angelically.

"Thee wouldst plant arachnids upon our Sir Vincent. Thee trow our lord's fear of such creatures," Prince Edward laughed loudly spinning Leticia around to look at him. "We wouldst naught told thee, wouldst we learn thee wouldst use thus fear against thy betrothed."

"Thee trow!" Leticia sighed. "My Lord Prince. Thus knight be deserved of such punishment for crimes."

"Crimes?" Prince Edward chuckled. "Whence crime deserved such punishment of terror?"

"Our betrothed leads us for belief of love, duty, and honor toward us," Leticia stated angrily. "Hence thy noble knight cur mongrel took mistress."

"Our Sir Vincent? Mistress? Nay!" Prince Edward objected vehemently. "Our noble knight wouldst naught conspire so!"

"Our eye hath seen such. Our ears heard such!" Leticia pouted.

"Whence wench doth lie with our liege?" Prince Edward countered. "We wouldst naught believe such! Give us name!"

"Thy liege and noble knight hath taken Lady Juliet to warm thus pallet!" Leticia groused stamping her foot.

"Nay, we wouldst believe naught thus tale," Prince Edward denied. "We wouldst stir thus waters and find troth!"

"We trow tis troth!" Leticia pouted.

"My Lady, allow us time for investigation," Prince Edward requested. "Wouldst thee allow us time, we wouldst naught tell thy betrothed about whence came arachnids."

"Thee wouldst naught tell?" Leticia gasped.

"Nay, we fear reprisal and fearful cats amok for our rooms," Prince Edward teased and then put his finger thoughtfully on his lips. "We wouldst equal thus score with snakes?"

Leticia swatted Prince Edward lightly on his forearm. "Prithee, tell our betrothed naught."

"We wouldst naught. My vow upon thus sweet fostered sister," Prince Edward assured. "We ask thee for time. We wouldst find out about Lady Juliet.

Thee wouldst make oath for us.  Thee wouldst naught punish our knight thusly evermore."

"We take oath," Leticia smiled.  She may not use arachnids again, but perhaps frogs?

"Come, thee wouldst minister for thy battle wounded knight," Prince Edward laughed loudly taking Leticia's arm and escorting her to Vincent's room.

Later that evening Prince Edward and Leticia shared a trencher.

Vincent was still groggy from the medicine Queen Phillippa had given him to help him relax and sleep.  Leticia had dutifully cared for him during the day and fed him supper before she and Prince Edward left for the Great Hall to dine.

King Edward asked Leticia about Vincent's well being, "Thy betrothed recovers?"

"Yea, our Lord High King," Leticia answered.  "Our betrothed wouldst be capable to join thy hunt on the morrow."

"Our Goodwife be most unclear to Sir Vincent's ailment.  Arachnid bite?" King Edward queried.  "Hath such bite festered?"

Queen Phillippa leaned over and spoke to her husband.  "Good fortune and medicines hath prevented such travail.  Methinks our house received good cleaning for such and naught such creature be bother anon."

Lady Leticia and Prince Edward started to spasm with mirth as they held back the laughter.

"Private jest?" Queen Phillippa asked her son observing his humor.

"Yea," Prince Edward answered.  "Tis private jest and crimes accused for investigation."

"Thus mystery doth be," King Edward chuckled.  "Some den thee wouldst share thus jest?"

"Merrily," Prince Edward replied and concentrated on eating venison from his trencher.  "Our food be tasty!" Prince Edward declared changing the subject at hand.

# Chapter 9

Feeling a little guilty, Leticia had a difficult time sleeping. Yes, Sir Vincent deserved her little lesson, but during the day she tended him he had been soft spoken and kind. He asked her to read to him and many times quoted a verse line by line. He was a sensitive man as well as a brave knight. Leticia did notice the scratches on his hands and did not mean for him to hurt himself in any way. She would make it up to him by bringing him food to break the fast before he went hunting with the king. The next day her monthly flow would cease and she would join them.

Leticia woke early in the morning well before dawn and went to the kitchens. She knew the servants would be up and starting the food for their lords.

Millicent, the oldest of the scullery maids greeted Leticia cheerfully, "dost thee greet us for morn? Wouldst thee start cleaning out our arachnids once more?"

"Nay," Leticia answered stifling a giggle. "We wouldst obtain trencher for our betrothed."

"Tis great relief for us," Millicent snorted. "Thee wouldst again renew our queen's command for more work cleaning keep."

"Thy pardon," Leticia apologized. "We wouldst naught want more work for thee."

Millicent busied herself preparing a trencher and tankard of ale for Leticia's betrothed. The entire time she did so, Millicent was snorting. She had heard about the big brave knight fainting at the sight of spiders. She also knew where the spiders had really come from, but servants never had such conversations with their lords or ladies. Instead she had shared the information with her husband and they laughed until tears streaked down their cheeks.

Leticia took the tray with tankard and trencher from Millicent. A devilish glint in Millicent's eye and broad smile gave it away to Leticia that Millicent knew the truth about the spiders and Sir Vincent de Courtenay. Leticia returned an impish smile and thanked Millicent for the tray.

Balancing the tray in her hand, Leticia knocked on the door.

"Enter," Vincent bellowed.

Leticia greeted Vincent with a warm smile.

Vincent's foul expression changed at once to delight when he saw Leticia enter carrying a tray for him. "My Lady!" Vincent exclaimed and walked to her side in two strides. He took the tray from her and gave her a kiss upon her brow. "We be highly pleased with thy countenance."

Leticia replied happily, "we be pleased with thy countenance this morn."

"Thus be so quaint and considerate of thy betrothed, Sir Vincent," Lady Juliet oozed stepping from the shadows of a darkened part of the room. She walked to the door straightening her gown giving Leticia the impression she had shared Vincent's bed last night.

Innocently, Vincent agreed with Juliet, "Yea, our betrothed be most considerate." Vincent had absolutely no concept of female cattiness and innuendo.

Leticia ground her teeth with anger. *Wouldst thus convince thee, Prince Edward?*

"We wouldst wait for thee upon the field," Juliet uttered with dominance.

Leticia looked at Vincent as he seated himself and began eating the food in his trencher. She then looked at Juliet. Angrily she asked Vincent, "Lady Juliet wouldst wait for thee upon the field?"

"Yea, we shouldst ride in hunt with our liege," Juliet answered for Vincent.

Again not thinking of any intrigue, Vincent nodded in agreement. He continued to eat his food. Juliet had come in the morning to let him know she had been invited to ride in the hunt and wanted to let Vincent know. She asked if she could ride near him because she had heard of the falcon contest and believed Vincent's falcon would win. It hadn't even occurred to him to ask how she learned of the contest and he didn't bother to ask who had invited her on the hunt.

Juliet watched Leticia turn crimson with rage. Smugly Juliet left the room. She was thrilled she had irritated and angered the beautiful maiden betrothed to the knight she wanted.

"Thee wouldst hunt with Lady Juliet?" Leticia queried quietly covering her jealous rage.

Vincent looked at her strangely and cocked his brow at the question, "Lady Juliet wouldst be with us on our hunt."

"Cur!" Leticia shouted reaching for the tankard of ale. "Mongrel!"

Vincent grabbed her wrist before she obtained the tankard. "Wench! Whence causes thy vexation?"

"Wench! Thee dare name us, wench!" Leticia shouted shaking angrily. "Thee sleeps like a mongrel dog with bitches and thee dare name us wench?"

Leticia jerked her wrist with strength she and Vincent were not aware she had. Leticia stomped out the room and slammed the door with such force Vincent's Shield Crest fell to the floor from its hanging place on the wall.

Vincent suddenly realized what Leticia's temper tantrum was all about, or at least he thought he understood. A tiny bubble started in his abdomen working its way up to his chest, and then to his throat. He let loose with a giant laugh that shook the field on the floor and made it rattle.

"My Lord?" Maynard queried. "Thy lady dost act most strange and suddenly thou breaks out with mirth. Whence be thus strange behaviors?"

"Good squire," Vincent answered shaking with laughter. "My lady be jealous! Tis wonderful she be so jealous."

"Thee believes evil emotion be good?" Maynard asked with shock.

"Yea," Vincent responded. "My lady dost care for us e'er she wouldst not behave so."

"Tis strange such happenings of late," Maynard shook his head solemnly.

"We wouldst soothe my lady's fears this eventide," Vincent added feeling confident and certain of his capabilities.

Leticia stormed out of Vincent's room muttering every curse she knew under her breath. She stormed through the castle passages to her room where she slammed the door and put down the bolt so as not to be disturbed. Leticia felt the rage turn to frustration. She flung herself on the bed and cried for several hours. Leticia then fell asleep and slept most of the day. She did not hear the knocking or calls of Lady Rosamund, Lady Agnes, or Lady Organa. All three handmaidens heard her cries, but could do nothing. Instead they made excuses for Lady Leticia when the queen had sent for her. They feared Leticia would get in trouble with the queen for not appearing when ordered. They told the queen it was her flow and thank the lord it was the last day. Queen Phillippa ordered a large portion of spinach and potatoes sent to Leticia's room. The handmaidens ate the food telling the queen that Leticia was thankful, but now wished to sleep. They waited until Leticia finally woke up and opened the door.

"My Lady," Lady Rosamund breathed with relief when Leticia walked out. "Wouldst thee eat for us?"

"Nay," Leticia replied wetting her swollen eyes with a damp cloth. "We wouldst naught be hungry."

"Wouldst thou tell us whence vexes thee so?" Lady Rosamund questioned hoping to give Leticia some comfort with her upset.

"Dost thee care, in troth?" Leticia sniffed wanting to share her turmoil.

"Verily, in troth," Lady Rosamund replied. Rosamund felt a deep and genuine fondness for Leticia. She felt almost like her mother.

"All present worry for thee, my Lady," Lady Organa added taking Leticia's hand lovingly.

"Tis my betrothed," Leticia sighed heavily. "For the morn, we brought our liege faire to break the fast. We found Sir Vincent shares pallet with wench." Leticia was not about to tell her handmaidens the name of the woman. That would never do. She just wanted sympathy and someone to listen to her heartbreak.

"No!" the two handmaidens gasped at Leticia's shocking news.

Lady Agnes chortled, "Thee wouldst naught expect such handsome face faithful to thee? For nuptial alone? Be naught a fool! Accept thee God's nature of man."

"We wouldst naught agree wholly with Lady Agnes," Lady Rosamund stated. "We trow whence thee wed thee wouldst be more agreeable to thy knight."

"Yea, whence thee be wed wouldst such happenings be changed," Lady Agnes agreed.

"Tis such possibility?" Lady Leticia asked hopefully.

"Thee be far more beauteous in soul and face," Lady Rosamund assured. "Be thee beauteous for thus pallet."

Rosamund then shared her experiences and knowledge for pleasing men. Rosamund's new shared experiences and with the queen's previous instructions, Leticia hoped she would keep Sir Vincent faithful.

When conversations had finished and the handmaidens had properly dressed Lady Leticia for the evening meal. They combed her hair and were about to put her wimple upon her head when they heard a knock at the door.

Lady Agnes opened the door to view the subject of their conversation.

"We bring our Lady foods for us to share our meal," Vincent announced. He walked in the room and opened the door wide. Maynard ushered in several servants that carried trays of food, goblets of wine, trencher, bench, and tables.

After everything was prepared, Leticia rose from her chair and walked to Vincent. "Whence be thus special favor for thy betrothed?"

Vincent took her hand and brushed his lips lightly over her knuckles. "Our person noticed thee be naught about upon our return from our hunt. We queried to learn thee wouldst be suffering. We worried for thee and thought to bring our meal to thee."

"My noble liege," Leticia addressed. "Thee wouldst be so kind and thoughtful."

"Merely thy servant, my lady," Vincent replied graciously. He walked her to the table and pulled the bench for her to sit. When she was seated he took her place beside her.

"Thus behavior be most strange," Leticia whispered in Vincent's ear as he cut a slice of meat from his trencher for her.

"Whither speak such words?" Vincent asked nearly choking on the wine he had just drunk from the goblet.

"Thee wouldst share thy pallet with wench for night and court us for den," Leticia whispered into his ear.

Vincent did choke on his drink of wine and coughed horribly for several minutes. Finally catching his breath he asked, "Whence wouldst thee hear such tales?"

"Tis naught tales, my lord," Leticia whispered once more. "We see with our eyes thus morn. Lady Juliet be in thy room."

Vincent placed his knife upon the table and crossed his arms. "So thus be in troth a reason for this morn's temperament!" He couldn't help himself and started laughing.

"Wouldst our liege share thus humor?" Leticia growled testily. She was not all amused by the fact she caught Lady Juliet in his chamber.

"Thee be jealous!" Vincent kept on laughing. "My lady, we wouldst naught share our pallet. The Lady visited us in morn. The Lady told us of joining us for thus hunt."

"We be naught jealous. We be concerned over thy righteous name," Leticia shrugged off. She had to admit to herself she was relieved to find out Lady Juliet was not his bed partner.

"As thee wishes," Vincent chuckled. "We be pleased our lady shows concern over our name."

Lady Rosamund stifled a giggle. It was obvious to all of the handmaidens Lady Leticia had thrown an enormous tantrum in a fit of jealousy. These two would be happily wed for certain. They both cared for each other. They just didn't want to show it, yet!

Vincent cut a piece of meat from the trencher to offer to his future bride. "Wouldst thee be joining us for hunt on the morrow?"

"Yea, we adore hunt. We be waiting patiently for recovery to join thee," Leticia replied happily. In fact, since a child she had participated and loved falconry. At Okehampton she kept and trained her own falcons.

"Wouldst thee ride by our side?" Vincent asked tentatively.

"Wouldst thee wish so?" Leticia queried.

"Yea," Vincent replied shyly. Deep down he still remembered his mother's rebuff. He had to admit he was always afraid of loving a woman. She might reject him as his mother had done.

Leticia feared loving a man. She was afraid he would treat her as her father had. It would be an interesting time for those people surrounding the couple.

"We wouldst ride with thee and carry thy colors," Leticia offered.

"Thy words please us," Vincent smiled and covered her dainty hand with his large one.

The warm gentle touch sent shockwaves through Leticia. It was a good feeling. It was a happy feeling. It was a sensual feeling.

"Wouldst Lady Juliet wear your colors?" Leticia slipped in question. She knew she shouldn't ask, but she just had to know.

"Nay, thus lady wore naught our colors or another's," Vincent replied finishing his trencher. "Thus dost surprise us since we trow naught who invited Lady Juliet."

"Thee invited her naught?" Leticia breathed happily.

"Nay," Vincent answered. "Thou art lady of our heart. Thee and thee alone." He said the words. He hoped he wouldn't regret them.

"Thus pleases us," Lady Leticia smiled placing her soft hand on his muscular shoulder.

Vincent and Leticia finished their meal. The servants quickly removed the makeshift dining room and Vincent sat on the largest chair facing the fire. "Wouldst thee read to us?" he queried Leticia handing her a book of lyrical poetry. A troubadour had given him the book as a gift for escorting him safely to London.

Leticia took the handwritten leather bound book and smiled happily, "we wouldst love to read for thee."

As Leticia was reaching for the book Vincent took her arm and guided her to his lap. Using the light from the fireplace and the setting sun, Leticia read the poetry. She had never felt so cherished and loved. It was a wonderful feeling and she felt herself nestling comfortably into Vincent's inviting arms. There was no question in her mind about being jealous anymore. She would rake any woman's eyes that dared tried to take away this man from her. Could she be falling in love at last? Her answer was yes. It was true that this was a marriage of royal decree and political, but she found Sir Vincent to be considerate of her feelings and gentle. Yes, she could learn to love this man and learn to be a Goodwife.

Vincent was thinking he had never been so content. Lady Leticia was gentle, intelligent, and still a vibrant woman with a temper. He found himself asking if he were falling in love. When he first had been told he would marry, it had been in his mind a convenience to obtain title and land. Then he saw Leticia. He felt protective and loving. He wanted her to love him. In this quiet evening before the fire he felt content and looked forward to being married.

When Leticia had finished reading the lyrical poetry she laid her head on Vincent's chest. A small sigh escaped her lips as he enclosed her frame with his large muscular arms.

Vincent gently brushed his thumb across Leticia's cheek and brushed her hair with his fingers. "Thou art beauteous," he whispered. "Beauteous in thy body and thy soul."

Leticia looked up into his eyes to find them staring into hers lovingly. "Thee be wonderful and fair of countenance, my liege," Leticia returned softly.

"Thee wouldst keep us content," Vincent stated dreamily. Waiting for this nuptial was beginning to take on eternal waiting. The thought of the nuptials and bedding immediately brought response to his manly organ.

This time, Leticia didn't notice. She was too content and happy.

Vincent rose from the chair keeping Leticia in his arms. Gently he allowed her to slip down his masculine frame.

It was then Leticia felt his need as the hardened muscle pressed against her belly. After her talks with Lady Rosamund and Queen Phillippa she found she wasn't embarrassed, but excited.

"We wait for morn," Vincent breathed huskily. "Our hunt." Vincent really didn't want to leave, but what was on his mind at the moment wouldn't be acceptable to his lady or the king. He looked at his squire, Maynard, and chuckled. Maynard had fallen asleep in Lady Organa's arms. Vincent addressed Lady Organa, "My lady, wouldst thee wake our squire and send him to our rooms?"

Organa blushed crimson and nodded. "We wouldst wake thy squire my lord." Gently she nudged the squire who was quite sound asleep.

Vincent left the room after he brushed Lady Leticia's lips with a soft kiss.

Organa quietly worked on waking Maynard. Together they left the chambers and walked toward Vincent's rooms.

Lady Rosamund and Lady Agnes assisted Lady Leticia with a late bath.

Leticia fell asleep in the large canopied bed almost immediately. It was late, she felt clean from the bath, and quite content about her evening with Vincent. She would wake up early, dress, and be with Vincent for the hunt in the morning.

Leticia almost skipped to Vincent's rooms. A light tapping on his door brought heavy steps for the answer. As the door opened, Vincent's smile was a welcoming golden sunshine of warmth.

"My Lady, enter," Vincent welcomed. "We wouldst be nearly ready. Hast thou come to enjoin us for breaking the fast?"

"Thee dost us great honor for invitation yester eve," Leticia replied warmly as she entered his chamber.

Vincent leaned over and brushed her lips with his, "Nay, thee dost us great honor."  He turned and walked toward Maynard allowing him to attach his mantel.

Another knock at the door was heard.

Leticia walked to open it.  She was surprised to see Lady Juliet standing there.

"Lady Leticia?" Juliet inhaled with her own surprise.

A wicked grin crossed Leticia's lips.  This was the perfect time to even the score on feminine wits.  She smoothed her gown exactly as Juliet had the day before, indicating she had spent the night with Sir Vincent.

The gesture was not lost.  In a pique Lady Juliet queried, "Whence be Sir Vincent?"

With evil intent, Lady Leticia replied suggestively, "Our Lord doth finish dressing. Whence be thy reason for intrusion?"

Juliet's face turned flame red with fury.  Holding back her anger she replied venomously, "We wouldst accompany Sir de Courtenay for breaking the fast.  We wouldst then accompany our lord for hunt."  It never occurred to Juliet that a simpleton girl raised in a convent would be interested in falconry or hunts.

"Our lord, Sir Vincent spent eve with us.  Our lord requested us to break the fast and ride with Sir Vincent for hunt," Leticia replied haughtily.  "We be our lord's betrothed, my lady."

Vincent approached the door and Juliet immediately cooed, "My lady, we wouldst naught comprehend thy wroth.  We wouldst accompany Sir Vincent believing thee be travailed."

Leticia felt Vincent's arm embrace her shoulders and cooed back, "My Lady, whence wroth dost thee speak?  Sir Vincent requested us to join breaking the fast thus morn.  Thus be all we dost speak for you."

"Lady Juliet?" Vincent questioned in surprise.  "Whence dost thee come to our chamber thus morn?

Smiling deceptively Juliet replied, "We wouldst naught be told thy betrothed wouldst join thee thus morn.  We only came to offer thee our company for breaking the fast and hunt."

"Thee be so considerate," Leticia oozed sarcastically.

Vincent was completely unaware of the battle conducted in his presence.  With ignorance he stated, "Indeed, thee be so considerate.  In troth, we be enjoying company with our betrothed thus den and other den of our hunt.  Mayhap our squire wouldst accompany thee?"

"Thy squire hath already offered to share trencher with Lady Organa," Lady Leticia informed delightfully.

At the insult of being paired with a squire and then to find out she was usurped by another lady, Juliet replied,  "Worry naught, we wouldst be off to our chambers.  Our meal already prepared.  We wouldst be concerned for Sir Vincent's company alone."  She turned and left the betrothed couple quickly.  Anger and insult moved her legs faster than ever before.  She returned to Sir Bolin's chamber to share his trencher as he offered before she left his rooms.

# Chapter 10

"Thy falcon be beauteous, Sirrah," Leticia admired Vincent's falcon as
he held it waiting for the dogs to flush out the partridge and ground grouse. She
had enjoyed sharing his trencher breaking fast since he was most attentive.
These several hours of the hunt Leticia couldn't help but be proud of the
magnificent specimen of manhood he was. The only other man she had ever
known to win this type of appreciation had been, Prince Edward, the Black
Prince. It was obvious to all on the hunt Sir Vincent de Courtenay was envied
for his countenance, Destrier, and hawk. Leticia had heard of the bounty for the

hawk bringing in the most birds on the week hunt. Because of her prank, Vincent was a day behind, but in these two days on the hunt Elizabeth had brought in eight birds. Sir Bolin's hawk had brought in eight for three days. King Edward's hawk had brought in ten birds.

"Dost thee trow falconry?" Vincent queried. He had heard that several women, especially noblewomen had also trained and hunted with hawks.

"Yea, we wouldst raise and own two falcons in Okehampton," Leticia bragged. "Our Romulus and Remus wouldst be competition for thy Elizabeth."

"Ho! Thus wouldst be challenge?" Vincent chuckled raising Elizabeth and setting her upon the birds as the dogs flushed them out.

"Yea, we wouldst challenge thee. Thus wouldst be our nuptial feast at Okehampton," Leticia gurgled with glee. "Romulus challenges Elizabeth for our hunt."

"Done!" Vincent agreed. He was feeling confident once more in this marital decree. Every day he found he admired Leticia more. When she walked into his rooms wearing his colors, a sky blue woolen gown, he thought he would burst with pride. She was not only beautiful, she was intelligent, loved hunting, knew medicines, and was a true lady. Those few kisses he had stolen he found her to be responsive and not cold as he feared. This hunt was even more enjoyable as she rode by his side. He found he was no longer jealous but actually enjoyed the envious looks the other knights shot at him with Leticia next to him. She was his betrothed. "Thee wouldst naught challenge our Elizabeth with thy Remus?"

"Nay, Remus hath lover character. Remus wouldst attempt to woo thy Elizabeth," Leticia laughed throwing her head back in mirth. "We found Remus fails training whence surrounded by such lovely lady."

"A fate most men, such as we be burdened with," Vincent replied in uproarious laughter.

The other knights looked at the strange and unusual laughter from the sober knight. They knew it had to be the beautiful Lady Leticia's influence. They would be as happy with such a lovely wife.

"Tell us in troth, whence name thy birds after god twins of old Rome?" Vincent asked.

"We read thus tale and our birds born of same nest fit such names," Leticia smiled.

Her smile melted Vincent into butter. Elizabeth came back with another bird and now it was time to rest at a camp and eat the mid day meal. Vincent was looking forward to that time with Leticia. Vincent called Maynard and gave him the hawk gauntlet, Elizabeth and bird. "Nearby wouldst be special place for thee to visit," Vincent said to Leticia.

"We hope thus naught be another lake to for swim," Leticia chuckled. "We suffered travail for such swim most recent."

"Nay, tis too cold for swims," Vincent laughed. He reached over and took her Palfrey's reins to lead her to a mystical place he found while hunting with King Edward last year.

Neither Leticia nor Vincent noticed Lady Juliet riding by Sir Martin Bolin's side. They were too happy and involved with themselves.

A few minutes later Vincent stopped in a clearing. He reined in his Destrier and tied it to a heavy oak branch. He walked Leticia's Palfrey mare to another tree and tied the reins to a branch. Vincent lifted Leticia from her mount as if she weighed nothing and gently set her down upon the clover and grass.

"Whither be thus place?" Leticia marveled as she looked around. There were walls 2 feet thick and 4 feet high. They were crumbling, but in a semicircle. The rocks were of pure white polished marble. In the center was a round table. The base was made of the same polished marble. The tabletop was a round smoothed and polished rose quartz. Leticia noticed there were flowers in circles surrounding the table in the clearing. Wild fragrant flowers of all kinds and colors permeated the air. Against the semi circular wall were many rose bushes. The blossoms were pink, red, and white. The rose bushes were wild and uncared for, but large and filled with the elegant blooms.

"Tis said thus be worship glen for many Druid sects in times before Roman conquest of Britain," Vincent explained. He placed his arm around her shoulders and led her to the semicircular marble benches facing the rose quartz table. Gracefully he set her upon his lap as he sat down on the bench. There was great pleasure for him placing her there. No explanation was needed. He just liked it. Leticia seemed to like it also. "A peace seems to surround hither."

"Yea, peaceful and fragrant," Leticia remarked. "Tis strange knight so powerful and noble enjoys such as thus."

"We see much pain, blood, and sorrow in battle," Sir Vincent shared. "Tis important for us to find such respite."

His gentle and honest words endeared him to Leticia. She placed her hands on his cheeks and offered her lips as more consolation.

With magnet force, Vincent placed his lips over the offered ones. Slowly and gently his tongue delved into the sweetness of her mouth. Deftly his hands began opening the buttons of her gown. Soon his hand had entered her chemise and was massaging the soft feminine globes of his betrothed. His kisses became more needful and wanting.

Leticia was losing reality and entering a world of sensation. As Vincent's thumb and finger squeezed her nubs she felt a sensation of euphoria. Her body began to pulse rhythmically.

Vincent left the sweetness of Leticia's lips and wandered down to the curve of her neck. There he stayed for a moment as his hand retrieved a breast and pulled it from the containment of her gown. Vincent tentatively laved his tongue over the nipple. When it hardened to a tantalizing nub, he boldly began to suckle.

When Vincent's warm mouth covered her breast, Leticia whimpered in ecstasy. These feelings shot through her with unbelievable pleasure. The feelings were waves through her entire body. Queen Phillippa had told her about this thrill. The queen was right.

Leticia's whimper caused Vincent to break from his delectable delight and look up to her face. She was smiling down at him and took his head in her hands placing it back to where he had been and arched her back to provide him better access to her rosy nub.

Vincent was overjoyed that Leticia responded in like kind to his passion. She may have been raised in a nunnery, but his companions were wrong about such woman. This woman was different. She matched his fire and responded passionately. He thought that this was going to be a wonderful marriage. He was certain he would enjoy the bed as much as his king enjoyed his queen in their bed. He chuckled a little thinking about having nine or ten children. He pictured his Leticia large and breeding his heir, no many heirs. He moaned a little himself as his manhood stretched to new lengths of need. When he thought how much he would enjoy filling Leticia with his seed for breeding the damn thing grew more.

Leticia recognized Vincent's moaning. She had heard this before when she wandered about the convent at night and her home in the secret halls and passages. She realized that sound was the sound of what she was feeling, a physical need. She wanted Vincent to touch her all over. She wanted him to feel the fire he had ignited in that secret place of her womanhood. Leticia raked her fingers through Vincent's hair as she arched more in to his suckling. Her body began writing rhythmically of its own accord. Leticia lost all sense of propriety. She wanted Vincent to touch her and kiss her all over. She raised her skirt and took his one hand placing it gently between her thighs. Leticia could no longer function or think rationally. Vincent had driven her to realize her own physical need.

Taken up in his personal pleasure, Vincent placed his thumb upon the sensitive tissue between Leticia's feminine lips and thrust his finger into her womanhood. Massaging her sensitive tissue and thrusting his finger rhythmically to match Leticia's writing machinations he felt her warm discharge of orgasm. Leticia's moan and body convulsion followed the evidence on his finger. She possessed a fire and passion he dared hope for in his wife. She was his! She was only his! Vincent realized at that moment his Leticia would be his passion and obsession. "Leticia, Leticia," Vincent whispered hoarsely. "Thou conquered our heart and our spirit. We be thy slave."

Leticia barely heard him, she was convulsing in a physical and spiritual experience that was beyond simple pleasure. It was ecstasy. Breathing heavily, Leticia tried to calm her racing heart. Vincent would be hers and hers alone. She would not allow any other woman to enjoy her husband in this way. She groaned and pulled his lips to hers. Leticia opened her mouth permitting Vincent to cover her lips and begin a duel of tongues.

Their breathing was heavy. Their bodies were on fire and any moment Leticia was certain she would lose her virginity in this magical mystical glen and she didn't care. They were married already by king's decree. The legalities were for the tally makers and the priest's blessings.

Vincent was also beguiled by this mystical moment. He was about to lay Leticia on the flowered grass carpet and bed her. He didn't even think about right or wrong, propriety and legality. Vincent only thought about sharing this ardent moment with his Leticia.

Their moment was shattered by loud sounds of growling, hissing, and snorting.

Vincent recognized the sounds immediately. He stood quickly and gently placed Leticia on the marble bench. He warned her quietly, "Stay here! Move naught!"

"Whence…?" Leticia barely said before Vincent placed his finger over her lips.

"Speak naught and stay," Vincent whispered with commanding tone. Vincent moved swiftly to his Destrier. He pulled his broad sword from its sheath.

Leticia was disoriented and began walking toward Vincent when she heard horrible cries of pain and agony. Stopping she looked toward a large hedgerow to her right and saw movement. Frightened to her wits, Leticia moved toward the disturbance.

The agonized cries ceased and a huge boar with bloodied tusks emerged from the hedgerow.

Leticia stopped. She was frozen with fear.

The boar smelled her fear and after pounding his hooves a moment, charged Leticia.

A muscular knight brandishing a large sword came between the boar and Leticia. The blade found its target and the boar was killed instantly.

Leticia felt faint and her knees buckled under her. "Sweet Jesu!" Leticia exclaimed. "Thee be brave and noble knight, Sirrah."

Vincent removed his sword from the boar's heart and turned to find Leticia on her knees. He imbedded the sword in the grass and lifted Leticia. "We dost merely provide our trencher's meat thus eve."

Leticia looked into Vincent's eyes, sighed, and laid her head upon his chest. "We be pleased to be thy Goodwife."

Vincent held her shaking body in his strong embrace and breathed softly into her hair, "We be pleased to be thy lord and husband." This boar had stopped him from ravaging his future bride. Vincent was almost grateful. When he would bed his Leticia it would be on silken sheets. The bedding would be lengthy and loving.

Moments of silence continued as Vincent embraced Leticia in that magical mystical glen. The two realized this was the beginning of a spiritual bonding between the two of them.

Suddenly they heard sounds of mournful crying. Vincent retrieved his sword and together he and Leticia walked toward the hedgerow. This time a little gray kitten with long hair emerged. The kitten was the size of Vincent's hand.

"Sirrah, tis tiny mewling!" Leticia exclaimed kneeling to retrieve the kitten with her hands.

Vincent moved the hedgerow with his sword and spotted the mangled body of what apparently was the kitten's mother. "Tis orphaned."

"Oh little darling," Leticia cooed as the kitten snuggled into Leticia's opened gown near her breast. "We wouldst keep our mewling."

Vincent smiled and stated, "Yea, thus mewling hath found new mother. We wouldst naught allow thus mewling our share of thy lord's possession." With those words he gently returned Leticia's exposed orbs to their containment in her gown. As deftly as he had opened her gown, he buttoned it closed.

Leticia petted the kitten and spoke quietly to it, "Mewling, thy name be Mystic for this magical and wonderful glen."

Vincent smiled at the motherly instinct in his future bride. "Come, we wouldst be missed and it be the hour for our meals. Our belly dost grumble like thus angry boar."

Leticia laughed with innuendo, "Yea, we hath created effort to build our appetite."

"Yea," Vincent agreed in the same mirth. "We hath built such an appetite to devour this great beast Jesu hath given us." He walked her to the Palfrey mare and lifted her to her mount so she would not disturb the sleeping kitten.

Leticia waited patiently on her mount and secured the sleeping kitten as Vincent turned his woolen hunting mantel into a bag for transporting the dead boar to camp.

Arriving at the hunting camp, the couple was met by Sir Lionel Tyndale.

"We thought mayhap we wouldst need send out dogs to track you," Lionel greeted.

Vincent leapt from his Destrier and embraced his best friend. "We missed your countenance, Goodman!"

"We missed thy countenance as well," Lionel replied returning the embrace.

"We thought thee wouldst meet us at Okehampton?" Vincent asked. "Whither bring thee hence?"

"Our good king sent messengers to Okehampton. We are all called to attend thy nuptials at Surrey," Sir Lionel explained.

"All?" Vincent asked with delight.

"Yea, all of thy knights, squires, and men at arms," Lionel answered. "The king hath included thy father and sisters."

"Sir Gaylord?" Vincent gasped. He adored his father and had not seen him in two years.

"Yea, with thy sisters, Morgan and Megan," Lionel responded knowing such news would bring joy to Vincent. "We accompanied Lord John de Redvers and his Goodwife, Maude."

Vincent cocked a brow. "Methinks our Queen Phillippa doth demand grand ceremony for thus nuptials."

Lionel whispered. "We heard our queen doth love thy betrothed dearly as her own daughters Joan, Mary, Blanche and Margaret."

"'Tis troth," Vincent chuckled. "We hath suffered and been reprimanded most soundly by our queen for our unwitting errors."

"Do things fare well with thy betrothed?" Lionel asked in concern.

The broad smile on Vincent's face answered the question without a reply.

"So good?" Lionel laughed uproariously.

"Yea," Vincent responded in laughter. "Hath thee brought thy goodwife, Sara?"

"My Goodwife wouldst naught permit us to leave for thy nuptials without our Sara's presence," Lionel answered still laughing. "In troth, we wouldst naught leave our Sara. We find we enjoy thus company in our pallet."

"We hope to learn thus warm company soon," Vincent shared wickedly. They walked to Lady Leticia who was waiting patiently for her betrothed to help her dismount.

Lifting his love from her mount Vincent told her, "Sir Lionel brings us good tidings. Thy mother and father await thee at Surrey with our father and sisters."

"Your father and sisters?" Leticia quizzed. In their conversations he had many times talked of his father with admiration and love. She never heard him mention his mother or sisters. Leticia asked boldly still cuddling the kitten in her arms as Vincent lifted her. "Thee hath naught spoken of sisters. Doth thy father bring also thy mother."

Vincent stiffened but calmly replied, "Our mother passed to God last Michaelmas."

Leticia felt Vincent's sudden tension but had no time to question it. She spotted Prince Edward approaching with her father's two favorite men at arms, George and Damian. Leticia craned her neck looking for Lady Organa. Vincent's squire, Maynard, was helping her dismount. "Lady Organa," Leticia called excitedly. "Come hither anon!"

Organa responded quickly to her lady's pleading call.

"Lady Organa, take our mewling to our pavilion with haste!" Leticia ordered nervously.

Vincent's betrothed's behavior caught his attention. "Whence travails thee my lady?"

Leticia passed the kitten into Organa's hands and replied. "Naught my liege. Our Prince Edward approaches and we trow our lord fears mewlings as thee dost fear arachnids."

Vincent's intelligence did not miss that remark. "Whither wouldst thee trow we fear arachnids?" Two plus two calculated into four. Vincent wasn't certain to laugh or throttle his vivacious betrothed.

Leticia realized her slip of tongue and did the only thing possible. She ran. She ran right to Prince Edward.

"Dearest foster sister," Prince Edward greeted. "Thy father hath sent men at arms to escort thee back to Surrey. Thy mother anxiously awaits thee, and our mother misses thee most dearly. Our dear sister, Margaret cries with colic. Our mother stays with her. We trow our mother prefer the hunt with father."

"We wouldst return with haste to greet our mother and assist our queen," Leticia replied. She ran towards her pavilion mainly to avoid Vincent. She didn't dare respond to his question of her knowledge of his fear.

Vincent walked to Prince Edward chuckling as he watched his betrothed dart across the field to her pavilion. Prince Edward had been his squire and Leticia's childhood friend. Prince Edward was the only one who knew of Vincent's great fear of spiders.

"Ho! Sir Vincent!" Prince Edward greeted cheerfully. Elizabeth had brought in two more game birds and was certain Sir Vincent would win the prize. He noticed servants helping Maynard release the boar carcass. "We doth naught be aware this be a boar hunt!"

"The boar merely desired to be supper's food," Vincent chuckled. "We wouldst naught deny thus boar's gracious gift."

"We wouldst have great feast on the morrow," Edward stated.

"Tell us in troth dear friend," Vincent asked cocking an eyebrow. "Whither be thus our betrothed trow our fear of arachnids?"

Prince Edward turned pale against his black armor. "Thee trow thence?"

Seriously Vincent answered. "Yea! It wouldst appear our betrothed enjoys trickery!"

"Wouldst thee beat her?" Edward asked in concern. He would protect her even from Vincent if he had to.

"Nay, we wouldst not harm our lovely Goodwife, thus occurrence!" Vincent replied teasingly. "But mayhap thus be trickery for her we might use for future reference. So do tell us dear friend! We learned thee fear mewlings."

Edward paled once more and then laughed, "So be it! Our lovely maiden hath dread fear of snakes."

# Chapter 11

Maude was walking in the keep to obtain certain herbs for Queen Phillippa spotted her daughter approaching with George and Damian.

Leticia saw her mother and reined her Palfrey toward Maude away from the castle courtyard. George followed her and realized she was heading toward her mother. He ordered Damian to take Lady Organa, who was holding the kitten, to the castle. Reining in front of Leticia, George nodded to Lady Maude and jumped from his Destrier to assist Leticia off her mount.

A few minutes of hugging, kissing, tears, and touching followed the reunion.

"We longed for thee desperately," Leticia confessed hugging her mother so tightly Maude could barely breathe.

"We desired thy loving countenance in our sorrow," Maude wept. "Thou art our only surviving child."

Leticia had forgotten her brothers had just recently been killed. She understood her mother's grief although she felt nothing. As a mother, wouldn't she feel the same pain at the death of her children? "We wished to be at thy side," Leticia sympathized. "We love thee, mother."

Maude sniffed back her tears, "We love thee, our daughter."

"Come hither, let us assist our queen," Leticia suggested.

"Our queen bade me select peppermint from the gardens to assist Princess Margaret's colic," Maude replied walking to the gardens.

Leticia and her mother retrieved the requested herbs and spices and returned to the queen. Leticia was introduced to Morgan and Megan. They were the twin sisters of Vincent de Courtenay. Unlike Vincent, the twins were not fostered out but instead took tutelage inside the de Courtenay keep outside of Exeter. For the past six years, the thirteen year old twins had helped care for their ill mother. Morgan and Megan were identical twins. They looked so much alike and wore the same clothes one could not tell them apart. Their father instructed their handmaidens to comb Morgan's hair in side braids and Megan's hair in back braids so he could tell which twin was which. After several deceptive episodes, Sir Gaylord ordered handmaidens to accompany the twins everywhere lest they change their hair to deceive.

The next few days were set aside for sewing the nuptial clothes and preparing for the great feast. Between caring for Margaret, time for her husband and other children, Queen Phillippa was a whirl of energy planning the feast.

Leticia and Maude assisted when they could. Leticia spent time with Morgan and Megan. She laughed when they shared their stories of deceptions and trickery used as twins. These two girls had the de Courtenay looks of their father, Sir Gaylord. It was also obvious Sir Vincent resembled his still handsome father. Leticia marveled at the family resemblance and wondered what their mother had looked like. Leticia, Maude, and the twins became instant friends.

Maude took over as a temporary mother image with Morgan and Megan. Leticia couldn't help but think this was going to be a very happy family. She even had spent time with Vincent's father, Sir Gaylord, and developed a deep fondness for him.

Vincent enjoyed the rest of the hunt with his best friend, Sir Lionel. Elizabeth had brought in two score and eight birds. The king's falcon brought in two score and ten. Sir Martin Bolin's falcon brought in only two score. The twenty crowns were taken by Sir Vincent and on the Sabbath day coins were dispensed to the poor after mass. King Edward admired his knight for the charity. But King Edward, Vincent, Lionel, and Prince Edward noticed a difference in Sir Bolin. They all noticed Sir Bolin was no longer unkempt and odorous. He bathed regularly, kept his clothes cleaned and mended. He began spending his hoarded monies on fine cloth and well-tailored clothes. Even his attitude began changing. Vincent commented that Sir Bolin actually appeared happy and content.

King Edward had been so impressed with Sir Martin Bolin's personality change that he discussed with his royal advisors sending Sir Bolin to Wales as temporary Lord of a fief there. If he did the job wisely, King Edward would bestow it to Sir Bolin. The catch was, Sir Bolin would only be told he would be sent as a temporary steward.

Even though Leticia hated sewing, this was different. Leticia, her mother, and the twin sisters of de Courtenay worked continuously on the fine gown for Leticia and the tunic and hose Sir Vincent would wear for the nuptials.

Leticia selected a gold shimmered damask of silk for her gown and Vincent's matching tunic. Her trumpet sleeves were lined with white satin. The sleeves and collar of her dress were edged with white ermine. Sir Vincent's shirt worn under his tunic was white satin. The high collar and trumpet sleeves were edged with white ermine. The light blue heraldic crest of the de Courtenay's was sewn on the tunic chest and side of Leticia's gown. Both the tunic and gown crest were embellished with elaborate embroidery stitches of fine golden and silken threads of many colors including red, blue, yellow and green. Precious stones of rubies, pearls, and emeralds were sewn into the embroidered crest. Maude and Leticia decided not to wear a wimple or dress the hair in any way other than a small golden circlet to be worn on the crown of her head with her hair flowing freely down her back.

"Thou art in troth happy with this contract?" Maude questioned her daughter as she worked fine embroidery stitching to the crest on her daughter's gown.

"In troth, most happy!" Leticia bubbled in the excitement of the pre nuptials. It would be only two days and the holy day of St. Giles would be here. On that day Sir Vincent would take her as his legal wife. "We find Sir Vincent to be kind, fair, intelligent, and quite gentle."

Maude smiled and was happy for her daughter. She loved her husband, John, in the same happiness. It was unfortunate John de Redvers put no interest in his lovely daughter until now. Maude realized John had never realized what a beautiful and intelligent child he had begat. Leticia even resembled her mother and John had often commented on how beautiful his wife was. "In troth daughter, thou must naught forget Sir Vincent also be a knight and warrior for the king," Maude warned hoping her daughter would understand.

"Yea mother, in troth we forget thus," Leticia sighed. "We see our lord as man and naught knight. To think of Sir Vincent thus causes us fear our lord wouldst reject our care as our father hath."

"We pray thee wouldst forgive thy father's errors," Maude said quietly. "We pray thy lord wouldst love and care for thee and thy seed always above all else."

Leticia stopped sewing on Vincent's tunic and looked directly into her mother's eyes. "Dost our father care for thee over duty?" Leticia queried. "Hast thee trow love or emptiness as our person?"

"In troth my daughter," Maude replied stopping her embroidery and looking directly back. "We hath known great love from thy father. Our heart breaketh whence we see his treatment of thee compared to his sons. Thy father be truly a kind and loving man."

"We wouldst make every effort to persuade our Lord Vincent to love us and our kinder!" Leticia declared firmly. "Regardless of whence gender they be born. If we be blessed with sons or daughters. We wouldst naught foster kinder, but raise kinder in our love. We hath enjoyed such love with our Queen Phillippa and her children. We believe we wouldst do naught less."

"We wish we wouldst take back time," Maude responded. "We wouldst kept thee closer to us."

"Thee dost offer us love, mother," Leticia assuaged. "Tis thy love helped us through lonely days."

Queen Phillippa entered the room then with Morgan and Megan. "Tis so lovely!" she declared describing the nuptial garments.

"Whither be Princess Margaret's complaint?" Maude asked politely.

"Our daughter sleeps soundly and comfortably this night," Queen Phillippa answered with a chuckle. "As we hath slept well this past eve with our king."

Morgan sat next to Leticia and hugged her. "We be so happy thee be our new sister."

Megan took a seat next to Maude. "We hope our brother trow whence fortune doth obtain with thee."

"We wouldst speak to father about our brother's good fortune," Morgan agreed taking up the gown to help Leticia finish the stitching.

"We love thee in like kind," Leticia grinned with joy. She was looking forward to the nuptials. The twins spent the rest of the day gossiping and sharing stories of their brother with Queen Phillippa, Maude, and Leticia.

Vincent spent his days in tactical and physical warfare training with his good friends Lionel, Gifford, Hugh, Tobias, and William. On occasion his father would join the practices. Sir John de Redvers still recovering from his wounds would join the men after the evening meal for wine and mead in front of the fireplace. Lady Juliet seemed always to be present providing fresh goblets to all the men including Sir Bolin, who smiled consistently with her presence.

Vincent admitted only to himself he missed seeing his betrothed. Leticia, Queen Phillippa, his sisters, and Maude took meals in their chambers. He once tried to visit his Leticia but was shooed away by the handmaidens of Leticia and the Queen. He was told the ladies were not to be disturbed.

The evening before nuptials Vincent sat solemnly before the fireplace apparently in deep thought.

"Whither be thy thoughts, Goodman?" Lionel asked taking a chair next to Vincent and sitting. "Dost thee first comprehend thee wouldst be permanently shackled in thus morn?"

"We be thinking of our bedding," Vincent whispered sharing his thoughts with his trusted and good friend.

"Anxious art thou?" Lionel guffawed.

"Nay, thus be naught our thinking," Vincent countered. "We wish to make thus bedding special and wonderful. Our betrothed be unlike the nunnery raised ladies we hath heard of in stories. Our betrothed be passionate and shouldst have special care. In troth we be uncertain we can control our lust."

Lionel looked at Vincent as if he grew two heads. "Whence thus be worry of man? God hath given us women to fill our needs. We give to wives our seed for breeding. They be happy with our kinder. Thus be a noble circle of life."

"Nay, thee naught be taught well, Goodman," Vincent corrected. "We hath felt passionate fire our betrothed keeps within her heart. We hath learned from our good king that small cinder, if brought to raging fire in pallet, brings great satisfaction for both man and wife."

"Methinks we need more instruction from our king hence tactical warfare," Lionel stated intensely.

"Yea," Vincent chuckled in agreement. "We be planning our strategy for our nuptial bedding."

"Wouldst thee share thy great wisdom with us," Lionel requested with interest. "We wouldst learn thus and use in our own pallet."

Vincent did share his plans in soft whispers. Whenever anyone approached he would remain silent until they left until he completed relating his plans to Lionel.

Lionel sat back in his chair and accepted a tankard of mead from Lady Juliet who openly flirted with Sir Vincent as she served him. "We hath learned much this eve," Lionel said thoughtfully. "We wouldst watch thy bride's face next morn to watch if thy strategies hath worked. We in troth believe thy plans wouldst prove fruitful."

John de Redvers and Gaylord de Courtenay joined Vincent and Lionel.

"Whence plans be discussed?" Gaylord asked his son.

Vincent blushed with embarrassment.

Lionel replied for him, "we be discussing warfare strategies."

"Yea, tis good subject to calm a man's fears before nuptials," John stated cheerfully.

The rest of that evening was a sharing of battle tales won and lost.

Early in the morning, several servants, the king, his father and his future father in law wakened Vincent entering his chambers. Two of the queen's handmaidens carried in his completed nuptial ensemble. He was breathless when he viewed the satin shirt, damask tunic, and light blue hose with matching velvet slipper shoes. "Who hath created such finery?" Vincent asked with awe pointing to the wedding clothes.

"Our daughter with fine needle," John de Redvers bragged. "Thus our Leticia created with assistance of our dear Goodwife, queen, and thy sisters."

"Even we as king hath naught such finery for our nuptials," Edward laughed. "Thou art wedding to a fine needle indeed. Thou dost see how fortunate to wed a lady nunnery raised."

"Yea," Vincent agreed with astonishment. He remembered Leticia had told him how much she hated needlework, but she had created this fantastic garment for him. Vincent reached to touch the soft fabric. It was soft to his touch. He marveled that such fabric would cover his body shortly. Lionel and Maynard assisted Vincent with his bath. Gaylord, John, and King Edward sat in his room and made joking remarks about the upcoming nuptial.

When completely bathed and dried, Vincent was helped to dress. The king offered a blue garter for his hose to be worn above the knee. The garter was embellished with a jeweled piece in the shape of square set with diamonds and sapphires.

Gaylord produced a soft light blue mantel with white ermine edging that Morgan and Megan had made for their brother's nuptials.

Lionel stood several feet from Vincent to view him. He suddenly began guffawing.

"Whence be thy great humor?" Vincent growled testily. "Wouldst thee share thus humor?"

"Thee," Lionel answered continuing to laugh holding his ribs. "Thou art beauteous!"

"Enough!" King Edward ordered barely hiding his own mirth. "Tis time to enter our Great Hall and begin nuptial contract."

The men walked to the Great Hall where the tally maker, royal steward, and priest awaited Vincent to begin the compilation of contractual agreement and estates.

The listing took hours as the royal steward scribed all the holdings, castles, keeps, fiefs, manors, knights, men at arms, incomes, farms, serfs, and coffers. The rights and lands that would be held by Leticia on Vincent's demise should it happen to him before her were listed. Vincent's personal wealth and lands were also included in the compilations. The compilations continued on well past the mid day meal.

Leticia waited patiently in her rooms with her mother, Vincent's sisters and Queen Phillippa. She would stay in her rooms until the contract had been signed and sealed with the royal stamp. Leticia would be summoned when it was time to attend the chapel service and obtain blessings for the marriage contract from the attending priest.

At last they heard a knocking at the door. It was Maynard. He had been sent to bring the ladies to the chapel for blessings.

Queen Phillippa, Maude, Morgan, and Megan walked into the chapel and stood to the left of the altar. Vincent remained standing on the right with King Edward, Gaylord De Courtenay, and Lionel. He looked to the chapel entrance after the women had taken their places. His bride entered holding the extended arm of her father, John de Redvers.

Vincent stopped breathing and his legs buckled under him. Lionel quickly aided his friend with support. Vincent's bride was incredibly beautiful. The gold shimmering damask sparkled like heavenly hands touched it when the sun's beams peeking through the windows sprayed upon the cloth. Her hair glistened like spun gold. His crest sewn upon her dress took his breath away. At last she was his, truly his alone. Leticia was a vision of angelic perfection in his eyes. A moan suddenly emerged from his lips. Vincent's control was lost already. How could he ever control his lust in the bedding? Vincent was already hurting in lustful need.

John de Redvers was asked by the priest, "Who giveth thus woman to thus man?"

"We doth give our daughter to care of Sir Vincent de Courtenay," John de Redvers replied and took Leticia's hand to place it on the extended arm of Sir Vincent de Courtenay.

Vincent trembled as Leticia's hand was placed upon his arm. Fortunately Lionel still gave Vincent support.

The priest commanded the couple to kneel for the blessing.

It was then Vincent turned his head and looked at Leticia's face. She looked so calm and serene. Leticia looked up and their eyes locked. She was so very beautiful and angelic. Her eyes were rich deep brown full of love and passion. If only he could be capable of fulfilling all her needs both physical and emotional.

They stared at each other for several minutes speaking in a silent understanding.

The priest ended his blessings and they were joined at that moment by a nuptial contract and church protocol.

Together they left the chapel to walk toward the Great Hall. Servants were preparing for the celebration feast. Nobles and knights with their ladies were filling the hall in anticipation of the nuptial celebration.

Vincent's arm stayed protectively around Leticia's shoulders. He didn't want to stop touching her. He wanted everyone present to know she belonged to him officially. Leticia was now his wife!

As they entered the Great Hall, servants approached them with golden goblets studded with jewels and filled with wine. Each took a goblet and Vincent toasted his new bride, "A toast for our beauteous Goodwife! God Bless our nuptials, provide us with many kinder, and keep us happily together through eternity."

Leticia and Vincent drank entwining their hands and drinking from each other's goblet.

"To our husband, may thee be loving and kind for us and our kinder through eternity," Leticia toasted raising her goblet.

Again their hands entwined and they drank from each other's goblet. This time they stared deeply into each other's eyes. Leticia and Vincent burned each other with their expressive passion reflected in their souls.

When they finished their sips of wine. Vincent placed his lips upon Leticia's and delicately tasted her sweet wine flavored lips. In a few moments he covered her lips with his and delved deeper. Leticia responded and whimpered softly. He fired her passions with his kiss and touch. She was looking forward to the bedding as much as Vincent.

A cough, followed by several coughs interrupted their world.

"We wouldst appreciate a kiss for our new bride," Prince Edward announced. "Mayhap thus dance?"

At that moment the musicians began playing and Leticia took Edward's Hand. They joined arms with other dancers twirling in a circle in the center of the Great Hall. Vincent joined the dancers on the other side of Leticia. There was laughing, dancing, toasting, and more drinking. Leticia received goblet after goblet of wine. For a young woman raised in a nunnery, Leticia was not used to a large volume of spirits. She felt warm and giddy, but continued taking the goblets of wine until finally the food was served. Vincent noticed the change in his young bride's demeanor. He was concerned that his well laid plans for the bedding might be useless if his young bride was completely inebriated. Vincent picked Leticia up and carried her to the great table and placed her on his lap. Vincent wanted to make certain Leticia would get solid food in her belly.

The trencher was served. Vincent began to cut a slice of meat for Leticia when she reached for the goblet of wine.

"Nay, thee hast drunken enough!" Vincent ordered dropping the knife and removing the goblet from Leticia's reach. He turned to the servant and commanded him to bring a tankard of fresh cold well water.

Leticia wiggled on his lap and stretched once again reaching for the wine goblet.

"Nay, Goodwife!" Vincent stated firmly and put the goblet farther out of her reach.

"Whensh doth thee order (hic) thy wife? (hic)," Leticia slurred. She stood up and weaving slightly, attempted to place her hands on her hips in a stance of defiance. Her hands never quite made it to the hips. "We naught (hic) be wed a den and thou becommmmmst a beascht!"

# Chapter 12

Prince Edward bit his lip so not to laugh at his inebriated friend. John de Redvers was in shock at his daughter's behavior. Fortunately Maude and Queen Phillippa were occupied elsewhere and did not witness the scene. Morgan and Megan giggled loudly.

"We hope we wouldst enjoy such giddiness when we wed," Megan whispered to Morgan.

"Yea, we wouldst enjoy being as light hearted as besotted man," Morgan agreed and giggled more.

Vincent merely took his bride's hand and carefully guided his bride back to the bench. "We wouldst only seek to give thee solid food," Vincent said gently. He had been inebriated enough to know it was best never to argue with someone drunk.

"We wouldscht be of greeaaatt th..th..(hic) irst!" Leticia slurred in response.

"Yea, our lovely little bride," Vincent answered trying not to laugh. "We bring thee fresh cold water to soothe thy thirst."

"Nay!" Leticia replied with a thick tongue. "We wouldscht (hic) delighscht in our drinkth!"

King Edward was laughing openly, but turned his head hoping to hide his guffaws from Leticia, who unfortunately was quite serious. He had truly never seen an inebriated woman to this extent of drunkenness.

Lionel whispered to Vincent, "Prithee, wouldst we appear such as this whence we be inebriated?"

"Yea," Prince Edward answered for Vincent. "Thee dost appear so whence thee be inebriated. Mayhap worse."

Lionel covered his face with his hand and moaned, "Sweet Jesu!"

Vincent managed to place the slice of meat in Leticia's mouth and she began to chew. He then offered her some bread with water. "Our venison be tasty?" Vincent persuaded offering more meat.

"Yeasch, (hic)" Leticia replied savoring the meat in her mouth. Leticia realized she was hungry. "Ooooh, thus venison be (hic) wooonnnddeerful!"

Patiently Vincent cut small pieces of venison, game hen, boar, bread, and potatoes to feed Leticia.

Leticia was feeling quite tipsy and cuddled into Vincent's strong arm that held her in place and prevented her from reaching the goblet of wine he had set away from her grasp. "Thee be sooo good (hic) husband," Leticia cooed. "Sooo kind, (hic) sooo sweet, (hic) sooo big!" Leticia spread her arms in animation to describe the word big and her arms dumped the trencher into Vincent's lap and Prince Edward's wine onto his royal tunic. Prince Edward jumped hoping to avoid the spill and dumped Lionel's trencher and wine onto Lionel's lap. Lionel jumped up setting off a domino affect of spills and dumped trenchers down the line of the table.

King Edward was laughing so hard at the sight he almost fell off his chair at the table. Queen Phillippa, who was now sitting next to her husband, bit her lip so hard controlling her laughter it turned bright red. Maude's mouth dropped open at her daughter's behavior. John de Redvers was in catatonic shock. Morgan and Megan were laughing so hard they left the Great Hall to catch their breath.

"Our brother wouldst be challenged," Megan roared in laughter.

"Yea, tis time," Morgan agreed. "Until thus, our dearest brother hath only proper maidens without heart pursuing him. Lady Leticia be real heart and doth behave most peculiar."

"A funny peculiar," Megan confirmed. "Methinks we love Lady Leticia dearly."

"Yea, we love our Leticia also," Morgan said. "Tis happiness with real heart she brings to our family."

Gaylord watched the scene with delight. He was happy for his son. Vincent's mother was so stern at times he thought his wife was granite. Vincent would have a wife of challenge, humor, vivacity, and what appeared to be stubbornness. Yes, Leticia would keep Vincent's love with challenge and consistent change.

Vincent helped her drink more water hoping to sober her a little more. He had succeeded. Leticia's hiccups had stopped and she was slightly more coherent, but she was indeed still happily tipsy.

Another round of dancing began after the meal and Leticia joined in with whole heart. Vincent watched proudly as she twirled, kicked, and clapped with great exuberance. She turned no one away. Leticia even danced with Sir Bolin. In Vincent's eyes, she was beautiful. He loved her hair floating in the air as she twirled in dance. Her cheeks were bright pink with heat from the dancing. Most of all the red luscious lips revealed smile after smile of happiness.

Those thoughts were enough to bring his lust to attention and his plan for the bedding to action. The day had slipped well into the night. The moon was beginning to rise high in the sky.

Vincent moved to the dancing Leticia and swept her up into his strong arms.

Leticia automatically put her arms around Vincent's neck.

Swiftly before too much notice, Vincent walked toward the staircase leading to his rooms.

Maynard watched his lord's movements and ran to the chambers. Vincent had shared a portion of his well-laid plan with his squire. At least what Maynard was expected to look for and then accomplish. He took his place behind the door in Vincent's rooms.

Lionel watched his friend head toward the stairs and shouted to the crowd, "Ho look they leave for the bedding. Let us assist our liege undress!"

Two thirds of the Great Hall was on Vincent's heels. This was half the fun of the nuptial guests. They were expected to chase the bride and groom into the rooms removing as many of their clothes as possible. It was expected of the bride and groom to avoid this nuptial tradition if possible.

"Maynard!" Vincent shouted from the hallway near his room. "Ready!"

Vincent entered the room and Maynard slammed the door shut and bolted it firmly.

Vincent placed Leticia on the canopied bed and sat next to her catching his breath.

Still tipsy, Leticia swayed a little and chuckled, "Wouldst my lord husband need witness or assistance for our bedding?"

Vincent choked, "Goodwife, thy language!"

Leticia would not be dissuaded. She pointed to Maynard. "Tell us troth husband, wouldst thee need witness or assistance?"

Vincent didn't answer. Instead he pushed her down on the bed and holding her with one hand, raised her gown's hem to reveal her shapely legs and garter. Vincent removed both garters and her hose. He threw them to Maynard and chuckled, "Goodwife, be assured we need no assistance or witness. Our squire will take thy garter and hose to the awaiting masses to give us peace and privacy!" Vincent rose and when Maynard was in proper position, he opened the door enough to push Maynard through the door into the crowd. He slammed the door shut and bolted it from the inside quickly.

Leticia heard the yells and whoops of the people outside the door and then heard them leave the hall. Boldly she questioned Vincent, "in troth, wouldst we naught be taken to our chamber where our handmaidens await to prepare us for our virginal sacrifice?"

Vincent choked once more, "whence dost thee learn such language?"

"'Tis naught troth?" Leticia asked innocently and then burped quite loudly.

"'Tis naught our troth," Vincent laughed at his wife's expected happenings and her belch. "We wouldst naught use thee as any sacrifice. We wish to share our bodies and souls this eve with joy, happiness, and pleasure."

"We be told we would suffer pain in the losing of our virginity," Leticia countered. She couldn't seem to stop giggling or belching. She started to rise from the bed and walk toward the wine bag and goblets left by the fireplace. "Mayhap we need more wine to dull our pain."

"Mayhap thee hast drunk too much wine and wouldst naught feel much this eve," Vincent said as he walked in front of her determined path. "Instead let us enjoy our bodies. First, help us undress. Learn our body. We wish thee to touch and explore our person."

A wicked smile plastered itself on Leticia's lips, "Thee wouldst enjoy us exploring thy tall, strong, handsome body?"

"Thee dost consider us handsome?" Vincent questioned. He never once considered himself in that description.

"Yea," Leticia answered when her hand reached to touch his face. "Thou art fair of face, deep soulful blue eyes, perfect nose, strong cheeks, and handsome square jaw." Her other hand started untying the laces on the side of his tunic. "We wish to explore thus strong chest and thy powerful arms."

Leticia's inquisitive hands burned into Vincent's body like a branding iron. A soft moan escaped his lips. What had he intended? His brain was lost. His body took control. Wait! Hadn't he promised himself he would control himself so Leticia would be pleasured? "Sweet Jesu!" Vincent uttered in agony.

"Hath we injured thee?" Leticia questioned with concern as she began to lift his tunic.

"Goodwife, we hear of virginal pain, but my lady, thou art inflicting great pain on our person," Vincent replied huskily. He lifted the tunic off and quickly removed his satin shirt. He took her hand and placed it upon his hardened manhood that was still restrained in his braies. "Thou dost create great burning hence."

Leticia's other hand touched the nipples on his chest, "We hath never seen a naked man. Thou art beautiful naked man."

Vincent moaned once more in agony. He closed Leticia's open hand to envelope his erection that was growing harder. He rhythmically moved that erection she held in her hand.

"Let me see thy manliness," Leticia breathed heavily. She was falling into the sensual sexuality of her own body's yearnings.

Vincent released the knotted draw cord on his braies. They fell down his thighs and slid over his calves to the floor.

Leticia's eyes widened in wonder and asked breathlessly, "Whence dost thee put such a large powerful rod."

Vincent chuckled at his bride's innocence. Of course she would know nothing of procreation and the body of a man. His hands lifted her gown to her waist. With one hand holding the gown in place he released her braies letting them fall to the floor. His free hand began massaging her sensitive nub between her feminine lips and inserted his index finger into her womanhood. "Our manhood be placed hither."

Leticia totally absorbed in the sensations currently attacking her body asked, "Wouldst thus large manly rod fit into our little body?"

"Yea," Vincent replied barely breathing. He continued the rhythmic inserting and removing his finger in her womanhood. The problem was, he was losing control. He stepped back and retreated to a chair by the fireplace.

Leticia looked at him questioningly. Her mind was swirling. Her body was heated with strange new desires, and Vincent leaves her standing alone with her legs barely able to keep her upright?

"Goodwife, let us view thy sacred body," Vincent ordered lovingly. He tried to calm his desire. After all, he planned this moment for days and he was focused on making this night a wonderful experience for both of them. "Remove thy clothing and let us gaze upon thy beauty."

Leticia stood still and untied the laces to her gown. She let it drop to the floor. Looking at Vincent wiggle on the chair made her laugh.

"Whence be thy humor?" Vincent queried.

"Thee sits on thy chair as thus be dreaded irritation on thy bottom," Leticia replied giggling. She untied her shirt and when that fell to the floor her body was revealed through a silken translucent chemise. Her breasts revealed tantalizing pink teats with hardened nubs inviting Vincent for a taste. Her body was perfectly formed with small waist, slender hips, and long shapely legs.

Vincent growled and lunged at Leticia pulling her to his body. He returned to the chair holding Leticia and placing her on his lap.

Leticia's thin translucent chemise was no barrier between her passion warmed bottom and his erected manhood. The sensation of the touch was

94

thrilling to both of them. Leticia arched her back in excitement as Vincent released her breasts from the confinement of her chemise. He tenderly massaged a hardened nub with thumb and forefinger as he bent his head allowing his lips access to suckle the other breast. For several minutes Vincent concentrated on Leticia's feminine globes. He massaged, touched, pinched, manipulated and suckled her breasts moving from one to another and back again.

Leticia felt that warmth between her legs once more and moaned softly. This time the warm feeling was accompanied be a strange wet feeling. A new aroma emitting from her body permeated the air around them.

Vincent inhaled and groaned, "Sweet Jesu give us strength!" He carried his Leticia to the bed ripping her chemise to shreds along the way. Gently he placed her on the bed.

Leticia was moaning in her own wanton need when Vincent surprised her be placing an arm over her abdomen and positioning his head between her legs. If it were not for the arm holding her in place she would have flown of the bed in sensation as his tongue delved into the feminine lips between her legs. Deeper and deeper Vincent's tongue penetrated. Leticia's body became hotter and hotter and wetter and wetter. Sensations raced through her body as light flashing from sky to ground during a storm. Flashes of desire and body heat were overwhelming. Vincent's tongue continued its exploration accompanied by grunts, groans, and moans of the both of them.

Vincent could no longer control his desire or needs. Slowly his tongue traced a path from her apex to her navel, upward to her breasts, and finally stopping on her shoulder and neck. He bit her shoulder gently with his teeth and then laved the area behind her ears.

"My lord," Leticia cried softly. Her body was taught with need. "Thee hast created a burning within us. We need thee, we need thee!"

"Yea, we need thee," Vincent responded. He positioned himself over her bracing the bulk of his body on his forearms that he laid on each side of her.

She felt his satiny tip at the entrance of the place burning with fire. Instinctively she arched into him.

Her movements positioned him for entrance and Vincent could no longer hold himself back. He thrust into his Leticia and felt her barrier. Slowly he retreated.

Leticia whimpered, "Nay, Nay! We need thee." She reached for his head with her hands and pulled his lips down to meet hers. They exchanged passionate kisses and Leticia would not release him when he came up for air. Her hands caressed the taut muscles of his back.

"We need thee!" Vincent repeated. He put full power into his next thrust and the barrier ripped. Vincent felt her warm virgin blood surround him. Slowly and lovingly he provided Leticia with his rhythmic machinations relieving the tension and physical need both of them were enduring jointly.

Leticia felt something but her body was indeed numbed by the wine. When Vincent continued his movements, she responded with her own movements in synchrony. Both uttered moans and groans of pleasure and ecstasy.      What started slowly increased in movement and need.   Leticia suddenly arched and trembled emitting a quiet growl of ecstasy.   Uncontrollably she raked her nails down Vincent's back.

When her body stiffened her womanhood tightened around him, he moved rapidly in pleasure.   It was then Vincent fulfilled his body's demands with magnificent release. His seed spilled inside of his bride with several muscular spurts.. Vincent roared in agony and ecstasy.   He collapsed breathing heavily in her ear.  His heart pounding and racing with a thundering in his ears he had never heard. "Leticia," Vincent breathed heavily. "We love thee!"

"We love thee," Leticia whispered. "Thus bedding be wonderful. Wouldst we enjoy each other thusly every eve and all our lives?"

"Yea," Vincent replied still trying to reach a level of reality with his pleasure.

A few moments later Vincent heard Leticia breathing evenly and softly. He raised his body to look at her and found her to be sound asleep.   Vincent laughed observing his sleeping bride and the smile on her face, "Tis man to fall asleep thus!   Especially falls to sleep with yon smile upon one's face."   He rolled to her side and tucked her into his body placing her back to his chest.   He placed his arm over her arm and cupped her breast possessively in his hand. "Thee be in troth our Goodwife!"  Vincent marveled at his good fortune. Vincent admitted silently he had been fortunate and blessed with this nuptial.  A man dare not ask for more than a sensual and passionate bride that happens also to be beautiful.  With a sated smile, Vincent quickly fell into a contented sleep of his own.

Vincent woke to moaning.   He sat upright and focused his eyes on the moving robed figure in the shadow holding her head with her hands.   "Whither travails thee Goodwife?"

"Must thee shout?" Leticia shouted back and then groaned in pain. "Our head feels like it be pealing bell in the monastery."   She groaned and sat down in the large chair by the fireplace.

Vincent chuckled at his bride's suffering.   His poor bride had a hangover.   He had suffered enough of his own hangovers to be somewhat sympathetic.   Vincent pulled down the covers and swung his large thick legs over the bed.   Standing up he stretched a little and walked to the pan of water on a chest.   He picked up a linen cloth from the chair next to the bed and placed it in the cool water saturating it completely.   He offered the cool rag to his bride, "Place thus upon thy forehead."

Leticia looked up at Vincent and grinned wickedly as she took the cloth.   "Must thee wander about like thus?   Thee wouldst excite thy young travailed bride!"

"Ah," Vincent cooed and knelt next to Leticia.  "Thou dost like whence thee owns!"

"Thy head appears to be as large as ours," Leticia moaned and sat back laying the cool cloth on her forehead.

"Whither head dost thee speak?" Vincent roared with laughter. His manhood had once again turned rigid in attention of his lusty bride's dialogue."

Leticia lifted a corner of the cloth and peeked out to see Vincent standing in his full glory. "We be naught certain of whither head be larger," Leticia giggled and then held her head for the pain.

"Mayhap we might offer another remedy for thy malady," Vincent crowed with mirth.

"Our malady? Thee dost appear in dire malady," Leticia replied sarcastically once again laying her head against the back of the chair and enjoying the cool cloth upon her forehead. "Wouldst thou be kind and fetch for us drink of water. Our mouth feels as dry as harvested farm in summer's end."

"Yea," Vincent replied and retrieved a goblet of water from the clay pitcher. He presented the goblet to Leticia and then waited patiently as she drank it.

Again Leticia peeked from under the cloth. "Thy malady wouldst travail thee sorely?" Leticia asked touching the satiny tip delicately.

"Yea, gravely my lady," Vincent moaned truthfully.

"We wouldst be Good wife and ease thy suffering," Leticia suggested sensually circling Vincent's manhood with her hand. "Tis our duty."

"Yea, tis thy duty my lady," Vincent inhaled deeply as Leticia stroked his erection. "Our suffering be dire."

It wasn't until late in the day and just before the mid day meal Vincent and Leticia finally emerged from behind Vincent's locked chamber door.

# Chapter 13

"Thy Romulus hath once again bested our Elizabeth," Vincent whispered to his young bride. He had ridden his Destrier next to her Palfrey taking her hand in his and squeezed it tenderly.

"Tis troth as we told thee," Leticia smiled happily as she replying. "We trained our falcon with love and devotion. With devotion and love doth our falcon serve us."

"As thee hath trained us in few den," Vincent grinned. "We dost respond well to love and devotion."

"Thee be an indulgent and kind husband deserving of our love and devotion," Leticia answered lovingly. "Thee dost see to our feeding and care most wonderfully."

"We wouldst see to thy care again thus eve," Vincent answered wickedly cocking an eyebrow.

Leticia laughed loudly and the two rode hand in hand to Okehampton castle. They made this day a special day. On Sunday it became their habit to rest from the burdens of their responsibility by hunting together. Vincent and Leticia shared many things, but falconry was a love most treasured by them both.

They had spent two wonderful months together. It took two weeks to arrive at Okehampton castle from Surrey Castle and the rest of the time was spent settling in to their new home.

Leticia felt a tremendous joy at beginning her duties as mistress of Okehampton Castle. Not only was she free of childhood fetters and domination, she found she enjoyed running the household. She also found she enjoyed being Vincent's wife.

Morgan and Megan adored her, as Leticia adored them. They spent many daylight hours together as Leticia taught them everything they needed to know to run a household.

Vincent was kept busy in the office he made in the keep. Vincent would study Okehampton Castle inch by inch every day. From his daily rounds, he returned to make schematic drawings of military improvements for the keep and castle battlements. Lionel and Vincent's father, Gaylord, worked laboriously with Vincent by adding their own knowledge. Vincent found he couldn't be happier in his life. He loved being the Lord of Devon and husband to Leticia. He was so content he wanted to put aside his knightly duties to the king, but knew that would be impossible. King Edward had told him to ready Okehampton quickly. King Edward had informed Vincent he would spend these next months in preparation and would attack Calais after the winter months. Vincent knew King Edward would call him later in the spring after his attack on Calais. Vincent was fully aware he had only the winter months to build Okehampton to King Edward's tactical orders and this was the worse time of the year to start the building projects. Vincent really had no choice. Many nights he and Leticia would discuss the projects after they made love. After the lovemaking was a special euphoric time for them that they learned to enjoy sharing everything of their days and their thoughts. It had been Leticia's idea to build mud and straw huts around the building area as shelters for the workers. The make shift shelters proved viable for the necessary remodeling. The workers were shielded from the cold winds and kept warm by peat fires as they worked. Vincent had been very happy he listened to his beautiful and intelligent young wife.

Whenever they walked from the livery through the gardens after their Sunday hunt, Mystic would meet them. No one understood just how Mystic would know when to meet his mistress, but he always met her at the entrance to the garden when she and Vincent returned from the hunt, regardless of the time they returned.

"Thy mewling trails thee as shadow," Vincent commented watching his wife kneel to pick up her kitten.

"Mystic only shows affection for us, husband," Leticia replied as she stood cradling Mystic in her arms.

"He dost demand much of thy attentions," Vincent growled quietly under his breath.

"Husband? Wouldst thee be envious?" Leticia teased. She stroked Mystic's head and his purring was so strong it could be heard by anyone nearby. "Envious of a mewling?" Leticia began to chuckle.

"Thee hath naught ordinary mewling," Vincent complained. "Thy mewling covets our pallet and we fight each eve for our place next to thee."

Leticia stopped and her eyes widened in surprise and humor. "Thee dost jest with us? In troth thou dost naught believe Mystic fights with thee to near us in our pallet?"

"Tis naught jest!" Vincent replied sharply. "Hath thee naught seen our wounds?" He lifted his sleeve and showed the scratches on his arms. "Thy mewling protests with claws whence Mystic be removed from our pallet."

"Husband, tis normal for mewling to scratch in protest if handled roughly," Leticia tried to explain without laughing too hard. "Tis more troth whence Mystic be taken from warm pallet and tossed to thus cold ground."

"Thy mewling dost not protest! Yea, thy mewling fights ferociously," Vincent denied. "Mayhap thee wouldst watch carefully this eve."

Holding down a grin and chuckle, Leticia nodded her head and replied, "We wouldst attempt to be more observant, husband."

When they entered the keep from the first level and crossed the gateway into the chapel, a shadow in the connecting tower caught their eye. Quietly Vincent walked toward the tower. Since he was wearing his soft leather boots, he was able to be very quiet. Expecting to surprise some servants of the keep, it was Vincent that was surprised. In the shadow of the round tower he found his sister Morgan in a fondling embrace and deep serious kissing with fifteen year old, Quintin, who was his friend Gifford's squire.

Vincent saw red and reacted in the speed of light. Quintin was raised several inches off the floor as Vincent grabbed Quintin's tunic and roared angrily, "wouldst thee defile kin of thy Lord and liege?"

Leticia jumped at the ferocity of Vincent's voice.

Morgan quaked in fear. Her knees were knocking so loudly, Leticia could hear them.

"Be Gone!" Vincent shouted at Quintin as he put his feet back on the floor. "We wouldst speak with Sir Gifford for thy misbehaviors!"

Then Vincent turned to Morgan. "Whither sister be thee? Morgan or Megan?" His rage was evident in his burning eyes.

Morgan suddenly felt nauseous adding to her shaking body's terror. Tears began to flow down her cheeks and as small whimper escaped her mouth.

"Ho, we see by thy silence, thee be Morgan. Sister, hath thee naught sense? Hath thee naught regard for thy good name?" Vincent shouted. "Thy virtue be priceless! Mayhap a belting might bring thee back to thy senses?" Vincent removed his sword belt and began to remove the solid buckle on his tunic belt.

Hearing Vincent's threat, Leticia ran and stepped between Vincent and Morgan. Still holding Mystic in one arm, she raised one hand with palm out to prevent Vincent from punishing Morgan. "Nay, touch naught thus child! We beg of thee! Whence happened here? Naught! Only thee hath terrified thy delicate sister. We think our sister may faint and be ill." Leticia looked toward Morgan who was pale and terror stricken. Morgan really did look like she would faint. "Husband, hear thy Goodwife. We pray pardon for our sister. Let us take Morgan and talk."

Vincent left his tunic belt in place and picked his sword belt up from the floor. "Be gone to thy rooms, Morgan. Consider thy errors. Understand value of thy virtue," Vincent growled menacingly. "Our Goodwife hath saved thee belting. Later we wouldst send our Goodwife to thee for lessons of lady! We wouldst naught allow our sister to be named strumpet or concubine."

Those words cut into Morgan's terror and broke her heart. She ran from the tower sobbing.

Leticia faced her husband and reprimanded him quietly, "Consider thy harsh words husband. Thee broke thy sister's heart and sliced thus with thy sordid tongue! Wouldst thee tolerate being named bastard, mongrel, cur from one thee adores?"

"We wouldst recall thee hast called us thus many times naught long ago," Vincent retorted. "Understand our love for our sister. We wish to protect our sister."

"We trow thee dost love thy sister and she loves thee," Leticia replied somberly. "Dost thee need to cut her heart and break her soul with thy cruel tongue?"

"Nay," Vincent sighed in disgust and anger with himself. He truly only lost his temper because he did love his sister. "Go, be with our sister and tell Morgan thus reasons for our wrath."

Leticia stood on her tiptoes to plant a kiss upon Vincent's chin. "We dost love thee, husband." She left Vincent when they entered the Great Hall. Vincent took the stairs on the left to return to his office and find Maynard. He would send Maynard to fetch Sir Gifford for him so he would talk to the boy about fondling the Lord's sister.

Leticia went to the stairway to the right and walked the stairs to the fourth floor of the keep where she would find Morgan in her room.

Morgan ran into her rooms sobbing hysterically and into the surprised and open arms of her twin, Megan.

"Whither travails thee?" Megan queried holding her sobbing sister in her arms. Megan patted Morgan's back comfortingly.

"Our bbbrooother," Morgan wailed. "He, hee called us concubine!"

"Shhh, we be certain thee misunderstood our brother," Megan reassured stroking her sister's long dark hair.

Still sobbing Morgan shook her head, "Our brother meant thus words. Vincent threatened to belt us."

"Our brother surely wouldst naught belt thee," Megan gasped in surprise.

Morgan pulled away to look at her sister and nodded. Her eyes were puffy, her cheeks soaked with tears and trembling with fright. "He, he threatened us with beating."

Megan sat back in surprise and marveled, "Whence dost thou anger our brother to such words and threats? Hath thee slain our brother's favored Destrier?"

"Nay," Morgan sniffed loudly. "We be in company with our dear Quintin."

"Wast thee naked?" Megan chuckled. She couldn't see Vincent getting that upset with Morgan being with Quintin unless they were caught fornicating.

Morgan stomped her foot and railed, "Tis naught humorous sister. We be just snog."

"We dost naught comprehend our brother's rage," Megan explained. "Unless thee and Quintin hath been comprised, thence wouldst naught be such melee."

"We dost naught comprehend our brother's rage," Morgan sniffed. "We wouldst be snog. Naught more."

"Come sit beside us," Megan offered. "Dost our brother raise hand to thee?

"Nay, our sister Leticia wouldst come between us and prevent our brother," Morgan hiccupped and sat next to Megan. "Lady Leticia stalled our brother's hand and allowed us to run to our chambers."

"Dost our brother raise hand to Lady Leticia?" Megan questioned fearing something would happen to Leticia.

"Nay," a voice came from the door outside the chamber. Leticia then followed the voice into the twins' chamber. "Thy brother's wrath covered the fear and love for thee."

"Mayhap thee couldst explain to us that calling our sister a concubine be love?" Megan questioned.

"At times thus tongue doth slip and evil words be emitted," Leticia concurred walking to Morgan. She sat next to Morgan and cradled the still upset girl in her arms. "We believe thy brother regrets thus words anon."

"Tis troth our sister merely be snog Quintin?" Megan asked Leticia still a bit confused at Morgan's upset and her brother's unusual behavior. Vincent was always kind, thoughtful, and loving. They had never seen him angry or heard venomous words come from his mouth.

"Tis troth," Leticia replied taking her hand and tilting Morgan's face up to look at her. "Thy tears be so great for such small infraction."

"Our brother despises us," Morgan wailed.

"Nay," Leticia reassured. "Thy brother loves thee. He be only concerned that thee and Quintin be comprised. He be concerned about thy virtuous name."

"Tis naught fair," Megan hissed. "Our brother as man be concerned for virtuous name of our sister, yet all men misthink and behave as stallion."

"Yea, tis one of the inequities of gender," Leticia agreed. "We must be virtuous and chaste. Yet man behave as stallion. Still sweet sister, tis good in thus nuptial bed whence thy husband be experienced."

"Wouldst thus be better wouldst our gender be experienced in bed as well?" Megan asked after contemplating Leticia's statement.

"Thus be excellent question," Leticia replied. "Mayhap we wouldst ponder upon thus and query others."

"Mayhap we wouldst query concubine of court next time we be visiting Surrey Castle," Morgan replied as she regained better spirits.

"Hence be concubines of knights in our bailey," Megan blurted out with excitement. "We wouldst query thus dames."

"Whence hearest such things?" Leticia gasped in shock. Even she did not know about prostitutes in the bailey.

"Dost thee naught hear of camp concubines who follow pavilions?" Megan returned. "These dames hath followed our brother's pavilions since Vincent be knighted and followed our good king. Thus dames hath serviced our brother and knights devotedly."

"Megan!" Morgan declared. "Dost thee forget thy tongue and remembrance our Lady Leticia be the Goodwife of our brother?"

Realizing her faux pas Megan said hesitantly, "We only heard thus stories."

Leticia laughed, "Tis troth in thus stories. Thy brother be naught ignorant of love. Thy brother dost learn well from someone. Yea, the learning be over and in past."

"Doth our brother be calm once more?" Morgan asked sheepishly. "And be our brother's wrath placed abed?"

"Yea," Leticia replied without doubt of mind.

"Whence be our brother?" Megan questioned.

"Our husband hath returned to keep offices," Leticia answered. "Come let us prepare for dinner meal. Our falcon hath brought great feast to our table."

"Wouldst cook allow us sweet?" Morgan queried hopefully rising with Leticia and taking her hand.

"Cook wouldst allow us several sweets," Leticia responded holding Morgan's hand and heading toward the door. "Wouldst thee join us, Megan?"

"Nay," Megan replied quickly. In her mind she had her own agenda.

Several hours later, Sir Phillip dragged a doggedly stubborn Megan into Vincent's office. Vincent had just finished speaking to Sir Gifford about his squire, Quintin.

"Whither be our sister in thy hand?" Vincent queried when he looked up at his knight at arms. "Be thee Morgan or Megan?"

Megan straightened and stared coldly at Vincent. She crossed her arms over her chest and took a stance of defiance.

"Megan!" Vincent recognized.

"Thy sister wouldst naught tell us name," Sir Phillip stated. "Whither thee trow thy twin's name?"

"Morgan be shy and fearful," Vincent replied holding back his chuckle and pride. "Megan be defiant and stubborn!"

"Hence thus be Megan," Sir Phillip conferred.

"Be reason to bring our sister to us?"

"Yea, we found thy sister in most unusual place," Phillip answered. "We believed thee wouldst wish to be appraised thy sister be found with Dame Tamar."

"Wouldst thee appraise our brother about how thus be thee wouldst find us in such place?" Megan snarled. "Mayhap thee dost come to use Dame Tamar's service?"

Phillip did not reply but blushed crimson.

"We thought as such," Megan uttered triumphantly.

"Whither be thee with Dame Tamar?" Vincent countered angrily.

Megan fluttered her eyes and responded quietly, "Mayhap brother, thee trow the Dame Tamar and her services?"

Vincent lost his tongue and he too blushed crimson.

Assured of her victory, Megan stepped forward to her brother's desk and placed her hands palm down upon it. "We merely inquired of Dame Tamar simple question."

"Question Dame Tamar?" Sir Gaylord offered entering the room sending her a scathing look. "Whence wouldst thee need to inquire of thus Dame?"

Vincent released a breath of relief. "Father, we hath numerous trials with thy daughters thus den. We be relieved thee hath returned to deal with thus trials."

Gaylord didn't respond to his son but sat on a chair and continued, "We be waiting for thy explanation daughter."

Megan had lost all her bravado. Her brother was one thing, but her father was quite another. This time Megan blushed crimson.

"We see thee wouldst naught discuss the matter so freely with thy tongue in our presence," Gaylord reprimanded. "Still, we wouldst require thy answer."

Thinking quickly Megan began, "Our brother nearly belted our sister for innocent snog and…"

That was as far as she got when Gaylord interrupted and raised his hand palm forward, "we require of thee answer for thy presence at Dame Tamar, naught whence occurred with thy sister."

Taking a deep breath Megan felt she could only be truthful and answered, "We queried of the Dame Tamar, 'wouldst thus married bed be better if lady wouldst need greater experience of fornication?'"

Gaylord although incredibly shocked by his daughter's answer remained calm.

Vincent sat down immediately and Phillip left the rooms.

Gathering his wits, Gaylord asked his daughter, "wouldst thee explain whence thus inquiry arrived in thy mind?"

Megan braced her shaking legs against Vincent's desk as she faced her father. "After our brother caused our sister great sorrow by calling Morgan concubine, we talked of thus inequity of gender. Tis troth man behave as stallion, but lady must be virtuous and chaste. Our sister, Lady Leticia commented a man be better lover for experience. We thought to ourselves it might be better for man if lady wouldst obtain experience. We merely asked someone with such experience."

Vincent once more felt his face warm crimson. His wife discussed with his sister what a good experienced lover he was. That was good, but very embarrassing.

How Gaylord managed to keep his wits about him was a miracle. How could he explain these things to a daughter? This was a wife's job. Worse, in reality there was no good answer. Finally a response came to Gaylord. "Daughter, we understand thy need to find response to thy inquiries, yet thee didst find thyself in dangerous places. We be fortunate thee be naught mistook for handmaiden and abused. We wouldst be deeply sorrowful if thee wouldst be wounded in any way. Henceforth, come to us with thy question and we wouldst assist you in the finding of answer."

Megan bent her head in submission, "Yea father, we wouldst inquire of thee first."

A small smile crossed Gaylord's lips and he asked Megan, Hath thus Dame Tamar give thee answer?"

"Yea!"

"Wouldst thee share thus answer with us?" Gaylord questioned.

"Dame Tamar told us for lady to have knowledge before nuptial bed wouldst inhibit wonder and thrill of thus new body experience. Man be more ignorant of spiritual thrills so man requires more experience to please thus lady."

Gaylord could not hold back. He let out a belly guffaw that rocked the room.

Vincent responded in like kind and rolled back into his chair.

"Tis troth thus Dame Tamar doth tell thee," Gaylord said laughing uproariously. "Tis troth. Be thee satisfied with thus inquiry?"

"Yea."

"Leave us and return to your sister," Gaylord ordered Megan and then turned to Vincent seriously and queried, "Whence be reason for calling our daughter, Morgan, concubine?"

Vincent explained he did not call Morgan a concubine but attempted to warn her about keeping her virtuous name and keeping chaste for her betrothed. He told his father everything that happened.

"We hope Sir Gifford dost naught punish Quintin severely," Gaylord commented. "We wouldst speak to Quintin about intentions. Thus boy dost come from noble stock."

"Tis troublesome being older brother to thy daughters, father," Vincent sighed.

"Learn well my son, for thee wouldst be father anon," Gaylord laughed.

"We wouldst naught procreate daughters!" Vincent complained. "We wouldst request Leticia issue us only sons."

That statement started Gaylord laughing once more and he actually had to leave the room leaving Vincent wondering what he had said that was so funny.

# Chapter 14

At dinner Gaylord approached Quintin.

Quintin did not know if he should run or face the father of his love. He decided to stay. Gifford had reprimanded him regarding wooing his lady love since she was still a child as was he, and she happened to be the sister of the Earl of Devon. Quintin was determined. He realized they were both young but their feelings for each other were strong.

"We wouldst speak with thee," Gaylord said confronting Quintin. "Tis our daughter, Morgan, we wouldst discuss with thee."

"Yea, my lord," Quintin replied stoically. He would not be intimidated. Morgan would be his betrothed. He would see to it. His father was a powerful noble in the King's Court and he would speak to him the next time they were in Surrey.

"Be naught travailed," Gaylord soothed. "We wish only to ask thee of thy intentions regarding our Morgan."

Firmly Quintin replied, "Sirrah, we may be young and kinder in thy eyes, yet our love for each other be powerful. Whence time arrive we obtain our spurs and become knight, we wouldst ask thy blessing on our betrothal."

"Thy father, Richard be our friend," Gaylord responded. "We wouldst send him our greetings and speak to him of betrothal. Whence dost thee expect to achieve thy spurs?"

"We be ten and seven years my lord. We wouldst achieve our spurs next Michaelmas when we be ten and eight," Quintin answered. "We wouldst betroth to thy daughter then and wait our two next Michaelmas before our nuptials. Thy daughter wouldst be of thus marriageable age of ten and six. We wouldst acquire time to accrue monies to support our lady. We be our father's heir and wouldst inherit large manor."

"We be aware of thy blood and inheritance," Gaylord assuage. "We be concerned for our daughter's heart. Thee would inherit a portion of our keep with marriage to our Morgan. We wish our daughter to be happy."

Quintin smiled and bowed. "We wouldst keep thy daughter's heart with gentleness and love. We wouldst love thy daughter as we wish thy daughter wouldst love us."

"Hence thus matter be settled," Gaylord grinned and put his arm around Quintin's broad shoulders. "We wouldst send message to thy father and thy betrothal wouldst be decreed."

Leticia entered the Great Hall with Megan and Morgan. All three looked in astonishment at the sight of Gaylord embracing Quintin and smiles were on their faces.

"Whence occurred hence?" Morgan whispered to Leticia.

"We dost naught trow," Leticia whispered in return.

Megan said nothing. She was certain her encounter with her father and brother this afternoon had the desired affect. She was certainly pleased with herself and although she had shared Dame Tamar's answer with Leticia and Morgan, she didn't tell them the entire story.

Vincent rose to greet his wife and together they sat to enjoy the evening meal. Vincent had determined this would be a short dinner since all the conversations of fornication had only made him focus on the bed and his wife.

Since Vincent never allowed servants into their chambers at night Leticia helped him undress. Vincent loved this time because the way Leticia undressed him fired his body. He was about to undress Leticia when she pulled away from him.

Seeing the puzzled look on his face, Leticia quickly stated, "We feel great sorrow for thy wounds endured by our mewling, Mystic. We wouldst remove him from our pallet for thee." Leticia strode silently to the bed and gently picked up Mystic where he was laying, on Vincent's portion of the bed. She stroked Mystic's forehead and whispered assurances as she walked to the door and gently placed him outside. "Gentleness, husband. Gentleness." She turned from the door to walk into the brick wall that was the body of her husband.

"Yea, gentleness," Vincent agreed. Slowly and sensually he undressed his wife. Within moments they were in the bed and enjoying each other's lustful needs.

After their hearts had calmed came the time for their special talk time.

"Husband, whence occurred with thy father and Quintin?" Leticia queried running her finger up and down Vincent's arm.

"Our father told us later thus wouldst announce betrothal of Quintin and Morgan. Tis the troth of matter, Quintin dost love our sister, Morgan."

"Tis wonderful to love before betrothal," Leticia sighed.

"Dost thee have regrets?" Vincent worried.

"Nay, husband," Leticia reassured. "We be most happy with our marriage. We be all different and since we hath been kept in convent. Thus be naught way to love thee afore betrothal. Be assured, Sirrah, we love thee most dearly and be most happy. Thee dost conquer my heart."

"Yea, thee hast conquered my heart," Vincent stated kissing Leticia's face lightly. "We be most content with thee as our master and lady." Vincent rolled to his back pulling Leticia under his arm. "We wouldst miss thee on the morrow."

Leticia bolted upright and asked fearfully, "Whence wouldst thee miss us?"

Vincent smiled and pulled Leticia back to the crook of his arm. "We wouldst go to Exeter. We wouldst install Phillip as sheriff there. We wouldst observe any and all weakness of Exeter's armaments. Exeter would be prize for French attack. We wouldst be gone only fortnight."

Leticia giggled, "Hence be thus case, we wouldst naught miss thee."

"Thee wouldst naught miss us? Thy mewling Mystic wouldst give you enough company for fortnight?" Vincent asked sadly. He had hoped Leticia would miss him as much as he would miss her.

"Nay, our mewling wouldst miss us, for we wouldst accompany thee to Exeter," Leticia answered lovingly. She kissed Vincent's chest tenderly. "We wouldst naught allow thee to leave our person for one den."

"Wouldst thee naught be bored accompanying us?" Vincent queried. Tis nearly Winter Solstice, wouldst thee naught be chilled?"

"Nay, we wouldst enjoy shopping in Exeter whilst thee be burdened with labor," Leticia giggled. "We wouldst be chilled staying at Okehampton. We wouldst naught be chilled ever with thy arms about us."

Vincent closed his eyes and hugged Leticia. Lord how he loved his little wife. He was truly a happy man. He hoped King Edward would change his mind about attacking Calais. He really did not want to leave Okehampton, His wife. His family.


"Whence wouldst thee tell thy husband about thy breeding," Lady Rosamund asked while helping Leticia bathe. "Thee dost show thy condition anon."

"We dost naught remember," Leticia replied testily. She was angry with herself. She wanted to tell Vincent but things kept happening that made her forget.

"Naught remember?" Lady Rosamund chided. "Thee art blooming with seed of thy husband. Such joy to share and thee dost forget? Thy middle be thick and grows."

"We be so inclined to bless thee graciously for reminding us we be fat!" Leticia growled rising from the tub and wrapping herself with the flannel cloth used for drying. "We wouldst tell our husband thus den on our way to Exeter."

"Thou shouldst naught travel whilst thee breeds," Lady Rosamund reprimanded.

"Be still, we hath only missed three flux," Leticia argued. "We feel wonderful. Our Queen Phillippa hath gone to war whilst heavy with child."

"Every lady be different," Lady Rosamund countered. "Our queen be of sturdier stock than thee!"

"Enough!" Leticia ordered.

"The winter cold be upon us," Lady Rosamund continued.

"Enough!" Leticia ordered once more. "Help us to dress and be silent."


Lady Leticia and Lady Rosamund walked down the stairs and into the Great Hall to a great surprise. In the center of Phillip, Gaylord, Lionel, Gifford, and Vincent was Lady Juliet. Leticia became more worried when she saw the sour look on Vincent's face. She nearly flew to Vincent's side. "Husband?"

"Lady Leticia," Juliet cooed wickedly. "Tis a great news we bring to thee. We find we be breeding Vincent's son."

"Liar!" Leticia shrieked in disbelief and horror. This couldn't be happening. She was Vincent's wife and carrying Vincent's child, not this whore.

Lady Rosamund stood back and immediately walked to Gaylord de Courtenay. Together they had found a soothing companionship and she immediately sought his strength at this news. Earlier in the week Rosamund had confided to Gaylord that Leticia was breeding.

Juliet merely smiled and softly replied, "Tis troth. Confirm to thy wife our happy news. We be so happy to carry thy son."

"Liar!" Leticia shrieked once more raising her hand to strike the blatant concubine.

Vincent grasped her hand and held it more firmly than he meant too, but he was upset at the news of the impending bastard. He had always been so careful not to leave bastards. He didn't remember love making that night. He didn't love Juliet. Hell, he didn't even like Juliet, but he promised himself he would always care for his children. "Tis troth," Vincent confessed sadly.

"Noooooo!" Leticia heard herself cry in pain. She turned on Vincent and began pounding her little fists onto his muscular chest until her hands hurt. "Clod Pate! Thee dost behave as stallion and cause us shame in our keep!"

"Enough!" Vincent barked grabbing both hands firmly. "Be still little Goodwife. We wouldst shelter Lady Juliet during thus confinement."

"Thee be bastard as thy seed," Leticia seethed. "Thee be cur, mongrel!"

"Enough!" Vincent growled. "Goodwife be silent. Thee wouldst obey our order and care for Lady Juliet tenderly."

"Bastard! Care tenderly for thy own bastard!" Leticia cried out. What came over her even she didn't understand. This behavior was not like her. Perhaps it was because she wanted her baby to be special and now Vincent would have a child from the beautiful and enchanting Juliet. Would he love Juliet's baby more? "We wouldst naught allow thee to defame our name by placing thy concubine in our keep."

"This be our sovereign," Vincent countered bitterly. This was bad enough and Leticia's behavior embarrassed him more in front of his friends and father. "Thee wouldst obey us."

Fighting Vincent's grip with all her might and tears streaming down her face Leticia cried out, "Nay, we wouldst naught have thy concubine in our keep."

Vincent's upset at the Juliet's news compounded with Leticia's behavior brought a rage from him that he had never felt before. His nostril's flared and his eye's bulged out red from their sockets. He was about to release Leticia and strike her when Leticia cried out in pain.

"Husband, release us! Thou be hurting us! Thee wouldst break our bones in our hands!"

Vincent released her hands as if he had released hot coals. Before he hurt her and made matters worse he bellowed, "Be gone! Go to thy rooms anon!"

Juliet smirked triumphantly and casually palmed her belly.

Gaylord recognized the fury in his son's manner. "Take Leticia away anon," he whispered to Rosamund. "Our son be full of wroth. Our son mayhap wouldst hurt our lady."

Rosamund lunged to Leticia before Leticia once more opened her mouth and pulled her out of the Great Hall whispering, "Be silent my lady. Thy husband be confused and full of wrath."

Vincent still full of fury spotted Lady Agnes and ordered her, "Lady Agnes, thee wouldst be handmaiden to Lady Juliet. Care for Lady Juliet tenderly in thus confinement and thee wouldst be rewarded handsomely. Take Lady Juliet to thus rooms outside our offices."

Lady Agnes obeyed dutifully. She reached for Juliet's hand to lead her to the rooms.

"My lord, we wouldst be hungry," Juliet complained. "Wouldst thee allow us to eat? Thy son be hungry as well."

Vincent once again addressed Agnes, "Whence thee hast taken Lady Juliet to thus rooms come down and make for thus lady trencher to eat in thus rooms." Vincent then squared his shoulders and addressed Lady Juliet. "We wouldst prefer thee remain in thy rooms for thy confinement. Thee wouldst be tenderly cared for hence."

"Son?" Gaylord entreated. He wanted to talk to Vincent hopefully to calm him.

"Nay father, we dost naught spare thee time," Vincent responded. "We wouldst deal with our shrewish wife anon." Vincent was furious with Leticia's behavior and the embarrassment she caused him. He was furious about the entire situation.

"We beg thee," Gaylord implored. "Calm thy wrath e'er thee confronts Leticia."

"Our Goodwife embarrassed us in front of our peers. She hath revealed a wicked tongue that must naught be allowed to surface again," Vincent grumbled. "We must be assured our Goodwife doth understand our position and commands." With those words Vincent left the Great Hall to return to the Lord's private chambers. He unbuckled his sword belt along the way and removed his tunic belt.

Leticia was distraught and her tears uncontrollable. This couldn't be happening. The only woman she was jealous of had successfully bedded her husband and they had created a child. To make matters worse, Vincent was keeping her in their home. Terror ran through Leticia. Would she be put aside and would Vincent keep his concubine to share his amorous needs?

Rosamund tried to console and soothe Leticia to no avail. Rosamund felt real terror when Vincent walked into the chambers and in his hand was his tunic belt. She knew her Leticia was in danger. "My Lord, have mercy, please..." Rosamund pleaded hoping to tell Vincent that Leticia was also with child and breeding.

"Be Gone!" Vincent thundered. He pointed to the door.

There would be no talking to him Rosamund was certain. She fled the room and jumped when Vincent slammed the door behind her.

Leticia stood frozen while watching her husband. Which was the more fearful, losing Vincent to Juliet or receiving the belting that was inevitable? The answer did not matter. Leticia could not utter a plea or move. In a flash she found herself being held firmly by Vincent and bent over his body. Suddenly there was a hot sting and she cried out. Again and again Vincent's belt found its mark upon her bottom.

Rosamund heard the belt slapping Leticia's bottom. She heard her lady's cries of anguish. She wondered what she could do. She could not stop Vincent. He was so big and strong.

"Whence be happening hence?" Morgan asked Rosamund fearfully.

Rosamund jumped. She had been so distraught she did not hear Morgan approach. "Our Lady receives belting from our lord and we can do naught to stop thus."

"We may stop thus!" Morgan declared. "We wouldst naught allow thus belting. Our lady saved us from our brother's wrath. We wouldst save our lady!"

"Whence wouldst be done?" Rosamund asked trembling as she heard another blow.

"Hurry, we wouldst find our father," Morgan offered running toward the Great Hall. "Our father wouldst end thus bestiality."

Vincent threw the belt aside. In his mind he had counted six trespasses and he would only belt his wife once for each trespass. It was when he looked at his wife he felt extremely guilty for raising his hand. Never had he inflicted pain on a woman and it bothered him tremendously.

Leticia was pale, sobbing, and hiccupping. Tears flooded her face. She looked forlorn and terrified. "Wouldst thee, hic, be finished with thy hic, beating?"

"Dost thee understand reasons for thy punishment?" Vincent questioned quietly.

"In troth, hic, nay," Leticia cried raising her arm to her face to wipe the tears. "We discover thee created bastard child and we be beaten. Nay, hic, we dost naught understand."

Vincent picked her up. He sat on his chair near the fireplace and set Leticia upon his lap. "Thy sharp tongue sliced us in presence of our peers. Thus wouldst naught be allowed by wife of lord!" Vincent explained adjusting her in his arms. "We in troth must speak of Lady Juliet and thus news, but thus must be conducted in privacy of our chambers."

"We repent of our (hic) trespass," Leticia whimpered. "We wouldst request we speak of thus in privacy, but we wouldst, hic, naught understand why only such feminine person be punished."

"Thus be naught troth," Vincent answered gently. "We be punished most severely by our Queen Phillippa and thee whence we embarrassed thee before our king. Dost thee remember? Thus another time whence we received thy wrath for unknown reason and we be covered with arachnids until we be bloody to dispense of them."

Leticia looked up into Vincent's eyes and replied, "yea, thee dost receive punishment for thy trespass. Hic! We repent."

Both jumped when the door slammed against the wall and Gaylord strode angrily to the fireplace. "Thee wouldst tell thy father thee hast naught beaten thy lady!"

"We applied discipline," Vincent confessed. He did feel guilty for belting Leticia and his father's anger was righteous. Still he was Lord of Devon and could not allow anyone including his wife to challenge his authority.

"Thee be ignorant and fool!" Gaylord growled at Vincent. He bent on one knee and took Leticia's hand. "Be thee well? Hath our beast of son hurt thee or thy child?"

Vincent's mouth dropped, "Leticia, be thee breeding?"

"Yea my lord," Leticia confessed. "We missed three flux and our middle grows thick. We be certain we be breeding."

"Whither hath thee naught told us?" Vincent questioned nearly in tears. "If thy breeding be known, we wouldst naught punished thee thusly."

"We be punished more with such fear thee wouldst prefer Lady Juliet to us," Leticia responded. "Thy belting hurt naught as much as our fear and broken heart."

"Leticia, our love," Vincent cried outputting the truth of his own fear. "We be spurned as kinder by our mother. As young lad we troth oath to love our seed be thus son or daughter, bastard or heir. Understand my love, thus be our solemn vow to love our seed. We love naught Lady Juliet. Our love be thine alone."

"Thee wouldst love our babe?" Leticia asked understanding Vincent's vow. It was similar to the one she had made as a child to love her children, son or daughter. She too knew what it meant to be spurned by a parent.

"We love our babe whilst thus seed grows in thy belly and whence we hold thus babe in our arms," Vincent answered joyfully. He took his large hand and spread it over Leticia's abdomen. "Thy belly be thicker. We wouldst notice thus difference."

"Yea, our son be ignorant," Gaylord agreed.

Lady Rosamund entered the room and knelt next to Leticia. "Wouldst my lady be well?"

"We be well, Lady Rosamund," Leticia reassured. "thee wouldst naught to dread or fear."

"We be ignorant but logical," Vincent chuckled and addressed his father. His mood had completely changed. His wife was carrying his child and he was thrilled. When Juliet told him the news of his parentage he was distraught. "Hence thee trow of our breeding lady. So thus appears thee and Lady Rosamund have found happiness together."

"Yea, Lady Rosamund told us of Leticia's confinement," Gaylord confessed. "We find comfort in Lady Rosamund's person."

"Wouldst thee be angry for thus?" Rosamund queried Leticia.

"Nay," Leticia sighed and snuggled into Vincent's arm. "We wouldst wish thus news naught be given thusly, but we be naught distressed."

Gaylord took Rosamund's hand. "Tis in troth we find love and comfort with thee. Wouldst thee accept us and become our Goodwife?"

Rosamund choked out, "Yea. Yea, Sirrah! Thus dost please us."

"Sweet Jesu," Leticia cried out joyfully. "We shouldst prepare thy wedding in Exeter at Sir Gaylord's manor whilst we visit there. Morgan and Megan wouldst be happy for thee and must now accompany us thus den." She leaped from Vincent's lap only to be grabbed by the waist and brought down on his lap.

"Thee wouldst not accompany us to Exeter for thy confinement," Vincent countered firmly.

"Husband, if our babe dost survive thy anger, surely our babe wouldst survive our love," Leticia implored. "We wish to be near thee."

"We must confess we wouldst miss thee sorely," Vincent grinned releasing his hold on Leticia. "Yea, go prepare our sisters for thus happy journey."

Just for reassurance Leticia turned back to Vincent and asked, "Dost Juliet stay at Okehampton?"

Vincent nodded his head, "Yea!"

Leticia left the chambers relieved she would not have to deal with Juliet and felt a bit more secure from her fears of being abandoned by her husband. She sought out Morgan, who was outside the door, and Megan who was later found antagonizing the alchemist. Leticia's belting caused only a little discomfort and she had her saddle padded when she and the family rode to de Courtenay manor outside of Exeter.

# Chapter 15

While in Exeter Leticia had been true to her word, she spent nearly all the time shopping for furniture, draperies, curtains, cloths, foodstuffs, condiments, and fragrant soaps. The wedding of Gaylord de Courtenay and Lady Rosamund only dented a small amount of time off Leticia's shopping spree allotment. Exeter was well known as the seaport for all international trade goods.

Once Vincent spent the day shopping with his Leticia only to return home exhausted and fell sound asleep right after the dinner meal. The day was worth it because he was proud of how frugal and knowledgeable Leticia was about costs and values of all items she purchased. There was not one merchant that got the better of his wife. Up until this day he sat for an hour with a tallyman going over Leticia's expenses and marveled at the articles purchased for the amount spent. He was very proud of his wife. He was also proud because his wife did not spend money on personal jewels, clothes, or artistic items. Her purchases were practical and for the benefit of the keep and its residents.

Morgan, Megan, and Lady Rosamund accompanied most of the shopping events. They all agreed Okehampton would be their home. They participated and shared ideas for most of the purchases.

Vincent placed Sir Phillip, as Sheriff of Exeter and the De Courtenay manor would be his rented residence. Sir Phillip had shown the greatest capability of all the knights for this pressure position. Sir Phillip was delighted, because he had wanted to settle down and start his own family. Soon he would find the woman meant to be his wife and have his lord, Sir Vincent decree the betrothal.

Vincent spent more time with Leticia than both thought could be possible on this trip. It was what one could call a vacation. They grew closer to each other. Not only did they discover more about each other, they found they really enjoyed each other's companionship. Vincent was amazed with Leticia's intelligence, mathematical, linguistic, and logic capabilities. She was more than just a pretty face as were most noble women.

Leticia found Vincent to be strict, but loving, intelligent, kind, and generous just as Prince Edward had told her he was. She savored their private time in their rooms every evening. The private time that Vincent insisted upon was more than love making. It was their special time to discuss many things.

Vincent shared his childhood with her. She understood his thinking about Juliet and the child she carried. Leticia didn't like it at all, but understood it. She realized the punishment she received from Vincent was a result of her behavior. Leticia promised herself she would never embarrass her husband again. This was important because she found on this trip there wasn't anything she couldn't discuss reasonably with her husband during their private quiet time.

Vincent regretted his punishment and fawned over his pregnant wife in overcompensation. Leticia didn't mind his guilt. She actually enjoyed the consistent and loving attention of her husband. He also realized he was at fault for not explaining to her in the beginning the unwritten code of knighthood and lord of the manor. This was something that Leticia needed to know since she was raised away from court and the world in the Convent. More and more Vincent treasured his quiet time with his wife. It was addictive.

At the end of the fortnight sojourn in Exeter, everyone was anxious to return to home. The winter months were here and it was a perfect time for Vincent to plan the rearmament of the castles and Leticia to decorate the keep.

In the fortnight Leticia's middle nearly doubled in size and she felt fluttering of life inside her womb. She loved waking Vincent in the middle of the night to feel the movements of his child. When he did feel the slight movements his smile lit up the darkened room. Leticia could see his smile even through the curtained darkness in their bed. One of the things they talked about was raising their children. Leticia did not concede to his request of having only sons because they were not as difficult to raise. Instead he conceded to one daughter just for Leticia. He also promised to love her with all his heart, but Leticia needed to raise and discipline her. He couldn't see himself managing that.

Vincent's open honesty about childrearing and his vulnerability merely caused Leticia to love him more.

The return home seemed to be a short journey. Leticia squelched her fear of Destriers and enjoyed riding on Vincent's lap for most of the journey. It was time for them to spend even more time together. Leticia wasn't certain why every moment together was so precious but they both felt it. Deep inside Leticia felt Vincent was holding something back. That something she felt was something sad and she wasn't certain she even wanted to know. Leticia did know that Lady Juliet was no threat to her marriage and relationship with Vincent. Those thoughts kept her happy and from thinking about that something.

The traveling party returned to Okehampton at midday. Vincent had just lifted Leticia from her Palfrey when a gray streak appeared from the bushes near the livery and jumped into her arm.

"Mystic?" Leticia questioned. It didn't look like her cat. The gray cat's fur was matted and filthy as if sticky food had been poured over him. Her Mystic was half the size he had been when she left. Mystic looked dehydrated and starved.

"Meow," Mystic replied in answer.

"Thy mewling doth look afflicted with malady," Vincent observed.

"Yea," Leticia replied sadly. "We must take care of our mewling and return Mystic to health. We shouldst seek out Elena. She hath cared for our mewling. We must find whence travails our mewling."

Vincent kissed Leticia on the forehead. He loved her tenderness and gentleness, even with the scruffy cat he never cared for. "Go find thy Elena and tend to thy mewling. We wouldst see to unpacking of all thy treasures."

Leticia looked up at Vincent and when their eyes met it was with a loving understanding, "Bless thee lord. We wouldst seek out our Elena and care for our mewling anon."

Leticia left the traveling party and walked briskly up the path of the bailey toward the keep. The winds were strong and frigid. She cuddled Mystic in her arms protecting him from the chilling winds, regardless of his filthy condition. A cold drizzling rain began to fall and Leticia was grateful when she entered the keep. When Leticia entered the Great Hall she expected to see both fireplaces extending their glowing warmth and the tables filled with food. Instead she gasped to see one fireplace lit and only one log upon it. The Great Hall was freezing cold. The servants looked half starved and were shivering from the cold. The head table was near the burning fireplace so it would be warm, and it was the only table with a feast of food upon it. The other tables held only one small trencher with small amounts of meat and vegetable in them. There was only one large tankard in the center of each trestle table. Leticia also noticed the rushes on the floor appeared to be more than several days old. It was her mother's instruction and her instruction to the steward to change the rushes daily, even in winter. The Great Hall reeked of foul odor. Leticia knew it had not been cleaned in some time. She would locate Durand Alwins, her steward, to find out what was happening here after she took care of Mystic and talked to Elena.

Leticia's next stop was the solar. She was horrified to see the windows had not been shuttered against the blowing winds. The fireplace appeared exactly as she left it a fortnight ago. Not one cord of wood had been used. The chambers she shared with her husband were freezing cold, unwelcome, and even ice crystals had formed on the walls. It would take days to warm their solar. Leticia was furious. She found a warm flannel toweling to wrap her cat in and placed him on the apron of the fireplace hearth. She lifted several cords of wood and put them in the hearth. Striking the flints to create sparks she finally started a blazing fire. Leticia placed Mystic closer to the fire to keep warm. Mystic meowed in gratitude. Leticia then found the clay bowl contain stones and put them very near the fire to warm them. She would place them under their bed to warm it.

"Sweet Jesu, Mystic. We be in troth confused for understanding of thus occurrence hence," Leticia whispered to her cat. Her breath created a warm vaporous cloud near her mouth. "Wouldst thee tell us, Mystic?"

"Meow," Mystic replied and snuggled deeper into the flannel being warmed by the fire.

"Thee must be hungered," Leticia said softly to her cat as she petted Mystic gently. "We wouldst obtain sustenance for thee anon."

Mystic mewed gratefully. If animals could talk he would have told Leticia how happy he was to have her home again.

"My Lady!" Elena shrieked when she saw Leticia sitting at the fireplace next to Mystic. Tears of joy flowed from Elena eyes. She ran to Leticia and taking her lady's hands in hers and pressing them against her tear stained cheeks.

"Elena, whence happened? Thee look gaunt and with malady?" Leticia queried observing her chambermaid. "Whence happened in our keep? Our conditions be sorrowful."

"Tis Lady Juliet, my lady," Elena replied. "On very day thee left for Exeter Lady Juliet argued with thy steward and released Durand's duty. Listening to Lady Agnes' whispers, Lady Juliet commanded thus keep and we hath suffered terribly."

"Lady Juliet released our steward?" Leticia gasped with shock. "The Lady Juliet hath naught authority for thus! Surely thee all trow such fact?"

"The Lady Agnes agreed to Lady Juliet's rule. She carries the child of Sir de Courtenay so in thy absence Lady Juliet wouldst rule thus keep," Elena whimpered. "Tis a sorrowful plight we hath suffered thus fortnight. Lady Juliet complained we servants were given too much food. Our rations cut by more than half. Our duties be doubled. Our firewood hath been taken from us. We worked more with less food and naught warmth. Lady Juliet decreed thus castle fireplaces be naught used with exception only to occupied rooms of thus noble household. Tis **waste** Lady Juliet said."

Leticia sat back in shock. It was difficult to believe all this occurred in the short time they had been in Exeter. "Whither wouldst thee naught send messenger to inform us of thus abominations?"

"The Lady Juliet set only certain knights to watch Okehampton gates. Naught one wouldst enter or leave without Lady Juliet's notice," Elena answered.

"Doth Lady Juliet be aware we hath returned?" Leticia queried.

"Nay, her sentry wouldst naught think to announce thus return of lord," Elena responded still holding Leticia's hands. "We heard noise in thy solar. Thinking thus might be Mystic, we entered hoping we wouldst care for Mystic."

"Yea, Mystic looks starved and ill as thee," Leticia observed. "Hath Mystic remained hidden during our absence leading to his condition?"

"We tended Mystic thus first days until Lady Juliet found us caring for thy mewling. Lady Juliet warned us to leave thus animal fend for itself or we wouldst be punished harshly for thus care. Lady Juliet threw hot porridge upon Mystic in temper one den and whenever Mystic neared Lady Juliet wouldst spill foul things upon thy mewling. Tis thus past weeks Mystic hath remained hidden even from us."

"Go to our stables and fetch Mystic some fresh milk from our goats," Leticia ordered removing her hands and stroking Elena's hair. "We wouldst command thee to get warm soup and bread from our cook for thy person. Whence be the Lady Juliet anon?"

"We saw Lady Juliet walking toward thus kitchens. Thus be Lady Juliet's way before our meal. Lady Juliet wouldst check on all portions," Elena told her lady. "Thus lady watches all and accuse all of waste and thievery."

"We wouldst confront Lady Juliet anon," Leticia said rising from the fireplace. "Fetch fresh milk for Mystic. We wouldst deal with Lady Juliet."

"Yea, my lady," Elena said quietly. "We wouldst wait until thee deal with Lady Juliet before we wouldst seek our hot soup."

"Fear no more," Leticia answered gently. "Thee wouldst find our Lord Vincent at livery near stable. Request of our lord to meet us in Okehampton kitchens."

"Yea, my lady," Elena replied walking quickly and leaving the chambers heading toward the stables. "Before the night we will groom Mystic. Soon our home be happy once more." Elena decided she would find Sir Vincent first and then get fresh milk for Mystic. Elena wasn't certain her Lady Leticia was really aware of how strong willed the Lady Juliet was. Elena determined it was best to make sure the Lord of the Manor was there to issue commands and protect her Lady Leticia.

Leticia descended the stairs in the frigid stairwells. She wrapped her fur mantel about her to maintain her body warmth. Stepping once more into the Great Hall, Leticia noticed Eugenia Alwins tending the tables. The knights entered expecting their food. Some were grumbling about the cold and the ration.

Leticia pulled Eugenia's arm and queried, "Prithee Eugenia, whence be thy husband, our steward?"

Eugenia's eyes opened with joy. Their dull sad appearance lit up with joy as they saw the face of their mistress lady. "Sweet Jesu!" Eugenia screamed with happiness. "Thou art returned. We prayed daily for thy return and rescue."

"We be hence at hearth and keep," Leticia returned graciously. "Prithee, whence be Durand?"

"Our husband be in hiding in stores of our keep," Eugenia grinned with a secret knowledge she was about to share. "We trow things be righted upon thy return."

"Yea, things be righted," Leticia decreed angrily as she looked around her at the unkempt and foul appearance of her Great Hall. This would be most embarrassing if the King or the Black Prince had decided to visit. "Fetch our steward and inform him to once more begin his duties anon. Our Durand wouldst begin with the cleaning of this foul smelling hall. Inform our steward to once more light all hearths and warm our keep. We wouldst prevent thus icy fingers of frost from cracking our very walls."

"Yea, my lady," Eugenia bubbled and regardless of her age, two score and nine years, she ran like a young child to bring her husband and let him know he could resume his duties.

Leticia walked with determination to the kitchens. She descended the stairs with a powerful mission. Before her stood Lady Juliet's back. She was tasting some soup and holding a large wooden stirring spoon.

"Old woman," Lady Juliet addressed without feeling. "Add one more pinch of salt."

Alice, the cook's helper reached into the salt box and added a large pinch of salt.

"Addled fool!" Lady Juliet snarled and raised the wooden spoon to strike the cook's helper. "We told thee to add but small pinch! Thee wouldst be punished for thy waste of so precious spice!"

Alice raised her hand in anticipation of the expected blow. Juliet seemed to enjoy showing her authority in that manner.

A hand stayed the blow.

"Nay Lady Juliet, thee wouldst not strike our Alice," Leticia said with deceiving calm. "Lay down thy spoon and give thus to our Alice."

Juliet recognized Leticia's voice and turned quickly to peruse the kitchen and see if Vincent was there with her. She still held the large spoon firmly.

"Whence dost thou trow knowledge to run household? Thee be raised in convent!" Lady Juliet replied indignantly. "We see thy methods and thus pitiful wastes!"

Leticia did not feel the necessity to point out Lady Juliet's method of running a household would cause damage to the castle itself and sickness to the servants. When servants were ill, the costs to run the keep were even higher. Instead she simply replied, "We be lady of Okehampton keep and we wouldst run our household as we see fit and methods of de Redvers."

"This be de Courtenay keep and we be running thus keep for benefit of our Lord's coffers," Lady Juliet sneered. "After all, we be breeding our lord's son and heir."

Vincent was unaware of anything that had occurred in his Okehampton or the confrontation of the two women in the kitchen. Elena had only run to him and asked that he hurry to the kitchens at Lady Leticia's request. When he entered the Great Hall his nose was offended by the stench. He mumbled to himself that he would speak to Durand about the current condition of the Great Hall. By the time he entered the servants had lit the second fireplace and both hearths were now blazing welcome warmth. They had recognized Lady Leticia talking to Eugenia and knew the household would return to normal. The servants took it upon themselves to begin the standard operations of the former de Redvers household.

"Lady Juliet, thee be whore," Leticia snapped angrily at her inference with disrupting the smooth running household and that she used carrying Vincent's heir to do so. "Thy babe growing in thy belly be bastard."

Juliet was furious. That was not the way she saw herself. She slammed the wooden spoon with great force against Leticia's cheek.

Stunned, Leticia ignored the hot sting upon her cheek and fought to maintain her balance.

Alice stood frozen in shock that the Lady Juliet dare to strike the Lady of the Keep.

Gaining her balance Leticia moved quickly and yanked the wooden spoon from Juliet's hand. Once she had secured the spoon she pushed Juliet to the floor.

It was that moment Vincent walked into the kitchens.

Juliet saw him enter and stayed on the floor. She hugged her abdomen and began crying in pain. She cried out, "Whence dost thee hate us and our child so thee wouldst do thus to kill Sir Vincent's son?"

Leticia stepped back and looked at Juliet in confusion. She had no idea what she was even talking about. Leticia automatically put a hand to the heat and pain still burning her cheek where Juliet had hit her with a wooden spoon. Then she saw Vincent's form kneeling at the side of Lady Juliet.

Juliet grabbed onto Vincent's arms, "My lord, we be in great travail. We fear for thus life our unborn. Help us."

Vincent immediately placed one arm under Juliet's knees and one firmly about her back. He lifted her with ease and walked to the kitchen stairway carrying her. Without turning he addressed Lady Leticia, "We be uncertain of happenings here. Yea knowest thus, thee wouldst expect explanation when we have returned the Lady Juliet to her rooms and tended her."

Leticia was furious at the act Juliet had put on. She promised to remain calm and discuss this reasonably with her husband. She trusted Vincent to allow her voice and be fair. He would soon learn exactly what had been happening under Lady Juliet's household. Leticia sat down on a bench and took deep breaths to become calm.

Alice rushed to Leticia's side. "Let us tend to thy wound, my lady!"

"Wound?" Leticia questioned. Then she tasted the blood seeping into her mouth from her lip. Her lip had begun to swell. "Yea, sweet Alice. Bring some ice from outside and place thus in flannel cloth."

Vincent carried Juliet to her pallet and laid her carefully upon it. He grabbed a large quilt from the end of the curtained bed and covered her. "We wouldst fetch for thee physician."

"Nay my lord," Juliet protested weakly. "We wouldst naught cause thee troubles. If we wouldst just rest, and trow thee care for us be all thy child and us require."

"We wouldst always care for our child," Vincent replied rising from the bedside. He didn't want Juliet to believe he cared for her. He didn't. "'Tis naught trouble. We wouldst fetch thee physician."

Lady Agnes entered the chambers from her private room. "My Lady?" she asked with true concern. Agnes ran to Lady Juliet's beside.

Vincent noticed Agnes was wearing new and expensive clothes. He then looked about Juliet's rooms and noticed new expensive furniture. A chest had been left open and he noted expensive cloths. Again his mind went to Durand Alwins. He would question him as to the funds released to Lady Juliet for expensive luxuries.

Juliet knew Vincent's reputation enough that it was never wise to accuse anyone of anything. Instead she pretended weakness and wept, "Our lord hath carried us to thee for thee to attend us. We wouldst naught understand our Lady Leticia's anger toward us."

# Chapter 16

Vincent spoke to Agnes, "take thy lady's care. Inform us of any crisis. We wouldst send for court physician." With those words he left Juliet's rooms and retraced his steps returning to the kitchen.

He found Leticia still sitting on the bench with her back facing him. She had removed her fur mantel because all the fireplaces in the kitchens had been lit and the room was warming. He noticed Alice, the cook's helper, hovering over his wife. Briskly he walked around the bench to face his wife. He found that one third of her face was covered with a cold wet flannel cloth. "Whence be thus?" he queried and gently removed the cloth from Leticia's hand. His knees weakened when he viewed the swollen and bloody lip. The left side of Leticia's face was swollen in the shape of a spoon and already turning blue with bruise. He roared at Alice, "Whence occurred hence? Be it troth or thee wouldst suffer severely."

Alice seemed to ignore the lord of the keep when she retrieved the cold cloth from Vincent's hand and gently dabbed the drying blood on Leticia's lips. Alice slowly replied, "Lady Juliet struck our lady with great force and avarice to cause our lady harm. Twas but thus moment thee entered whence our lady defended our lady's person by pushing thus evil woman away."

Vincent knelt next to his Leticia, "Tis troth? Lady Juliet caused thus wound upon thy person?"

Leticia only nodded. It was not the time to discuss all that had occurred at Okehampton in their absence, or her showdown with Juliet. The time would be later tonight during their quiet time and not in front of servants. "We ask of our lord to find the steward Alwins. Discuss with him the happenings of this fortnight of our absence. As lord, thee must right many things."

"We wouldst first carry thee to thy rooms and tend to our Goodwife," Vincent replied.

Leticia stood and stated firmly, "We hath many things to right. We wouldst naught waste time for thus wound. Tis naught grave or grievous wound so concern thyself little. Find our steward and learn thus occurrences in our absence from thy servant."

Vincent gave Leticia a dubious look.

"Tis troth our lord," Leticia said soothingly. "Our wound be naught of serious nature. Thee hath much to do."

"We wouldst discuss all thus eve during our time," Vincent responded kissing Leticia gently on her right cheek. "Alice, run and fetch Lady Rosamund. We wouldst request our new mother to tend to our Goodwife. The Lady Rosamund be at livery with our father, Sir Gaylord."

Alice nodded and taking a warm woolen cape ran outside to find the Lady Rosamund.

The cook, Urban finally made his appearance. He had been hiding in the servant quarters off the kitchen. He stayed there whenever Juliet entered the kitchens. Paulin his other assistant was usually sent to deal with Juliet. Juliet had sent Paulin back to the stores with two chickens that she had determined would not be cooked. Alice had accidentally walked into the kitchen not knowing Juliet was there. With the security that the Lord and Lady of the Manor returned and Juliet was removed, he appeared to finish the Midday meal.

Leticia found several servants and walked through Okehampton Castle ordering cleaning and the lighting of fireplaces. With the winter winds blowing, she also saw to the shuttering of the windows. Every bedchamber was warmed with blazing fires and rocks were heated ahead of time to warm the beds for the evening.

Leticia also saw to it that more food was prepared and hot meals were given to all the servants. The castle was still chilled from the lack of blazing fires but was warming. Leticia felt they had returned just in time or their household would soon be suffering from dropsy and weakness.

It was two hours later and Leticia was feeling tired. Lady Rosamund had tended her bruise with poultices and questioned Leticia without end. Leticia wasn't certain if the constant questioning wore her out or righting Okehampton. There was so much Juliet had undone. Lady Rosamond finally left her. Leticia hoped she had given up trying to persuade her to go to bed.

Leticia was also worried about Mystic and decided to return to her chambers to rest and be certain it would be ready for her husband in the evening. Leticia walked into the chamber carrying a hot trencher for her own meal and was determined to share some of the added meat with Mystic. She found Elena combing Mystic's matted coat and the cat was purring contently. Mystic's ears twitched in recognition as his Leticia entered the room.

Leticia placed her trencher on the hearth and as she ate her food she offered Elena a share and gave Mystic tiny bits of meat.

Lady Rosamund returned to badger Leticia into going to bed. Leticia conceded and found she was really tired. She drifted quickly into a sound sleep.

Elena remained in the chambers and every hour changed the warming rocks to keep Leticia's bed warm.

Vincent paced his office back and forth while listening to all of Durand Alwins reports and tallies. He was beyond angry and into furious rage. Vincent's hands raked his hair angrily as he heard of all that Juliet had taken from his coffers and taken through exchanges by denying rations for servants, selling those rations. Vincent wasn't sure what to do. He couldn't throw Juliet out. She was in confinement carrying his bastard child. He wanted to belt her thoroughly but couldn't do that for her breeding condition either. He had to punish her somehow. The punishment had to fit the crime.

"We be grateful for thy accurate accounts, Alwins," Vincent appreciated disguising his fury. "Whence wouldst be the count of coins left in Lady Juliet's hands?"

"We count five crowns, 30 shillings, and fifty pence," Durand replied quickly handing the calculation records to his lord.

"Thus be all left?" Vincent groaned. "Lady Juliet took more than 40 crowns alone from our coffers, not withstanding her trades in rations."

"Yea, my lord," Durand agreed. "Lady Juliet hath expensive tastes."

"Tis our punishment for preparing naught for our departure," Vincent growled in self-loathing. "We wouldst leave orders for Lady Juliet's arrest on our next departure."

Gaylord burst into the room, "Prithee, enlighten us on our Goodwife's fury? Whence be thus business about the Lady Juliet stealing and worse, causing injury to thy Lady?"

Vincent placed Alwins' parchment down upon the desk. He folded his hands into tight fists and placed them on either side of the table bowing his head. Vincent took several deep breaths and slowly raised his head. "Alwins, thee may leave us."

Durand Alwins sensed the disguised anger of his Lord and with Vincent's father now in the room, it was time to depart. The Lord would need advice from an older and wiser man.

Vincent continued to lean on his closed fists. "Whither explanation wouldst thou desire, father?"

Gaylord knew his son well. He took at seat in the chair across from the desk and folded his hands palms together creating a steeple and placing his index fingers under his chin. "We wouldst first desire thy explanation regarding Juliet's theft. We sense thou wouldst erupt as volcano for thus subject!"

"We just received all tallies regarding thus matter. Lady Juliet denied rations to servants trading such rations for goods. Thus lady ceased firing of hearths in all but occupied rooms and sold thus other cords. Lady Juliet released our steward from duties and opened our coffers taking our coin for selfish purpose," Vincent snarled.

"Whither be tally?" Gaylord questioned calmly.

"Over 100 crowns," Vincent replied handing Alwins' account calculations to his father for perusal.

Gaylord took the parchment and studied the numbers silently.

Vincent stood straight and slammed his right fist into his left palm.

"Hath thee considered punishment for thus theft?" Gaylord asked placing the parchment back on the desk.

"Nay," Vincent replied in disgust. "We wish such punishment to be equal in pain to thus crime."

"Thus shows thy lady to be filled with greed," Gaylord advised carefully. "For ones with greed in heart, whence wouldst cause most pain?"

"Yea, father," Vincent smiled because he understood his father's meaning. "Tis greatest pain for greed by sacrificing thus whence be taken."

Gaylord returned the same smile to his son.

"We wouldst go to Lady Juliet with our tally and inform thus lady of her punishment," Vincent announced.

"Nay," Gaylord countered. "We wouldst learn about thy Lady's injury? My Goodwife railed me thoroughly. We wouldst demand of thee to see retribution for thus."

"Tis most difficult with two ladies under one lord," Vincent complained shaking his head.

"Tis thy folly and reward," Gaylord reproved. "Bastard be naught conceived without dalliance and male seed. Wouldst thee cast thy seeds about, such seedling doth appear."

"In troth," Vincent replied sighing heavily and sitting down. "In troth we endure doubts of thus bastard's parentage."

"Prithee, thee doubts thee be father?" Gaylord questioned leaning onto the table.

"Yea," Vincent shared. "We be naught certain. We hath no memory of such bedding."

Gaylord said nothing but raised his brow in question.

"We drank most heavily upon our return from Neville Cross celebrating our queen's victory. We wake in thus morn with Lady Juliet sharing our pallet, naught else."

"When thus babe be delivered, thee wouldst trow in troth," Gaylord assured his son and patted his arm. "Dost thy Goodwife trow of thy doubt?"

"Nay," Vincent told his father. "Thee be our only confessor."

"We wouldst share thus with none other save thy Goodwife," Gaylord agreed. " Hath thee determined the Lady Juliet's punishment for thy lady's injury?"

Vincent nodded and started walking toward the curtained door. "We wouldst see Lady Juliet anon.

Gaylord rose from his chair and returned to his chambers and looking forward to sharing his bed once again with his fine new wife.

Vincent did not knock but burst into the Lady Juliet's room unannounced. He did not find her in the bed, but burrowing through her new cloths folded in her large chest.

"Thee hath recovered?" Vincent queried sarcastically.

Jumping with surprise and turning to face Vincent, Juliet took a moment and deep breath to respond, "Yea my lord. We needed only rest."

"Sit thyself upon chair," Vincent ordered showing no more concern. "We be informed thee hath taken coins from our coffer. Thee hath traded rations for goods and thee hath sold cords from our fires."

Juliet couldn't believe Vincent would find out what she had been doing. With the steward discharged, there would be no one to keep account. Juliet nearly fell into the chair.

"Hath thee lost ability to speak?" Vincent prodded.

Juliet's mind raced, she needed to justify her acquisitions. "Thee dost speak evil of our earnest effort to run thy household." That answer gave her a minute or two to think.

Vincent cocked his brow. The affectation was de Courtenay. "Thee wouldst explain thus to us."

"We wouldst assume our person be responsible for household upon thy departure with thy Goodwife," Juliet attempted in explanation. Inside she actually felt fear. "We saw waste. We wouldst be frugal with our household."

"Dost our frugalities include our coffers and fifty crowns?" Vincent growled menacingly.

Juliet quivered a little with fear. How could he know how much she took? Where was he getting this information? How could she answer that question? "We be proud of our frugality and rewarded our person."

Vincent suddenly burst out laughing for the contradiction of it all. "Sweet Jesu! By our arms blood and bone!" Vincent cursed. "Wouldst we e'er hear such tale in our life. Lady, but for thy breeding thee wouldst receive beating for thy thievery."

Juliet froze. "We attempted frugality."

Vincent tossed his head back with bitter laughter. He regained his composure and showed the tabulated account parchment. "Dost thou see balance for five crowns, 30 shillings, and fifty pence?"

Juliet leaned forward to look at the accounts. They were written by Durand Alwins' hand. She was found out. Apparently Durand had remained hidden and still kept counts. "So thy tallies say."

"Thee wouldst take thus coin and donate for our poor this coming holy mass," Vincent instructed firmly. "We wouldst accompany thee on holy day seeing to thus matter."

Juliet's face cracked. She felt tears stream down her cheeks.

"We see thy pain be great," Vincent chuckled triumphantly. He rose and gave one more command. "Thy punishment for striking my Lady and Goodwife causing her injury wouldst be confinement to thy room." Vincent turned to the Lady Agnes who was standing nearby. "Thy Lady be most generous with thee. Our eyes hath naught missed thy expensive clothing. Be confined with thy Lady."

"Hence be our confinement?" Lady Agnes choked out timidly. She would need to leave in early spring for a number of days.

Vincent was walking toward the chamber door and turned abruptly, "Thee wouldst be confined til our wroth be eased!" He left the room and slammed the door. The two women heard shuffling of guardsman feet and a loud thud as a bolt was dropped into place.

Vincent heard Juliet crying hysterically inside as he watched the guard drop the bolt outside the rooms and a smile appeared on his lips. He knew he had selected the right punishments. Lady Juliet would find it difficult to part with her luxury money and not being able to walk about freely announcing her position would really hurt her ego.

Vincent went to the Great Hall and his dinner. He was expecting to see Leticia, but couldn't find her. He ordered a chambermaid to take trenchers to Juliet and Agnes. He found Durand Alwins and instructed him to take food for every meal to the confined woman and allow chambermaids to take care of their personals, but Juliet and Agnes were not allowed to leave their rooms until further notice. He also informed Durand to schedule a guard by the door lest the ladies attempt bribery.

Vincent took his seat at the head of the table. All began to eat their plentiful and hot food in a warm and cleaned Great Hall. Vincent nibbled at his trencher and turned to his left side and queried his new mother, "Whence be our Lady?"

"Thy Lady required rest. We left thy lady fed and abed. Her injuries tended," Lady Rosamund informed Vincent.

Vincent nodded and finished his meal. This was their special time. It was their quiet time. He finished his meal and left the Great Hall heading directly to the solar. Entering their chambers he found Elena sleeping curled up on the hearth wrapped in Leticia's warm fur mantel. Leticia was sound asleep and there was Mystic curled next to his mistress on Vincent's bedside. Gently he roused Elena and told her he would care for his lady and she could leave. Vincent had not forgotten Mystic's condition earlier and he carefully picked Mystic up and placed him on a warm flannel cloth in front of the blazing fireplace. Mystic purred gratefully. Silently Vincent undressed himself and climbed into bed with his wife. He held her tightly in his arms and determined to let her sleep.

Leticia woke to her husband's soft breathing on her neck. Sunbeams peeked through the slatted shutters. She touched her cheek and found it still was tender, but the puffiness had disappeared. Leticia lifted the covers and attempted to leave the bed without disturbing Vincent. There were many more things she wanted to tend to upon her return from Exeter including some redecorating in their solar. As she moved Vincent's grip on her abdomen tightened.

"Wouldst thee depart from us?" Vincent asked sleepily.

"We believed thee to be asleep," Leticia replied snuggling into her husband once more. "We wouldst naught disturb thee."

"Thee disturbs me most often," Vincent answered huskily. He nibbled on her ear lobe.

"Thee still finds us attractive? We grow thick quickly and hence our face be scarred with wound?" Leticia teased but hoped his reply would be yes.

"Thy belly and face be naught our attraction," Vincent teased in return. His hands were already playing with her feminine globes. "Wouldst appear thy teats grow larger with thy belly. Thee wouldst have plenty milk for suckling our kinder."

Leticia turned to face Vincent. Little teardrops formed in her eyes, "Thee finds us fat and ugly!"

Vincent laughed, "Nay, we find thee beauteous." He brushed his lips lightly across her lips.

Leticia knew this was the right time to ask the question for the answer she feared. "My Lord, if we wouldst have female child and Juliet wouldst have male child wouldst thee love thus male child most?"

128

Vincent took his thumb and forefinger to lift her chin. He wanted her to look into his eyes when he replied, "Thee be our dearest love. Hear me well and believe this troth, we wouldst love our child be female or male. We wouldst maintain our doubt regarding the parentage of Juliet's bastard."

Leticia wanted to shout for joy but Vincent placed the palm of his hand over her lips. "We wouldst prefer thee issue us only sons. We find ourselves plagued with too many ladies in our household."

"We wouldst attempt obedience to our Lord's preference," Leticia replied. "Dost thee in troth doubt thee be Juliet's bastard's father?"

"We in troth doubt," Vincent responded. "Whither be father remains for proof. We do our responsibility for honor and name. Dost thee comprehend?"

"Yea," Leticia said once more snuggling into her husband's muscular chest.

"If thee comprehends, thee wouldst trow to care for Lady Juliet in our honor and name," Vincent reminded. "Give us thy oath."

"We take oath," Leticia promised. "We love thee."

"We love thee," Vincent repeated taking his wife's lips with his own.

Between sweet kisses Leticia questioned, "Whence thee walked in to our kitchens and thee watched me push the Lady Juliet, wouldst thou believewe meant to harm?"

"For thus moment, we thought thee meant to harm," Vincent whispered lovingly. "In troth when we saw thy wound we trow thee meant to defend thy person." Vincent once more began to concentrate on relief for his now painful erection.

Leticia responded to his needs enjoying the same wonderful sensations and pleasures she had come to need as much as her husband.

Later, Vincent rolled to his back savoring his satisfaction.

Leticia snuggled to his side and boldly questioned, "Dost Lady Juliet receive punishment from thee? We felt, most sorely, thy wroth."

"We wouldst apologize many times for our error in thy belting," Vincent sighed with regret. "We wouldst naught laid hand on thee for thy confinement."

"Juliet naught receive punishment?"

"Dost thee remember thy oath?" Vincent teased rolling to his side and gently brushing his hand across Leticia's thighs.

Leticia nodded. "Juliet wouldst be punished only if naught be breeding."

"Nay, Goodwife," Vincent chuckled. "Juliet be punished most severely and whence thus doth hurt most. Thus lady must offer alms to poor thus coming holy mass. All thus be left from Juliet's thievery wouldst be offered in alms. The lady and her chambermaid be confined to rooms err we feel enough for punishment."

Leticia smiled broadly, "In troth most severe punishment for Lady Juliet. Tis more severe than brief, yet painful belting."

✦

"We offer thee apology. Dost thou forgive us?" Vincent pleaded still heavy with guilt.

A knocking at the door interrupted their conversation. It was Elena, Lady Organa, and Lady Rosamund come to check on Leticia and Mystic. It was time to rise from bed and face all duty required of the Lord and Lady of Okehampton.

# Chapter 17

Vincent was dressed in velvet green tunic with matching colored hose and soft green colored slippers when he walked into Juliet's room. "Be thee prepared for holy mass of St. Nicholas? We celebrate the Christ Mass. Tis opportune thee wouldst select thus day to bestow thy wealth to alms for poor."

Juliet straightened her velvet and satin gown. "My Lord, forgive us, we could not find thy total." She had been worried about this all morning. In the arrest to her rooms she worried continuously that Vincent would throw her out and she really had no where to go.

Vincent arched his eyebrow.

"We hath procured four crowns, a score shillings, and fifty pence," Juliet said meekly holding out the coins in her hands. To her surprise Vincent pulled out his coin purse and added the missing coins until it matched the accounts of Durand Alwins. He gently placed those coins in Juliet's hand.

"Verily Lady Juliet, thee be in our care and we be responsible for all thy actions," Vincent addressed. "If thee wouldst need coin. Thee wouldst ask us. Shouldst we deem thee be in need we wouldst open our purse. Dost thou comprehend?"

Juliet bowed her head and nodded. She realized that Vincent was fair, kind, and a good lord for everyone. At the moment Juliet started to look inwardly at who she really was.

"Tis good. Hence there be naught need to steal from thy protector or from others," Vincent stated solemnly. "Come our Lady awaits us in our Great Hall. We wouldst attend Christ Mass thus day at our cathedral in thus bailey." Vincent did not extend his arm for Juliet, but turned and left the room expecting Juliet to follow, which she did.

When she entered the Great Hall Juliet saw Leticia without cover of mantel for the first time since their return from Exeter. Leticia was large with child. Juliet tugged at Vincent's arm. "Thy Lady Leticia be breeding?"

Vincent turned toward his back just slightly and replied, "Yea, our Lady Leticia be breeding with our seed."

Juliet was shocked and disappointed. Juliet noted the pride Vincent intoned when he told her it was his seed. This was devastating news. Her plan had been to eventually take over as Vincent's Lady by right of heir. She didn't believe the little girl raised in a convent would breed so quickly. Yet, Leticia stood there with a larger abdomen than her growing abdomen. Juliet started looking inwardly once more at who she was and what a delicate position she was in.

A page placed a white velvet ermine lined mantel about Leticia's shoulders. Lady Organa wrapped it properly and pinned it. Vincent's squire, Maynard placed a green velvet mantel lined with mink about his Lord. A page came to Juliet with a red velvet mantel lined with fox and placed it about her shoulders. Lady Agnes came to adjust it properly and pin it.

To Juliet's surprise Sir Malcolm, a loyal knight of the de Redver's household of Okehampton offered his arm as escort. Juliet noted that Leticia glanced her way and smiled to Sir Malcolm. Juliet realized Leticia was kind enough not to embarrass her by forcing her to walk to the cathedral alone. Juliet also noticed that although the servants had no ill will or hostility toward her. The protection and strength of Vincent de Courtenay was powerful. Juliet realized how wonderfully the lord and lady of Okehampton treated her. She promised herself to give thanks to God for her saviors.

The mass seemed endless but at last ended. Vincent escorted Leticia to the courtyard where the aged, widowed, hungry, and ill serfs met them. Leticia opened her coin purse to give to the aged and widowed in need. Vincent opened his purse and gave to the hungry and orphaned.

Vincent told Juliet, "Give the contents of thy purse to our poor with malady."

Malcolm escorted to Juliet to where the diseased and lepers were standing with open hands. Malcolm was ordered to protect her, but see to it she gave to the ill.

Juliet was repulsed by the diseased and lepers but opened her purse and dropped the coins in the outstretched hands. Juliet made certain not to touch them or let them touch her. In her heart she suddenly felt warm inside for helping these poor dredges and cast offs of society. Soon she felt as if she was being watched. She looked to find both Vincent and Leticia smiling at her. Proudly she took the last of the coins and gave a full crown to a young crippled boy.

Vincent finally relented on his imprisonment of Juliet January 21$^{st}$ the holy day of Saint Agnes. Juliet was then allowed to wander the keep and take meals once more in the Great Hall. She was also obligated to assist in duties for the keep. Leticia suggested she spend time with the servants and instruction of proper spinning, weaving, and sewing. The twins learned about tally records and candle making.

Leticia spent many hours of every day running the household. Her schedule was as demanding as her husband's in running the keep, bailey, and properties. Even in the cold winter months there were constant visitors and problems were solved regarding all the properties, manors, keeps, and trades.

Vincent found himself spending long hours settling disputes and arranging for guardianships and marriages of his vassals. Many nights he would share these problems with his wife. He would chuckle at how heavy these responsibilities were. He couldn't imagine the responsibilities of King Edward III. He would always whisper to Leticia he was happy the king arranged his marriage.

Leticia grew larger and larger with child to the point that in early spring she had to curtail many of her activities. Leticia actually looked with a little envy at Juliet. Even though Juliet was supposed to be further in pregnancy, Juliet did not seem to grow as large or cumbersome.

Juliet was enjoying the freedom of the keep and the protection of Vincent, but underneath a strong jealousy of Leticia remained that she continued to fight. She wanted everything that Leticia had knowing she would never have it. That included the devoted attention of Vincent de Courtenay. Juliet was forced to ask Vincent for any coin, and he never seemed to deny her requests, but Leticia had free access. That proved Vincent really loved and trusted his wife. Juliet determined to keep herself busy and now since she was caught in her own web of deceit, she would make the best of it. She was assured a place in this household. She had food, shelter, and clothing. Juliet determined to become grateful and squelch her jealousy.

"My Lady seems troubled," Lady Agnes noted one evening as she assisted Juliet in preparing for bed.

"Nay," Juliet replied removing her tunic. She gently palmed the chemise covering her growing abdomen. "Our babe be moving," she sighed. Who would have believed a child growing in her womb would begin to mean more to her than a royal court, money, property, and love.

"Tis sorrowful Sir Vincent seems to care not for thee or babe," Lady Agnes said irritably. "Sir Vincent seems to care only for Leticia and her babe. Thus lady grows fat!"

"Lady Leticia be Sir Vincent's wife. She carries heir," Juliet replied sitting on the edge of the bed and removing her slippers. "We carry only bastard child, but thus be our child."

Agnes came to Juliet's side and started combing her hair in preparation for the cap. "Tis be better if de Courtenay show more interest in thy babe."

"We did thus to our person," Juliet confessed. "Tis our folly and responsibility, no other. We only wish to be loved and dost seem our babe wouldst be our love."

"Wouldst thee be happier if thee were the lady of de Courtenay?" Agnes asked.

"We be naught certain, Lady Agnes," Juliet answered. "Whence we arrived our answer be yea. Today, we wish only to hold our babe. Tis certain the de Courtenay be most happy with his Leticia."

"We believe thee wouldst be lady of Okehampton," Lady Agnes insisted. She stopped combing Juliet's hair and wound her hair for the cap.

"We believe Okehampton be too great for us," Juliet excused. She realized she had failed completely when she ran Okehampton in Leticia's absence. "We be trained as gentle lady for noble lady. Our frugality caused great upheaval."

"Nay," Agnes disagreed placing the bed cap upon her head. "Twas only misunderstood, and time for thee to learn. Trouble naught thy soul with such thoughts."

"Thee dost care for our person and we be grateful," Juliet appreciated as she swung her legs up on the bed and allowed Agnes to cover her with a heavy fur sided quilt. It took Juliet several moments to become comfortable.

"Be thou comfortable?" Agnes asked tucking Juliet in and beginning to close the curtains.

"Yea."

"Thee art becoming fond of de Courtenay's seed growing in thy belly?" Agnes asked curiously.

"We begin to love our kinder most affectionately," Juliet sighed heavily. "Our kinder wouldst be all thus we wouldst hold."

"Hence be always hope," Lady Agnes replied almost with sinister tone. "Sleep well my lady."

Juliet yawned and fell sound asleep peacefully. No matter what, she did have the child that was growing in her.

Agnes slipped out of the room silently.

It was in early spring a messenger from King Edward III arrived at Okehampton. Vincent de Courtenay was informed that Calais had been captured and he was to report to Calais as soon as possible for policing duties. Edward had won the battle but the knights that accompanied him were tired and some needed to go home. Edward was sending Vincent to complete the conquest and assist in establishing Edward's rule in Calais.

Leticia learned at the meal that evening that Queen Phillippa had accompanied King Edward and returned home in time to deliver a baby boy, Thomas. Leticia was not included in the discussion regarding Vincent's orders that would take him away to Calais for a time.

"Come sit with us," Vincent requested of Leticia. He was sitting in front of the hearth watching the flames as a man hypnotized.

It was their quiet time and Leticia recognized Vincent's mood of contemplation. When these occurred she would wait until he spoke to her by sewing curtains, tunics, or swaddling for their expected child. Leticia jumped when Vincent spoke to her. "My lord?"

"Come sit with us," Vincent repeated beckoning her to sit on his lap.

Leticia placed her sewing on the floor and awkwardly sat on Vincent's lap. "Our babe seems to make us most big for thy little lap."

"Nay, our lap be large enough for thee and all our heirs thee wouldst provide," Vincent contradicted. He helped her get comfortable and holding her tightly lay his chin upon her head.

"Whither troubles thee husband?" Leticia questioned.

"Dost thee think we be troubled?" Vincent teased still holding her tightly.

"Nay, tis troth thou be troubled," Leticia insisted laying her head closer to his chest and listening to the comforting beat of his heart.

"We must inform thee and remind thee of our duty as noble and favored knight of our King," Vincent said softly into Leticia's hair.

Those words were a knife digging into Leticia's heart. She knew what he meant. She knew he was being called to duty. Covering her emotion as best she could, Leticia asked, "Whither wouldst thee be sent?"

"We wouldst be sent to Calais," Vincent answered picking up Leticia's chin. He wanted to see her face and look into her eyes. He wanted to know what she was really feeling and how she would react.

"Tis most confusing," Leticia managed to say holding her tears. "The King hath conquered Calais. For what reason doth our King send thee?"

"We be noble knight to represent the King and establish King Edward's throne," Vincent answered. He saw those tears forming. He would miss her as much as she missed him.

Bravely Leticia uttered, "We wouldst accompany our husband."

"Nay," Vincent countered. "Thee wouldst stay safe here and care for our Okehampton."

Tears flowed freely now as Leticia argued, "We wouldst miss thee painfully. We wouldst be with our husband. Whither thee goest, hence we wouldst be."

"Thee be breeding," Vincent reminded. He would not have his little wife risk miscarriage on such duty.

"Our Queen Phillippa accompanied our king to Calais and our queen be breeding," Leticia pointed out.

"Yea, tis troth," Vincent agreed on the one point. "We wouldst answer in troth to thee. Leticia my lovely Goodwife, thee be quite cumbersome. We wouldst naught see thee even fit upon Palfrey and tis too dangerous to ride thee seated upon our lap on our Destrier."

Tears really flowed and sobs choked Leticia's words, "Thee thinks us sow! Thee be ashamed of thus large girth!"

Vincent pulled Leticia even closer. He lovingly replied, "We love thee Leticia, with all our heart, our soul, and our being. We wish thee to stay and be safe for us. In troth Okehampton needs thee to run such more than us. Thee dost understand thy duties? Be there any person we wouldst trust but thou? Queen Phillippa and King Edward have all of the ladies and knights to run royal domain. Leticia, we hath only each other."

Leticia nodded her head. "We trow thy words to be troth, but we wouldst miss thee most desperately. Naught hath this person been happier in her life hence with thee."

"Thy words make us happy," Vincent responded gently kissing Leticia's forehead. "We be naught happier in our life. Thou art our life. Thee dost carry our kinder. Take care of our heir for us. We ask thus of you. Stay safe. Stay here at Okehampton. Make me worry naught for thee lest we lose sight of our duty and suffer for it. Dost thee pledge to us?"

Leticia nodded, but did not answer. Instead, she laid her head upon Vincent's chest and let her tears drop onto his shirt. Her fingers squeezed the linen of his shirt. Even she could not believe the difference in what a few short months had made in her life. She was happy, she loved Vincent, and she was going to have a baby. It was Vincent's baby. She had grown accustomed to Vincent's company and suddenly she was being left alone again. She was being left alone and kept apart from the one she found she loved most dearly. The thought of his leaving and possibly going into battle frightened her. If something happened to her Vincent, what would she do? Leticia buried her face into Vincent's chest. She inhaled the scent that was Vincent. She wanted that part of him with her always.

They sat together silently.

It took Vincent great will to keep his feelings composed. As Vincent sat on the chair with Leticia on his lap feeling her tears wet his shirt he could only think of his own fears. He was leaving his happiness and his heart at Okehampton. Before every call to duty was a thrill and challenge he looked forward too. This duty was painful. He had grown used to Leticia's company. She was not only his wife; Leticia had become his confident and trusted friend. The thought of his never seeing her again sent a sense of terror in his thoughts. He was leaving his soul and his child. He wondered if he would ever see his child grow. He wanted to train his child, love his child, and watch his child grow. Yes, it was his and Leticia's child. He had vowed to care for Juliet and his supposed child, but he had to be truthful to himself. He was most concerned about Leticia and seeing their child grow to manhood. Thinking over his obligations, his fears, and his duty he realized his Leticia had fallen asleep in his arms. Carefully he carried his wife to their bed and gently laid her upon it. He carefully covered her and stood watching her sleep for sometime. She looked so beautiful and so peaceful. He engraved that vision in his head so he could remember her the entire tour of duty. Sadly and slowly he undressed himself and climbed into bed next to his dear Leticia.

Mystic mewed quietly by the hearth. He had forgotten all about Leticia's cat and it seemed even Mystic seemed to understand their need to be close. Mystic curled next to the fireplace and purred until he too fell asleep.

Leticia woke the next morning to find herself secured in Vincent's strong arms. She craned to kiss Vincent's lips. She whispered, "We love thee. Thee hath conquered our heart."

A smile grew on Vincent's lips and he held her tighter. Without opening his eyes he responded, "Thy heart be most difficult conquest. Our duty in Calais wouldst be quite easy in comparison."

"Fie upon thee cur," Leticia teased. "Thee wouldst be sleeping."

"With thee in our bed we keep alert lest we find arachnids or frogs as pallet companions," Vincent teased in return.

Leticia started laughing and warned, "Thee be most intelligent to stay alert and prevent such pallet companions."

"Yea, a most intelligent man to take thee as Goodwife," Vincent responded lovingly. He bent his head to kiss Leticia deeply and passionately.

Leticia pulled back for breath. She took her hand and stroked Vincent's cheek. She asked, "Whence dost thee journey to Calais?"

Vincent took her hand and turned it to kiss her knuckles. "We wouldst depart for Calais in four den."

"Must thee depart so quickly?"

"Yea," Vincent answered. "For sooner we leave for Calais, sooner we wouldst return to our love's side. We wish to be with thee whence our kinder be delivered."

It was if the babe heard its father's words.

"Sweet Jesu!" Vincent exclaimed. "Whither dost thee bear beatings thus child offers thee?" He threw off the covers and with wonder stared at the movements very visible within Leticia's abdomen. "See hand, and foot, and foot, and foot, and hand?"

"Tis thy babe for certain," Leticia giggled withstanding stoically the intense movements. "Thee be restless as such whence thee sleeps in our arms."

Vincent stroked her abdomen with his large hand. "We protest thy mother's words! We wouldst not cause such travail for thy mother. We wouldst thee honor thy mother in like manner and give such rest."

As if magic, the active movements slowed and then ceased.

"Thee must return home to discipline thy child," Leticia whimpered. "Still unborn thy child trow father's law and dost obey."

"Yea, we wouldst be certain we wouldst be here to discipline our kinder," Vincent chuckled wickedly. "All of them. Thus be our first."

Leticia knew he was comforting her. She didn't realize he was reassuring himself as well. She replied passionately, "Wouldst thee need practice for the seeding?"

"Yea," Vincent whispered into her ear.

Again the servants had to wait until the door opened allowing Mystic to find his good friend, Elena. Mystic's daily routine started with Elena a bowl of food in the kitchens. The rest of the day would be spent following his Leticia or sitting upon her lap and being stroked and petted affectionately.

While they dressed this morning they discussed the duties that were currently on their minds. This mindset included Juliet.

"Thee wouldst accompany us to Lady Juliet's chambers," Vincent told Leticia as he allowed Maynard to place his red woolen tunic over his white linen shirt. "Together we wouldst tell her of our journey to Calais. We wish thee to be present whence Juliet be told of obligation to thee as mistress of Okehampton. We wouldst bear naught doubt of who resides as Lady of Okehampton."

"We wouldst be by thy side," Leticia answered obediently. There had been subtle changes in Juliet's behavior since her punishment. Leticia also noted that Juliet seemed very interested in her baby and movements. There were times she heard Juliet talking to the unborn telling it how much she loved it. Leticia was convinced Juliet was changing in this pregnancy from a selfish shrew to a caring mother. Leticia was convinced that Juliet wanted only to find love. It was obvious that love would never be Vincent. Leticia believed Juliet would love her baby and be a good mother.

"We wouldst then speak with our father," Vincent continued. "Our father wouldst remain at Okehampton and take over our duties as Lord of Okehampton."

Leticia nodded. Vincent continued discussing his plans even after they were dressed and as they walked into Juliet's chambers.

Payton Lee

✦

# Chapter 18

Vincent opened the door to Juliet's chamber and gently pushed Leticia into the room first. He followed her into Juliet's room and stood behind her when she stopped just short of the large curtained bed on its raised dais.

Juliet came out of her privy. Her hair was a mess. Her tunic was being worn on the wrong side. She stopped in a start at the sight of Leticia and Vincent in her room.

Leticia couldn't help but notice Juliet's hapless condition. "Whence be thy handmaiden, Lady Agnes?" Leticia asked looking around the room for her.

"Agnes begged us for leave to visit cousin and family thus live nearby," Juliet replied while attempting to smooth her messy hair.

"Her surname be Tillet," Leticia commented. "We trow of naught family of such surname to live nearby."

"Mayhap they moved hence," Vincent suggested and realizing Juliet's need for assistance turned to Lady Organa. "Fetch for us Lady Mildred. Inform the lady of new duties as handmaiden for Lady Juliet."

Organa looked to Leticia for her ladies approval of Vincent's order.

Leticia smiled with understanding of her lady's devotion. "Our Lord be gracious and wise to fetch help for our Lady Juliet."

With those words of approval, Lady Organa went to the sewing rooms of the keep to bring Lady Mildred.

Vincent then returned to his purpose of visit. "Lady Juliet, we wouldst inform thee of our tour of duty. We wouldst leave Okehampton in four den for such new throne of Calais."

Juliet being well versed in knightly duty accepted the news calmly. "We wish for thee safe journey and quick return."

Leticia smiled at Juliet. There indeed was a change in Juliet's personality with this pregnancy.

"We wouldst thee trow our commands in absence," Vincent continued. "Our father, Sir Gaylord de Courtenay wouldst be lord in our absence. Our steward wouldst be Durand Alwins. If thee need of anything, request thus of our Lady Leticia or our steward. Within reason, thus wouldst be given to thee. Knowest our Goodwife hath final word on all in our keep including our steward. We wouldst give our Goodwife same authority as our person. Dost thee understand?"

"Yea," Juliet replied. "'Tis noble and righteous for our Lady Leticia as thy wife and mistress of Okehampton."

Vincent cocked a brow. He still couldn't believe this selfish and self-serving woman had made such a change. "We wouldst do our utmost to return in time for the birthing."

"We wish thee to be hence," Juliet replied. "Yea, we do understand if thee wouldst naught be present."

Vincent was surprised once more. Could it be a possibility she had changed?

Leticia walked forward to Juliet and said, "If our husband be detained thy person wouldst still be cared for most tenderly. Thus be our oath."

Juliet whispered a grateful, "Bless thee my lady. We lay naught only our life, but our babe's life in thy hands."

Vincent beamed in pride at his wife's great gesture.

At that touching moment, Lady Organa returned with Lady Mildred.

"Lady Mildred, thee wouldst be upgraded to handmaiden of Lady Juliet," Vincent commanded. "Upon Lady Agnes' return thee wouldst still remain to help care for the Lady Juliet. We wouldst naught allow Lady Juliet to be unassisted in this time of most need."

"Bless thee, lord," Juliet appreciated. She thought she could handle things herself. She had been afraid to ask Vincent for help after she allowed Agnes to leave. She found her pregnancy to be more cumbersome than she thought. "Whence be thy sojourn in Calais?"

"We wouldst be in tour of fortnight," Vincent replied. "'Tis naught too long."

"'Tis eternity," Leticia blurted out. She would miss her Vincent every moment.

Vincent appreciated his wife's comment. Could it mean she truly loved him nearly as much as he loved her? Tenderly his strong hands that had been stationed on her shoulders gave a gentle squeeze.

"We wouldst leave thee anon. Thy maid servant may attend thee," Leticia offered politely. Poor Juliet looked so pathetic. Leticia was certain Juliet would appreciate a hot bath, gentle hair brushing, and attendance to dress as soon as possible. "Dost thee feel well?"

"Yea, we feel wonderful," Juliet replied with a small smile. She stroked her large abdomen. "Our babe reminds us daily of such presence."

"If thee wouldst need anything or physician, merely ask of us," Vincent volunteered.

"We bless thee for all thy kindnesses," Juliet returned with a broad smile. She sat on her bed as Lady Mildred began brushing her hair.

Leticia and Vincent left the room to be met by Morgan and Megan.

"Thee wouldst leave us?" Megan questioned Vincent bluntly.

"Our lord hath duty to throne, Megan," Leticia defended quickly.

"Whither dost thee learn of our journey?" Vincent queried the twins. "'Twas Quintin, Morgan?"

Morgan blushed crimson.

"Yea, we trow thus be Quintin," Vincent chortled. "Dost our father trow of thy devotion to squire?"

"'Tis naught thy concern," Megan snapped in protection of her sister. "See how thee upsets our sister?"

Vincent raised his eyebrow in discipline.

"Use naught thus affection with our person," Megan returned with bravado. "We dost naught tremble in thy presence."

"One den we wouldst take belt to thy person," Vincent threatened. "Mayhap thus den wouldst be thus fortuitous day." Vincent stepped forward and began removing his sword belt.

"We be happy thee leave us," Megan shrieked and began running down the staircase. She shouted back to Morgan, "We told thee he cares naught for thy feelings."

Vincent grabbed Morgan before she ran and held her arm firmly. "Whence troubles thee sister? Dost thee need us to intervene for thee?"

Morgan began trembling and cringed, "We dost naught offend thee. Prithee, belt us naught."

"Morgan!" Vincent replied in irritation. "We wouldst trow thy reason for addressing our person in regard to our journey?"

Shaking Morgan whispered nearly choking, "Wouldst thee bring Sir Gifford and our Quintin with thee on thy journey?"

Vincent suddenly started laughing and released his hold on Morgan. "Thee trow in troth anon thus answer. Yea, we wouldst have Sir Gifford and Quintin join us."

Morgan sank to the floor near faint with fear of her brother but folded her hands and begged, "Prithee, take naught our Quintin with thee."

Leticia bent over Morgan taking her hand to help her stand. "Morgan, thee wouldst trow such duty is required by throne. If thee wouldst be wife to knight, such separations be necessary. Necessary, but sorrowful and lonely."

Vincent adored his Leticia at times like this. Today he was a very happy man. He realized Leticia would miss him as much as he would miss her.

Leticia wound her arms around the still trembling Morgan in comfort. She brushed Morgan's cheek with the palm of her hand. "We wouldst be keeping each other company in our loneliness. Such sorrowful lot of women we be."

"Yea," Morgan whimpered snuggling into Leticia even though it was a little difficult with the expanding pregnancy overwhelming Leticia.

"Come with us to thy father," Leticia invited to her young sister in law. "He wouldst be our liege in our husband's absence."

Vincent embraced Leticia and she held Morgan's hand as they walked to the chamber used as Vincent's office. They knew Gaylord would be there at this time in the morning waiting for Vincent.

"Ho, we be waiting for thee," Gaylord greeted merrily. "We heard of our journey to Calais."

Vincent removed his arm from Leticia and walked to take his seat by his desk. "Nay father."

"Thee be naught reporting to Calais for throne?" Gaylord asked in surprise. "Our King Edward hath commanded thee to thy knight's duty."

"Father," Vincent replied patiently. "We wouldst fulfill our duty to our King. Thee wouldst naught accompany us on thus journey."

Gaylord stood up with anger and indignation. "Think thee we be too old for our duty to throne? We think naught. We wouldst still best thee in joust."

"Father, we wouldst naught challenge thee and we think naught thee be too old," Vincent chuckled raising his hands in defense. "We need thy wisdom and strength to protect Okehampton. We wouldst charge thee to be lord of Okehampton in our absence. We have our Goodwife, kinder, and even thy own daughters to defend and protect from any and all harm."

"Thee wouldst naught allow us to accompany thee on thy journey?" Gaylord questioned glumly.

"We need thee to protect Okehampton and our household from all invaders," Vincent repeated. "We require thee to be lord of Okehampton in our absence."

Gaylord plopped into his chair. "Yea, we trow thy meaning. We wouldst stay behind and miss the adventure. We wouldst be lord of Okehampton."

"Bless thee father," Vincent said gratefully. There was really no one he trusted more than his father to guard and protect his family and Okehampton.

Morgan timidly asked her father, "Wouldst thee allow us to accompany our brother to Calais?"

Gaylord arched his eyebrow in the affectation of the de Courtenay men. "For the purpose thee naught be separated from thy Quintin?"

Vincent marveled at the great wisdom on his father.

Morgan meekly replied, "Yea, father. We wouldst miss our Quintin greatly."

"Thee must become acquainted with such separation," Gaylord responded with fatherly firmness.

"If Quintin be slaughtered…" Morgan wept wringing her hands.

"Thus be the hand of God," Gaylord interrupted. "'Tis fate wouldst take our hand. We wouldst hear naught more of thus nonsense."

Morgan left the room in tears.

"We must look after our sister," Leticia stated beginning to leave the room and go after Morgan.

Vincent's command stopped her. "Nay, we wouldst speak to thee with our father together."

Leticia walked closer to Vincent and sat in a chair. "As thee wishes."

Vincent reached across the space to touch her cheek. "'Tis our wish." How he wanted to make everything perfect for her. He had dreaded this call of duty. Inwardly he had hoped through the winter months that he wouldn't be called. He had inwardly hoped he would be at Leticia's side for the entire length of her pregnancy. "Father, we charge thee to care for our Leticia and all needs our lady wouldst have."

"We must include thy Juliet," Leticia added quietly.

Both men looked at her as if she had grown two heads.

"We understand the need for protection and care being in breeding ourselves. 'Tis not a point of bastard child or naught. 'Tis point of care. We understand," Leticia explained for the surprised men.

A grin covered Vincent's lips, "Yea, we wouldst include Juliet for thee to care and supply all need."

"We commit ourselves to thy will," Gaylord complied reluctantly. He still wished to go off to the adventure of knighthood in a place called Calais.

"We wouldst begin to review all our household with our Goodwife and our steward, Alwins," Vincent announced retrieving papers from his table. "Alwins wouldst be here anon with our tallyman."

"We need such instruction for the care of the keep," Gaylord agreed. "Our own manor be nothing like thy keep."

Alwins appeared at the door with the tallyman at that moment. The entire day and the next two days were spent in preparation for Gaylord to manage the keep as Lord Protector.

The last day Vincent and Leticia spent together behind the closed doors of their chamber. Vincent spent most of the time just holding Leticia and enjoying the movement of his baby still encased in her womb. They talked of many things and nothing of importance. They discussed poems and read to each other. It wasn't until late into the night Vincent broached the subject both had avoided.

"Mayhap we wouldst naught return.." Vincent attempted to say.

Leticia placed her finger upon his lips. "Nay, thee wouldst return. We wouldst hear naught other."

"Goodwife, interrupt us naught," Vincent reprimanded removing her finger. "Mayhap we wouldst naught return, we dost make thee our heir of all Devon until our heir reach proper age. We hath instructed our father and left the legal papers."

Leticia turned her face. "Nay, we wouldst naught think of our life without thee."

"Dearest heart of mine," Vincent replied holding her face in his large strong hand. "We wouldst also ask that thee take care of Juliet and the bastard she wouldst bear. Thus be our wish."

Leticia wrapped her arms around Vincent and sobbed, "Thee hath our oath, but leave us naught."

Vincent nuzzled Leticia's ear and whispered, "Our intent be to return to thee anon without mishap." Vincent squeezed his eyes closed and thought very deeply. Before his marriage to Leticia, tours of duty were an adventure. He looked forward to every call from the throne. He would not have believed that in less than a year he would dread leaving his wife, his child, and his keep. Leticia had changed his world completely. He hoped she would never learn the power she held over him. He was nothing without her and she had done this to him in less than a year.

Leticia nestled herself comfortably in Vincent's embrace. She couldn't begin to imagine what the next fortnight would be like. They had shared their evenings and bed everyday since their marriage. How could she face nights alone? How could she even

think of never having Vincent near her again?

The sun was in mid heaven when Leticia and Vincent walked hand in hand down the steps of the keep and into the bailey where all the knights, squires, horses, pavilions, and wagons were waiting for their lord. Vincent did not wear armor suiting. Instead he wore only mail under his tunic. He wore his light blue heraldry crest. The de Redvers knights that were staying behind with Sir Gaylord moved aside for the couple as if presenting a private archway. Servants stood watching their lord and lady as they stood in the bailey to wave farewell to their lord and wish blessings for his journey. In the short time Vincent had been Earl of Devon and Lord of Okehampton, he had won the servants hearts. All of Okehampton would miss their lord. That included his twin sisters and Juliet.

Vincent stopped to face his sister Megan. "Dost thee wish to send us blessings? Or dost thou wish to vex us yet once more before we depart?" Vincent addressed his younger sister with a chuckle.

"Brother, thee dost trow we love thee," Megan replied sincerely. "We send thee blessings and beg thee to return anon. For without thee, we wouldst naught enjoy banter. Thee dost challenge us and we wouldst miss thee dearly." With those words she stretched on her tiptoes to plant a sisterly kiss upon Vincent's exposed cheek.

"We take thy love and blessings with us dear sister," Vincent replied. "We wouldst miss thy sharp tongue and verbose challenges." He looked around for Morgan. "Whence be our sister, Morgan?"

Megan pointed to a figure standing near the squire Quintin on his palfrey. "Tis our sister's farewell to her love," Megan expounded sarcastically.

"Dearest Sister, such time wouldst arrive whence thee wouldst be so captivated by thy heart," Vincent teased.

"Nay!" Megan scolded sharply. "A fate of marriage thus female might endure, but love? Hah!" She folded her arms defiantly.

"We thought of same mind not so long ago," Vincent shared. "Look at us hence. We be lost soul without our love." The exchange of looks between him and Leticia told all present of their devotion to one another.

Megan only smiled at her brother and sister-in-law. She remarked affectionately, "Tis for all to see thy love for one another. Thee hath indeed become a changeling." Megan then walked to her father and new stepmother's side.

Vincent released Leticia's hand and whispered, "Tis here we wouldst speak our adieu." He kissed her gently on her lips. He picked up her hands and brushed his lips over her knuckles. Vincent then bent down and kissed her extremely large and bulky belly. "Take care of our babe." Vincent then turned and walked to his father who was standing next to his Destrier.

Lady Rosamund stretched on tiptoes to place a sweet kiss upon Vincent's cheeks. Gaylord said nothing to his son, but did embrace him.

Maynard assisted Vincent to mount his Destrier.

Vincent then reined his Destrier, motioned the entourage forward. The gates to the bailey were opened and the drawbridge was lowered.

Leticia stood watching in silence as Vincent disappeared in the horizon. She didn't see Juliet approach.

"Come inside with us," Juliet offered taking Leticia's hand. "Together we wouldst weep for our lord's absence from us."

Leticia was startled but regained composure. "We saw thee naught upon our lord's departure. Prithee, wast thee about?"

"We trow we be embarrassment to our lord. We respect Sir Vincent and love Sir Vincent for such kindness. We hid in thus midst," Juliet answered. "Come inside with us. We wouldst rest our bodies from our heavy burden."

"Of breeding? Or of melancholy?" Leticia asked as she took Juliet's hand and walked toward the keep.

"We wouldst decree, both," Juliet answered. The two women to the surprise of the throng walked hand and hand into the keep.

# Chapter 19

Thirty days of lonely nights had passed for Leticia since Vincent went to Calais. Mystic had been her bed companion curling up in a ball next to her every night. Vincent's absence had left Okehampton Castle quiet as if mourning for its master. All the servants knew how much Leticia missed her husband and their lord. As Leticia progressed into the last months of her pregnancy it became more and more difficult for her to move.

Sharing in their pregnancy, Juliet and Leticia grew to become close friends. Juliet and Leticia spent many hours together talking of the babes growing inside them. Juliet shared many secrets of her heart with Leticia. These secrets included her childhood and how she came to think she loved Vincent de Courtenay. Once Leticia understood Juliet and Juliet understood Leticia, they found they could like each other.

Megan and Morgan assisted Leticia getting up from bed. They helped her sit down and get up from meals. The twins became more excited about the arrival of their brother's child.

Sir Gaylord continued with all of Vincent's plans to reinforce the batteries and walls of Okehampton. He also took good care of his son's holdings. Gaylord and Rosamund even made certain Leticia would never be alone at night. They continually prodded her with tiny details of nonsense every night to keep her in conversation with them until it was bedtime.

Lady Rosamund would take Leticia for a walk in the garden every morning Leticia was able. "Whither dost thee bother with thy husband's concubine?" Lady Rosamund asked Leticia during a stroll in the Okehampton Castle gardens. "All of our keep be talking of it."

"Then let such prattle," Leticia chided. She continued walking and petting her cat, Mystic.

Mystic was even more of a presence with Leticia since Vincent had departed a month ago.

"Prithee, tell us thy reason for befriending Lady Juliet," Lady Rosamond pursued. "Lady Juliet breeds thy husband's bastard."

"Yea, tis troth," Leticia conceded. "Verily Lady Juliet has opened her heart to us thus past season. Our lady realizes such wouldst naught love our husband, or e'er wouldst love our Vincent as we do. Thus lady only wished to be loved. Lady Juliet came to Okehampton hoping our Vincent wouldst love such person since our lady be breeding Vincent's child. Lady Juliet dost learn anon Vincent wouldst love such child and not Juliet's person. Lady Juliet tells us such be content with thus babe. All Lady Juliet wish be someone to love her. Juliet realizes one must love first and hence loves thus babe. Lady Juliet tells us such be all our lady really want and desire."

"Thee dost believe thus?" Lady Rosamund queried skeptically.

"In troth we trow thus," Leticia stated firmly. "We love Lady Juliet for loving our husband's bastard. This be true Christian love."

"We still trust the lady naught," Lady Rosamund said petulantly. "Thee be far greater woman for us."

Leticia gave Lady Rosamund a small smile. She was about to reply when they both turned to see Lady Mildred running toward them and calling frantically.

Leticia stopped and waited until Mildred caught up to them.

Breathlessly Mildred uttered, "Our Lady Juliet hath begun travail of delivery."

Leticia did not ask why Mildred came to her. Instead she began retracing her steps back to the keep as fast as she could carrying her own large burden. "Hast thee sent for our midwife?"

"Yea," Mildred replied still breathless. She was finding it hard to keep up with the two women because of her own run to find them. "We sent for physician and midwife."

"How long hath thy lady travailed in pains?" Lady Rosamund asked.

"In troth, thus pains began last eve," Mildred answered. "Our Lady Juliet said naught to be concerned for they were naught too difficult."

"Whence dost our midwife say?" Leticia queried as they approached the stairs to the keep.

"Our Lady sent us to find thee anon whence the midwife came into the chambers," Mildred answered. She maintained her speed only by adrenaline. She was exhausted. It had taken her some time and plenty of running to finally locate the Lady Leticia as Lady Juliet had requested of her.

Once in the keep they were up the castle stairs and in the hallway outside Lady Juliet's chambers. Lady Organa was there and Leticia handed her Mystic. "Take Mystic to our chamber," Leticia ordered. Once she had passed the cat to Organa, Leticia opened the door to the chambers. She was met with Juliet's whimpers of pain. Leticia moved quickly to Lady Juliet's side and held her hand. "We be near for thee."

Juliet's sweaty face and tear filled eyes answered a grateful thank you. Juliet squeezed Leticia's hand until it was white as another contraction lasted a full minute.

Rosamund sat on the other side of Juliet and wiped her brow with a cool cloth. Even the skeptical Rosamund couldn't hold a grudge against a lady delivering a baby.

The labor continued on for several hours before the midwife took Lady Juliet to the birthing chair. Lady Mildred had finally caught her breath and had rested. She was prepared with the knife and string the old midwife had boiled. The old midwife had also readied a tub of hot water to clean the baby and sweet smelling rose oil to cover the newborn's fragile skin. Lady Juliet's lovingly prepared swaddling was also ready for the new arrival. A large shallow bowl had been placed under the birthing chair to collect the waters, blood, and placenta.

Finally, after coaxing from the midwife, the newborn entered into the world.

"Tis female child," the midwife said casually. She motioned Mildred to take the baby and wash it thoroughly. After assisting with the removal of the placenta and afterbirths, the midwife cleaned Lady Juliet.

Lady Juliet was more concerned over her crying baby. "Let us hold our daughter," Juliet pleaded continually throughout the midwife's cleaning.

Leticia marveled at the birth. She was amazed and thrilled with the little girl. Leticia assisted Juliet in dressing for bed instead of holding the newborn. Rosamund prepared a freshly sheeted pallet for Juliet and assisted Leticia in placing Juliet in bed and covering her.

In the meantime, the midwife covered the newborn with fresh sweet rose oil and wrapped the baby in swaddling.

It seemed like an eternity before Juliet held her daughter. She just stared at the life she had brought into the world and knew at that moment exactly what true love really meant. She loved her daughter.

"Look at thus red hair," Rosamund commented. Her husband Gaylord had confided in her of Vincent's doubts of parentage. When she saw the red hair she was convinced this little baby girl was not Vincent's child.

"Tis beautiful child," Leticia said to Juliet lovingly. As far as Leticia was concerned, parentage didn't matter at this moment. The world had just received a very pretty little girl that Vincent would take care of and love.

Juliet's finger wandered over the baby's face and stopped at the cheeks. "She's so beauteous." Juliet looked up at Leticia with wonder and sighed, "Tis love for us."

Leticia removed an errant lock of hair from Juliet's face and answered, "Yea, tis troth thee hath thy love. We be joyous for thee."

Juliet placed her hand on Leticia's hand and offered, "Thee wouldst give birth to our Lord's child anon and trow thus wonderment and blessed feeling."

"Wouldst thee allow us to hold thy daughter?" Leticia asked.

Juliet extended the arm she was using to hold her daughter allowing Leticia to hold her baby.

The newborn moved restlessly in Leticia's arms. The little pink face contorted and the mouth made funny little movements. Leticia giggled with marvel. "Hath thee thought of a name for thy daughter?"

"Yea, we wouldst name her Reine for our daughter doth rule our heart," Juliet replied happily. Her fingers gently stroked the curly red hair on Reine's little head.

"Welcome to our life, Reine," Leticia said softly to the newborn.

Little Reine opened her eyes and fixed upon Leticia.

Leticia was enthralled and kissed the baby's forehead. She gave her back to her mother. "Vincent wouldst be most pleased with thy labors," Leticia told Juliet. "We wouldst only hope we provide our husband with such beauteous gift."

"Humph," Rosamund remarked. She wondered just what Vincent would do when he saw the red headed baby. It was obvious to her Vincent was not the father.

Leticia shot an angry glare to Rosamund. She quickly returned to Juliet and spoke gently. "Allow thy Lady Mildred to take our Reine. Thee must be weary. Thee must rest. Sleep now, dear Juliet." After she spoke the words, Leticia tucked the large quilt around Juliet after she allowed Mildred to take the sleeping Reine.

When Leticia and Lady Rosamund left the rooms, Rosamund spoke her mind, "Why wouldst thee declare our Vincent be pleased with Reine. Tis obvious Vincent be naught father."

"Juliet said our Vincent be the father," Leticia corrected.

"Whence the lady say and whence be troth be in conflict," Rosamund argued.

"Our Vincent bid me swear oath to care for Juliet and babe. Our Vincent took responsibility as father and we wouldst abide by our lord's word," Leticia countered. She then took Rosamund's hand making her look at her in the eye. "Sweet Rosamund, if our Vincent care naught for Juliet and Reine, who wouldst? Our Lady Juliet hath nowhere to go but hence under our protection. Doth thee understand? We wouldst hear no more of it."

"Yea," Rosamund accepted. In truth she knew what Leticia said was right. Vincent had taken responsibility and Juliet had nowhere else to go. She also would abide by Vincent and Leticia's wishes. Rosamund still wondered about what Vincent would say and do when he saw little Reine's red hair.

The two women saw Lady Agnes walking up the stairs in a hurry. She was still wearing her traveling clothes and appeared to be in a great hurry.

Agnes saw Leticia and Rosamund above her on the stair landing. "We heard our lady doth travail in delivery. Tis troth?" Agnes shouted toward the two woman standing at the head of the stairwell.

Leticia placed her finger over lips for quiet and replied, "Yea, thy lady hath given birth to our beauteous daughter, Reine. Our Lady Juliet sleeps anon."

Agnes stopped in surprise. Leticia had referred to the child as *our beauteous daughter*. What had happened here in her sojourn? "We wouldst attend our lady."

"Nay," Leticia ordered firmly. "Wash thy journey from thee, rest, and attend thy lady whence thee be clean."

"Our lady must need us," Agnes replied.

"Thy lady hath needed thee for fortnight," Leticia scolded. "Whence Juliet allowed thee to visit thy family thy lady wouldst naught trow thee be gone fortnight."

"From such looks of thy travel mantel," Rosamund added. "Thy travel be farther hence from our village. We smell scent of great waters."

"We stayed near our coast with other family," Agnes excused. "Our lady dost give us approval for our family visit."

"Thy lady dost naught consider thee wouldst leave her fortnight!" Leticia exclaimed. "Our lord Vincent hath assigned thy lady another handmaiden, Lady Mildred."

"Our Lord Vincent be most kind to our lady," Agnes said humbly. "We wouldst wash our journey from us and thus assist Lady Mildred with our lady."

"And new daughter," Rosamund added.

Agnes hurried down the stairs to bathe in the communal servants privy.

"We wouldst lie down anon," Leticia said to Rosamund. "We be most exhausted."

"We wouldst assist thee," Rosamund replied. She was concerned Leticia might have over expended herself in assisting Juliet's childbirth. Leticia was so tiny and fragile and Vincent's baby seemed to overtake the tiny little body. Rosamund was afraid the baby might burst her little Leticia.

Leticia was finding it more and more difficult to go about a normal day. This particular day she was very tired. Rosamund helped Leticia remove her tunic. Wearing only her chemise, Leticia climbed into her bed. In moments she was asleep. Rosamund and Megan, who showed up a few moments before, covered her and left the room. Mystic immediately took his position next to Leticia. Curling into a ball upon the quilt, he purred next to his mistress and fell asleep.

Rosamund sought out her husband, Sir Gaylord. She found him outside near a battlement that was being reinforced. It was early evening.

"Goodwife," Gaylord greeted with a large smile. "We missed thee at our mid day meal."

"Lady Juliet hath given birth to daughter," Rosamund announced. "We and Leticia hath spent thus den with Juliet."

"Ah, we heard rumor as to delivery," Gaylord answered watching the workman. " Daughter eh?"

"Daughter with red hair!" Rosamund declared.

Gaylord raised an eyebrow and looked directly at Rosamund. "Tis troth, thus babe be naught seed of our Vincent."

"Yea," Rosamund answered. "Lady Leticia hath commanded us to speak naught of it. Our lady commands we honor Vincent's order to care for Juliet and thus babe. Our lady speaks of noble cause. *We wouldst protect Juliet and the babe for thus lady hath no place else to go.'*"

"Wouldst such be terrible thing to do?" Gaylord answered stroking Rosamund's cheek. "Whence the child be Vincent's seed or naught? Wouldst it be most difficult to provide the mother and kinder with warm hearth, food, and protection?"

"Nay," Rosamund answered taking her husband's hand and kissing it tenderly. "We wouldst trow where all this nobility and love first hath begun."

"Yea," Gaylord teased. "Forget thus naught!"

"We wouldst still worry for our Leticia," Rosamund continued. "Our Lady be so large for breeding. Vincent be tall and strong one, but thus babe seems so huge!"

"Yea, Leticia be large indeed," Gaylord agreed.

"Our Vincent returns in ten den," Rosamund stated. "We hope our Leticia be well for such return. We placed our lady in bed anon. Leticia be so tired. Dear heart, we worry greatly for our daughter."

"Wouldst we send for physician?" Gaylord suggested.

"Nay, our Leticia wouldst hear naught of it," Rosamund informed. "Our Leticia states firmly thus be well."

"Thee worries yet," Gaylord understood. "Yea, we worry with thee." Gaylord embraced his wife and walked toward the Great Hall. "Come let us eat our supper. Thee say our Leticia be asleep?"

Together they walked into the Great Hall. "Mayhap we wouldst send our Vincent message with courier. We wouldst ask Vincent to make attempt to return forthwith," Gaylord suggested seating his wife at the great table.

151

"Bless thee," Rosamund thanked. "Wouldst thee send parchment on the morrow?"

"For thee, we wouldst send parchment and courier thus eve," Gaylord answered slicing a bit of meat from his trencher for his Goodwife. "We be worried with thee."

Vincent sat in the captain's room aboard the ship. He had been slightly wounded in the shoulder and was recovering. A king's personal physician had accompanied the de Courtenay knights on their return to England and stayed with Vincent to tend his wound. Fortunately for Vincent, Sir Henry was a talented and capable physician. He had not wanted Leticia to worry for him. The next day they would arrive in London and he would rest there a day or two before returning with entourage to Okehampton.

The tour at Calais was a quiet one. They had only three skirmishes to deal with and the throne had been completely entrenched. He received his wound while protecting Sir Martin Bolin who had also been sent to Calais. The king was pleased with Bolin's change and running of the manor in Wales.

Bolin was very grateful to Vincent for saving his life. Vincent offered a quick visit to Okehampton to see what had been accomplished as a guide for Bolin's Welsh manor. King Edward had given the manor to Bolin for reward. Sir Martin Bolin was now a favored, titled, and landowning knight. Martin told no one, but he was looking forward to returning to England to take Juliet as his wife. He had waited to this time to prove his capability.

Maynard assisted his lord walk down the gangplank after the ship arrived in England. The De Redver courier waiting at the docks met Vincent. "My lord, a message from Okehampton sent by Sir Gaylord."

Vincent winced as he opened the sealed parchment. His arm wound was still painful. He read the message and his brow creased.

"My lord?" Maynard queried.

"We be off for Okehampton anon," Vincent stated.

"My lord, tis eventide," Maynard reminded.

Vincent looked at the dark smoke clouds and remarked to the courier, "Dost thee stay in London thus den?"

"Nay," the messenger responded quickly.

"Tis foul odor in such air," Vincent noticed.

"Yea, tis plague. Thus ravages city," the messenger acknowledged. "We learned thee wouldst return thus den upon arrival. We stayed with our Palfrey in livery near thus docks. We wouldst naught enter city, my lord."

"Whence be our king?" Vincent worried.

"Our King hath departed to Surrey," the messenger informed. "Tis too late for his three and ten daughter, Blanche. The lass died of plague, as well new son Thomas. Thus plague runs rampant my lord. Be warned my lord. Stay out of city."

The news dumbfounded Vincent. He remembered Blanche and adored the little girl. The death of the King's new son also caused him trouble. His dear Leticia was carrying his child and the missile told him his father was worried about Leticia's pregnancy. He wanted to take off immediately. There would be no real rest until he was by his wife's side. The missile also told him Juliet had been delivered of a female child. Now hearing London was covered with the plague that had just finished ravaging Europe. The plague had killed almost two thirds of the French population alone.

"We leave for Okehampton in thus morn," Vincent said testily. He fidgeted nervously. Thoughts of his Leticia ill worried him. His baby, his wife, could they have been touched by the plague. Is that what his father meant when he said he worried for Leticia and their baby. Was Juliet causing grief? His mind could not stop racing and imaging the worst of all possible situations. He didn't hear Prince Edward approach. The Black Prince had been on another ship that had just docked.

"We heard of plague. Our sister and brother hath been taken," Edward shared somberly. "Tis best we stay away from London city. On the morrow we wouldst journey to Surrey."

"Our Leticia wouldst need us anon," Vincent choked out. His mind was filled with horrors imagined. "We wouldst ride straightway to Okehampton. Wouldst thee follow us with our entourage and pavilions?"

"Yea," Edward promised. "We wouldst follow thee after we see to our father and mother, our King and Queen. We be most concerned for our parents, brothers and sisters."

"Bless thee," Vincent said embracing the Black Prince. Both of the men were concerned and understood the fear they felt for their families. "Tonight tis advised for us to stay with our Destriers in livery and away from London city."

# Chapter 20

Vincent was awake before the sun peeked over the horizon. He woke his squire Maynard and his friend, Lionel. The three would journey much faster on their mounts alone and not burdened by slower pavilion wagons. Maynard had pre-packed saddlebags of foodstuffs for the journey. When Vincent awakened him, Maynard quickly prepared the Palfrey with the saddlebags and saddled his Palfrey. Maynard was beginning to understand his lord and moods.

The worry etched on Vincent's brow warned Maynard that his lord would readily leave him behind if he did not hurry and keep up.

Vincent gave free rein to his Destrier. Both Lionel and Maynard were hard put to keep up. Lionel finally forced Vincent to slow down at a stream where their horses rested and drank water. In one day they had already arrived at Surrey Castle. Vincent had not eaten any meal during the day, or even stopped to drink. He only allowed that privilege to his Destrier.

"Thee are driving thy Destrier and friends to death like crazed man," Lionel chided when they entered the gates of Surrey Castle.

"Our Leticia," Vincent began to say but was cut short.

"Yea, and our Sara and Maynard's Organa. We be aware all of us. We fear all of us, for our family and loves. Killing our person and our mounts wouldst naught help any person," Lionel lectured. He suddenly held his head high and sniffed the air. "Tis sustenance! We wouldst eat food anon. Trow thus well my friend, we wouldst eat and naught take our mounts in thus darkness. Meet our king, conference with our king and we wouldst leave in first light. If thee wouldst dispute our words thee wouldst be in dire danger for thus growling of hunger in our belly."

King Edward met the three knights in the bailey. "Whence be thy entourage and pavilion?"

"We left them to follow with thy son, our Black Prince," Lionel replied. "We ride for Okehampton. Learning of thus plague we worry for our family."

"Yea, even our own house be in mourning for our kinder," King Edward responding showing his own emotion. "Our daughter Blanche and infant son, Thomas, be taken by plague. Our queen be most distressed and cries woefully each day. Prithee, be our son, Edward in good health?"

"Yea, thy son be in good health," Lionel answered. "He wouldst be hence in one or two den. He hath already heard of such loss of his kinder and worries for thee and his mother."

King Edward placed his hand unknowingly upon Vincent's wound and noticed his grimace. "Whence travails thee?"

"Our Vincent be wounded saving Sir Bolin," Lionel explained. "Thus wound still be healing. Our lord wouldst naught take time to recover."

"We wouldst be with our Leticia," Vincent stated. "We received message from our father who be concerned for our lady. Leticia be breeding our heir." Hearing about the death of the two children from King Edward's mouth frightened Vincent even more. The deaths and horror of the plague was even more frightening to Vincent's concern for Leticia. Vincent's mind raced with images of all possible disasters.

"We dost trow. Thus de Redvers messenger spent one night with us hoping to locate thee," King Edward shared while leading the men to the great hall. "Come eat, rest, and then continue your journey in first light. We understand thy need for thy urgency. We wouldst be lost soul without our Phillippa. Even today we be more concerned for our Phillippa's grief than our own."

Vincent understood all to well what the king said. Vincent didn't want to even think about not seeing Leticia again. He would be there. He would be by her side in just a few more days. The urgency in his mind returned full force. It was only his hunger and the night that prevented him from once again mounting his Destrier and riding toward Okehampton.

King Edward recognized the look of worry on his knight and comforted, "We wouldst trow wouldst anything happen to thy Leticia. We heard naught. Come in and eat and rest. Thy journey wouldst begin on the morrow."

Leticia missed supper the evening before and awoke to a growling stomach. Mystic nuzzled her as she attempted to get out of her bed. Fortunately Organa and Morgan had peeked in the room to see their lady trying to rise from bed. With help of her handmaidens and sister she was dressed and walking down the stairs for breakfast. Nearly starving, Leticia ate twice her normal portion of food. After breakfast she stopped in to check on Juliet.

Juliet had just finished feeding her new daughter when Leticia walked in. "Come in and visit with us," Juliet greeted cheerily. She picked up Reine and proudly showed her to Leticia as she spoke to her new daughter, "look see little Reine, tis our Lady of Okehampton come to visit you."

Mystic followed his mistress, Leticia, into the room.

"Tis not good to let animal in our chambers with newly born," Agnes complained loudly.

Mystic stopped and looked at the voice. He then continued on to sit near Leticia's feet giving the impression of ignoring the rude woman.

"Thy Mystic be thy shadow attached," Juliet commented lightheartedly. "Reine minds naught of thy shadow. See? Our Reine likes thy mewling."

"Tis troth," Leticia smiled as she took little Reine in her arms.

Agnes huffed out of the room and disappeared for several hours.

Several days later every movement seemed to be a discomfort to Leticia. She spent more time in her chambers. If there were something that needed to be discussed with Leticia, the steward, staff, or Sir Gaylord would have to come to her. Leticia's feet began to swell. It was painful for her to walk long distances and it was more and more difficult for her to climb and descend stairs. Morgan and Megan began picking up the details of running the castle that Leticia had instructed them. Lady Rosamund also helped with the duties of running the household and kept Leticia informed of all functions.

Lady Agnes noted Leticia's absence at the Great Hall, but she also noticed that Vincent de Courtenay was not present either. For several days Agnes noted Sir Gaylord and Lady Rosamund sat at the great table. Agnes knew Leticia was remaining in her chambers, but exactly where was the Lord and Knight Protector of the Castle? She finally asked Lady Juliet about the absences of the Lord de Courtenay. "Tis thus Lord of Okehampton about such manors for inspections?"

"Nay, Sir Vincent be about our throne's duty," Lady Juliet replied. Juliet was so enthralled with her new daughter she didn't really think about Lady Agnes' questions. It really would be no concern of a handmaiden if the Lord Knight Protector were not in the castle.

"The throne's duty?" Agnes pursued. "Dost thee mean building more battlements about such lesser manors?"

"Our lord be in Calais on our throne's duty," Juliet answered lifting a sleeping Reine into her arms. "Methinks we wouldst take our Reine out in thus garden on the morrow. We wouldst show our daughter thus beauty of our gardens."

"Calais?"

"Nay, our garden," Juliet replied confused as to Agnes' question.

"Thee tells us Sir Vincent be in Calais," Agnes insisted.

"Yea, tis Sir Vincent's duty tour," Juliet replied. "Tells us Lady Agnes, dost thee believe our little Reine wouldst love Okehampton garden?"

"Thy daughter wouldst love Okehampton garden," Agnes assuaged. She was plotting how to send the information of the missing lord to her brother. "Tis good for thee to leave these chambers for a small walk in such sun."

Juliet smiled at Agnes in agreement as she gently rocked her sleeping baby. "Come Reine, we wouldst visit our Lady Leticia. We be certain our Lady miss us and be lonely locked away in her rooms."

"My lady," Agnes addressed politely. "Wouldst thee be angered with us if we wouldst naught accompany thee on thy visit to Lady Leticia with Mildred? We wouldst have small errand to attend."

"Thee wouldst naught leave us again for fortnight?" Lady Juliet queried with concern. Juliet knew Leticia had been none to pleased at Agnes' last long sojourn.

"Nay, my lady," Agnes answered quickly. "We have small duty to attend outside our bailey in thus nearby shire. We wouldst be gone from thee only until sun set."

"See to such quickly," Juliet requested. Since Vincent had assigned Lady Mildred as her new handmaiden, she hadn't really missed Agnes at all. Juliet did know Vincent or Leticia would not appreciate an excessive absence of Agnes. Juliet was happy and content with her new baby girl. She did not want any strife of any sort.

"We wouldst leave anon," Agnes already had her plan for the day. She would inform her brother of the fortuitous situation at Okehampton Castle, and cover her purpose by buying a present for Reine. Agnes took her light travel mantel and ran to the livery to obtain a Palfrey for a quick ride into the shire. She would ask one of the lesser knights to accompany her. Agnes would then lead him to the local inn for a drink of mead. Agnes was proud of her quick thinking and was anxious to speak to her brother waiting for her in the shire.

Vincent grudgingly spent another night at an inn with his companions. They had ridden hard and long, but his wound once more started to bleed. A few of the physician's stitches had been pulled out and Lionel forced him to stop and have another physician repair the damage in a nearby shire. It also gave Lionel and Maynard a chance to eat a midday meal as well as rest. Vincent was a very unpleasant companion at the supper table. They had wasted half a day of travel to re-sew his wound. They were now forced to spend the night in the shire.

"We wouldst arrive at Okehampton in two den," Lionel said reassuringly to Vincent. "Thus be sooner wouldst we have brought entourage and pavilion."

"Yea, we wouldst be in Okehampton anon," Maynard supported.

Vincent grumbled and put a piece of bread in his mouth.

"Thy wound be repaired and thy Leticia wouldst see thee alive and well," Lionel chided. "Thy lady wouldst need thee alive and well, naught filled with malady and weak."

Vincent glared at his friends. He would not be comforted with their words. He was only concerned with being with Leticia. Two more days would be an eternity.


Lionel and Maynard were still hard put to keep up with Vincent. In the morning they left, Lionel had a piece of bread in his mouth as he mounted his Destrier. Maynard was still trying to finish putting on his boots when Vincent was already mounted and riding.

"Sir Vincent be crazed man," Lionel muttered under his breath. He stropped his Destrier in an effort to catch up to Vincent. Maynard too, muttered under his breath. They were all concerned about their family, but something seemed to drive Vincent even more.

Vincent's imagination had taken hold of his reason. To make matters worse? Vincent had always counted on his instincts in battle and this seemed to be no different. Vincent's finely hewn instincts told him there was trouble at Okehampton. He instinctively knew Leticia was in some danger and it wasn't only the message from his father. Underneath there was his gut instinct.


Leticia felt much stronger when she woke up on this morning. For the past several days she had felt weak and tired. This morning of energy was a wonderful change. Leticia asked herself if she felt better because Vincent would be coming home soon. "Yea, we feel better for our Vincent's return," she said aloud in the empty room.

Mystic mewed in agreement.

Leticia rolled from her bed. She used the washbowl to freshen herself. To her own surprise she efficiently dressed herself with a large tunic over her chemise. There would be no form fitted gowns on this day. Nor had there been any form fitted gowns for several months. The thought made Leticia laugh as she smoothed her tunic.

While brushing her hair Leticia walked to the un-shuttered window. She realized she had slept in late. The sun was already in mid sky. Funny, she didn't even feel hungry. She also wondered why Rosamund, Organa, or one of the twins hadn't woken her up.

Rosamund and Megan had checked in on Leticia several times in the morning, only to find her sleeping. They both had agreed to let Leticia sleep because she had been feeling so miserable this past month.

Finishing her hair by binding it with a ribbon and letting it flow down her back, Leticia left the room with an intention to visit Juliet and Reine. Then Leticia would find something to eat in the kitchens.

Rounding the hallway to Juliet's chambers Leticia heard male voices. She stopped short and listened. Not only were they strange male voices, the strange voices were speaking French.

Once Leticia recognized they were speaking French she concentrated on what they were saying.

"Jean wouldst bring our force on the morrow," Claude informed Jean's sister, the Lady Agnes.

"We wouldst open thus postern gate within three hours of thy attack. In that time we trow such forces be concentrating on your siege," Agnes told the Frenchmen. "We have sketched for our brother location of postern gate on thus parchment. Place thus sealed parchment in our brother's hand."

"Yea," Robert complied taking the parchment from Agnes. "We wouldst depart anon for Jean's camp. We be only few leagues from hence and wouldst lay siege on the morrow."

"Let us depart," Claude ordered standing to his full six-foot height. "Okehampton wouldst be in our hands on the morrow. Tis most fortuitous the Okehampton defending lord protector and knights be on throne's duty."

"The throne hath taken Calais. In retribution, we wouldst take Devon," Agnes snickered wickedly. Her positioning in the court of King Edward had proven its worth at last. She inwardly looked forward to becoming the mistress of Okehampton. In the short time she had encouraged Juliet to take the power of mistress in the de Courtenay's absence for Exeter, she had enjoyed her power and wealth immensely. It was a taste she savored and wished to obtain.

Leticia inhaled sharply. Whispering to herself she couldn't believe the words, "Traitors in Okehampton." Her large girth proved to bulky for her position. In an attempt to leave unnoticed and tell Sir Gaylord of the impending attack, Leticia bumped right into a table toppling a brass urn of flowers onto the floor. The clatter was deafening as it fell onto the floor and bounced several times.

Claude and Robert bolted from the room towards the noise. There had been no one near when Agnes had led them to Juliet's chambers. The two men had been hiding near the keep masquerading as tradesmen. Claude and Robert were waiting for Agnes to talk to them.

Agnes waited until Juliet had taken Reine out to the sunny spring gardens of the keep. Following her lady as a dutiful handmaiden she slipped away silently and located the two French spies. Taking them into the castle had been easy. She discussed repairing a door in Juliet's chamber. Once in the privacy of the chamber they discussed their plans. Agnes had been certain no one was about until they heard the clatter.

Robert was the first to grab Leticia. He held her tightly. Holding his prey firmly he chuckled menacingly, "Whence be thus?"

Agnes moved swiftly from the room to identify the intruder. Recognizing it was Lady Leticia, the mistress of Okehampton, a plan came to her mind immediately. Speaking in fluent French she spoke, "Tis Lady Leticia, our Lady of Okehampton." Agnes walked up to Leticia and addressed her, "Come! Come! Tell us troth. We trow thee speak French. We trow thee understand our words."

"Yea, we trow thy words," Leticia replied calmly contradicting her wildly beating heart. "We come to visit our Lady Juliet and little Reine. Whence be our lady?"

"Think thee thus lady heard our planning?" Claude asked quietly while approaching Leticia and scrutinizing her from head to toe.

"In troth, we believe our lady hath heard and trow our planning," Agnes answered.

"Thee hurt us," Leticia grimaced as Robert tightened his grip.

"Wouldst we kill thus lady?" Robert queried the group with a menacing tone.

"Foul cur! Mongrel! Wouldst thee turn into lady killer?" Claude reprimanded angrily. "We be noble knights of noble ideal and training. Nay, we wouldst harm thus lady naught." Claude looked at Agnes and questioned, "Trow thee hiding place to keep thus lady until our siege?"

"Yea. We trow of such secret place," Agnes replied. This would be the perfect time to reveal her plans for the Lady Leticia now they had found her listening. "We wouldst also keep our lady for ransom. Queen Phillippa be most interested and fond of Lady Leticia."

"Thus be most interesting," Claude pondered. He picked up Leticia's chin with his thumb and forefinger. "A beauteous face," Claude commented moving Leticia's face from one side to another. "We wouldst hope thy throne be naught in haste to ransom thee. We wouldst desire to use thus fine body whence thee drop thy burden."

As Claude dropped his kiss upon Leticia's lips she bit his lip.

Claude backed off and laughed wickedly. "A shrew to be tamed. Thee wouldst be a delightful challenge for us. We wouldst enjoy our times with thee."

There was no misunderstanding to his meaning and Agnes retorted quickly, "More like the Falcons she trains." Agnes was swept up in jealousy. "Watch thy body for thus scratches." Over several years of knowing Claude Monte Pierre, she had developed a fantasy for him. Agnes had even discussed the marriage of her and Claude with her brother when she had spent those weeks with Jean in France. Jean had agreed and would proclaim the marriage of Agnes with Claude. This proclamation would occur in conjunction with Jean winning Okehampton and naming Claude Monte Pierre, the new lord of Devon.

The very idea of her Claude using Leticia as a concubine was intolerable to the jealous Agnes. Of course she must wait for all to fall in place first. Claude had no idea, nor had been made aware of Agnes and Jean's plans for him. The important thing now was to get Leticia out of Claude's sight and safely hidden from everyone in the keep. "Bring the lady," Agnes ordered Robert. Carefully she walked ahead of the two men and their captive. She looked from side to side avoiding all encounters. Agnes eventually led them to an unused small chamber on the third floor of the keep's western tower. This tower overlooked the outside walls over the postern gate. A heavily forested glen was approximately a half-mile from the castle wall. Large rocky ledges rambled across the land prohibiting an easy access to the moat and tower.

Robert pushed Leticia into the room.

Leticia stumbled and nearly fell, but managed to steady herself and took a seat on the chair near the unused hearth. She and her mother had come to this room many times. In this room was the de Redvers secret. As a child, Leticia had played here many times. The room was usually used only as a spare chamber for guests when other rooms in the keep were in use. Leticia also realized this room would not be used in an attack. The room had only a small observation hole. The parapet above would be the one actually used in battle.

Agnes believed she had selected a perfect temporary prison for the Lady of Okehampton. She walked from the room taking Claude's arm and ordering the two men, "Leave quickly and bring our brother. Tis naught simple to keep such lady hidden for long."

Both men agreed with Agnes. "Yea, we depart anon."

The noise of the bolt being dropped into place startled Leticia. She was alone and in the dark. Only a small light from the observation hole gave her any light. A small smile crossed Leticia's face. Agnes didn't know the de Redvers secret.

# Chapter 21

Leticia knew this tower room wouldn't be used in the coming attack. The natural environment protected Okehampton Castle on the western wall.

Leticia jumped when she heard the thud of the bolt being secured. She listened for footsteps to fade away. She was suddenly aware of a purring sound near her feet.

"Mystic!" Leticia cried as she seated herself on a bench near the hearth. Mystic jumped onto Leticia's lap, or at least what was left of it.

Leticia felt a strong band of tightening around her abdomen. When she woke she had been aware of weak bands, but this hurt. "Sweet Jesu!" Leticia cried. "Vincent, we need thee." She knew the bands meant she would deliver Vincent's child. "Mystic, we be alone and our lord's child desires to be born. We wouldst naught stay in thus chamber. Wouldst thee be our companion as we traverse such passage to freedom from our prison."

Mystic mewed sympathetically. "Let us begin," Leticia said with resolve. Leticia walked to the hearth. It was clean. No one had used this chamber room for several years. It was used only when there was a guest overflow in the castle.

Agnes thought she had provided the perfect prison. She hurried down the stairs and led the two men through the halls until she had them safely outside the keep. "Hurry to Jean," Agnes commanded. The two men went to the livery to get their horses and leave the keep.

Agnes didn't know the de Redvers family had recognized this special protected side of Okehampton a long time ago. They had used this room as their secret escape route in case of the castle losing a siege. If the postern gate would be breached, the family would see it and flee to the safety of the wooded glen.

At the hearth Leticia reached under the fireplace mantle to feel for the latch that would open the secret hearth panel. Somehow as a child this had always been a lot simpler. Finally she found it and yanked it down with all the force she had.

A scraping on the stone floor was heard. She looked at the hearth and saw the opening. It was only a crack opening. Leticia remembered as a child how she pulled the panel open. "Thus opening looks much smaller," Leticia said with levity to her cat. "Methinks thus opening dost become smaller."

Mystic mewed.

Leticia's burden became quite awkward when she went on her knees and crawled closer to the opening on the stone floor. With all her might she pulled at the panel and moved a few more inches.

Mystic walked into the passage encouraging Leticia to follow him. Mystic sensed this was very important. He knew his lady was in trouble and this was a path for escape. He peeked out back at her and mewed for her to follow.

Leticia took in a deep breath and pulled the stone panel once more. This time the stone panel opened as far as it would go. It looked so small now compared to when she was a child. To make the matter worse, she was now a grown woman. She was very pregnant. "We must!" Leticia said to herself in encouragement.

Putting her legs in first she immediately felt the cool dampness of the passage. Slowly she wiggled through the hole. Halfway she found she was wedged tight. It was then another band tightened around her. "Nooo!" Leticia didn't move for several moments until the banding ceased and then wondered what she could do to get the rest of her body into the passage.

Mystic continued mewing in support.

"We be coming," Leticia answered her mewing cat. "We trow naught how we dost thus, but we be coming." Leticia moved side to side until she was in a little further. Her hands grabbed on to the top of opening and pushed her body through. Sliding onto the damp floor sent shivers up Leticia's body. Leticia carefully rolled to her knees and turning back to the chamber took several minutes to close the open panel. In case Agnes returned, Leticia did not want her or her Frenchmen to find her secret escape route. "We be hence, Mystic." She stood up in the passage and saw the darkness before her. Leticia stretched arching her back in a bow and placing a hand on the small of her back. Mystic became her strength and her hope as well as her means of communicating her emotions. "Mystic tis dark and hence naught be any flint to light thus torch. We must traverse thus dark halls together. Thee must help us to see."

Taking a small step toward the stair Leticia slipped on the slippery damp fungus floor. Leticia braced herself on the wall. "Mystic, we wouldst be most careful and walk slowly. There be three stairwells and then the locked gate. All be slippery and dangerous."

Mystic ran up and down the stairs mewing for Leticia to begin. Slowly Leticia edged to the first step. The pungent stale air made her nauseous. She took one step carefully putting one foot and then bringing the other next to it. Leticia managed to get halfway down the first step when another band stopped her. She had to sit until the pain ceased. A few minutes later she stood to try again. With her hand against the wall she felt something sticky. The sticky mass wrapped around her fingers and she felt eight tiny legs walking upon her hand. "Our Lord Vincent wouldst faint," Leticia laughed with forced humor. "Sir Vincent be terrified of arachnids." She had to grab on to something to keep her mind from her own dire situation and fears.

It took a quarter of an hour to get down the one flight of steps and now she sat in the pitch-black darkness of the landing for the next stairwell. Leticia allowed herself several tears. Mystic purred at her feet.

Carefully stepping on the next flight of stairs Leticia heard scratching of long nails on the floor in front of her. She heard Mystic hiss and spit and begin chasing the creature before her. "Mystic? Hath thee found mouse or rat? Good boy!" A tightening band gripped her again. "Sweet Jesu!"

As Leticia was making her way down the second stairwell Vincent, Lionel, and Maynard entered the bailey of Okehampton. Disregarding any pedestrians, Vincent galloped his Destrier right to the keep and leaped from his saddle landing with a thud. Taking the stone steps two at a time he craned his head toward his companions that had followed him and shouted, "Maynard, take our steed to livery." Vincent ran into the keep and first looked into the great hall. He saw only normal kitchen servants. Moving quickly up the stairs he came upon Lady Rosamund mounting them to check on Leticia. "Whence be our Goodwife?" Vincent bellowed.

"Vincent!" Rosamund shrieked in surprise.

"Whence be our Goodwife?" Vincent repeated anxiously.

164

"We wouldst be on our way to look in on our lady," Rosamund replied. "Our lady naught be well these past den. We hath let our lady sleep."

"Hath thus plague visited our land?" Vincent asked in fear for Leticia.

"Plague?" Rosamund choked. "Nay!"

Vincent didn't respond. He bounded up the stairwell toward the solar. Reaching the door he noticed it was open. If his wife had been sleeping the door would have been kept closed. He burst into the solar and looked at the bed. It was empty. He scanned the room with a keen eye. He didn't see Leticia. Vincent walked to the privy and opened the door. The privy was empty also. "Leticia?" Vincent uttered uselessly.

Rosamund entered the empty room, as Vincent was about to go down the stairs in search of his wife.

Vincent stood erect and accused angrily, "Thee told us our Leticia be in thus solar sleeping! Our Leticia be naught hence! Thee wouldst naught be caring for our lady as thee gave oath!"

Rosamund stood dumbfounded. "Our lady be naught in thy solar? We wouldst let our lady sleep!"

"Whence be our Leticia!" Vincent roared in hostility. He was scared and felt dread right down to his bones. The uncanny sense of dread he felt when he first received his father's missile had just been compounded a hundred fold.

"We trow naught," Rosamund babbled in a fear from the sense of fear she felt in Vincent. Thinking quickly she replied, "Mayhap our lady dost visit Lady Juliet and Reine."

Vincent didn't even hear the second name. He stormed out of the solar and stomped toward Juliet's room.

Vincent burst in upon Juliet's room with a thud of the door slamming against the wall. "Our Lady Leticia?" Vincent shouted. He looked around the room searching for his wife. His concentration was broken by the wail of a newborn.

Juliet who had been in shock at Vincent's entrance now ran to the cradle of her baby. Reine had been sleeping and the noise and roar of Vincent's strange angry voice woke her. The voice scared Reine. She began crying loudly.

Vincent stood still and focused on the cradle and the crying moving object in it.

"Mongrel Cur!" Juliet cursed. "Thee hath frightened our Reine."

Agnes walked into the room behind Vincent and was surprised to see the Lord of Okehampton standing before her. This was not a good omen for her brother's plans. Vincent de Courtney was well known for his battle prowess.

Juliet kneeled at the cradle and lifted her daughter. She held Reine stroking her little back and spoke to her soothingly, "Tis fine, cry naught our little darling. Thy mother be hence and holding thee. Thy mother loves thee."

Vincent peered over Juliet's shoulder. "Thee hath delivered?"

"Yea," Juliet answered brushing her cheek along Reine's soft cheek. "We hath delivered our beauteous daughter, Reine."

Speaking more softly Vincent agreed, "Thy daughter be beauteous. Hath Leticia delivered?"

Juliet looked at Vincent strangely and queried, "Thee wouldst trow thy wife still be breeding. Surely thee trow thus before thee came into our chamber."

"Whence be our Leticia?" Vincent asked quietly but with great worry.

"We wouldst naught see Leticia thus den," Juliet responded. "We wouldst be with our daughter in Okehampton garden thus morn and in our chambers for rest. Tis troth our lady doth visit us every den. Thus den we hath naught seen our lady."

Rosamund came into the room pushing Agnes aside. "Juliet, hath thee seen our Leticia?"

Juliet was worried now. "Nay! Tell us our Leticia be naught lost?"

Agnes choked hard. Vincent had returned unexpectedly. Everyone was realizing Leticia was missing. Certainly Vincent would tear this castle apart until he found her. How long would she have before he located her in the tower room? "Mayhap Lady Leticia hath gone into Okehampton gardens looking for thee," Agnes offered.

"Rosamund, tell our father to search thus keep," Vincent ordered. "We wouldst be about our garden." Vincent left the room as quickly as he entered it.

"We wouldst take our Reine and look for our lady," Juliet volunteered.

"Nay," Rosamund disagreed. "Tis soon time for feeding. Stay in thy room and take care of Reine. We be certain Lady Leticia wouldst wish it."

"We wouldst assist thee," Agnes volunteered. She thought she would tell them she would search the western towers and thereby not find Leticia in the tower room. "Lady Mildred wouldst stay with thee, Lady Juliet." Agnes did not wait for approval but left the room quickly. *What wouldst we do?* Agnes thought. *Our brother trow naught of thus lord protector's return.* She hurried down the hall and went to the western tower. She spoke to all servants letting them know the Lady Leticia was missing and she would be searching the west towers.

Leticia made it down the third stairwell. She had to stop several more times. The banding was growing with intensity and duration. She was becoming more and more frightened. She couldn't go any faster. The deeper she went into the castle walls, the more damp and slippery the stairs had become. Moving about in the narrow staircases with slippery stairs was difficult enough. Leticia starting labor slowed her down even more. She had to stop and carefully sit down with every contraction. It had taken her nearly two hours to reach the last stair well. Leticia blindly wiped the tears from her cheeks and leaned against a wall. "Vincent!"

Vincent stopped dead in his tracks as he rounded the Great Hall. It was as if he heard Leticia calling him. He swore he heard her crying. She needed him. He knew his Leticia was in great peril. Standing still for several minutes he hoped he would hear her voice once more and then find her. Vincent waited a few more moments. He heard nothing. Vincent left for the Great Hall and the gardens. He would find her if he had to bring in the dogs.

It took nearly another half hour to find the locked gate leading to the underground passage that led to the wooded glen. For fifteen more minutes Leticia fumbled in the darkness trying to find the keys that would unlock the gate. "Mystic, thus be much simpler as kinder and with torch light."

Mystic wound around Leticia's leg as reassurance he was still close to her and listening.

Leticia sat down for ten minutes for the next contraction. It was exceptionally painful and she needed time to rest. Once more she stood and fumbled for the keys. Leticia had forgotten that the keys were a stretch reach as a child, not as a grown woman. After another half hour of trying to find the keys she slid her hand down the wall in exasperation. Her hand slid over the peg and the keys. "Mystic, we forget we be much taller," Leticia began to laugh almost hysterically. Continuing to fumble in the dark Leticia found the lock and placed the key inside of it. The key had to pushed into the rusted lock. Finally Leticia heard the click. She felt spider webs and other tiny little crusted forms of life about her. Leticia heard Mystic hissing and spitting again. "Vincent! Prithee, we wouldst naught go on!" Leticia sobbed leaning against the wall and enduring another labor contraction.

Mystic returned mewing his arrival so not to frighten his mistress. He mewed loudly and walked down the passage. He returned again and again trying to tell Leticia she couldn't stay here.

Vincent combed the castle gardens. He couldn't find Leticia anywhere and no one had seen her. It was mid afternoon and no one had seen her. No one. Returning to the castle he found his father.

"Nay," Gaylord responded worriedly. "We hath naught found trace of our Leticia. Tis almost magic."

"Nay, naught magic," Vincent answered in terror. "We believe our Goodwife hath been taken. Tis some foul deed. We trow thus."

"Whence person wouldst come into Okehampton during thus light of den and take away our lady unseen?" Gaylord countered in logic. In his heart he really believed his son was right.

"We trow naught!" Vincent shouted. "We trow our Goodwife be danger."

"We hath searched the entire castle," Gaylord informed. "Naught a soul hath seen Lady Leticia since morning. If our Leticia be taken, how wouldst our lady be removed from Okehampton?"

"We must find our Leticia!" Vincent shouted slamming his fist against a wall. "We wouldst bring the dogs. Organa, fetch one of our lady's gowns. Maynard bring the dogs and hound master."

"Vincent," Gaylord pleaded. "Calm thyself. We all fear for Leticia. Thee trow in any action tis best to retain a calm head. Come inside and have drink of wine."

Reluctantly Vincent acquiesced. He fidgeted as he drank the wine and waited for the dogs to be brought into the Great Hall.

Leticia walked gingerly behind the soft sounds of her mewing, Mystic. The stone floor of the passage way was even more slippery than the stairs. Her contractions were coming every few minutes. It was late into the afternoon when she came to the wooden plank that covered the stone stairs leading to freedom into fresh air and light. Resting for several minutes after another contraction, Leticia climbed the stone steps and using her back tried to push open the sod covered plank. It was heavy. The plank was heavier than she remembered as a child. Leticia whimpered as she saw daylight and smelled the fresh sweet air of the forest. Leticia couldn't lift the plank anymore. She was exhausted.

Suddenly a confused male face appeared before her as he lifted and pushed the plank aside. "Be thee witch?"

Leticia cried in relief, "Nay, we be Lady Leticia de Courtenay of Okehampton. We be in great danger of French siege."

The man assisted Leticia from the passage. A muddy cat followed her.

"We wouldst trow thy name kind Sirrah?" Leticia queried.

"Turold, my lady," The strong muscled man answered. "We be Devon shire's woodcutter." Once Leticia stood he saw she was extremely pregnant.

Leticia bent over as another contraction slammed her.

"My lady," Turold asked nervously. "Whence travails thee." He was a father of three children and knew Leticia was in labor.

"Tis appear thus Lord de Courtenay's child desires to be born," Leticia said in short broken words between the pains of her body.

"We wouldst take thee to our Goodwife, Clarice," Turold offered picking Leticia up in his arms and carrying her to a small house nearly hidden by all the trees. "Tis appear thee hath little time before thy delivery."

"Nay, we need to return to Okehampton Castle," Leticia objected. "We must speak to Sir Gaylord de Courtenay. There be traitor in Okehampton castle. Thus French wouldst arrive in siege on the morrow. We all be in danger!"

Turold replied walking faster to his house. "Tis thy danger anon." Nearing the house Turold spotted his wife outside washing clothes in the stream. "Clarice! We wouldst need thy aide!"

The woman turned placing her hand upon her breast in surprise. Her husband was carrying a dirty pregnant woman. The tone of Turold's voice warned her something was amiss. "Bring thus lady into our dwelling!" Clarice called back. Taking her youngest son's hand she returned to their cottage.

Once Turold had placed Leticia on their rough bed pallet, Clarice saw the reason for her husband's concern for the lady. It was obvious the woman was in term and ready for delivery.

Leticia drew short and steady breaths during a long and hard contraction. "Prithee, we need thee to warn our father of impending siege. The French be coming to take Okehampton. Wouldst thee help us traverse to Okehampton?" Leticia begged trying to rise.

"Nay my lady," Clarice countered gently. "Our God hath determined thee must give birth to his child. Thee wouldst naught go to Okehampton during thy travail."

"We must warn…" Leticia's plea was broken by a long and hard labor contraction.

"Thee wouldst first be cleaned," Clarice ordered. "Thee wouldst naught give birth to healthy child in thy present state." Clarice turned to her husband and ordered him, "Hasten to thus river and bring us clean water to boil. We wouldst clean our lady. Make Haste! We share little time." Clarice then went to her small chest and pulled out a clean chemise for Leticia. Fortunately for Leticia, Clarice was a pudgy woman and there was enough room in the clean chemise for Leticia's larger girth.

Turold took their two oldest children with four buckets. They filled them with water and then poured two of the buckets into a large pot over the fire in the hearth. Soon the water began to boil. Clarice took a large ladle and added the boiling water to a bucket of cold water. She then took a clean woven homespun cotton cloth and dipped it into the warmed water bucket. Clarice looked at her husband and ordered him to leave the cottage, "Out with thee. This be our work!" Hurrying to Leticia, Clarice removed the filthy tunic and chemise. Clarice had already removed Leticia's hose and shoes.

Leticia received a warm and wonderful feeling sponge bath from Clarice. Every part of Leticia was thoroughly cleaned from head to foot. Leticia cooed between a contraction, "God bless thee dear lady. We be grateful to thee for thy kindness."

"Dost thee hath name?" Clarice asked while putting the clean chemise on Leticia.

"We be Leticia de Courtenay of Okehampton," Leticia replied reveling in the fresh clean scent of the chemise.

Clarice gasped, "Thou art Lady of Okehampton. Thee be our Liege? Whence caused thus travail for so high a lady?"

# Chapter 22

"Thus be our reason for returning anon to Okehampton," Leticia sighed in exasperation. "Our person learned of upcoming siege. We be taken as prisoner and held for ransom. We escaped." Leticia then remembered Mystic and called for him, "Mystic. Dear Mystic."

A gray muddy fur ball crawled out from under the bed and mewed.

"Whence be thus?" Clarice queried stepping back from the dirty cat.

"Tis our cherished pet, Mystic," Leticia introduced noticing another band surrounding her abdomen. She laid back on the bed and whimpered, "Without our Mystic, we wouldst naught escape our prison."

"Mayhap as we wait for thy birthing, we wouldst clean thy pet," Clarice chuckled. "Thy mewling be as much a muddy mess as our lady."

"Prithee Clarice," Leticia pleaded. "We must send word to Okehampton. Wouldst thy good husband, Turold go warn Okehampton for us? Even we naught be safe in thy cottage during French siege."

"Yea," Clarice soothed the anxious Leticia. Clarice went to the door and called her husband into the cottage.

Leticia breathed out short words during another long contraction, "Kind Sirrah, make haste to Okehampton. Thee must find our father, Sir Gaylord de Courtenay. Tell him thus French plan siege on the morrow. Tell him whence we be. Prithee!"

"My lady, de Courtenay be thus Lord High Protector. Thee wouldst naught be about. Whence wouldst such person as de Courtney listen to our words? Yea, even admit our lowly person to thus keep," Turold complained. In fact it would be difficult for a serf to enter the keep of Okehampton. "Wouldst such high lord believe thee be in our dwelling in birthing? Wouldst naught high lord believe we hath taken thee? Wouldst.."

"Enough!" Leticia raised her hand in protest. "We wouldst naught ask thee allowing only for our current providence. Take our pet, Mystic. Place our pet in thy sack and carry Mystic to Sir Gaylord de Courtenay. Our pet be recognized. All about trow our pet wouldst naught leave our side unless we be in great peril."

"Yea my lady," Turold conceded. Bowing his head he asked, "Whence wouldst our lady command us to say to Sir Gaylord de Courtenay if our head remains still upon our shoulders?"

"Sir Gaylord be noble man," Leticia assuaged. "Thy head be safe. Tell our lord a traitor be in midst of Okehampton. Quietly prepare for French siege on the morrow. Trust no one save our de Redvers and de Courtenay knights. Tell our lord we be busy in birthing at thy cottage for reason of our escape and thee finding us."

Mystic had allowed Clarice to wipe off most of the mud with a cloth and he allowed Turold to place him in a sack.

Turold than placed the sack upon his back. He set out for the mile walk to Okehampton Castle.

"Make haste kind Sirrah!" Leticia called out after Turold. "Make haste! We naught hath much time."

Vincent was beside himself with worry. He had been told the entire castle, towers, and bailey had been searched with no sign of Leticia. Maynard had brought the dogs and the huntsman. Vincent allowed the dogs to sniff a gown of Leticia's. The hounds were trained for the hunt by scenting their prey. The dogs had proved to be just as worthless in finding Leticia. Even with her scent from the gown, when the dogs were let loose in the bailey they found no trail.

Sir Gaylord was worried as much as Vincent. The entire castle was tense with fear. How could the Lady of Okehampton disappear into thin air? Many whispered it was evil and black magic.

"Truly thus devils about wouldst take such goodness," several servants whispered in agreement.

"By God's teeth," Vincent cursed angrily. "Whence trickery or deceit we find in thus castle we wouldst remove such heads with our sword blade."

"Mayhap we wouldst query all in thus keep," Sir Gaylord suggested. "Mayhap threat of thy anger wouldst frighten person to reveal troth."

"So be it!" Vincent roared. He stomped to the Great Hall. "Bring everyone to our Great Hall! All knights, squires, pages, ladies, servants, all in thus keep wouldst appear before us at vespers!"

The servants and Maynard trembled at Vincent's wrath. No one had ever seen their lord this enraged before. They quickly hurried to bring all the staff together including Megan, Morgan, Juliet, Reine, and Agnes.

Vincent sat at the high table. His face was set with rage. His skin tone was crimson. One by one he began interrogating every servant and member of the house.

Turold entered the Great Hall meekly. Once the guard at the gate recognized Mystic he allowed Turold entrance as Leticia's messenger. The guard personally walked with Turold into the Great Hall.

Durand Alwins, Okehampton steward, stopped Turold, "Whence be thy purpose?"

"We come for Sir Gaylord de Courtenay," Turold announced bravely. "We hath message from Lady Leticia."

Alwins gasped. He couldn't imagine what message a lowly woodcutter would carry from the Lady Leticia.

"Tis troth," Turold said boldly. He opened the sack holding Mystic.

Mystic peeked out and meowed.

"Tis troth. Our Lady sent with us her pet as seal," Turold stated calmly. He was no longer afraid of consequences. The guard had chased away all his fears when he showed him Mystic. Lady Leticia had been right. Everyone about Okehampton that knew Lady Leticia knew her pet Mystic.

"Come with us anon," Durand Alwins ordered pushing through the crowded Great Hall. In so doing he created turmoil.

Vincent looked up from his interrogation and spotted Mystic peeking from a sack on the woodcutter's shoulder. "By God's teeth!" he roared. Jumping from the bench onto the high table and leaping onto the floor he pushed aside any body in his way until he reached the woodcutter. Picking the man off the floor by his tunic Vincent growled, "Whence be my lady? Speak or we wouldst separate thy tongue from thy head!"

Turold took a mystical bravado that came from no where and he whispered to Vincent, "Our Lady sends me to Sir Gaylord de Courtenay with message and her Mystic. We must speak to Sir Gaylord her father. Art thee Sir Gaylord?"

172

Vincent placed him on the floor still holding his tunic. He motioned for his father.

In a moment Sir Gaylord was by Vincent's side. He too had recognized Mystic.

"Our woodcutter speaks only to thee, father," Vincent said. He turned to the woodcutter. "Tis our father, Sir Gaylord de Courtenay. Give us thy message."

Turold whispered once more, "Our lady commanded us to speak in privacy."

Vincent nodded and led his father and the woodcutter to the keep chapel. Once the three were in the chapel, Vincent shut the door and bolted it.

Turold looked warily at Vincent and then addressed Gaylord, "Wouldst thee trust thy knight, Sir Gaylord de Courtenay?"

The tenseness of the situation made Gaylord burst out laughing, "Sirrah, thus knight be Lord of Okehampton, Sir Vincent de Courtenay. Sir Vincent wouldst be Lady Leticia's Lord husband."

"We be told thee were about Calais on our throne's duty and naught scheduled for return for many den," Turold replied skeptically.

"We came back for our Goodwife and our worry for her," Vincent replied hotly. "Whence be our lady?"

"Firstly, our Lady desires us to warn thee of traitor at Okehampton," Turold began. "Our lady also warns thee of French siege on the morrow."

"Whence be our lady?" Vincent loudly insisted. "Wouldst thy words be troth, whence be our lady? Hence be thee to trow of all thus?"

"Thy lady be in our cottage inside thy forest. Thy lady be delivering thy child. Thus be reason our lady be naught hence to tell thee," Turold said quickly.

Vincent's face turned white. Suddenly everything the woodcutter told him became clear. His wife was having their baby and she sent word to warn them of an impending French Attack. "Tell us all thee trow!"

Turold complied, "We be in our forest gathering old fallen branches for fire start when we saw thus ground near us move. We heard whimper of lady under thus ground and see her face. With haste we lifted such ground to see such was opening to passage. We pulled thy lady to find thy lady be in birthing travail. We bring thy lady to our cottage for care by our Goodwife, Clarice. Thy lady insists we make thee trow of thy lady's imprisonment and escape from traitor in thy castle. Thy lady insist thee be warned of French siege on the morrow. Thy lady tells us we wouldst be safe whence we bring Mystic."

"Father, prepare our Okehampton for attack anon. Be prudent and careful in thy methods. We wouldst need to find thus traitor. Close our gates! Naught person be allowed exit or entry save us," Vincent ordered. "We wouldst accompany thus woodcutter to cottage for our Leticia anon." Vincent believed the woodcutter immediately. The story was too unbelievable to be made up by any serf valuing their head.

Turold straightened his back in pride. He had accomplished all requests and revealed the dangers to the Lord of Okehampton. He would soon take the high lord to his wife. The best part of all of this was he hadn't lost his head in the process.

"Dost thee hath name?" Vincent questioned Turold while leading him out of the chapel.

"We be Turold."

"We be most grateful to thee, Turold," Vincent replied. "Whence it be far to thy cottage?"

"Tis only in thus woods on west side of Okehampton," Turold informed.

Durand Alwins had dismissed all of the servants and household when Vincent took the woodcutter in the chapel with Sir Gaylord. Agnes remained in the Great Hall as the kitchen servants prepared food for supper meal. She watched as Vincent and the man left the chapel. Her heart was racing. She thought she would be taken any moment if the man truly did know where Leticia was. Agnes inhaled quickly after holding her breath. Sir Vincent and the woodcutter left. No one took her. Perhaps the woodcutter had found Mystic wandering around and they thought Leticia might be near. *The fools*. Agnes smiled knowing her plans were still safe. She stayed in the Great Hall for the coming meal.

Agnes had no idea Mystic had been locked away with Leticia.

Sir Gaylord slipped away unnoticed by any save his wife Rosamund. She hunted him down to find out the news. Together they prepared the castle for siege with trusted servants and knights.

Vincent took Turold to the livery. He also brought Sir Lionel with him. They mounted their Destriers and Turold was given a Palfrey.

Leticia was sitting on the artistically hewn birthing chair built by Turold. "Ahhhh," Leticia screamed as she bore down and pushed.

"Thus be full of wonder my lady," Clarice encouraged. "We see head of thy child. Bear down once more and thy child will enter our world."

With all her might Leticia pushed and screamed, "Arghhhh!" She felt the head and shoulders forced from her body.

Clarice took the dark haired babe and placed it in a soft woven piece of material of swaddling she had used for her own children. "Tis male child!" Clarice announced. "While we wait for afters, we wouldst clean thy son."

Leticia panted heavily. A son! She had secretly wanted a daughter, but Vincent ordered her to have a son. She was certain Vincent would be pleased. It really didn't matter if it were a boy or girl. Leticia promised herself she would love their child.

Clarice washed the newly born child in the warm water her two older children had prepared. Just as Clarice placed the protesting infant on the pallet they heard the thundering of horses hooves outside. "Turold brings thy Lord. We wouldst clean thee."

The door suddenly opened wide with a thud.

Leticia looked and couldn't believe her eyes. It was Vincent in the doorway.

Vincent straightened to his full height after bending to enter the doorway, Vincent looked around the cottage. He saw his Leticia sitting on a chair and her legs were bloodied. Vincent almost fainted until he heard the squalling of a newly born child.

Lionel saw Leticia and pushed Maynard out of the cottage. The two would remain outside until they were told they could re-enter. Lionel realized immediately Leticia's need for privacy.

Leticia tried to speak, but a hard band and an urgency to push once more stopped her.

"My lady," Clarice uttered with concern. "Thy afters! Thee hast naught expelled thy afters."

"We still be in travail," Leticia whispered in exhaustion.

Clarice raised an eyebrow and muttered a mild oath, "By my honor!"

Vincent raced to Leticia's side. He covered her face with soft kisses. His arms attempted to embrace her.

"Arghhhhh!" Leticia spewed out angrily as the pains urged her to push once more. She pushed away Vincent's arms and screamed. "We be a bit occupied my lord!"

"Bear down my lady," Clarice chuckled. "We wouldst naught be finished in thy delivery."

"Whence be happening?" Leticia screamed as she bore down with all the strength she had left.

Vincent stood back at his wife's admonitions and watched in amazement as a baby emerged from his wife. Vincent had witnessed the birthing of animal stock, but never a human birth. This was also the birth of his child.

"Tis another male," Clarice announced to Leticia. Clarice took the baby in her apron and walked toward the hearth to clean this boy.

Leticia bowed her head and wiped her brow of perspiration. A small need to push released the placenta into the basin under her chair. She was worn out.

Vincent knelt next to her and kissed her hand, "Leticia, my love and heart, be thee well?"

Leticia turned to look into her husband's worried eyes. Weak from childbirth she took her hand to his cheek, "Be thee our Vincent and naught vision?"

"My conqueror. My heart. Tis thy Vincent," he answered tenderly. His heart was swelling with love. Vincent stayed by Leticia's side and embraced her in his arms. He held her tightly for several minutes not even being aware of the two crying infants nearby. There would be time for that later. Right now he needed to hold his Leticia in his arms.

"Get thee hither," Clarice's voice ordered into Vincent's mists. "We wouldst care for thy Lady. Go look after thy sons."

"Sons?" Vincent queried. It hadn't occurred to him there were two screaming babies on the bed pallet.

"Yea," Clarice laughed pointing to the bed. "Thy sons lie on yonder pallet. Mayhap thee wouldst tend to them as we tend to thy lady." Clarice began washing the blood and afterbirth from Leticia's legs.

Vincent walked as if in a daze to the two tiny bundles on the bed. He looked in wonder at the tiny babies. Both looked identical. They both had dark hair like his. These were his sons. Vincent picked up one and then the other. In his arms the boys stopped their crying. The coming French siege didn't enter his mind. He was holding his sons. "Our King Edward wouldst be proud of us," Vincent announced cheerfully. "We be ordered to give heir for Okehampton and by God's teeth we hath done so. Twice over!"

Leticia turned to look at her husband. She grabbed one of the bloody towels near Clarice and threw it at Vincent's leg. "We travailed and provided the birth of heirs thee Churl!" Leticia shouted. "Thee ordered us birth thee son. We gave thee two sons. Prithee, tell us which obeyed our commands!"

Vincent laughed loudly. It was more of a joy of relief from worry and tension. "Thee be noblest of thus realm dear Goodwife. Thou art truly most noble."

Clarice helped Leticia to the pallet and covered her with a soft rabbit fur coverlet. "Thee wouldst rest now, my lady."

"Nay, we wouldst naught rest until we speak to our husband of coming French siege," Leticia muttered wearily. "Vincent, we must warn thee of traitor."

Still holding his sons, Vincent sat next to Leticia lying on the pallet. "Tell us whence thee came to be in thus cottage."

"We overheard three voices speaking in French inside Juliet's chamber," Leticia began.

"Lady Juliet!" Vincent growled. "Yea, we wouldst trow it be thus villain."

"Naught Lady Juliet," Leticia chastened quickly. "Thus traitor be Lady Agnes. Her brother, Jean Tillet leads army to Okehampton from French shores. Tis reprisal for our King Edward taking Calais."

"We hath heard of thus knight warrior in Calais," Vincent shared. "Tis brave and noble Frenchman devoted to throne of France as our person be to throne of England. Tis strange we hath naught connected thus name to Lady Agnes until hence."

"The Lady Agnes found our person listening and confined us to western tower room," Leticia continued on. She was tired and wanted to tell Vincent everything before she fell asleep. "Agnes trow naught thus be room of de Redvers hidden escape passage. With Mystic as our guide through darkness, we escaped. In our woods such good and kind Turold took our care. We give thee sons…" Leticia's voice trailed off into sleep.

Vincent looked up worriedly at Clarice and asked, "Our lady?"

"Thy lady requires rest. Wouldst thee naught be tired after travail delivering naught one but two sons?"

"Yea," Vincent answered sheepishly. Once more he concentrated on the two babies in his arms. There was no doubt these would be his sons. They looked just like him and the thought hit him. They looked liked Morgan and Megan when they were born. He couldn't help but laugh. "In troth our lady wouldst require much rest if thus be like our twin sisters, Morgan and Megan." He rose and took the bundles to show off to Lionel and Maynard who were still waiting outside.

Lionel had been sitting on a tree stump outside the cottage. He was hungry and his stomach was growling, but he would not leave Vincent. Not after he heard about the French siege. As the door opened and the bent form of his friend emerged he noted two small bundles in his arm. Lionel nudged the sleeping Maynard and rose to meet Vincent. "Ho, whence be in thy arms my lord?"

"Leticia doth give us naught one, but two sons," Vincent beamed proudly. He walked to his friends and showed off the two boys.

"Thy lady be most virtuous," Lionel noted. "Wouldst naught thy lady prefer to give birth to thy sons in Okehampton. Be hence reason to birth in a woodcutter cottage?"

"Our lady escaped from her prison room," Vincent explained. "Fortuitous for us she escaped or we wouldst naught be holding our sons. We also owe much to Turold, his Goodwife, and Leticia's Mystic. Our lady's pet led her through darkness of escape passage."

"So thus be traitor," Lionel understood.

"Yea, thus siege be on the morrow," Vincent replied seriously. "We wouldst stay with our Leticia and sons. Go with our squire and bring our Lady Elena, Lady Organa, and three wagons to bring our Leticia and sons with our woodcutter and family to our haven of Okehampton."

"We wouldst go anon," Lionel acknowledged. "Tis nearly dark, we wouldst return by torch."

"Upon thy return, place Lady Agnes in containment," Vincent ordered. "We wouldst tend to thus traitor in thus morn."

"Lady Agnes?" Lionel gasped with shock.

"Yea, Lady Agnes be thus traitor," Vincent answered. "Thus lady be sister of Sir Jean Tillet of France. We heard of thus knight in Calais. Tis revenge on King Edward's taking of Calais."

Lionel moved quickly to his Destrier, "We return anon."

# Chapter 23

Vincent returned to the inside of the woodcutter's cottage.

Turold was sitting at the table by the hearth pouring stew into a bowls. He had fed his children because his wife was busy with the Lady Leticia. He placed a bowl in front of his wife. "Wouldst thee take sustenance my lord? Surely thee must be hungered," Turold asked the lord holding the bowl of stew in offering.

"Yea, we be hungered," Vincent accepted. He walked to the pallet and lay the two sleeping babies next to his sleeping Leticia. He couldn't help but note how beautiful and serene she looked asleep. He bent over his wife to brush a kiss upon Leticia's cheek. She moved slightly at his touch and a smile appeared on her lips. In her sleep she mumbled, "Tis wonderful kiss my lord."

Vincent smiled. His lady was dreaming about him. He walked to the table and consumed not only one bowl of stew. He consumed three bowls. He was indeed hungry. When he finished he addressed Turold and Clarice, "We owe thee much. Thee hath saved life of our Goodwife and our sons. We wouldst reward thee for thy honor."

"We be happiest to see thee united with thy lady," Clarice replied. "We wouldst need no more reward."

"Tis troth," Turold agreed. "Clarice and our person be most happy and content hence. Thee and the de Redvers hath been good and kind lords. Tis little more we wouldst need for our happiness. We be most happy to serve our lord in his need." Turold placed their youngest child on his lap and cuddled the boy. "We be most happy and be joyful thee hath discovered joy of thy newly born sons."

"Thee be good and kind people. Thy goodness and kindness must naught go un-rewarded or we wouldst naught be good lord," Vincent said firmly. "We wouldst reward thee handsomely." He pulled out his purse from his tunic and gave the entire pouch to Turold. "Thus be only partial payment. We wouldst make certain our steward, Durand Alwins wouldst purchase only thy woods for our fires."

Clarice looked to Turold with pride and joy. Turold took the offered purse and handed it to his Clarice. "Thee hath committed most wondrous goodness on this den. Thee hath delivered our lord's sons safely and taken care of our lord's Goodwife. We wish thee to buy finest gown for thy person."

Clarice's eyes watered with pride and love. Her husband Turold was a wonderful man and just reminded her of the many reasons she was happy being his wife.

"We be most pleased with thy labors," Vincent agreed. "Tis most appropriate for thee to take our purse."

When darkness fell Vincent heard the wagons approaching. He had spent the time with Turold finding the passage that Leticia had emerged from and they replaced the sod-covered plank. No one would be aware of its presence should the French happen to come into the forest. Vincent listened carefully to all Turold had told him about what Leticia had told him and his wife. Vincent had also informed Turold and his family to pack some of their belongings. Vincent would take them to Okehampton for protection during the siege. He told Turold he would also need Turold's knowledge of the forest to help in the preparation of a plan Vincent had in mind.

Vincent greeted Lionel, "Goodman, thee hath brought all we requested. Hath thee contained Lady Agnes?"

"Yea," Lionel replied. "Thus Lady turned into devil spouting curses upon us. Agnes be most definitely thus traitor. Sir Gaylord hath contained her in tower room near thy keep."

Lionel's stomach growled loudly.

"Be thee hungered Goodman?" Vincent teased.

"Wouldst thee be concerned? For thee we hath naught taken sustenance since midday," Lionel responded testily.

"We be concerned for thee," Vincent chuckled. "In thus cottage be delicious stew. Thee need only request of such from Clarice."

Lionel smiled and went into the cottage quickly. Vincent assisted the Lady Elena while Maynard helped Organa down from the wagon.

Elena began asking Vincent questions, "In troth, be our lady well? Tis in troth our lady hath given birth to twin sons? Dost our lady sleep? Hath our lady eaten?"

Vincent held up his hands in surrender, "Lady Elena, if thee wouldst stop thy chatter and go hither into cottage, thee wouldst answer all thy questions."

Elena ran into the cottage to side of her sleeping lady. Lady Organa was on her heels. Leticia slept through all of it. Elena picked up one baby and Organa the other. They walked outside to the waiting wagons.

Vincent helped Lionel, Maynard, Turold, and three other de Courtney knights load the woodcutter's belongings onto the wagons. Turold, Clarice, and their children climbed onto one of the wagons. Elena and Organa with the twin boys sat waiting in another. Vincent returned to the cottage and carefully picked up his sleeping Leticia. He had Maynard prepare several wooden boxes so he could easily mount his Destrier without releasing his Leticia. Once seated on the Destrier, Vincent settled the sleeping Leticia in his arms. He tucked in the rabbit coverlet surrounding her.

Leticia still sleeping snuggled into Vincent's arms. In her sleep she recognized his manly scent and slept comfortably. On the torch lit march back to Okehampton, Leticia did not wake once. Vincent's protectiveness emanated to all who watched their lord carry his lady back to Okehampton.

Vincent waited until Maynard had once more prepared the boxes for his lord to dismount. Carefully he descended from his mount and carried Leticia into the keep. He carried her into their solar and laid her gently upon their bed. Removing the rabbit coverlet he handed it to Lady Rosamund who had followed him. "Return thus to Turold and Goodwife, Clarice. Make such family comfortable in our keep. Give such our finest hospitality, fit for King Edward. Thus family saved our Leticia and gave aid to our sons."

Rosamund said nothing. She took the coverlet and went to find the woodcutter's family.

Lady Organa and Lady Elena brought the twins. Morgan and Megan followed them. The twins were ecstatic about the birth of the twin boys. They were pestering Organa and Elena to hold their nephews.

Vincent addressed the young women, "Go find wet nurse for our sons thus eve. We wouldst naught disturb our lady until morn." When they left Vincent closed the door to the solar and undressed. He climbed into bed with his Leticia. In the morning he would leave and prepare for the French siege. He would let the women care for his Leticia and change the rags soaking her blood after childbirth. Tonight he would sleep with his precious and treasured wife in his arms. He heard a mewing and laughed, "Verily Mystic, we wouldst allow thee portion of our pallet thus eve." His voice disturbed Leticia's sleep a little. She snuggled into his arms. "For thus eve thee be in our arms," Vincent whispered to Leticia. He soon fell sound asleep after days of worry and little rest.

The sunbeams entered the solar chamber casting their dancing lights on Leticia's eyes. Her eyes fluttered and focused on the face of her husband. Her fingertips touched his cheeks and lips, "Tis naught dream vision. Thee truly be hence," Leticia whispered. "Thus be real!" Leticia then remembered the night before and the birth of her sons. She sat straight up in bed and cried, "Our babies! Our sons!" She placed her hand on her now empty womb. "Whence be our sons? Tis naught dream!" Leticia was about to remove the covers and leap from her bed in search of her babies when a strong hand pulled her gently back down into the pillows.

"Our sons be with wet nurse under watch from Lady Elena and Lady Organa," Vincent informed quietly. He felt her unease and tried to reassure her of the twins care.

"We desire our sons by us," Leticia replied firmly. Why didn't Vincent understand the babies were supposed to be with her, not her handmaidens?

"We wouldst send for them," Vincent responded. "Be troubled naught. We wished only for thee to sleep well thus night."

"We be in woodcutter's cottage," Leticia said shaking her head trying desperately to remember everything. "Thee brought us to Okehampton?"

"Yea," Vincent answered while leaning over Leticia and gently kissing her brow, eyes, and cheeks. "We carried thee to our solar last eve. Thee be worn thin by delivery of our twin sons. We let thee sleep."

"We wish to see our sons," Leticia insisted. She was so exhausted last night she didn't even get to hold them. She had loved holding Reine, Juliet's daughter, and she hadn't even been given the chance to hold her own babies. Unknowingly she pouted and her lower lip began to tremble. Everything was so supposed to be wonderful and perfect when she had her baby. Nothing had happened as it was supposed to. Even though Vincent was once again near, nothing seemed to matter more than holding her babies in her arms. The natural instincts of motherhood took control of Leticia. Nothing would feel right until her babies were near her and under her protection. "Whence be purpose to remove our sons from our care?"

Vincent kissed Leticia's forehead and apologized, "We offer regret for our error. Our love conquered our heart to allow thee rest. We thought naught correctly with our mind." Vincent rose from bed and wrapped a long silken robe about him. He went to the door and ordered his squire, Maynard to fetch Lady Organa and Lady Elena with his sons. Vincent also ordered Maynard to bring two well-armed knights to guard Leticia and his sons. They were to be ordered not to leave their posts even during the oncoming siege. Vincent then returned to Leticia's side. "Our sons be brought to thee anon."

It was then all the terror and emotions that Leticia had suffered through yesterday burst open like a reservoir behind a cracked dam. She clung to Vincent and sobbed hysterically. "We thought we wouldst naught see thee again. We thought we wouldst die and our babes die with us," Leticia wailed. "We thought our castle lost to traitors. We feared for our shire, our people, our husband, our life, our babies." Leticia cried full tears and deep sobs.

Vincent embraced Leticia and let her cry without rebuke. His terror these last few days had manifested itself in reality. On the ride back to Okehampton he thought of the terror and pain his young beautiful wife had just endured. He realized he could have lost her and his precious twin boys if not for her fortitude and resourcefulness. When she was calmed he would take the time to tell her how proud he was of her. For right now, all she needed was his arms and their babies.

After several minutes of sobbing and hysterics, Leticia stopped crying. She wiped her eyes with her hands. She sniffed apologetically, "Thee must believe us to be kinder!"

"Nay, we believe thee to be brave and resourceful Goodwife," Vincent answered. "We be prideful of thy courage. We adore thee! Thee dost hold title of most bravest Goodwife thus knight trow."

"Even greater hence our Queen Phillippa?" Leticia sniffed hopefully.

"Yea, score braver and resourceful hence our good queen," Vincent replied honestly and quickly without thought.

"In troth?" Leticia brightened.

"Yea, in troth," Vincent reassured. "Thee be our bravest!"

Elena walked in with one sleeping baby boy and Organa with the other. Lady Rosamund followed the two handmaidens.

Leticia brightened like the dawn when she saw the babies. She attempted to get up, but was kept down by the firm arm of her husband.

"Nay, Goodwife," Vincent countered in authority. "Thee hath suffered much. Thee must rest and stay in our pallet. We order thee to remain abed until thy strength be fully recovered." He motioned Elena and Organa to bring the twins over to Leticia.

Leticia obeyed and lay against the pillows. Elena placed one twin in the crook of her right arm. Organa placed the other twin in the crook of her left arm. Leticia looked from one baby to the other and said in wonder, "our issues be beauteous."

"Most beauteous," Vincent agreed running his finger over one sleeping baby's thick black hair. "Thus sons remind us of Morgan and Megan at birth."

"Hath thee given thought of naming?" Rosamund asked Leticia admiring her new grandsons by marriage.

"Yester den be holy mass of St. Austin," Leticia replied and lifted her right arm. "Thus be thy given name dearest son, Austin." She then looked at the left arm and declared, "thy name wouldst be Aleyn for our honored father's father."

"Bless thee dearest Goodwife," Vincent chuckled. "For one moment we feared thee wouldst call our sons, Romulus and Remus."

Leticia gave Vincent a blank stare of unbelief.

"We trow thee love thy Falcons thee trained," Vincent said innocently.

"Thee tease us," Leticia giggled.

"Yea," Vincent admitted. "We wouldst suggest thee tie a blue ribbon on Austin's foot and a red ribbon on Aleyn's foot. Hence we wouldst trow which son be which."

"Tis troth," Morgan said entering the solar. "Our dear father and servants wouldst naught be able to tell us apart. Only our mother wouldst trow which twin be which by some magic. We be certain our brother wouldst naught tell which twin be which. Sir Vincent to this day wouldst naught recognize which twin be which."

"Nay," Vincent argued. "Thee be our Morgan. Thee be soft spoken and gentle. Our Megan be slicing with tongue and rough as a new squire in training."

Leticia laughed and spoke to Austin and then Aleyn, "Dost thee hear thy father? Until thy spirits reveal which child be which, we wouldst put ribbons upon thy feet."

"Our father hath us dress in different colors and hath our hair done differently," Megan added when she entered the room. "Tis easy to switch when servants be naught aware."

"Tis thus evil twin," Vincent chortled. "We wouldst discipline our sons. Our father failed to discipline thee dear Megan."

Megan stuck out her tongue at her brother and went to sit on the floor by Leticia's side of the bed.

Mystic came from under the bed and meowed at Elena's feet.

"Lady Elena," Vincent addressed. "Wouldst thee feed our Mystic fresh cream thus morn? Some treats of partridge? We owe our Mystic much for aiding and saving our Goodwife and heirs."

"As for heirs," Rosamund asked. "Whence son be born first?"

"Austin," Leticia said raising her right arm.

"Hence wouldst thee trow?" Vincent asked curiously.

"We be hence at thus birthing," Leticia replied. "We trow our Austin be thus first born. Thee came in time to see our Aleyn's birth."

Vincent bowed dutifully to his wife in acquiescence.

Austin's eyes opened and his face moved toward his mother's breast. His little mouth began to suck on her chemise. When the boy realized he was not getting the wonderful nourishment he had only a few hours ago he began a wailing that woke his brother Aleyn.

"Tis time for thee to suckle thus newly born," Rosamund stated walking to Leticia. "We wouldst teach thee."

"Tis time for thee to leave us women, brother," Megan taunted.

"Thus children wouldst leave with us, Morgan and Megan," Vincent returned. "Come hither."

Megan stuck out her tongue at Vincent once more.

"Be of care sister," Vincent warned. "One den thee wouldst bite thus tongue and thee wouldst make such bleed."

Just as Megan was about to make a sarcastic remark, Sir Lionel called Vincent from the doorway, "Sir Vincent, thus French be half league from Okehampton. We received word from our watch."

Vincent turned to tell Leticia he loved her when he saw his sons suckling. Austin suckled the right breast and Aleyn suckled the left breast. His eyes watered. Here was born hope and joy, but he could not stay. He had to defend what he held most dear. Instead he leaned over and kissed his wife on the forehead. "We wouldst return anon."

Leticia shielded her sudden terror. The French were almost here. After all she had been through, the thought of losing Vincent frightened her immensely. Instead she smiled and told Vincent, "We wait for thy return anon. All be wonderful and happy in our love. Tis naught any foreign power to conquer our hearts."

Vincent grabbed his tunic, chausses, and mail. He would dress quickly in his offices. Lionel waited for Vincent outside the door. When Vincent emerged from the solar the two men talked of the battle and the plans. Vincent was relieved he had ordered the reinforcement construction of Okehampton upon his arrival and through the winter. The castle was fortified and formidable against siege. It was while he was dressing he remembered Turold and why he had brought him to Okehampton. Turold knew the forest and could help with Vincent's plan to use the very same passage Leticia had used in her escape. Then he remembered! "By God's Teeth!" Vincent swore. He finished dressing and returned to the solar.

Leticia was rocking Aleyn and Rosamund had taken Austin to change his swaddling. Both women asked in unison, "Whence be thy quick return?" Both were nervous at Vincent quick return. They were afraid something was wrong.

"Leticia," Vincent said softly. "Whence be thus tower thee used for escape?"

"Tis de Redvers escape passage in thus western tower of the keep," Leticia answered. "Tis thus same flooring as our solar."

"We hath visited thus room on our arrival at Okehampton," Vincent replied. "We noticed naught way out."

"Look under mantel of thus hearth," Leticia instructed. "Thus be handle thee wouldst pull down. A panel wouldst open on back wall of the hearth. Behind thus be passage to woodlands."

"Bless thee Goodwife," Vincent smiled and started to walk out of the solar.

"Husband," Leticia called after Vincent. "Take thee torches through thus passage. Whence be arachnids along thus passage. We trow thy fear of arachnids."

Vincent stopped and turned to look at Leticia. "Thee wouldst naught put arachnids hence in retribution for our absence at Calais?"

Leticia snorted, "Nay! Thus arachnids be hence by opportunity and naught our hand."

Organa, Rosamund, Morgan, and Megan looked at each other in confusion. They had no idea what secret meanings were behind Vincent and Leticia's comments. It was however obvious there were secret meanings to the conversation.

Vincent shot Leticia a large white-toothed grin and bolted from the room. "Stay abed and safe," he ordered as he disappeared into the hall.

"We wouldst naught leave our darlings," Leticia smiled cuddling little Aleyn. "We hath endured much adventure of late. We wouldst naught need more adventure."

Vincent nearly ran into Juliet as he left the solar and headed towards the office where Lionel waited for him. Vincent took hold of Juliet's arms and said quietly as not to wake the sleeping Reine. "Take thy daughter and stay in solar with our Lady Leticia."

"Tis troth hence?" Juliet asked with quivering voice. "We heard our Lady Agnes be captive as traitor and French come upon us?"

"Yea, tis troth," Vincent answered in honesty. "Fear naught for thee or thy daughter. Stay with our sons in thus solar and be safe with our ladies."

Vincent released Juliet and went to his office.

Juliet entered the solar with Reine and Lady Mildred behind her. "Sir Vincent ordered us to stay with thee in the solar," Juliet announced upon entering. "Prithee, we wouldst trow naught Lady Agnes treachery."

Leticia smiled at Juliet and said, "Fear not Juliet. We trow thee be naught involved in Lady Agnes' treachery. We trow thee be innocent. Come bring Reine hither to meet her brothers, Austin and Aleyn."

Juliet breathed a gasp of relief and replied, "We heard thee hath returned safely with Sir Vincent's sons and heirs. We rose early thus morn and gave prayer of thanks at early mass." Juliet sat next to Leticia and gave her a hug. "Thy sons be as beauteous as our daughter."

The movement and shouting of many knights, squires, and foot soldiers shattered the contentment of the women. Rosamund went to the open window that overlooked a castle wall and shuttered it. She then bolted it. "Tis command of our lord and husband, Sir Gaylord."

# Chapter 24

Entering his office, Vincent was greeted by Sir Lionel, Sir Gaylord, two younger knights that had served as scouts, and Turold. The men had been sitting around Vincent's table that served as his desk. They were studying a parchment that contained schematics of Okehampton, and the shires surrounding the castle.

Vincent took his seat between Sir Lionel and Sir Gaylord his top two advisors. At first he ignored the parchment to address one of the two young knights. "Gerard, whence be count of approaching French?"

"My Lord, we count five score knights upon Destrier including Sir Jean Tillet," Gerard replied quickly. He was anxious to impart his report knowing the French were less than a half league from the castle.

"And foot soldiers?" Vincent asked placing his fingers in the shape of a church steeple below his chin.

"We count ten score afoot," Gerard answered bowing slightly. He wanted to get to the ramparts and was fidgeting in his fervor to begin the battle.

Vincent allowed a small smile on his lips. This would be Gerard's first battle. He had no idea the horror and blood he would see as he or his friends would be wounded or killed. That is what would happen if Vincent's plan didn't work. "Take thee anon to thus ramparts. Raymond, go with Gerard and return to us whence thus French arrive."

After the young knights left the room Lionel commented, "Tis anxious for thus battle our young knights."

"Yea," Gaylord agreed. "Tis first battle for our lads. Our lads wouldst learn anon tis naught glory in battle."

"Yea, tis naught glory in death and pain," Lionel concurred.

"Whence be our force?" Vincent directed back to the intense moment at hand.

"Thy knights be with our Black Prince," Lionel responded. "The de Redvers armory be two score Destrier knights and four score foot soldiers."

"We be outnumbered two for one," Vincent said thoughtfully.

"We wouldst enjoy strength of Okehampton walls," Sir Gaylord reminded.

Vincent bent over the parchment and addressed Turold, "Show us whence thee discovered the opening upon the forest floor thee found our Lady."

Turold walked to the parchment and after studying the schematics he pointed to a spot in the middle of the forest near Okehampton. He understood the schematics enough to take Vincent's quill pen and draw a hole with it upon the parchment. Turold then sketched a box near the hole and announced, "Thus be our cottage."

"Thus be near center of forested glen," Vincent said thoughtfully.

"Whence be thy plan?" Sir Gaylord frowned. He knew his son well and was worried if the boy was plotting something dangerous.

Vincent seemed to ignore his father as he once more questioned Turold, "Be cover outside thy forest near thus field?" Vincent pointed outside of the sketched forest on the field facing the castle's drawbridge. He knew Jean Tillet's army would challenge his knights of Okehampton.

"Yea," Turold answered firmly. "Thus be wild outgrowths of hedgerows all on such outside of thus forest. Thus be nearly as tall as thee."

"Sweet Jesu," Vincent prayed with gratitude.

Sir Gaylord was more worried then ever. He rightly believed his son was about to do something daring and dangerous. "Thy plan?"

"Turold wouldst accompany us through thus de Redvers passage into our forest," Vincent replied. "We wouldst scout our forest and hedgerows for shielding our foot soldiers and knights."

"Thee be crazed," Sir Gaylord protested. "Our Okehampton be fortified to withstand assault."

"Yea," Vincent agreed. "Yet our knights and Black Prince return forthwith. We wouldst roust thus French ere our Black Prince's arrival."

"Our knights be thus finest in all kingdom," Lionel protested. "Our Black Prince and our knights wouldst roust all thus French interlopers."

"We be two for one. Our Black Prince be two for one," Vincent explained. "We wouldst roust French with surprise ere thus arrival of our Black Prince."

"Thee in troth believes thee wouldst surprise thus French?" Lionel questioned. He was more comfortable with the plan knowing about the surprise element. He would be comfortable if he were certain it would be a surprise.

"We wouldst study our forest, hedgerows, and fields first," Vincent replied looking at Turold. "Come hither with us. We wouldst inspect our advantages."

"Nay," Lionel objected. "We wouldst leave with Turold. We wouldst review our battleground."

Vincent laid his hand upon Lionel's shoulder. "Tis our duty. Tis our family we wouldst defend and protect. Father, thee wouldst stay and face French challenge. Our enemy trow naught of our return. Let thus believe so. We wouldst place all our knights and foot soldiers upon our ramparts. Thus French wouldst believe all our forces be on our walls upon such challenge. In darkness of night place helmets and shields for every other knight and foot soldier. Arm thus men well and prepare for our use."

Lionel opened his mouth to object. Vincent raised his hand for silence and walked to the doorway. "Come hither Turold."

Turold obeyed and followed Vincent to the third floor tower room. He looked about when they entered the room and asked, "Be a reason to bring us to thus room?"

"Yea," Vincent replied. "Our Goodwife told us thus be the opening for escape passage." He walked to the fireplace and put his hand under the mantel. He moved his hand up and down, and right to left until he found the handle. Once he found the handle he pulled it down forcibly.

Turold watched in awe as the panel behind the fireplace moved a crack revealing a passageway behind the hearth.

Vincent bent down on one knee to push the panel wide open. His strength was capable of opening the passage completely. Vincent noted the passageway was too small for a large man of his father in law's size. He surmised correctly. He found another handle that released another panel directly over the smaller passageway. The handle released the top of the hearth allowing him to push it aside. The opening was now to his full height and width. From what Leticia had told him she had to push herself through only half of the passage. As a child she would not have known of the adult passage for height and girth. He marveled at his wife. It must have been a snug fit. The situation gave him all the more pride for the voracity of his young beautiful wife. Vincent peeked inside and with the light of the larger opening he spotted torches along the walls. "Turold, doth thee own flints in thy pouch?"

"Yea," Turold replied handing the flint stones to Vincent.

Patiently Vincent struck the flints near the oil soaked torches. At last a spark ignited the torch and bright flame revealed the circular steps downward. Vincent pulled two torches from the wall stands. He lit them both with the first torch. One he kept and the other he handed to Turold. "Follow us," Vincent commanded. Slowly and carefully he led the way down the slippery circular steps. Vincent lit every other oil lamp he found along the path. He saw the disturbed spider webs and saw the dried places where Leticia had sat only the day before. It must have been horrible for her. He would take time later to tell her how wonderful she was. Along the way he burned the webs and spiders with his torch. He heard the scurrying of feet with nails on the stones that fled before his arrival. "Sweet Jesu, Mystic," Vincent offered in prayer. "We be grateful thee stayed with our Goodwife. Thee protected our Leticia from thus rodents."

The stairs were narrow and slippery. The large men had to be very careful while walking down the steps. "Tis unbelievable thy Goodwife made it through thus passage," Turold commented. "Tis dangerous and slippery."

"Yea," Vincent agreed. "We wouldst keep these oil lamps burning for our knights and foot soldiers. Thus burning wouldst dry out thus dampness, freshen thus foul air, and light our path. My lady suffered naught of such luxury."

They reached the locked iron gate that Leticia had opened. Vincent easily pushed it open and the men continued through the stone floored dirt passage.

They walked the next half-mile lighting oil lamps bolted to the walls. Vincent saw the steps leading to the ground above. He handed his torch to Turold and easily moved the sod-covered board revealing the floor of the forest. Once upon the forest grounds they heard the thunder of the Destrier's hooves. It was the French army arriving.

Turold now led the way. With knowledge of every tree in the forest, Turold led Vincent to the edge of the forest. They saw the tall wild hedgerows weaving in and out of each other. Vincent smiled broadly. It was perfect cover for a surprise attack. The two men moved in and out of the hedgerows until they were only a few hundred steps away from the French army.

Vincent and Turold listened to Jean Tillet address Sir Gaylord with his challenge.

Shouting to the walls of Okehampton Jean addressed, "Come hither Sir Gaylord, hear our demand."

Gaylord took his position upon the highest rampart facing the French Army. He saw the crimson pennants flying in the wind. A black raven emblem resided on every flag and upon the crimson tunic of Jean Tillet. "We be Sir Gaylord de Courtenay," he shouted in return. "Whence be thee addressing us."

"We be Sir Jean Tillet," was the reply. "In such name of our throne of France we claim thy lands."

"Thee be trespassing upon our throne of King Edward," Gaylord resounded heatedly.

"Give up thy lands or face our siege," Jean warned. He was confident of the battle for his sister had promised to open the postern gate. When two of his men had entered Okehampton they would overcome the guard at the drawbridge gate and allow entry of his forces. His sister had told his spies there were less than two score knights and foot soldiers. The majority of knights were with the lord of Okehampton in Calais. It would be a long siege against the formidable walls, but a quick victory once the drawbridge was lowered for his forces.

"Prepare for thy siege," Gaylord answered angrily. "Thee wouldst find our walls most formidable."

"So be it," Jean replied once more in fluent Anglo English. He reined his Destrier and ordered his men in French to bring up the catapults. He had a battering ram and belfry in reserve but believed he would not need them. Once in place, Jean ordered the catapults to begin sending the large stones to break the walls. Agnes had no knowledge of the reinforcements to the walls made inside and outside under order of Vincent de Courtenay. The large boulders merely bounced off the walls when they hit the subtle curves of the fortified walls. The curve was so soft on the wall it gave the illusion of being straight.

Jean Tillet cursed as the boulders bounded back with force toward his knights.

Vincent held back guffaws as he saw the frustration of the French knight.

It was near dusk and Vincent signaled Turold to return to the forest. They sprinted in and out of the hedges until they were safely hidden in the forest. The two men watched from the edge of the forest as the two spies walked to the entrance of the postern gate. Vincent drew his sword just in case the spies found out their entry was denied and it was really a trap. He could not allow the spies to escape and inform their lord.

The spies called out for Lady Agnes and the door opened slowly. They saw nothing but darkness when they entered. The door shut behind them and they heard the bolt drop behind them. The last man in felt cold steel pressed against his back. "En avant," a male voice ordered. The first man was about to turn when a lighted torch around the bend revealed two large and heavily armed knights in front of him. The two men raised their arms in defeat.

Vincent waited a few moments and when he saw the torchlight he knew the spies were apprehended. He and Turold slipped back into the heavy foliage of the forest. They sprinted back to the opening in the forest grounds and followed the passage back to Okehampton.

Returning to the castle Vincent emerged from the passage and was greeted by his squire. Maynard had stayed as guard during Vincent's trek into the passage and forest.

"Whence be Sir Gaylord?" Vincent inquired once he emerged.

"Sir Gaylord stay at watch upon our battlements," Maynard replied.

"Fetch Sir Gaylord and bring our father to our office," Vincent ordered. "Once achieved, bring Turold and us trenchers in our office."

Maynard obeyed immediately and ran to get Sir Gaylord.

Vincent upon the return to his office sat down and began sketching on the castle parchment.

Gaylord entered the room. Relief showed on his face when he saw his son had returned safely. "Thee hath scouted our forest and hedgerows?"

"Yea," Vincent answered not looking up at his father but still concentrating on the drawing. "Hath thee chosen for us score knights and two score foot soldiers?"

"Yea," Gaylord replied. "Thus be ready upon thy word."

"Send our force to rest," Vincent ordered now looking at his father. "We wouldst leave before sunrise on the morrow."

"Yea," Gaylord responded. "What armament wouldst thee set with our force."

"Our force wouldst be armed with battle sword, slashing sword, flail, and hatchet," Vincent said automatically. His plan was already played out in his head several times over. "We wouldst have all meet us in the third floor western tower room ere thus next morn's light."

"Thee wouldst naught lead thus battle," Gaylord barked furiously. "Thee be Lord of Okehampton. Thee be new husband and father of heirs. We forbid thus!"

"We scouted the battleground and we laid such plan," Vincent answered calmly. "Thence be naught other to lead."

Gaylord threw up his hands in frustration. "Thee be stubborn as our God's ass!"

Vincent rose and faced his father. "Thee trow we be great in battle and stratagem. We ask thee to give us faith."

"Thee be our only son," Gaylord choked out revealing his innermost fear.

"Thee hath naught one, yea, two sons of ours!" Vincent reminded cheerily. "Thus wouldst be raised with thy hand as well as ours."

Maynard came into the room carrying several trenchers and tankards of ale on a large brass tray. Lionel carrying his own trencher and ale followed Maynard into the room.

"Show us thy battle plan," Lionel requested tearing a piece of meat off with his teeth. "We wouldst know where to keep our enemy occupied whence thee began thy attack."

Gaylord glared at Lionel. "Dost thee trow our Vincent plans to lead thus attack?"

"Yea," Lionel answered breaking a piece of bread to eat. "Whence be another more capable to lead such attack save our person?" Lionel took a seat next to Vincent while placing his trencher and tankard upon the table.

"Hence thee lead thus attack," Gaylord grumped.

"Vincent hath scouted such battle fields," Lionel replied casually. "Show us thy plan."

Vincent took his tankard and took several gulps and between bites and drinks explained the plan to Lionel and Gaylord.

Turold sat at the table eating his meal and saying little. No one had said he would go into battle, but in his mind he was protecting his forest and he would lead the knights through the forest glen and hedgerows.

Lionel listened intently to Vincent's plans. He then explained to Vincent how he would conduct the battle from the interior of Okehampton. Because Vincent's attack was planned on the west side of the French Army, Lionel would concentrate a heavy barrage on their east side.

Several hours later Gaylord suggested they get rest.

Vincent realized he was quite tired and he did need sleep. He gave final orders sending his father to the chosen men and telling them to get some sleep.

Lionel saw to the armaments and rechecked the battlements before he sought out his Goodwife for the night.

Turold returned to his Clarice. She welcomed him with open arms and warm embrace. They spent a comfortable night together in a large canopied bed prepared for their comforts by several servants of the keep.

"We be treated as noble," Clarice commented to her husband when he climbed onto the bed pallet.

"Dost thee become accustomed quickly?" Turold teased.

"Yea."

Turold looked at his wife with searching eyes. Would she want to return to their happy little cottage?

"Dolt," Clarice laughed. "We only be happy with thee and our children in our cottage."

"In troth?"

"Yea," Clarice replied sensually. "Still naught harm for enjoying thus soft pallet."

"Grrrr," Turold snarled playfully. It was a little bit later before they fell asleep in the soft pallet.

Vincent entered his solar to find Elena and Organa sleeping upon his large chairs that were moved away from facing the fireplace. They were turned and near the hanging hammock cradle of his twin boys. In the twilight cast from the embers of the fireplace he noticed movement in the hammock. Walking as quietly as a fully dressed knight could, Vincent approached the hammock cradle. He quickly glanced behind his shoulder and saw his Leticia sleeping. "Thee look as if an angel," Vincent whispered quietly. He turned his attention back to the movement in the hammock. Looking down Vincent saw one twin sleeping soundly and one twin moving in the swaddling. The baby had managed to free one hand and was sucking on it contentedly while thrashing about in the swaddling. Vincent took the small hand away from his son's mouth and was surprised when the little hand grabbed firmly to his finger. The boy's head moved toward his father's finger and began suckling it. "Ho son, thee wouldst naught find sustenance hence," Vincent chortled softly. Vincent forgot about the French, the siege, and his upcoming attack. Vincent forgot about everything and marveled at the little lives he and Leticia had created. Vincent released his finger and carefully picked up the little bundle. "Whence son be thee?" Vincent asked softly.

"My Lord?" Elena asked sleepily.

"Yea," Vincent replied quietly. "Return to thy sleep. We wish only to coddle our sons." He felt small arms envelope his massive frame and the sweet scent of his wife wafted up to his nose.

"Thy son Aleyn appears to await such father's arrival," Leticia said lovingly. She moved to face Vincent. "Thee appears to be most tired and in need of sleep." Leticia released Vincent and lifted Austin from the cradle. "Organa!" she called to the sleeping handmaiden. "Wake and take our son Austin to our wet nurse with Elena and Aleyn. Our Lord wouldst need rest thus eve."

Organa jumped on Leticia's order and took the baby leaving the solar. Elena waited as Vincent brushed a soft kiss on Aleyn's head before he gave his son to the handmaiden.

Leticia began undressing Vincent and when she removed the mail tunic she gasped in horror, "Thee be wounded!" A long gash revealed fresh stitching and scab. "Thee wouldst tell us!" Leticia scolded. She went to the pot of hot water always kept over the fire and dipped a cloth into it. Leticia then went to her small leather medicinal bag and took from it a small box that she kept her salve in. Returning to her husband she made him sit down as she washed the gash and applied a special healing salve.

Vincent was too tired to protest. He sat quietly.

When Leticia finished applying the salve she helped Vincent remove his mail chausses and braies. They walked together to the bed.

Vincent lay down immediately and pulled Leticia next to him. Placing his wife on her back he pulled down her chemise and fondled her breasts. "We see thy womanly globes hath filled with milk for our sons."

"Yea," Leticia giggled. "Thy sons be most greedy and require much milk."

"Our sons be as thus father," Vincent teased taking her breast in his mouth to suckle. "We be in need of sustenance."

Leticia arched her back to allow Vincent full access to her breast. She patted his head as he suckled one breast and then the other as greedily as Austin and Aleyn. A large smile crossed Leticia's lips. "In troth thee be as greedy as thy sons," Leticia agreed. She heard the soft breathing sounds she recognized so well. Her Vincent was asleep in her arm. "Tis thy place to be," she uttered quietly. "Asleep near us. Remember thus on the morrow when thus siege begins once more."

# Chapter 25

Vincent felt happiness as he held his Leticia and watched their twin sons play in the meadow by the bailey. He was holding his wife close to him. "We love thee with all of our heart," Vincent whispered quietly into Leticia's ear. The sun was shining on the meadow and everything seemed to glisten with beauty. Suddenly a dark knight dressed in crimson riding on a Destrier thundered across the open meadow. The knight's sword flashed in the sunlight and came down upon one twin and then the other. Vincent cried out, "Nay!" It seemed like it was impossible for him to move. The crimson clothed knight thundered on his Destrier, closer, closer, until he was upon Vincent and Leticia. The crimson knight grabbed Leticia and carried her off. Vincent looked down to find himself unable to move. His legs up to his knees were stuck in a mud pit.

A thunderstorm appeared from nowhere and rained upon him. Struggling he called out over and over, "Leticia!"

"We be near," Leticia comforted trying desperately to wake Vincent up from his nightmare. He was moving violently in the bed as if struggling and calling her name.

Finally awake and in Leticia's arms Vincent pulled Leticia to his sweaty chest and held her closely. He panted trying to catch his breath. Vincent kissed her hair and stroked her soft body for several moments.

"Whence be thy dream," Leticia finally queried.

"We lost thee and our sons," Vincent answered still shaken from the dream. "We must arise and take care of Sir Jean Tillet thus morn. We wouldst naught allow thus French to take our Okehampton."

"Our love and faith be with thee," Leticia soothed. "Naught wouldst harm us or our sons."

Vincent kissed his wife with deep passion and tenderness. He felt the need to hold Leticia for several moments and then he rose from the bed. Vincent went to the door and called for Maynard. In moments the squire was helping him get dressed and prepared for battle. Once he was dressed he had Maynard get Elena and Organa to bring his sons.

Leticia watched from her bed. She squelched her natural fears and concentrated only on the fact that Vincent was here protecting her and their babies. He was a brave, noble, and feared knight. No one could defeat him. No one! Leticia brushed her tears aside when Vincent held his twins in his arms and kissed them tenderly.

"We offer our oath to thee Austin and Aleyn," Vincent said to the twins while holding them. "Naught wouldst harm thee or thy mother. We wouldst end thus siege for thee on thus den." Vincent gave the twins back to Organa and Elena. He commanded, "Take our sons to our mother. Let our sons stay in thus arms secure until our return." Leaving the room he turned once more to Leticia and told her, "We love thee Goodwife."

Holding in her fears and tears, Leticia responded bravely, "We love thee Husband."

Vincent and Maynard walked in the torch light to the western tower room. The knights and foot soldiers were just arriving. Patiently Vincent waited for all the knights, foot soldiers, and Lionel to arrive. When all were present Vincent and Lionel embraced without words. Vincent raised his head and ordered his small army, "Follow us!" Vincent then led the men into the passage.

Vincent knew the passage but he heard a great deal of clanging and banging as the knights followed him. It was apparent their swords were banging walls and many slipped on the steps even though most of the slippery moss had disappeared due to the flaming torches lighting and drying the passage all night. Vincent had to see the humor as he imagined some of his knights falling on their bottoms. Hearing many curses he couldn't stop laughing. Turold was the last to enter the passage and he could be heard warning the knights to be careful.

Vincent thanked the lord that silence was not necessary for this part of his planned attack.

Vincent opened the passage board to the forest floor and assisted every knight and foot soldier out to the forest floor. He cautioned each man to be silent and wait for his lead. When Turold appeared, Vincent knew all of his small army was present. Vincent allowed Turold to lead his band through the forest to the hedgerows. Once in the hedgerows Vincent positioned every knight and foot soldier personally. Vincent's attack force was in position as dawn broke on the eastern horizon. He watched as a half hour later Jean Tillet's troops arrived to begin siege. He noted they had not brought the battering ram. Vincent rightfully knew that the French believed their spies would lower the drawbridge once they began their attack.

Vincent held up his arm signaling all to remain silent and stay in position. He would wait until the French began their attack and Lionel responded with his rampart archers on the eastern wall. That is if the French began their siege by hauling the belfry towards the eastern walls, as Vincent believed they would.

Knights upon Destriers and foot soldiers began arriving slowly. It was too slowly for the knights hiding in the hedgerows. They wanted to begin the battle. It took several hours to line up Jean Tillet's knights according to his plans. It seemed forever as they lined up the slow moving belfries. It was mid morning before Jean Tillet gave the order to attack.

Lionel and his archers had been waiting patiently on the battle ramparts since dawn. His men had prepared both boiling water and flaming arrows. Their oil cloth wrapped arrows would be ignited from the fires under the boiling water pots and would be aimed at the wooden belfry. Vincent already had planned correctly for his opponent's siege tactics.

Jean Tillet and his knights remained in back as the foot soldiers ran towards the drawbridge expecting it to be lowered. They stopped at the moat edge when the drawbridge did not lower. Immediately Lionel gave orders for the archers to begin shooting. The foot soldiers ran back to the knights fleeing the barrage of arrows that took one of every five soldiers. Jean Tillet called his knights to defend the fleeing soldiers. Holding their shields the knights charged into their foot soldiers offering protection with their shields.

This was the moment Vincent had been waiting for. While Jean Tillet was busy protecting his soldiers it was the moment of surprise for Vincent's surprise. Vincent signaled his soldiers and knights to begin their attack. The French didn't have a clue as to how close Vincent's attack army was until they were upon them.

Vincent led the attack. His sword slashed and cut down French soldier after French soldier. The French mounted knights realized what was happening and turned back to attack Vincent's forces.

Vincent faced the charging Destriers. He realized it was at this moment he would lose most of his men. He stood straight as example for his men and prepared to do battle when shouts and charging Destriers appeared from the east. The banner in front of the force was that of the Black Prince. The French

196

turned their Destriers to meet the Black Prince. Vincent watched in gratitude when he saw his banner and his knights. To his surprise he saw Martin Bolin and his force riding next to the Black Prince. It was now the French force that was completely outnumbered. Vincent signaled his force to cut down the rest of the foot soldiers who were fleeing every which way. Some were even running toward the oncoming forces of the Black Prince. In moments French Knights and French soldiers that survived were surrendering.

Vincent removed his helmet as Prince Edward and Martin Bolin approached him.

"Hath thee lost thy Destrier?" Prince Edward teased.

"Nay, our de Courtenay hath always enjoyed thus leisure of walking," Martin Bolin responded lightheartedly.

"Nay, our de Courtenay hath lost his Destrier," Edward chortled leaning forward on his saddle. "Wouldst thee need mount? We be certain one be provided for thee."

Vincent grinned broadly and replied, "Since all our force hath lost their Destrier's we wouldst walk with them to our Okehampton."

"We trow naught," Edward stated. "Tis more fit our French Knight, Sir Tillet, walk as we wouldst take Tillet's Destrier for thy mount." Edward motioned to his squire. The squire brought Tillet's Destrier and behind him was a bound Jean Tillet being pushed forward by a foot soldier.

"We are in debt to thee," Vincent said seriously. The only casualties were the French. His men had only suffered minor wounds. They had taken many prisoners whose families would offer great ransom to King Edward.

Leticia and the women in her solar all heard the shouts of pain, agony, and desperation during the battle. Leticia showed bravery she did not feel. Her mind was focused on Vincent and his safety. She tried to stop visions of his being wounded out of her mind but it was difficult. Leticia held Austin tightly as he fed and then Aleyn. Reluctantly she gave each one up to her handmaidens after they had fed, but she knew holding her boys somehow gave them strength to endure the noise of the battle.

Morgan and Megan paced continually about the solar. Megan was furious. She had wanted to stay by her father's side as he captured the spies at the postern gate and then stay with him as he organized Okehampton's forces and the boiling of water for the battle. Morgan was biting her nails in trepidation. There still had been no word on the return of her Quintin. Morgan was terrified of the battle and perhaps never seeing her Quintin again.

Juliet held tightly to Reine. Her handmaiden Lady Mildred stayed on the floor next to her mistress laying her head on Juliet's knee.

Rosamund continuously peered out a tiny crack in the closed shutters that overlooked the battlegrounds. She told all the women what was happening.

"Dost thee see our Vincent?" Leticia would ask over and over again in the beginning hours of the battle.

"Nay, hence be naught forces revealed," Rosamund would continuously answer. She told them when the French started the attack of foot soldiers upon the drawbridge. When it didn't fall open to them, the women all laughed as Rosamund described the French fleeting Lionel's barrage of arrows.

Leticia remained silent and remained in her bed as her husband had ordered her to do. Leticia did not laugh on the French running from the arrows. She still had not heard that Rosamund had spotted Vincent. Her head ached as she thought a hidden French force waiting for Vincent in the forest might have slaughtered him. Tears continually threatened to fall. Leticia instead spoke calmly to the women and suggested maybe they should all pray. Leticia led the prayers and recited the rosary no less than five times.

"We see our lord!" Lady Rosamond screeched. "Tis our Lord Vincent leading such attack against thus French."

Leticia crossed herself and used every bit of restraint not to run to the shutter and watch her husband. "Sweet Jesu keep our Vincent safe," Leticia whispered. Instead of doing what she wanted she rose from the bed and took the fussing Austin from Organa's arms. Leticia paced back and forth soothing her baby while talking to him to comfort herself, "Worry naught our Austin. Thy father be thus strong and brave knight. Thy father wouldst defeat such French who dare threaten our Okehampton."

Rosamund described the attack throughout the surprise attack, "Thus French be surprised. Sir Vincent and our force be cutting thus French soldiers. Oh our lord be so brave and strong. He cut another and another. We be winning thus battle my lady!" Then Rosamund saw the mounted French Knights turn to attack the Okehampton knights. "Nay!" Rosamund screamed. "Look out dear Vincent. The French Destriers turn to attack thee."

Leticia's heart sank. She began once more to repeat her rosary. Austin was sleeping in her arms as she looked down upon him. He looked so angelic in her arms. "Keep us in peace, husband," she whispered into the air. "Return to us anon."

"By God's Teeth!" Rosamund screamed in oath, shaking the room with a piercing shrill. "Tis our Black Prince! He rides to attack such French from east side!"

Leticia handed Austin to Organa and ran to the shuttered window pushing Rosamund aside. Peeking through the crack she spotted the large force attacking the French. There were the banners of the Black Prince, her husband, and Martin Bolin. Even Leticia could see the French were now badly outnumbered. She scanned the battlefield until she saw her Vincent. "Be safe our husband!"

"Thee wouldst stay abed," Rosamund reprimanded pushing Leticia away and toward her canopied bed. "We wouldst watch for thee."

Leticia loosened her robe sash and walked back to her bed. The piercing scream of Lady Rosamund had woken Reine and Aleyn. Both babies were crying. Leticia picked Aleyn up from Elena's arms and carried him to her bed. There she opened her chemise and allowed Aleyn to feed from her breast. Aleyn quieted immediately.

Juliet followed suit and soon Reine was suckling peacefully.

Rosamund continued to describe the battle until its end. "Lady Leticia, thy husband just mounted Sir Tillet's Destrier. All our knights are mounting the Destrier's of such defeated French knights. Thus return to Okehampton. Sir Lionel be lowering our drawbridge. Vincent and Prince Edward are entering Okehampton. Thus defeated Jean Tillet be walking bound behind them."

Leticia jumped from bed leaving Aleyn sleeping peacefully on it. "We must prepare feast." Leticia went to her wardrobe and began looking for a gown that might fit. She was much smaller but had not regained her tiny figure yet.

Rosamund chased her and reprimanded, "We wouldst see to thus celebration with our husband, Sir Gaylord. Thee wouldst be back to thy pallet. Our Lord hath ordered thee to be hence upon our lord's return."

"Yea my lady," Elena agreed retrieving the sleeping Aleyn. "Thee hath only delivered past two den. Thee wouldst rest. Thee wouldst obey orders of our Lord Vincent."

Reluctantly Leticia returned to her bed. "Prepare thus greatest feast for our forces as Okehampton hath naught ere seen," Leticia requested. "Please send our Lord to us upon our lord's return."

Morgan and Megan were the first to leave the solar. Morgan was running through the keep to the bailey hoping to find Quintin. Megan ran through the keep to find her father and hear first hand of the battle from her own hero. Rosamund left the solar and begin gathering the servants to prepare a feast.

"We wouldst return to our chambers," Juliet offered generously. "We trow thee and Sir Vincent wouldst need time alone."

"Nay," Leticia replied. "Our Vincent wishes our family together upon return. Thus includes our baby daughter, Reine."

At that moment Juliet felt great guilt and was about to tell Leticia the truth when Maynard ran into the room announcing that his lord would be arriving immediately. Maynard looked sideways toward Organa and Leticia grinned.

"Organa, give us our son Austin and take our Maynard for drink and food," Leticia ordered knowingly. She knew Organa had been as worried for Maynard as she had been for Vincent. She graciously gave them some time alone.

Vincent took the castle steps two at a time. Although he was weary from the battle he wanted to return to Leticia and reassure her he was fine and the French were defeated. He had no idea Rosamund had been giving everyone a blow-by-blow description. He entered to see Leticia holding Austin, Elena still cradling Aleyn, and Juliet holding her daughter, Reine. Without another thought he ran to Leticia and took her in his arms. He kissed her passionately and then gently kissed the brow of his sleeping son, Austin. Motioning Elena to him, Vincent then kissed the brow of the sleeping Aleyn. Graciously he said to Juliet, "Bring us thy daughter for loving."

Juliet smiled and presented Reine to receive a kiss from her protector. "We thank our God thee be safe and victorious," Juliet said to Vincent.

Vincent was so relieved and grateful he had survived the battle and his forces finally showed up to turn the battle to victory, he didn't notice he was bleeding.

Leticia hugged her husband. When she released him so he could kiss Reine she cried out as she looked at her bloodied hand. "Thee be wounded!"

Elena took Austin from Leticia placing him in her other arm. Juliet handed Reine to Mildred. The two women removed Vincent's tunic and armor. Sword blades had once more slashed his shoulder and arm.

Leticia ran to her medicine bag. Juliet went to her sewing box and put needle and thread into the pot of boiling water kept over the fire. Juliet then put cloths in the pot to use for cleaning Vincent's wounds.

Vincent remained silent as the two women cleaned his wounds, sewed the slashed skin with fine stitches, and Leticia placed salve upon the wounds. When they had finished Vincent grumped. "Thy hands be gentle, but thus healing hurts worse for thus wounding."

"Tis better than thus wounds becoming foul with puss," Leticia countered immediately. "Thee wouldst heal faster with our care."

"Yea," Vincent teased. "We trow of thy special care only thee wouldst provide to ease our pains."

Juliet left the room silently. She knew what Vincent meant and it cut into her heart. All she had wanted from life was to be loved. She had Reine and she reminded herself that was all she needed. Mildred followed her lady.

Elena placed the sleeping boys in their cradle and left the solar as well.

Vincent looked about and chortled, "Tis dost appear we finally be alone." Observing their privacy Vincent took immediate advantage of it and pulled Leticia to the chair by the fireplace. He put her on his lap and there they remained for several hours. Together they watched the flames and just held each other without saying a word. They were at peace.

Below in the Great Hall there was a feast and celebration rivaled only by the King's court at Surrey Castle. Quintin and Morgan stole some time alone. Megan listened in awe to her father's description of the battle. Rosamund was by Gaylord's side. Her eyes were filled with love and pride. Maynard and Organa spent some time alone in the gardens. Juliet remained in her room with her Reine and handmaiden Mildred. Lionel, the Black Prince, Martin, and all the de Courtenay knights celebrated their victory.

The prisoners were put in chains and taken to the camp of the Black Prince to be taken to Surrey Castle for ransom. A messenger had be sent to Surrey Castle requesting a guard troop be sent to help escort the prisoners to Surrey.

Vincent finally descended from the solar to the Great Hall near the end of the celebration. The only reason he came down was to send food to Leticia and get food himself. He was tired and hungry and it was protocol to be there for the celebration. He noticed that Prince Edward was quite inebriated and was playing with an attractive kitchen servant. She was a blond haired young woman of sixteen. She was enjoying Prince Edward's attention. Vincent said nothing when Edward took the girl to his room in the keep. Such goings on never bothered him before. The difference must be was he was a married man with family and lord of the keep.

Slowly the celebration broke up and Vincent went to his solar. He found his Leticia feeding his sons. Vincent took a chair and watched as his wife fed the babies. It made his need for Leticia increase but he knew she still bled and his wounds needed to heal first. With resolve and control, he climbed into bed with his wife and his babies. The four of them shared the bed and slept peacefully through most of the night.

Vincent spent this night dreaming once again. This dream however did not turn into a nightmare. He and Leticia were enjoying a quiet moment together in the Great Hall of Okehampton while he watched their twin sons playing knight with wooden swords and horses. In this dream he was quite content. The Great Hall was warm, full of sunlight, and welcoming. He saw his father, stepmother, sisters, and friends. Everyone was smiling and all were engaging in laughter and watching the twins. Before his eyes the twins grew into boyhood, then manhood. The gentle coaxing of Leticia disturbed his dream.

"My Lord Husband, awake," Leticia repeated.

Vincent awoke to the aroma of a hot sandalwood scented bath. "Mmmm," Vincent mumbled.

"Thus be bath prepared for thee," Leticia cooed to her sleepy husband. "Come hither."

Vincent rose and obediently allowed Leticia to lead him to the hot tub. Without a doubt Vincent enjoyed the gentle machinations of his wife's bathing. At this moment the dream meaning was quite clear. He had changed from a devil may care brave knight to a husband, father, and Lord Protector. He could never go back and most importantly he never wanted too. He would be happy being just what he had become. As Leticia soaped his chest he pulled her into the tub with him and laughed. "Thee wouldst share everything with us dear Goodwife."

# Chapter 26

Organa and Elena walked in on a soaking wet floor. Leticia playfully splashing her husband with a wet cloth.

Leticia and Vincent were like little children laughing, playing, and teasing each other. They didn't even notice the two handmaidens walking in until little Aleyn decided to make himself known. They both looked up when they heard Aleyn scream for his breakfast.

"Give us Aleyn. Place Austin in thus cradle, " Leticia ordered taking Aleyn. "Send for Maynard to assist our lord."

Organa and Elena obeyed immediately. Mystic mewed and left his comfortable place by the hearth to follow Elena and get his morning's serving of fresh cream.

The family had settled into their normal routine once more and Vincent was pleased. Just how could he tell King Edward he no longer wanted to be called for service to the throne. He wanted to stay here with his family and protect Okehampton. He would discuss this with Prince Edward later today.

Once Vincent was dressed he kissed Leticia and told her he expected her to stay in the solar and rest. He explained his order was an order of love and caring. She had been through so much including the birth of two sons. It was time to rest and heal. "My love for thee is great and wish thee to heal quickly," Vincent told Leticia lovingly.

"And thee my lord?" Leticia queried. "Pray tell us about thy own battle wounds and giving thus time for healing."

Vincent chuckled, "Our healing be quicker for thy nimble fingers." With those words he left closing the door and allowing his Leticia privacy to care for his sons.

Upon his appearance in the great hall all the knights ceased conversations and eating to stand and cheer their lord. Even Prince Edward stood and applauded Vincent.

When Vincent took his seat next to the Black Prince all in the great hall sat and returned to their food and conversation. It gave Vincent the opportunity to question Prince Edward about his sudden but welcome appearance on the battlefield.

"We sent messengers before us," Edward explained. "Our messengers returned to camp whence such spotted thus French encampment near Okehampton. We be but league distance from thus French Pavilion."

"Hence thee trow of thus French siege," Vincent finished.

"Yea," Edward answered taking a bite of partridge. "We mounted our knights and rode in haste to thy aid."

"Most appreciated," Vincent said in gratitude. "Thy assistance came at our most dire need."

"Yea, we be fortunate for thee," Edward answered chuckling. He was enjoying this conversation as a full knight with his former mentor.

"Be aware my young friend," Vincent chided. "Thy head grows large and thee wouldst naught fit in thy helmet."

Prince Edward laughed and then suddenly turned serious. "We wouldst discuss the fate of thy prisoners."

"We wouldst send our prisoners with thee to Surrey Castle and thy father," Vincent responded. "Thus wouldst bring high ransom and wealth for our throne."

"Tis troth," Prince Edward agreed. "Whence portion of thus wouldst we ask of our father for thee?"

"We wouldst naught have a farthing," Vincent replied. "Yea, we wouldst request of our king and thy father request to stay at Okehampton for protection of our throne."

"Thee hath lost thy wanderlust?" Edward asked with surprise. "Thee hath lost thy taste for adventure?"

"Verily," Vincent answered quickly. "In our solar be our challenge, dreams, hope, and adventure."

"Our Leticia be most wondrous adventure," Prince Edward understood. "Leticia be our companion ere thy Goodwife." Edward sighed deeply. "We wouldst wish we find such love. We wouldst share with our father and king thy request."

"Tis most difficult for belief," Vincent grinned. "Frail maiden child hath conquered thus great knight with naught battle."

"And our Leticia doth give thee naught one, yea two sons," Edward noted. "We wouldst be of great joy whence we tell our mother thy news. Tis verily such surprise."

"Thus be surprise for us," Vincent laughed. "A most pleasant and happy surprise our Austin and Aleyn. Our king ordered us to provide heirs for Devon shire. We merely obeyed."

"To thy fertility," Edward toasted raising his tankard.

Vincent accepted the toast and then queried, "Whence wouldst thee return to Surrey?"

"We wouldst leave thus morn," Edward said taking another bite of meat.

"Wouldst thee be accompanied by Sir Martin Bolin?" Vincent asked.

"Yea," Edward replied. "Be thus reason for thy question?"

"We wondered reason for Bolin in accompanying thee," Vincent stated. He was really curious for the reason he came to Okehampton because King Edward had awarded him the manor in Wales. And even though he had invited Bolin to view refurbished Okehampton. But Vincent knew Bolin had always wanted property and Vincent thought he would return straight to his Welsh manor.

"Thus reminds us," Edward responded. "We heard Lady Juliet be thy concubine and bear thee bastard maiden child."

Vincent felt his face flush but responded with calm, "Lady Juliet be naught our concubine. Lady Juliet hath indeed delivered bastard maiden child. Thus be some concern of our true parentage."

Edward looked at Vincent thoughtfully. "Thus be some concern over thus parentage in our mind as well," Edward replied. "Thus be one more reason we bring Sir Martin Bolin with us. The second reason be our Sir Bolin requested thus whence he heard Lady Juliet took residence in Okehampton."

Vincent was about to ask Edward if he thought Bolin might be the father when the subject of their conversation entered the great hall. At the same time Juliet carrying Reine began to descend the stairs into the Great Hall. A knight was also bringing Lady Agnes into the hall to break her fast. What happened next occurred in a flash.

Lady Agnes pulled Lady Juliet's dagger from her belt and grabbed Reine from Juliet's arms. Agnes then began screaming for everyone to stand back. She held tiny Reine in one arm threatening the baby with the point of the dagger. Little Reine was wailing in fear and wiggling in apparent anxiety. Reine's little foot wiggled free from the swaddling and was flailing in the air.

Juliet's screams of terror and sobbing were heard echoing in the great hall. Sir Lionel had been behind her and restrained her in any foolhardy attempts.

Sir Martin Bolin saw Juliet descending the stairs. He began walking briskly toward her. He wanted to see the baby she carried. At Surrey when he learned from friends of Lady Juliet that she left breeding, he was convinced it was his child. He had intended to prove himself in Wales and then Calais. With the king's blessings he would return to ask Juliet to marry him. Bolin had received King Edward's approval and accompanied Prince Edward to do just that. A small battle with the French got in his way, but there she was. Juliet was his love. Suddenly the small baby was yanked away from his Juliet. The traitor Lady Agnes held the child hostage. Slowly he moved toward Lady Agnes. He saw the little baby's foot dangling and then he knew Juliet's child was his. He would save his baby!

Vincent stepped forward. "Give us Reine," he commanded coolly.

"Nay," Lady Agnes hissed pointing the dagger at the screaming baby's throat. "We wouldst kill thy bastard save thee give us and our brother safe passage."

Prince Edward addressed Agnes, "Woman, wouldst thee kill thus babe thee wouldst die in thus moment."

"Tis best to die quickly instead prisoner of King Edward," Agnes mocked wickedly. She pressed the dagger on the baby's arm. A drop of blood appeared. Reine shrieked in pain. Juliet fainted in Lionel's arms.

"Nay," Vincent cried. He couldn't stand the sight of Reine's innocent blood. He wouldn't let Agnes kill an innocent child.

"Thee wouldst give us safe passage," Agnes demanded. "Or thy bastard dies!" She raised her arm in warning.

Bolin saw his moment and from behind her he grabbed her arm. His grip so tight bruises showed immediately on Agnes' wrists when she dropped the knife to the floor.

Vincent bolted forward and caught little Reine as Agnes released her hold.

Cuddling Reine, Vincent did his best to calm her.

Bolin released his hold on Agnes to give her back into custody of the guard. He walked straight to Vincent and said, "Allow us to hold our maiden child."

"Thee claim parentage?" Vincent asked with surprise. He then realized both Reine and Bolin had the same color red hair. He noticed that Bolin and Reine showed remarkable resemblance to each other.

"Verily," Bolin stated proudly. "See thus foot? Thus kinder hath six toes. Tis Bolin's mark."

Vincent carefully passed little Reine to her father's arms. "We be joyous for thee."

"Tell us thus reason for Juliet trusting thee for delivery of our seed?" Bolin asked rocking the contented Reine.

"Mayhap we wouldst ask Lady Juliet?" Vincent suggested watching Lionel assist Juliet walk towards them.

Juliet fainted when she saw Agnes threaten her Reine with a dagger. The only love Juliet ever held might be destroyed. Blackness enveloped her with fear. When she came back to consciousness Sir Lionel was holding her and telling her Reine was fine. Juliet still was weak from her fright. Sir Lionel assisted her to Martin Bolin. "My Reine, my Reine, my Reine," Juliet cried taking her baby from Bolin's arms.

Once Reine was securely cradled in Juliet's arms, Martin queried, "Be reason for flight from Surrey to Okehampton to bear our kinder?"

"Thee left us," Juliet whimpered looking of Reine for any other wounds or bruises. "Thee left naught word and we be breeding."

"We believed best to be worthy of thee," Bolin replied apologetically. "We wished to offer thee land and title ere we request thee to be wife."

"Wife?" Juliet asked in unbelief.

"Yea, we love thee," Martin Bolin replied. "Whence we became titled with land, we petitioned our king for our marriage proclamation. Our King Edward approved."

Juliet stood straight and stared at Martin with surprise. "Thee love us?"

"Yea, with our heart," Martin replied sincerely. "We be more pleased with our Reine. We wouldst be family together."

Tears trickled down Juliet's cheeks. "All we hath wanted be love. We believed naught wouldst ever be our fortune."

"Thee be in our heart," Martin responded lovingly taking her in his arm. "Wouldst thee do us honor in marriage."

"Yea," Juliet sobbed. She snuggled into Bolin's embrace.

Vincent whispered to Prince Edward, "Mayhap we wouldst naught speak of Juliet declaring Reine as our bastard."

"Tis most wise," Prince Edward agreed.

Keeping Juliet and Reine in his embrace, Martin saluted Vincent, "We bless thee for thy tender care of our Juliet and Reine."

Juliet held her breath. Would Vincent tell Martin how she claimed him to be the father of her child? Everything had changed since she came to Okehampton. She was no longer the same scheming woman. She was Reine's mother and found she had love in motherhood. To be loved as a woman was her impossible dream. It was happening to her.

"We be most pleased for our Lady Juliet's care," Vincent answered quietly. He would not tell Martin about Juliet or even the problems he had with Leticia for it. He wouldn't hurt an obviously happy Juliet and she had changed. Instead he offered, "Our Leticia hath borne twin sons, Austin and Aleyn. Wouldst thee join us and see our seed?"

"Twins? Thee hath produced twice the heirs of our king's command," Martin joked. "Yea, we wouldst visit Leticia and thy twin sons."

Vincent led Prince Edward and Martin Bolin to his solar. Juliet and Reine remained in Bolin's embrace.

Juliet thought how long it had been since she was truly happy. She was grateful to Vincent for not revealing her deceit over parentage of Reine. Juliet was certain Leticia would not share her secret either. In the past months they had become close friends. Leticia was very kind and understanding especially after Reine was born.

The visitors found Leticia rocking Aleyn and singing a lullaby. Organa was humming the melody while rocking Austin.

Leticia looked up in surprise. She didn't expect Vincent to return so soon and she certainly did not expect to see Juliet and Reine in Martin's embrace. Her surprised look caused Vincent to make an explanation.

"Goodwife, our Sir Martin hath found Lady Juliet. Sir Bolin be most happy father to Reine," Vincent explained quickly. He walked to Leticia's side. A tiny mischievous grin revealed his true feelings to Leticia when he took her in his embrace. Holding Leticia and Aleyn tightly he offered, "Sir Martin, come hither and see our sons."

"Our Lady Leticia hath travailed much thus past den," Juliet told Martin sympathetically. She went on to tell Martin about Leticia's imprisonment, escape, assistance from Mystic, rescue by the woodcutter, and delivery of her twins in the woodcutters cottage.

Vincent told Martin and Prince Edward of Lady Agnes' treachery and relation to the French enemy, Jean Tillet. He told of how the woodcutter Turold helped him plan a sneak attack using a secret passage that Leticia used for her escape.

Prince Edward laughed profoundly, "Thee always loved the secret passages our dear sister of heart, Leticia."

"Yea," Vincent teased. "Thus passage provided our lady with favorite pet, arachnids."

"Thee wouldst yet play with arachnids my Lady?" Prince Edward prodded playfully.

"Only for our husband," Leticia bantered in return. "We wouldst naught find frogs for his pleasure in the passage."

Martin and Juliet looked at each other with bewilderment. It was obvious Prince Edward knew what they were saying to each other. He held his ribs in laughter.

When things were quieter, Juliet shared her proclaimed marriage with Martin Bolin and that she would leave on the morrow with her future husband.

"Nay," Leticia forbid. "Thee wouldst marry in our chapel thus den! We wouldst see to it. We give thee lovely gown, dress thee, comb thy hair,…"

Vincent interrupted, "Leticia, thee wouldst recover in thy solar for delivery. Thee be aware of confinement."

"Sweet Jesu," Leticia uttered. "We be fit and healthy. A good wedding be cheery and uplifting. Be gone, let us dress." Leticia fluttered her hands to the men in signal to leave. "Tell our priest to prepare for thus wedding on our hour!"

"Come hither," Vincent motioned to Martin. "We wouldst prepare thee as well."

Two hours later Martin Bolin and Juliet Bremond exchanged marriage vows in Okehampton Chapel. Lady Rosamund held Reine as she and Sir Gaylord witnessed the event with Vincent holding Austin and Leticia holding Aleyn.

Juliet beamed as a beautiful bride wearing the deep sapphire gown Leticia had given her to wear. Her hair was braided with blue ribbons and pearl circlet for her headpiece. There was a large feast for the mid day meal to celebrate the marriage. Mid day Prince Edward left with Lady Agnes and Jean Tillet as prisoners. Martin, Juliet, and Reine bid their farewells soon after Prince Edward. They would accompany Prince Edward for a time and then ride to Martin Bolin's manor in Wales.

The summer was beginning and the days were longer. It was nearly the equinox. Leticia had fed Austin and Aleyn and let Morgan and Megan take them for a while. It was after supper and the time she and Vincent usually spent alone.

Leticia waited for Vincent on their solar balcony overlooking the bailey. The sun was setting casting an amber hue over the land.

When Vincent entered their solar and finding only Mystic by the fireplace he knew Leticia had prepared for their special time. He saw her silhouetted by the amber hue of the sunset. She looked like a finely crafted golden statue. Coming behind her he placed his arms around her small waist and kissed her neck.

Leticia melted into his arms and sighed, "Tis a beauteous den."

"As beauteous as thee Goodwife," Vincent whispered into her hair.

"We love thee brave knight. Thee whom hath conquered our heart," Leticia said softly. "We wouldst thee naught leave us ever."

"We wouldst naught leave thee ever," Vincent vowed to Leticia and himself. He couldn't imagine being away from Leticia and his family ever again. "Thee be our conqueror of heart."

Nothing more was said. Nothing more needed to be said. They watched the sun set together and planned for their new day in the morning.

About the Author

A new author in the genre of historical romance, Payton Lee brings her characters to life. Twists and surprise turns lead her readers on to turn the page.

Read Payton Lee's Books:

Bear River Spirit
Smitten
Geneva's Hope
Geneva's Branch
Geneva's Return
Geneva's Promise
Geneva's Force
Geneva's Legacy
Five Star Affair
The Outsider
Firedrake of Cumberland
Conquer My Heart
Stone Heart
Novo Arkhangelsk
Coming Soon
Maui H.S.
A Mother's Love

Please donate to the Bear River Massacre Memorial Fund

Visit Payton Lee at her website:
http://www.paytonlee.com

Send Payton Lee an email at:
pyoung8@cfl.rr.com

Payton Lee lives in Orlando, Florida with her cats Ebony and Kirk. Ebony and Kirk also share the house with a pet dog, a rat terrier named, Peanut.